BROKEN
WINDOWS

ALSO BY PAUL D. MARKS

The Duke Rogers PI Thriller Series
White Heat

Stand-Alones
Vortex
L.A. Late @ Night

Anthologies as Co-Editor
Coast to Coast: Murder from Sea to Shining Sea
Coast to Coast: Private Eyes from Sea to Shining Sea

PAUL D. MARKS

BROKEN WINDOWS

A Duke Rogers PI Thriller

Down and Out Books, LLC
3959 Van Dyke Rd, Ste. 265
Lutz, FL 33558
www.DownAndOutBooks.com

Cover design by Zach McCain

ISBN: 1-948235-07-2
ISBN-13: 978-1-948235-07-5

For Amy

AUTHOR'S NOTE

Some of the language and attitudes in the novel may be offensive. But please consider them in the context of the time, place, and characters.

The world is a dangerous place to live, not because of the people who are evil, but because of the people who don't do anything about it.
—Albert Einstein

In a city, relatively minor problems like graffiti, public disorder, and aggressive panhandling, [James Q. Wilson and George Kelling write], are all the equivalent of broken windows, invitations to more serious crimes.
—Malcolm Gladwell, *The Tipping Point: How Little Things Can Make a Big Difference*

1994

April is the cruelest month.
—*T.S. Eliot, The Waste Land*

And November is the second cruelest month.

PROLOGUE

The Hollywood Sign beckoned her like a magnet—or like a moth to a flame. The sign glowed golden in the magic hour sun—that time of day around sunrise and sunset when the light falls soft and warm and cinematographers love to shoot. Like so many others, Susan Karubian had come here seeking fame and fortune, hoping to make her mark on the world. Oh hell, she had come to be a star like all the others. And she would do it, just not quite in the heady way she'd anticipated.

She had spent hours deciding what to wear. After all, this wasn't exactly in the etiquette books. Probably not the kind of thing you'd find in Ask Amy column. She finally decided on a tasteful dress with high-heeled sandals.

The young woman drove her Passat down Hollywood Boulevard, turning up Franklin, passing the Magic Castle. She turned slowly up Beachwood Canyon, past the low-rent area north of Franklin, up through the towering stone gates with their "Welcome to Beachwood Canyon" signs. Past the movie star homes in the hills—past where she thought she'd be living by now. She drove in circles, past piles of rubble from the earthquake several months ago, figuring that sooner or later she'd hit the right combination of roads and end up where she wanted to be.

The Passat crested the top of the mountain—mountain or hill? What was the difference anyway? A small concrete building with an antenna sat just below the road. No cars. No one around. As quiet as the Sherman Oaks Galleria on a Monday morning. She parked on Mt. Lee Drive.

She rolled up the windows, locked the car, set her purse on the floor by the gas pedal. The note she'd written in a steady hand tucked into her pocket. She hoped someone would find it quickly. Standing beside the car, she realized she'd have to hike down to get to the sign. She had thought it would be at the top of the mountain. She was buggin', as she treaded toward the edge of the road.

The nonstop rain of the last couple weeks had broken. The view from up here was incredible. You could almost see Mexico to the south and the Pacific glittering in the west. The city below, shiny and bright. Pretty and clean from up here. A million doll houses that reminded her of childhood, playing with dolls and making everything come out the way she wanted it to. Little toy cars down below, scooting back and forth. Swarms of ants scurrying this way and that on important business. Oh yeah, everyone here had important business all day and all night. Everyone but her. She gazed down at Los Angeles on the cusp of the millennium. The place to be. Center of the universe. Totally.

She hesitated at the edge of the road, her toe kicking some gravel down the hill. It clattered down, somehow reminding her of the industrial music in the clubs where she liked to hang.

Should she try to talk to him? What would be the point now? She was talked out. And he wouldn't forgive her. Why should he? She had hurt him. No, it was beyond hurt. There was no way to rationalize it.

She tentatively stepped off the road, pressing her heel in, testing its firmness. More loose gravel tumbled down the hill. Kicking off her Steven Madden heels, grabbing them by the straps in one hand, she made her way down. She walked and slid and finally made it to the landing—she didn't know what else to call it—where the sign rested. The city glowed, shimmering with hope and desire and people wanting to make their dreams come true. She knew this, because she was one of those people.

She had come here for the same reason. The Hollywood Dream. The American Dream. She had wanted to be in front of the cameras from the time her parents took her to her first movie-theater movie, *The Black Stallion*, in 1979 when she was five. After seeing the movie she had wanted a horse, but more than that she wanted to be in a movie. She hadn't yet heard of Hollywood, but by the time she was thirteen she was making plans to come here. And nothing could have stopped her. Her mom and dad told her how hard a career in the movies was, how few made it. But she had faith in herself. She was attractive, more than. Oh hell, she was *fine*, though she didn't want to come off conceited. And she had talent. She had been acting in school plays for years. She was the star, Juliet to popular Paul Bonnefield's Romeo, in middle school. Rave reviews. Fake gold acting awards. What did that mean in the big picture? She had come here gushing with hope and optimism. She still thought she could make it if she met the right people—what was the point now?

People looked up this way all the time, up to the sign. How many were looking at her now, as she climbed the scaffolding?

Higher and higher.

Her heart pounded through her chest. Her head throbbed.

Was she doing the right thing?

She reached one hand over the other, gripping the steel scaffolding. She held her shoes in one hand and the hard metal bit into her stockinged feet and palm. The pain felt good, like penance.

Would anyone notice? Would anyone give a damn that she was no longer here?

She gripped the scaffolding with all her strength and pulled herself up another rung.

"Don't look down." Her breath came in short bursts. She climbed higher. Warm blood trickled down her right palm.

She worried that the 6.7 quake last January had loosened the sign's footing. Would she fall before she even made it to the top?

Reaching the summit of the H, she pulled herself up and sat on top, balancing as best she could. The wind slammed her. She clutched a piece of scaffolding—warm to the touch—maintaining a precarious balance. A gust of wind hammered her. She began to topple, gripping the scaffolding with all her strength. She couldn't just fall off. It wasn't deliberate enough, didn't send the right message.

Her stockings ran. She thought this might happen, hoped it wouldn't.

She looked out again—the golden city. Los Angeles. Hollywood. Was that the ocean dancing in the distance?

She balanced on top of the H, a light breeze blowing her night-dark hair. She flicked it out of her eyes, put on her shoes, and talked to God. He didn't respond. If He did, she didn't hear it.

What had she done wrong? Was she in the wrong place at the wrong time? No, she had chosen her life.

The note she'd written was burning a hole in her pocket. She took it out for one last read. The wind blew up, snatching it away.

"Damn!" There was no time to write a new note and nothing to write it with.

She forced herself into a standing position. Unsteady in the breeze, she billowed in the wind like a sail. Her dress snagged on the scaffolding.

Scared to death, literally. That wouldn't last long. She held her breath until her head throbbed—pushed off as hard as she could. Shrieking. One shoe flew off as she plummeted downward. She waited for her life to pass by like everyone said. It didn't. The only thing whizzing by was the city below—the City of Angels. And devils. That was her life, so maybe they were right after all.

If she couldn't be famous in life, she would be famous in death. But she'd make her mark one way or another. She hoped her fall from grace would be graceful, even if her life hadn't been.

CHAPTER 1

I was famous.

*Dateline. 20/20. Primetime. Good Morning America-*famous. I didn't want to go on those shows, but I didn't have a choice. If I avoided them they'd have said what they wanted about me and I'd have had no way to set the record straight.

So now people knew my face. Knew my name. Stopped me on the streets. Some even asked for autographs. I hated every damn minute of it. I never wanted to be famous, just good at what I did.

But I was famous—for being a fuck-up, only most of the rest of the world didn't know it. They knew me as the private detective who had found promising starlet Teddie Matson's executioner. They didn't know I had inadvertently helped him find her to kill her.

Rita knew. Rita was Teddie's sister. We'd had a brief fling, for lack of a better word. It'd been two years and I was still waiting for the phone to ring. I would have called her but I didn't have the guts. You need someone to go down a dark alley with you, I'm your man. But the truth is, I was afraid to call her. Afraid she would reject me. Afraid she would hate me. Afraid she would see me for the fuck-up my father always said I was.

Sitting in my tiny den on the north side of the house, I tapped keys on my IBM 486 clone computer. I had only recently gotten rid of my Leading Edge 8088 computer with two floppy drives and no hard disk—true Stone Age technology—and already my 486 with its one hundred twenty-eight kilobytes of memory and twenty-megabyte hard drive, running Windows 3.1, was out of date. I was making decent money for a change, but why buy one of those new Pentium computers when it would be obsolete by the time I got it home from the store?

It had been two years since my dog Baron had been killed and I was finally ready to get another. I thought I might find one on the Net. Of course, no dog could replace Baron—that's why I waited so long—but I felt the need for the companionship only a dog could give.

Loyalty was something else. For that I'd have the dog and my bud Jack. We'd been to hell and back together. He had my back and I had his. But I couldn't curl up with him at two in the morning with an old black-and-white movie on Turner Classics.

The afternoon sun—the first sun I'd seen in three days, an eternity in Los Angeles—streaked through the window, through the old-fashioned, wide-slatted Venetian blinds, left-overs from when my parents lived in this house. They cast film noir shadows across the keyboard, a lineup of bars holding my fingers hostage. For a private detective I'm a pretty good typist. Took it in high school and it all came back when I needed it. Maybe the only thing I learned in high school that was really useful. Sure, I always loved history, but most of that I learned on my own.

What kind of dog should I get? Something big. Shepherd, like Baron. Rottie. Malamute. Dobie. Akita.

The radio droned in the background. A speech supporting Proposition 187 by one of our local SoCal congressmen. "...Proposition 187 is the answer to California's needs," Congressman Dan Wilkman declared, "It will stop the flood tide of illegal immigration into our state. A flood that is draining the resources for our schools, emergency rooms and other valuable services. If you don't want California to morph into Mexifornia, vote for Proposition 187—"

The bill was the latest firestorm to hit California. It was everywhere these days. On billboards, the television, radio, newspapers. You were either *fer* it or *agin* it. No middle ground. The vote was coming up in a few weeks. But I'd heard it all before. I hit play on the CD player. The radio switched off. Portishead's song "Sour Times" from their *Dummy* album came on. A little spacey but I liked it. I turned to the computer, dialed up the modem, tapped a bunch of keys, hoping to find a computer bulletin board system or newsgroup that might have dogs in need of a home. But it taxed my brain too much at this early hour. I picked up the paper and looked in the classifieds.

Thump. A noise on the south side of the house—the driveway side. I don't scare easily, but I don't like unexpected noises either, day or night. I grabbed the kit bag that held my Firestar 9mm that I carried from room to room— am I paranoid, maybe. In my line of business, you have to be paranoid. Headed for the back door. Wished Baron was heading there with me. I lived in a reasonably good neighborhood, the one I had grown up in. But both it and the city had changed. Besides, the bad guys were mobile. And they liked nicer neighborhoods.

Now it sounded like a tank pulling down the driveway. The only one who felt comfortable enough to come down my driveway was Jack. But he always rode his Harley and I knew its sound. I opened the door to see a desert camouflage Humvee there. What the hell?

The driver's door opened. I had my finger on the Firestar's trigger guard. Then Jack appeared standing above the car's roof. His ever-present wraparound shades hid his sniper's eyes and thousand-yard stare. He should never have left the service. He was a politically incorrect man in a politically correct time. And while he didn't always think or say the right thing, he mostly did it. He knew he was tough but he took no false pride in it.

We were opposites in many ways. He was six-two, built like the Rock of Gibraltar. I was five-seven, but tight and stocky like a mortar round. He wore his hair in a brush cut. Mine looked like I'd just gotten out of bed, no matter what I did to it. He was my friend. I could count on him, without ever having to think about it. How many people could you say that about?

"Like it?" he said.

"Sure, if you're going to war."

"I'm always at war."

That was for sure.

"Hummer. Military model?" I said.

"It's a Gulf War refugee. Makes your Cherokee look like the runt of the litter."

"Well, this model's not exactly street legal."

"Not exactly."

A yapping sound came from the car, though I use that term loosely. "Where are the .50 cals?"

"I wish," Jack said, opening the passenger door. A large rat scooted out the door, running in circles.

"What the—"

"For you. I found her in the wash, swimming her heart out."

This was one of the wettest years L.A.'d had in a long time. Rain every day, or so it seemed. Film noir weather. Perfect for Raymond Chandler's mean streets. Hell, if he thought they were mean back then, he should see them now. The wash, as Jack called the Los Angeles River, was normally a dry, cement bed, great for movie car chases and atomically radiated motion picture critters to come barreling down. But in these rains it was a raging river. If Jack found the pup in the *wash* she was lucky he'd come along or she might have been washed out to sea by now. At that I didn't know how he could have saved her. Half the time even the fire and rescue crews can't save people in the violent current.

"I think you should call her Molly."

"Molly?" I said, setting my kit bag, with the pistol in it, down on the stairs leading up to the back door.

"After the Unsinkable Molly Brown."

"C'mere, girl." The dog paid me no mind. She rolled on her back so Jack could pet her stomach. "Maybe you should keep her. She likes you."

"You'll grow on her. 'Sides, I can't keep dogs in my apartment. Got plenty of illegals though. Crammed in like sardines, otherwise how could they afford my neighborhood. Pretty soon we'll be living in Mexico *norte*. Gotta say I'm ready to move."

"You're over the top, Jack. And you're always ready to move. One-a these days you're gonna run out of places to move to."

Jack's hand glided across Molly's tummy. "Let's get her settled."

"What kind of dog is she?" Her fur was yellow-gold, with a black muzzle. Dark brown, inquisitive eyes and floppy ears.

"Don't know. Looks like she might have some Shepherd. Maybe when you take her to the vet you can ask."

When *I* take her to the vet. Well, I did want a dog and sometimes it works out better when things fall into your lap than when you go looking for them.

"Bring her in."

The first thing Molly did, of course, was pee on the kitchen floor. Luckily it was linoleum and easy to clean. I was going to let Jack do the honors when he said, "No, man, your dog, you gotta get used to it. Train her. I know she'll never re-place Baron, but I got a good vibe on her."

I did too; I'm not sure why. After peeing she looked up at me with those big brown puppy eyes as if to say, "Sorry, buster, but you know how it is."

I knew how it was.

"Hey, what's that shit you're listening to now?" Jack said.

"Portishead."

"Sounds like space-head music—space-*case* music."

"Don't you like anything post 1850?"

"Why don't you ever listen to anything classical?" Jack's idea of a hot composer was Scarlatti. If you wanted to push it, Grieg or Dvorak would do.

"Or that country music you listen to," I said.

"Cowboy, not country. Get that straight."

"Yeah, I know, Gene Autry, Roy Rogers."

"Tex Ritter. Rex Allen. Sons of the Pioneers. Cowboy. 'Sides, I told you, I'm starting to get into swing. Ellington, Goodman, the Dorseys. Got a thing for Jimmy Dorsey."

"A thing?"

"Not that kind of thing. He's just got a certain sound."

Okay, so I exaggerated earlier. He likes some stuff from the twentieth century. But hell, Tex Ritter, Jimmy Dorsey— they might as well have been from the eighteenth century as far as the rest of the world was concerned.

"Well, at least you've moved into the twentieth century."

"I'm a twentieth century man, but I hope to make it to the twenty-first century. Anyway, why don't you call the vet, make an appointment, she probably needs shots."

"Don't we need to take her to the pound, see if someone claims her?"

"Anyone who lets a dog like this get out deserves to lose it. Get on the phone."

I mock-saluted Jack, but I called the vet and made an appointment for the next day. Jack didn't hang around long. Molly and I were left alone. Flotsam and jetsam adrift on the convulsive tides of the L.A. River.

Baron's collar was too big for the pup, so I made a slip knot leash from rope, put it around Molly's neck, making sure not to pull too tight, and headed outside for a walk during a break in the rain. If it rained anymore we'd be getting into the forty days and forty nights kind of thing. Would it wash away the corruption? I doubted it.

The glare of the sun bouncing off the hard pavement made me squint but the air had that sweet, wet, new mowed lawn smell as we walked and I wondered what I'd feed her. Baron's food had long since been tossed and I didn't think I should be feeding human food to a dog. I'd pick up some puppy food on my next trip to the market. In the meantime I'd make do with something around the house.

It'd been two years since I walked a dog along my street. It'd been two years since I walked on my street. The dust had finally settled from the huge Northridge quake that shook L.A. on Martin Luther King Day in January. Most of the debris had been removed and chimneys fixed. A couple of houses on the street were still yellow tagged—meaning they were unsafe for more than supervised entry pending repairs. No red tags on my street—buildings unsafe for human entry and occupancy. I was lucky, the only thing that broke in my house was a prop vase from *The Big Sleep*. But right next door the chimney had come down in their driveway. I guess I was on the good side of the quake ripple.

I live in the heart of L.A., well it's the heart to me. Not far from Beverly Boulevard and La Brea. Not far from the Beverly Center. In the Spanish colonial house I grew up in. Today I live alone. Make that yesterday I lived alone. Today I had a new roommate, *Good Golly Miss Molly*.

We walked down the street, under the palms that looked like they were hoping for better weather, headphones from my Walkman tucked snug in my ears. Hot, dry Santa Ana winds blew; in L.A. the weather seemingly changed with the flick of a switch. Metallica's "Enter Sandman" played loud in my head: and like they say in the song, I always slept with one eye open. Good advice. Every other house had burglar bars on the windows. Seemed like every time I stepped out of the house these days, someone had put up a new set of bars on their windows. I hadn't succumbed to temptation yet. After all, this was a good Los Angeles neighborhood in the nineties. And I refused to become a prisoner in my own house.

Molly trundled along, sniffing everything there was to sniff. I smelled the neighbor's honeysuckle, sweet in the bright, fresh day. Then I saw a semi-familiar face, the house-keeper from a couple doors up, young, pretty, probably un-documented. But she'd been here at least two years 'cause I remember crossing paths back then, while I was walking Baron and she would walk her employers' two Yorkies—talk about rats.

"*Hola Señor* Rogers. Long time no see. You have a new dog." She spoke with a slight accent and an engaging smile. I tried to remember her name.

"*Perro,*" I said, trying out my rusty Spanish.

"*Sí, perro. Cómo se llama?*"

I remembered some high school Spanish so I knew what she had asked. "Molly."

"Molly, *qué bonita.* That's a pretty name."

"What are your dogs' names? I knew them, but I can't remember."

"Oh, they are not my dogs. They belong to my employ-ers. Their names are Hillary y Guillermo, William-Bill, after *el presidente* and his wife."

"*Esposa,*" I said.

Good thing Jack wasn't here. He wouldn't have ap-proved. He thought people should speak only English in the USA. He probably wouldn't even want Molly consorting with dogs named Bill and Hillary.

"*Sí,* wife." She smiled warmly. "It's good that you have a dog again. A man needs a dog."

I smiled at her, trying for friendly. I wasn't one of those people who could smile on demand. I was no actor, though in my business you have to be to some extent. "I'm sorry, I don't remember your name?"

"Marisol. It means, sunny sea."

Pretty name, but I didn't say it. These days you might get sued for some kind of harassment. Hell I might have been sued for smiling at her, if she was another person. Had to be on your guard. I wasn't as unPC as Jack. These things made him absolutely crazy. And he was starting from a farther point along the craziness scale to begin with. Jack leaned more to the right, while I tried to balance in the middle. It wasn't always an easy balancing act.

Marisol's face matched her name, pretty in an unadorned, wholesome way. Nice smile. Jet black hair trailing down her back. Bronze skin. Nice figure. Something else you didn't comment on these days.

We talked for another thirty seconds, then she went her way and I went mine.

The next day the vet told me that Molly was a Chinook, or mostly Chinook. A rare breed, used for dog sledding in Alaska. Another transplant to L.A. Almost everyone here is from somewhere else, even the palm trees aren't natives. On the way home I stopped at the pet store for a collar, food, and other supplies that I hadn't thought much about in two years.

To me a Chinook was a helicopter, so I looked up Chinook dogs. They were "invented" as a new breed of sled dog. Walden, the guy who created them, wanted a dog with power, endurance, and speed. But also one that would be gentle and friendly. He'd bred them from a mastiff and a Ningo, a Greenland husky descended from Admiral Peary's lead dog, Polaris. Sounded like a good line to me.

Powerful and friendly, my kind of dog. I liked big dogs. Tough dogs. Not junkyard mean dogs. I figured some breeds had a bad rep, Rottweilers and German Shepherds to name a couple. They could be friendly or they could be nasty, depending on how you raised them. Baron was the friendliest dog of all, kids loved him. But he was also protective of me and his turf. The perfect dog.

I turned to Molly. "You got a lot to live up to, girl." Right now she was about the same size as the Yorkies, but they were full grown. Molly would grow to be a monster. I scratched her ears and she rolled on her back for me to scratch her tummy. I guess we were going to be friends after all.

I had blown off almost two full days of work to bond with Molly. I was working cases, but I didn't give a damn about them. Ever since my seven minutes of fame with Teddie Matson's case, I had every two-bit producer who needed the goods on his wife or girlfriend or boyfriend, or all three, or had to know what the competition at the other studios were up to, wanting me to work for them. I had no end of cases to work. A lot of Hollywood riff-raff; the fact they might be worth a hundred million dollars didn't make them any less riff or raff. I was making good money for a change. And I hated every minute of it.

So many people in our society want to be famous these days. They don't realize they're making a bargain with the Devil when they ask for that. When they do realize it, it's too late. But most famous people aren't famous for doing anything important. I didn't want to be one of them. And fame is a double-edged sword. Sometimes it opens doors, but you also can't be anonymous. Some people ask for it—movie stars, then resent the price that goes with it. I hadn't asked for it. But maybe it was part of my penance.

Molly curled up in a ball next to me on the sofa. I picked up the newspaper and turned on the radio. Through the foggy blather the news announcer's voice came on strong:

"Not since aspiring actress Peg Entwistle jumped to her death from the Hollywood Sign's H in 1932 has there been another known suicide from the sign. Susan Karubian, twenty-one, wasn't believed to be depressed. 'It's like that poem Richard Cory—I learned it in writing class,' said Derek Futterman, a friend. 'You just never know what's going on in someone's head. Susan had everything to live for—why would she kill herself and why off the Hollywood Sign?' Ms. Karubian apparently jumped from the sign mid to late afternoon yesterday. Police are going through her car today. It's thought that she might have been an aspiring actress despondent over not hitting the big time. In other news—"

That caught my attention, not so much because of the young woman's suicide—after all, this was Los Angeles and I was a private detective. Ms. Karubian was just another statistic, one of seventeen deaths that weekend in La La Land. But I'd hiked up to the sign a couple times. I'd even read up on Peg Entwistle. Another starlet come to Hollywood to fulfill her dreams, expecting streets paved with gold, only to find them covered with things you wouldn't even want on your shoe.

Unlike the despondent Ms. Karubian, Teddie Matson's dreams had been coming true. I had never heard of her, but her star was on the rise.

I felt the urge to do something I knew I shouldn't. I walked to the office, pulled open the bottom drawer of the desk. Under a pile of papers was a yellowed newspaper clipping. Like someone reaching for a cookie they know they shouldn't eat, I reached in and pulled out that clip. And like someone who has that box of cookies when it shouldn't even be in the house, I shouldn't have kept the *L.A. Times* clipping.

PRIVATE DETECTIVE DUKE ROGERS
NABS TEDDIE MATSON'S KILLER

After a harrowing chase through the winding roads, hills and thicket-covered trails of Griffith Park, private detective Duke Rogers wrestled James Colbert over a wall at the Observatory. The two tumbled through the dense brush. Colbert managed to escape, jumped a wall and tumbled to his death.

Skimming ahead, I came to:

Hollywood hailed Mr. Rogers as a hero for achieving justice for one of their own. He is being feted at a party at Spago hosted by Aaron Spelling, producer of Ms. Matson's series.

They almost got it right. Good enough for the *Times*, I guess. What they didn't get at all was the backstory. They never asked; I never volunteered the info.

Teddie Matson was the co-lead on a successful sitcom and movie lights beckoned. Then one day a man—I called him The Weasel behind his back—walked into my office on Beverly Boulevard with a request to find an old classmate, Teddie Matson. It was quick cash. I gave the man his info and he gave me the money. A couple days later Teddie Matson's career was over, as was her life. I had taken the man at his word—that he wanted to look up an old friend. My blood boiled over when I read the newspaper and realized I had found her for him. I decided to drop everything and find him. It wasn't easy.

Teddie's family lived in South Central. I figured that was the best place to start in my effort to find The Weasel and I found myself there when the sparks hit the fan and the Rodney King riots broke out. Tiny, a friend of the Matsons, took me to their house, where I met Teddie's mother and brother and her sister, Rita. I couldn't tell them my unwitting part in Teddie's death, but I convinced them I was out to find her killer. And in the midst of the flames and fires and looting, Rita and I became friends, more than friends. We were each other's reassurance in that bad time, a black woman and a white man, together, telling each other, without words, that we could live together in peace, corny as that sounds. And I thought, and I think she did too, that we could have a growing relationship, one based on more than mutual need during a bad time.

I followed a trail that led from L.A. to Calexico on the Mexican border to Reno and back to L.A. But I found him. And he found me, or at least I think he did. I think he killed Baron to scare me and get me off his trail. We had our scuffle at the Griffith Observatory and now he won't be going after any more young starlets or killing any dogs or anyone else.

Eventually I told Rita the truth about my involvement with The Weasel. My unwitting aid in helping him find her sister. She didn't understand. She hated me at first, then the hate turned to indifference and she drifted out of my life and I haven't been able to call her. Every time the phone rings there's some faint hope that it might be her. But it never is. And every time I start to dial her, I hang up before punching in the last number.

So Susan Karubian's jumping from the Hollywood Sign somehow stirred these memories. I looked out the window at the sun glinting off the magnolia leaves, trying to peer up into the hills. I could almost see the Hollywood Sign from here—if I was on the street in front of my house, I could for sure. After two years, the smoke from the riots had cleared from the air—not so the bad feelings. Today, the smoke was clearing above the sign or was it just the fog? And it dawned on me, Susan Karubian jumped from the sign at the height of golden hour. A magical time for some, especially if you're making movies. Not so magical for Ms. Karubian. Nor for Teddie Matson. Golden hour is when she died too. Things happen at golden hour.

I stared down at the already-yellowing newspaper—definitely yellow, not golden. Oh yeah, I was famous alright.

CHAPTER 2

Eric Davies sat on the floor, smack in the middle of his one room apartment in Venice, mindful that the cockroaches might not like him intruding on their space. The sage green carpet under him was so threadbare he could see the wood floor beneath. Maybe someday he'd pull up the carpet, polish the floor, and pretend he lived in a decent place. Hey it had real plaster walls, not drywall. Of course that also meant it was old and in this case pretty decrepit.

The room was so small that his bed was on a cheap wooden platform against one wall so he could utilize the space underneath it. He was getting tired of climbing the ladder every night just to lay down. He wasn't an eight-year-old happy to be in a bunk bed, but a thirty-four-year-old man. Under the bed platform stood his battered desk, bought for fifteen dollars at a yard sale, a lamp that Edison himself might have built, and an old uncomfortable office chair he'd picked up off the street. It rolled, sometimes. More often it was like a shopping cart where all the wheels went in different directions. Sometimes he believed it was alive, with a mind of its own.

A couple of framed sailboat photos adorned the walls—they were clipped out of magazines. Ah, decorating. Two doors besides the front door, one led to a small closet, the other to a miniscule bathroom. The far wall held a book case and plenty of law books, remnants of a former life. Another wall entertained what passed for the kitchen. Sometimes he watched the little thirteen-inch, black-and-white TV that sat on an old crate and was illegally hooked up to cable. He'd watch the Home and Gardening Channel. Everyone on every show wanted a nice space for entertaining. Living room, kitchen, yard. All had to have the proper space for entertaining. Proper balance, proper flow, good colors, and placement of one's yin and yang. *Feng shui*. Eric looked at his apartment and tried to imagine entertaining here. Who would he entertain? The local gang bangers? He didn't believe in God, but he was grateful every time he made it from his car to the front door of his six-story apartment building and every time he made it from his third-floor walk-up to his car in one piece. He thought he should thank someone. The question was who?

He opened a window, could smell the briny ocean air and hear the waves booming in the distance. This was Venice, California—crammed onto the SoCal shore between tony Santa Monica and haughty Marina del Rey—but not the Venice of the tourists and beach people. And this certainly wasn't what Abbot Kinney had envisioned when he wanted to recreate Italy's Venice in southern California, complete with canals and gondoliers. No, Kinney must be rolling over in his grave these days. This was the other side of Venice. No canals here. No bathing beauties. Unless cockroaches had beauties in their midst, maybe to another cockroach. Miss Cockroach of 1994. Would she want world peace too? Or just a crumb of leftover bread?

Tourists loved to come here. Venice was very cosmopolitan. To Eric that meant it was a third world country of its own. And the tourists didn't have to sleep here. At least not in this part of Venice. There was a good part of Venice. He'd known that part once. Now he never got over that way, even though it was only a short walk.

If he looked out the window just right he could almost see the ocean a block away. He used to come down here when he was at UCLA and the world was his for the taking. The girls loved him, his deep blue eyes, his chiseled good looks, as his mother called them. What would she think if she knew where he was today, saw how he was living? Luckily for her—or was it for him?—she had passed several years ago.

He had never really known his father. He was killed in a freak accident when Eric was five years old. Some people idealized their prematurely lost love ones, even if they'd never met them. Some adoptees did the same to their birth parents. Eric never understood why. He didn't idealize his father. He didn't think about him much.

His mother had worked hard to support him and his sister, Kimberly. They'd repaid her by being good students. He and Kim hadn't been particularly close growing up. These days his sister wanted nothing to do with him. She could have offered to help him out until he got back on his feet. But why should she? She hadn't bothered keeping in touch when things were good? She sure as hell wouldn't bother now. At first that was fine, now he missed her. Missed any family contact.

Eric walked to his so-called kitchen, pulled a can of sardines off the shelf, and put them between two pieces of hard, stale rye bread. His grandfather had loved sardine on rye sandwiches. For him it was a treat. For Eric these days it was subsistence, one step up from eating cat food from the can or scouring dumpsters for dinner. He sat at the table with a glass of water from the sink, wondering if it was really okay to drink. And he opened the *L.A. Weekly* underground paper. Today was the day his ad was due out. He scanned a few pages until he came to it.

"Contact Eric," it said, and gave his phone number. So far the phone hadn't rung, but it was early. Breakfast time. He figured he'd sit by the phone today and hope for the best. If something didn't come along, he wouldn't even be able to pay the rent on this hell hole.

He looked at the phone, willing it to ring. When it didn't, his eyes shifted back to his ad, to the headline: "$$$ Will do anything for money. $$$".

CHAPTER 3

The Santa Monica Pier used to be one of my favorite places to go to while away time, do some thinking on cases when things weren't breaking right. I still liked it, but not as much as before. They'd remodeled it, turning it into a mini Disneyland, new rides, new chain restaurants. Just another mini-mall-amusement-park, but with a saltwater view, with kitschy chain restaurants featuring Cowabunga Burgers and a food court, for crying out loud. And a lot more people. Tourists. Families with their kids. Freaks of all kinds. Still, the air was clean. And I thought Molly should get a taste of it.

There weren't as many people as I thought there might be. They probably figured that if it was cold and overcast in their part of L.A., with just a hint of sun, it would be worse in Santa Monica and not worth the trip. And they would have been right. The biting ocean air stung my cheeks and I wished I'd brought a heavier jacket. Molly had her own jacket and since she'd been bred for the snow, I figured she'd be okay.

I bought a hot dog on a stick, my favorite thing when I'm at the beach. The first hot dog on a stick I'd ever had was just off the pier. My parents told me I shouldn't be eating any of the crap down here, who knew what was in it. But you know how kids are. I gave Molly her first taste. She took to it like mustard to a bun.

The smell of the hot dog mingled with the biting smell of the ocean. A catamaran bucked the waves. Breakers foamed to shore. The day was clean. I felt good.

The rides were open, but almost no one was on them. There's little that's more forlorn than an amusement park in the daytime with no one getting amused. We walked to the end of the pier to look out at the ocean. Jack and I had spent a lot of time in the ocean, diving, surfing. SEAL training. Besides, I was a SoCal boy. I grew up at the beach, in the Pacific. I think I learned to swim before I could walk. My father probably threw me in the pool and told me to either sink or swim when I was six weeks old. I don't remember it, but knowing my father, I believe that's what probably happened.

The gunmetal gray ocean stretched to the horizon, which today was also gunmetal gray down here. You could hardly tell where one ended and the other began. I looked out across the water, to infinity. I saw my past.

I blinked to pull a curtain down on that past. Tried to see my future, but that was an impossible task.

"Are you really unsinkable, Molly?"

She wagged her tail, lively brown eyes gazing up at me.

"You better stick around, pal. I already lost one great dog prematurely."

We headed back down the pier. In the distance a woman with coal black hair sat on a bench staring out to sea, her back to me. The wind pitched her hair over her face; she swept it away with a backhand. Something seemed familiar about her. When we got closer I saw that it was Marisol. She didn't see us and I debated whether to approach her.

"Days like this are my favorite time at the beach," I said.

She turned around, looking up at me through a tangle of hair. It looked like she had been crying, though it was hard to tell because the air was so damp.

"*Señor* Duke. What are you doing here?" Her eyes had a glossy look to them. And she didn't look like the sunny sea of her name.

"Are you all right?"

"Sometimes, you know, I wish I could just jump into *la mar*, the sea, and swim and swim and swim." Her voice was soft, I could hardly hear it above the waves crashing below. She reached down, let her hand skim across Molly's back. Molly returned the kindness by rolling over and offering Marisol her stomach. Marisol obliged and Molly looked like she was in puppy heaven.

Marisol didn't say anything for several minutes. She finally said, "Dogs are good. People are bad. Why cannot people be more like dogs? They don't hurt for no reason."

She was hurting, that much was obvious. I didn't want to pry so I hesitated, then she spoke some more.

"Someone killed Carlos, *mi hermano*, my brother. *Asesinado.*"

"Murdered?" I wasn't ready for that one. I thought maybe she was having problems with immigration or had lost her job, after all I hadn't seen her since that first time out with Molly.

Murder. I was used to it, if one ever really gets used to it. It was part of my job as a PI And as a Navy SEAL I'd dealt with death, but not murder and it's not the same. Marisol's pretty features seemed washed out. She looked older, like a refugee.

I asked her to tell me what happened.

"*No sé*, I don't know. I get a telephone call from *la policía*. They tell me he is dead. His neck is broken."

"How did it happen?"

"*No sé*. The police say it was *un accidente*."

"You don't think so."

She shook her head.

"So, they're not working the case?"

"I think not." She hesitated, as if she had more to say but didn't want to say it.

I thought I knew what it might be: "Because you're undocumented?"

She nodded. "They say it is because they have no, how do you say—"

"—leads."

"*Sí*, no leads."

"Maybe they just have too much to handle."

I debated whether to offer my services. I was, after all, a famous detective. A famous Hollywood detective in the tradition of Philip Marlowe and Lew Archer, maybe even some real private eyes like Anthony Pellicano, Fred Otash, or Nick Harris. Hell, I had solved Teddie Matson's murder two years ago.

I wanted to help Marisol. Even lawyers do pro bono work. I knew Marisol couldn't afford me, but I could do the job pro bono, help her find out what happened to her brother. I believed in what Einstein said about the world being a dangerous place not because of the evil people, but because of the people who stood by and did nothing. I was no hero. Maybe I'd watched too many old movies when I was a kid, where the cowboys had a code of honor. Maybe I wanted to make a tiny corner of the world a better place. Maybe I wanted to break the monotony of all the crappy cases I was working these days. Or maybe I wanted to continue making up for my part in Teddie Matson's murder.

She looked at me funny, startling me out of my reverie.

"Your name is Duke, as in the royal family?" she said out of the blue.

"It's a nickname."

"What is your real name?"

"Everyone calls me Duke. You can too." I told her my real name—Marion. My parents were John Wayne fans—and, believe it or not, his real name was Marion Michael Morrison. I can't count how many fights I got in as a kid because of what my parents did to me. Why couldn't they have named me John Rogers or even Wayne Rogers? Well, John Wayne's nickname was Duke and I took it too. Hell, Bartholomew would have been better than Marion.

"I will call you Mr. Rogers."

"How 'bout you just keep calling me *Señor* Duke?" I said half joking. "You know, I might be able to help with your brother. I'm a private detective."

"I know this. I hear my employers, Mr. and Mrs. Goldstein, speak this. But I cannot pay. I have to borrow *dinero* just to give him a proper funeral. The county will only hold onto his body for so long. He must be buried in hallowed, blessed ground. Only sinners are not." She crossed herself.

"Here or are you sending him back to Mexico?"

"We have no one there anymore. Our parents are *muerto*—dead. I will bury him here. But he must have a proper funeral."

What did it matter, I wanted to say. He was dead. He wouldn't know the difference. I didn't say it. Jack would have.

I wanted to stay with her, but she wanted solitude. Molly and I headed off. I looked back once and she was still sitting and staring out to sea.

When we got home, Jack was waiting for us in the kitchen, a glass of lemonade in hand. He was the only person I trusted with a key to my house. He and Molly greeted each other, while I stood at the double basin sink with a pill cutter snapping little yellow Valiums in half, hoping they wouldn't shatter into ten pieces. Jack moved to the table, to clean and oil his Colt .45 Officer's Model and a sleek black Sig 9mm.

Molly sat at *his* feet. What's wrong with this picture?

"Whadda ya need those for anyway?" Jack said.

"Help me sleep."

"Why don't you just take the whole pill?"

"I don't want to be a junkie. I take Benadryl to help me sleep. But when that doesn't work—"

"—You hit the harder stuff—Valium." The slide of the

.45 snapped back into place with a metallic bang.

"I don't think takin' a Valium or two makes me a junkie."

"They say it's more addicting than heroin."

"You're right, maybe I should just start mainlining H." I was trying to be funny, but I wasn't sure if Jack thought so. He had a certain kind of sense of humor.

"And when're you gonna get a real gun, something besides the Firestar?"

"It is a real gun." Jack thought my Firestar was a piece of garbage from Spain. It was from Spain, I didn't think it was garbage.

"You need a Sig or a Glock. Or a Colt .45."

I liked my little Firestar 9mm. It concealed nicely and besides, I wasn't planning on shooting anybody. At least not today.

"This is the wettest winter I remember in years," Jack said.

"Good thing we learned drownproofing. And now they can't bug us about the drought."

"The hell with that. As long as there's one illegal alien in this state don't tell me to conserve water or electric or any damn thing else. What about that Proposition 187? I can't wait to vote on that." Jack snapped the .45's magazine into place. "Can't wait to get outta my apartment either. They're cramming them in like in a clown car."

"There's gotta be zoning laws against that."

"Hell with that. I'm breaking my lease and getting out. I don't understand why they can't stay home or at least why we can't just enforce our borders?"

"Maybe they're desperate for work," I said, but there was really no arguing with Jack about this.

"Don't tell me you're buying into that propaganda."

Proposition 187 would have required California law enforcement, social services, health care, and public personnel to do a bunch of things nobody was doing or seemed to want to be doing, including verifying the immigration status of persons they came in contact with, reporting those persons to state and federal officials, and denying undocumented workers social services, health care, and education. And that was just a small part of what it said. Seemed that most of the state was for it and it looked good to pass. But there was strong and loud opposition. I guess I knew where Jack stood.

"One eighty-seven, isn't that also the penal code for homicide?" Jack grinned. He jacked a cartridge into the .45's chamber.

What could I say to that? So I didn't. Sometimes Jack seemed like my evil twin or the Devil on my shoulder from a cartoon, shouting in my ear to go against my better nature. He said things a lot of people wouldn't, but were probably thinking. Sometimes he said things I didn't want to think. But we were tight. Some people couldn't understand how I could be friends with someone like him. But he had my back in the Teams and he had it now—and I had his. If they couldn't understand, so be it.

I think most of us have a Jack in our lives.

"You take care of my girl," Jack said, bending down to give Molly a nice tummy rub. He packed up his guns and put my cleaning supplies away. "Remember, I have a stake in her too."

CHAPTER 4

Molly had a relatively quiet night, but I woke up to spots of what looked like blood everywhere. Jesus, what was wrong with her? I didn't want another Baron. He was murdered. It didn't look like anyone had broken into the house. So what the hell was wrong with Molly?

I leaned over her, running my hand through her fur. Her nose was covered with gunk; she was coughing. Wheezing. She had seemed fine just a few hours ago.

She looked up at me with pleading eyes. I scooped her up, jammed it to the Cherokee, and headed for the vet.

She spit up blood in the car. And some other vile-looking stuff. I approached Beverly Boulevard and Robertson, slowly. Damn traffic. Everywhere you went, any time of day. My hand almost pounded on the horn, the guy in front of me was driving like he was the only one on the road. And this intersection had one of those damn traffic cams. I was already famous enough, I didn't want any more fame, especially the kind you get when you're nosing out into the intersection three-tenths of a second too late.

"Move it, jackass," I mouthed. Unfortunately, he wasn't looking in his rearview mirror. Didn't look like he was looking at the road either. "Make the light, make the light."

He made the light—don't they always?—and I jammed into the intersection just as it turned yellow, smiling wide for the traffic cam, just in case. My left hand held the wheel. I thought about smiling for the camera with my right hand, or to be more precise the middle finger of my right hand, but it was busy petting Molly, who sat listless, in the passenger seat.

The vet's office was on Robertson, south of Olympic. And, of course, there was no parking in the six-space lot. Trying to park on the street would be a real nightmare. I found the closest space I could, carried Molly down the block, tucked under my arm.

"Mr. Rogers," the receptionist said, with a smile. Seeing Molly's blood-covered nose made the smile disappear. "What's wrong with Molly?"

"She's coughing up blood. And this other, dark stuff. I don't know what it is."

"I will get you into the doctor as soon as possible."

And she was as good as her word. I was in the examining room within five minutes, ahead of several unhappy looking people in the waiting room. The vet came in and gave Molly the once over. The first time I'd brought her here a few days ago she was eager, friendly. Today she was lethargic, hardly even lifting her head to say hello.

The doctor did a thorough exam. Helpless, I sat and watched as Molly was probed and poked. She did not look happy.

"I think it's kennel cough," he said. "Maybe parvo. That can be serious. I'll know more when I get the blood tests back."

"But she wasn't in a kennel."

"It's just a catch-all term. In the meantime, she's got fluid on her lungs."

Great.

"I want you to *coupage* her."

"What's that?" The name sounded familiar, maybe from my training. But at the moment I couldn't place it.

He held Molly up. "You steam up the shower as damp as you can get it, turn off the water, and put her in the stall with you. Then you reach around under her ribs like this."

He demonstrated, patting her lungs under her ribs. "And you tap lightly to break up the fluid that's built up there. Do it two or three times a day—three's better."

"Will she be okay?"

"I won't lie to you. I don't know. Right now it could go either way. But we'll do our best." He pulled out a needle and gave her a shot of antibiotics and a prescription for pills.

I carried Molly into the reception area, paid. I thanked the receptionist for getting us in quickly.

"*Buena suerte*," she said as I carried Molly outside into a glaring winter sun, glad it wasn't raining at the moment.

I tried to make Molly comfortable on the passenger seat. She looked up at me, then put her head down and went to sleep. I waded through traffic on the way home.

I pulled down the driveway, noticing a few more cracks in the cement than the day before, shut the engine off and went around to the passenger door. Molly's tongue lolled out of her mouth. Shit, I didn't want her to die. But I had just come from the vet. Besides, I wouldn't let her die. I lifted her from the seat, kicked the door closed and walked up the steps to my back door. Tucking her under my left arm, I managed to unlock the door, open it and walk in. I set her on the floor and she dragged tail to her favorite spot between the kitchen and breakfast room, where she promptly spit up blood and mucous. It hadn't taken her long to claim the little sunny area between the two rooms. In fact, she had a spot of her own in almost every room. I left her there while I went to the guest bathroom in the second bedroom, turned on only the hot water and let it steam up. And steam and steam. After several minutes, I retrieved Molly, under my arm again, went back to the head, reached into the shower with my right hand, turned off the water, and we stepped inside.

I set her on the pyramided deco tile floor. I could see her

mind wondering what the hell was going on. I bent over, held her with one arm, and *coupaged* her with the other. My hand tap-tap-tapped first one lung then the other, as we sweltered in the makeshift sauna.

"How's that, girl?" Her only response was to cough, sounding like an old man.

We walked back out to the breakfast area under our own steam and she lay in her spot. I looked at her, small and frail. Not the big Chinook she'd become, if she would become it now. Helpless.

I cleaned the mess she'd made, flipped on the radio. Another report about Susan Karubian. The news media, and I use the term loosely, love a juicy Hollywood story. But knowing Hollywood as I did, I almost couldn't blame her for taking the dive. I hated the people I worked for, most of them anyway, and especially the Hollywoodites. I had plenty of cases to be working. They didn't interest me. I was a victim of my own success, and guilt.

Everyone needs redemption. And I needed it more than most. I had caused a young woman's death, indirectly. But it still kept me awake at night. If I could help Marisol, maybe I could help myself. Maybe then I could call Rita instead of hoping one day the phone would ring and it would be her. Maybe one day I could look in the mirror and not see famous Duke, dragon slayer, savior of lost dogs and avenger of dead damsels. But just see myself.

I believed in the "broken windows" theory, which says that if you replace the broken windows in your neighborhood there will be less crime overall. The murder of Marisol's brother Carlos was a broken window that needed fixing.

And I decided right then: I would help Marisol, whether she wanted it or not.

CHAPTER 5

Two days now and the phone still hadn't rung.

Eric's journey had taken him from the tony thirty-third floor Century City law offices with movie star clients to a third-floor walk-up apartment in Venice, with cockroaches and gang bangers for neighbors. He looked out the window, angling to see the Pacific. He'd always wanted to live by the ocean—now here he was. Three stories up. If he jumped, would all the King's men and all the King's horses be able to put him back together again? Or would they take him off to some potter's field and bury him in a shallow grave? Did they even have potters' fields anymore?

Eric paced, fourteen steps this way, fourteen steps back. Every time he made a round trip, his room grew smaller. And every time he hit one end of the room he saw himself in the cloudy mirror, several days' growth of beard on his face. It wasn't like the Hollywood elite—trying to look cool, slumming. No, it was 'cause his last razor blade had cut the hell out of him and he'd thrown it away. He would give anything for a brand new one so he could shave and stop the itching. Look reasonably presentable.

Hollow eyes ringed with black half circles stared out at him under a shaggy head of hair. How different he was now. He looked at the bags under his eyes—suitcases he'd called them on his father when he was a child. And his father had laughed, saying he wished he had those suitcases full of nickels. But he had a house and a wife and two children. Eric had had that too, the American Dream, but his Dream went up in flames. And it was his own damn fault.

He stared at the apparition in the mirror, remembering back to his college days. The English lit course he hadn't wanted to take and T.S. Eliot's line about hollow men: "shape without form." He remembered the end of that poem too, "This is the way the world ends, Not with a bang but a whimper." And he wondered if that would be his fate.

He grabbed the bottle of forty-ounce Colt 45 off the counter. He hadn't yet sunk to the level of Thunderbird or wine with screw-on caps. But he liked to keep a constant light buzz going, something between inebriation and painful sobriety. Something to make the world a little more like looking through rose-colored glasses.

He gulped a mouthful of the bitter brew. A long way from having a sommelier open a bottle of wine, pour a taste in a crystal glass, and offer it to him for a sniff. Eric took a swig from the bottle of Colt. Right now he wished he had a different kind of Colt—a Colt .45. That would end it all with a bang and not a whimper.

How long had he lived in this dump now? The days, weeks, months all ran together. All this time and he still hadn't met his neighbors. From the looks of them that was just as well. Or was he being a snob? Some vestige of a former life? Did he ever have a former life? It was getting harder and harder to remember.

Maybe a little paint would brighten up the place. Yeah, that and a million bucks and he'd be set for life. At one time he thought he had been set for life; now that seemed like a different life, something he saw on a movie screen in a darkened theater once. Now he'd be lucky if he could make this month's rent on this crappy little place.

He listened to the waves crashing—or was it just the whoosh of cars? No matter, in his mind it was the ocean. That was good enough for now.

"Ring, Goddamnit. Ring!" He squeezed the phone in his hand, wanting to throw it across the room, smash it to little pieces. He had to consciously talk himself out of it. It was his only phone.

Eric reached into his pocket, pulled out his wallet. He felt the soft Spanish leather. This wallet had set him back three hundred dollars. His fingers brushed the surface several times before he opened it. Forty-four dollars. Not enough for rent. But enough for a pack of razor blades and a book at the used book store. If he didn't have something new to read he'd go nuts. He could go to the library but he was embarrassed by his appearance. At least if he bought a book he felt like a solid citizen—someone who could afford a book, even a used one. Besides, he had to get out of here. The walls were closing in on him like a coffin.

He wished he still had his mobile car phone. But at least he had an answering machine. He set it, grabbed his keys, and split like a fox running from the hounds.

The fog spilled off the ocean like a shroud. Eric walked to his car, vigilant. Head turning in every direction at the slightest sound. Gang bangers thought this was their territory. He'd heard about their initiation practice of having to kill a white person for no reason. He didn't want to be that person. Or maybe he was just being paranoid again. In all the time he'd lived here he hadn't been bothered by anybody except for a bum or two—or maybe he should call them homeless, since he might be one of them soon.

The Beamer's metallic blue paint was faded and cracked from the sun and salt air. The automatic door opener didn't work anymore. The tires were bald, the seats tattered. The floormats worn through to the floorboards. And the car was filthy. But it was his and, believe it or not, it still ran pretty good. He looked at it admiringly, remembering the day he bought it. How proud he'd been. His first new car. He should have sold it when it was shiny and relatively new. But he couldn't part with it. It was the only vestige of his former life. Besides, soon it might be his home.

He had thought he might go for a drive, then decided it was better to conserve gas and money and walked toward the Strand, the Venice boardwalk. At one time he'd laughed about the colorful characters down here. Now he was one and others were probably laughing at him.

The bleak sky mirrored his mood. It had been raining off and on, mostly on, for weeks now. Eric used to like the rain, now it just depressed him—now everything depressed him. This was Los Angeles, L.A., it was supposed to be sunny all the time. And all the people here were supposed to be sunny and optimistic and good looking and rich.

Not many people on the boardwalk today. The police bike patrol rolled on a couple hundred feet ahead. On one hand they gave Eric a sense of security. On the other, he felt guilty every time he passed them. Felt like they would stop him, question him, make him assume *the position*, just for being there. Just for being a bum in ratty clothes and worn out shoes.

The two cops wheeled toward him, nodding as they went by. Two Adonises, one black, one white. Youth and time on their side. They'd learn sooner or later that time waits for no one.

A few yards behind them, an old man, gray hair, prickly salt and pepper beard. Baggy, ripped cargo pants. But damn, what a nice blazer. Looked like something from Brooks Brothers or Nordstrom's. The man looked about Eric's size. He wanted that jacket. He wanted something to make him feel normal again. He contemplated shoving the man between a couple of buildings and taking the jacket off his hands. The distance between them closed. Eric's fists clenched. He wasn't as strong as he'd been, hadn't been to the gym in a long time. But he was young.

Ten feet and closing.
Eight feet.
Four feet.
Eric let the man come up on his right so he could use his right hand to grab him.
Two feet.
Side by side.
Now Eric was several feet past the man. He couldn't do it. Why not? Hell, the world sucked. It had cheated him. Screwed him. There was no justice. No right and wrong. Everybody out for himself and screw you. So why the hell couldn't he do it? Damn.

His fists slowly unclenched as he came on Small World Books. He reached into his pocket for his money and went inside.

He didn't really want to spend the money for a new book, but he liked looking. Liked the feel of a book in his hands. The smell. The way the pages crackled when he turned them. Nobody bothered him here, but he still felt out of place and walked out.

Down the boardwalk a ways a vendor had a couple of medium-sized folding tables packed with used paperbacks. This was more his speed these days. He stopped to look. The books were all well-thumbed. When he was buying books new he'd never crease the edges, even when he read them. Though he often didn't have enough time to read in the old days.

He paged through books by Tom Wolfe and Toni Morrison, James Ellroy and Charles Bukowski. He came to one called *Shoot the Piano Player* by David Goodis. The cover said it was originally titled *Down There*. Since he felt "down there" he picked it up. The spine was broken in a hundred places—it must have been bought and sold a dozen times already, judging by the various prices that were penciled inside the front cover. The last one—the one that wasn't crossed out—said thirty-five cents. Hell, Eric was a King—he could afford that.

"Good book." She was small, gamin-like. He'd seen her on the boardwalk before, though they'd never spoken. "Goodis is, uh, good. He writes about people like us. And you might try Dan Fante too. But don't get him mixed up with his father, John. Though they're both good."

Eric looked at the cover. "You've read it?" He knew it was a silly question as soon as it escaped his lips. She must have read it to know it's good. He felt like a moron. She smiled.

"I've been 'down there,'" she said.

"Down where?" Were they flirting? It'd been so long Eric didn't know.

"Down so long it looked like up to me."

He wasn't sure how to respond to that. "I hope you're not down that low anymore."

"If I am I don't know it anymore."

That frightened Eric. He worried he might start to feel like that too.

He started to pay her. She reached out a hand, then pulled it back. "I don't work here. Just browsing, like you. Pay that guy over there." She pointed to a man leaning against a wall, tottering on a folding green, white, and orange beach chair. Long, greasy hair dangled over his eyes. Eric could smell him from here. Not so long ago he wouldn't have gone near the man.

Eric paid the man, who said nothing, just nodded, sliding the money into a decrepit cigar box.

Eric sized the girl up. Too skinny. But skinny enough to be a top model with that heroin-chic look. Stringy black hair that set off a kabuki-white face. He looked for track marks on her arms. Didn't notice any.

"How 'bout if I buy you a soda?" She was young, maybe nineteen, maybe in her early twenties. But he longed for someone to talk to, companionship. Maybe they'd have nothing to say to each other, but it would be nice just to have a Coke with someone.

"You don't have to cheer me up."

"I'm not trying to cheer you up. But since you gave me a review on this book I figure I owe you." He winked. She agreed to have a soda with him. They walked down the boardwalk until they came to a hot dog stand. He splurged on hot-dogs-on-sticks and giant pink lemonades for both of them. She scarfed her hot dog down like it was the first food she'd eaten in three weeks—maybe it was. He bought her another. He still couldn't make the rent and buying a couple hot dogs and lemonades wouldn't make a difference one way or another.

"How long you been down here?" she said.

"I've lost track." But he knew every day that he'd fallen from grace, as if he was X-ing them off on a makeshift prison wall calendar.

"I thought you were a newbie."

"What makes you think that?"

"You don't have that empty look in your eyes."

He looked into her eyes, trying to see if she had the empty look. He couldn't tell for sure.

"What'd you do, lose your job?" she said.

"Something like that."

"Couldn't get another?"

He didn't want to go into the whole story. "Not in the same field and I'm not really qualified for anything else." He wanted to change the subject, away from him. What was the point of telling her his tale of woe? That he'd lost his law license. That it sent him into a downward spiral of cheap booze and feeling sorry for himself, even though he'd brought about his own downfall. That he was overqualified for most jobs, at least to the employers. But he knew he was really underqualified and under motivated. That he didn't want a real job, not if it didn't involve the law and there was no law firm in the city willing to hire him, not even as a paralegal. "What's your story? Are you out here on your own?"

"Damn straight."

"You're awfully young."

"You wanna hear my story? I'm twenty, came out here to be a moo-vee star like all the rest. That was a joke."

"Where do you live?"

She hesitated. "Anywhere I can. There's some squats I know about."

Eric knew what a squat was. Usually an abandoned building, no electricity. No running water, no toilets—the halls and floors served that purpose. Filled with a lot of lost kids with nowhere else to go, who would have had broken dreams if they had time to think about them.

"I know you don't know me, but you could stay at my place. It's not much, but—" he said.

"No thanks. And no offense."

They talked a little more, not saying much of consequence, except that she told him her name was Lindsay. They said maybe they'd run into each other again and went their separate ways. He hoped she hadn't thought he was coming onto her. He didn't care about sex—not now. He just wanted a friend. It'd been so long.

Eric sat on his bed, the new-used book next to him, feeling like a character in a Hopper painting, alone, and lonely in a cold light. He'd had an opportunity to buy an original Hopper sketch once. Jennifer said it was depressing and he let it go in favor of some no-name artist's work that hadn't appreciated but came highly recommended by her art guru. He wondered if he'd ever really see the girl again—Lindsay. He wondered if he'd ever get on his feet again. He wasn't qualified to do much and the one thing he was qualified for he couldn't do. Maybe he should be a janitor. Was it really beneath him at this point? Hell, he thought, you gotta be an illegal alien to do that work. That was a good enough reason not to try. He caught himself. In the old days he never would have thought like this, wouldn't have even used the term *illegal alien*. What the hell was happening?

He picked up the book, opening it to the title page, then checking the copyright notice. He always read the front and back covers, prefaces, author bios, publishing history, acknowledgments, the little blurb on what typeface they used, anything there was to read before he actually started a book.

He turned to page one: "There were no street lamps, no lights at all." Then the phone rang.

CHAPTER 6

Jack came by to see Molly. Brought her a rubber chew toy, but she would have been happy to see him anyway. He was her savior. I watched them. A good team. Like Jack and I. She was still sick, but the medicine seemed to be working, and her joy at seeing Jack seemed to push that into the background as she rolled on the kitchen floor. The room hadn't been remodeled since my parents lived here and I don't think they'd ever done anything with it. It still had its original nineteen twenties' deco tile and now-yellowed linoleum floor. But even that lent it a certain charm.

The Motels' "Only the Lonely" played in the background. I always figured Martha Davis, the chief Motel, could write the soundtrack to my life.

"And you talk about me listening to ancient music," Jack said.

"Hey, it's not that old."

"It's from the eighties, man. The early eighties." He adjusted his shades. Outdoors or in, the shades almost never came off. He saw the world through a polarized glass twilight that, in some ways, separated him from it by just enough distance.

"At least it isn't the sixteen eighties."

"Hey, that's the Baroque era. Now you're treading on thin ice, buddy."

"Well, 'Only the Lonely' was from eighty-two, if I remember correctly."

"Ancient history." Jack listened to the lyrics for a mo-

42

ment. Martha Davis wailed about loneliness. The shades came off for a moment—he looked at me with one of those piercing stares, the kind that could spear right through you and cause almost as much pain as if he'd been using a real spear—and just as quickly they went back on.

"What?"

"You're still carrying the torch for her, aren't you?" Jack said, his words weighted with concern.

I gave him my best I-don't-know-what-you're-talking-about shrug. But I did and he knew I did. Rita. "Can't I listen to what I want?"

"At least that Tortoise Head you listen to is current. Now you're sticking your head in the sand."

"Portishead."

Jack ignored my correction. But it dawned on me that since he knew the song was current, maybe he wasn't such a musical Neanderthal after all. He just liked to play one to get at me.

"A faint heart never won a lady. Why don't you call her before she forgets who you are."

Jack and I had been in many dark places together. So why the hell couldn't I do what he said and just dial her damn number?

"Gettin' closer all the time," he said, tugging on the chew toy, while Molly yanked at the other end.

"What is?"

"The vote on 187. It's gonna win. Meantime, I gotta go apartment hunting." And the subject was changed. He had said what he had to say about my calling Rita. No more for him to say. Now it was up to me and he was onto other things.

"I'm going to help Marisol find her brother's killer." Maybe it wasn't the smoothest transition. But he was talking about illegal aliens—Marisol and her brother fell into that category. It made sense to me at the time. I had told him about the housekeeper down the block whose brother had been killed. He grunted.

"Gratis?"

I nodded.

"You got all these Hollywood honchos comin' at you and you're gonna do a freebie for a bunch of illegals."

I knew if I didn't do anything about it Carlos would just be another statistic in L.A.'s infamous murder log for nineteen ninety-four. Just like Susan Karubian and so many others. She may not have been murdered in the traditional sense, but I had a feeling this city had murdered her, the way it does to so many who come here with big dreams and saucer eyes only to find out that the streets are paved with *mierda* instead of gold.

"Fucking wetbacks, they're taking over. You better start learning *Español*." He tore the toy from Molly's mouth, threw it across the room. She dashed for it. "Why?"

"Broken windows."

"That broken windows theory is BS. You know he, the brother, probably got fucked up hangin' with the wrong homies. When you lie down with dogs, you're gonna get fleas. Why not let sleeping dogs lie?"

"Is that a record for clichés in one sentence?"

Jack grunted again.

"Doesn't matter. Marisol needs closure," I said, holding my hands up as if to say that's that. "Closure is BS. There's no such thing."

"Not for me."

"You're doing penance. How long you gonna wear that hair shirt? And if you'd just take it off, you'd see what I'm saying about the illegals."

"Segue, Jack." That was our cue to change subjects. I didn't want a lecture on how illegals were screwing up the country every way possible.

"You're famous. A famous detective going after some

wetback's killer."

"I hate being famous. And I'm not that famous."

"'Spect you'll be wanting me to back you up."

"Your call." I knew he would. He'd do it for me. He'd do it for Molly, so she'd have a good home.

"So where do we start?"

With Jack gone, Molly and I enjoyed our steam bath together. The *coupaging* seemed to work. She still coughed up blood, but not as much.

"You stay here and guard the house," I said, as I picked up a notebook and the Pentel mechanical pencil I favored. I patted her head, closed the door on her. It's always hard to close the door on a dog. They have such expectations of you and are so sad to see you leave. But their eager reception when you get home makes it all worthwhile.

I walked up the block toward the Goldsteins' house, taking in the scent of honeysuckle and hoping I'd catch Marisol before they got home from work. I didn't know them very well—in L.A. it's a civil code that you are not allowed to know your neighbors. I hadn't walked Molly in a few days because of her illness and in just those few days it seemed that more bars had gone up on various windows. A lot of people who never thought they would had bought guns and put bars up after the Rodney King riots, then it seemed to quiet down for a while. Now it was like a land boom in real estate, everybody was buying.

One car, a white Lexus, was in the driveway, so I assumed one of the Goldsteins was home. The doorbell chimed. A minute later Marisol opened the door. She wasn't exactly beautiful, but there was something striking about her.

"*Señor* Duke."

"I'd like to talk to you about your brother."

"*Por qué?* That is very kind of you, but I cannot afford to hire you."

"I'll do it *pro bono*."

"*Pro bono*?"

"For free, I won't charge you."

"I cannot impose on you."

"I want to help."

She invited me in. I'd never been in the Goldsteins' house and there was no sign of either of them. Nothing unusual. It was nicely furnished in Danish modern, that might have been modern in the nineteen fifties. Still, it hardly looked worn. I assumed the Goldsteins had children and wondered if, when they were young, Mrs. G. had covered the furniture in plastic. Little porcelain gimcracks abounded. Hummel or Meissen maybe? I wasn't as up on my porcelain gimcracks as I should be. Why is it that when some women get to be a certain age they feel the need to acquire porcelain Bo Peeps? Something maternal? And when men reached that age they start wearing Madras pants of all colors with yellow Izod shirts or tall knee socks, white shoes with tassels, and Bermuda shorts, even if they don't play golf. Getting old scared the shit out of me.

We went back to Marisol's room at the back of the house. Small, neat, and very clean. Lived in—I wondered if she lived here full time. The only porcelain here was a small Virgin Mary on her dresser underneath Jesus on the cross. I sat in the blonde-wood desk chair and she sat on the bed. The powder blue walls were calming, though she didn't look very calm. A well-thumbed bible in Spanish sat on the desk. Travel posters on the walls, exotic places, Fiji and Jamaica. Sparkling blue water and palm trees. Clean white sand. Beaches, but somehow different from L.A.'s beaches.

"I like your posters."

"Someday I would like to travel." Her eyes lit up in anticipation. "I don't really believe that day will ever come."

"You never know."

She offered to get me something to drink; I declined. I wanted to get down to business. She was holding herself together pretty well, but I knew it would be hard for her.

"Tell me about Carlos. What's his last name, your last name?"

"Rivera, we are both Rivera." She stared up at the posters on her wall, as if wanting to escape into them. "It is very nice of you to make this offer, but truly you have more important things to do."

Chasing down dirt for the Hollywood crowd didn't seem important to me. "I'll just make a few phone calls, see if I can find something out for you."

Marisol stared at a Tahitian beach, was she already there in her mind? "Okay. What do you want to know?"

"Let's start with Carlos."

"He is one year older than me, but much less responsible. He doesn't want to hold a steady job. I help him when I can."

"Where did he live?"

"In East Hollywood. A not very nice area."

"And what did he do when he did it?"

"He was a day laborer. Sometimes."

"So you live here or you live somewhere else?"

"I live here. The Goldsteins are very nice. Good people to work for. They trust me and that is important."

"Where are the Goldsteins now? I saw a car in the driveway."

"They are at work. They drive in together most of the time."

"So you didn't live with Carlos?"

"Not since we first come here."

"When was that?"

"Two years."

I asked her where in Mexico they'd come from and where they lived when they got to the U.S.

"We are from Oaxaca. We come across the border at, how

do you say, Smuggler's Gulch, near San Diego. We don't stay in San Diego though. We come right up to L.A. We have to pay the man who gets us across the border, so at first we work and all our money goes to him. He takes us to a priest at the mission. The priest helps us, then we finally are free and Carlos works as a laborer and I work as a maid. I have worked three jobs before coming to the Goldsteins. We live together then until we get, how do you say, established and I move in here. We just want to work and make a life for ourselves."

"The American Dream."

"*Sí. El sueño Americano.*"

"And you're undocumented?"

"*Sí*, illegal." She squirmed at the word. "The Goldsteins are helping me to get my papers."

"When will that happen?"

"Soon, I hope."

"And Carlos?"

"He, too, was not legal." She looked down at the floor.

"Was someone helping him get his papers?"

"*No sé*, I don't know."

"Where was he killed?"

"I don't think anyone knows that answer. They find his body in the Los Angeles River, but one of the detectives says he thinks Carlos float there from the Arroyo Seco. I am not sure where that is."

"It's up near Pasadena," I said. "So somebody killed him, dumped the body, and he floated on down from the Arroyo Seco into the L.A. River." I immediately felt bad about using the phrase "dumped the body." Wished I had put it more diplomatically.

"*Sí.*"

"What was the cause of the death?"

She thought a moment. "They say his neck is broken."

"From the fall into the river? An accident?"

"This is what the police say."

"You don't think so?"

"I think not."

"Somebody broke his neck." Somebody who didn't mind getting close and personal to do his dirty work. "I'm sorry to go on like this, but I need to know the answers. Do you think it was a gang killing?"

"Carlos was not in a gang."

"I didn't mean to say he was. Just maybe he got in someone's way or made someone angry. If somebody tries to start a fight with you, you're in a fight whether you like it or not."

"I don't think so, but I do not know."

"Do you have any idea who might have killed him or why? Did he have a bad temper? Get in fights?"

"No, I don't think so. He was, how you say, laid back." Her hands cupped her face. "I am so guilty."

"Guilty?"

"*Sí*, he was *mi hermano*, I should have done more to help him. I should have been closer to him."

We talked a few more minutes. She seemed nervous, her eyes darting all over the room. Was it just talking about her dead brother or something else? I couldn't be sure. Before I left, I got Carlos' address and the name of the detective on the case, Courval. It wasn't familiar. She walked me to the door and I exited, turning back to say goodbye. It was later in the afternoon now and the sun had turned yellow, golden. She stood framed in the doorway and it seemed as if the frame was closing in on her like in some amusement park funhouse.

I checked on Molly. Called LAPD Detective James Courval. Left a message with my cellular phone number, grabbed my kit bag with the Firestar in it.

As I was getting into the Jeep, Marisol jogged down the driveway.

"If you are going to help me," she said, "I must pay your services." She handed me a hundred-dollar bill. I was about to protest, but she wrapped my fingers around it. I knew this would be a big job and a hundred bucks would barely cover a couple days' gas, but I took it. Thanked her. And I would fill out the paperwork, just like on any other job, and give her a receipt.

I hit the road as the skies were clouding up with dirty gray clouds that looked like Pittsburgh snow on a bad day.

Dribbles of rain landed on the windshield—just enough to smudge the dirt—as I turned north on my street, up to Melrose, then right, heading east. When I was a boy Melrose was ancient ladies and antique shops. Today it was one of the chic avenues of the city. Lots of little chi chi boutiques and places to eat that gave you portions of California cuisine that would barely fill a gnat's stomach. Not much evidence here of quake damage today. You might even see a movie star on Melrose. That was certainly more likely there than on Hollywood Boulevard.

At La Brea I turned north and then east on Hollywood. I could have gone a different way. But I liked driving Hollywood Boulevard. Used to be a ton of used bookstores up here. Now it was all discount electronics stores run by Iranians. Anyone who came to geographical Hollywood looking for *Hollywood* was in for a major disappointment, from the dirty streets to the tarnished stars set in the pavement.

I slammed on the brakes as I turned into a sea of red taillights. The light refracted in the mist, melding with the neon sign reflections on the street in a hallucinatory jumble of waves and lines. The Boulevard was backed up. As I inched my way east I could see throngs of people outside the Chinese Theatre. It used to be Graumann's, now it was Mann's. It lost something in the translation.

It wasn't unusual to see crowds outside the theatre, but these people carried Mexican flags and picket signs: "No on

187," "Gringos Go Home," and "Aztlan." Everybody was getting their two cents in. Aztlan was what some people wanted the Southwest of the US to become—a new Mexican homeland, Aztec-Land. Jack already believed he was living in Aztlan.

The movie playing at the main theatre was *Pulp Fiction*, which seemed appropriate. A blast of dialogue from the movie shot into my mind, where someone asks Bruce Willis what his name means. He says that Americans' names don't mean shit. But Marisol's name meant something, it meant sunny sea. Right now that sea was stormy. I hoped to bring the sun out again.

The Boulevard was down to one lane in each direction and it took thirty minutes to go one block. Protesters marched on the sidewalks and in the streets. I was ready if they touched my car. They can protest all they want but they better leave my car alone.

I got through unscathed. The street opened up after the protest and traffic flowed smoothly, or as smoothly as it does in L.A. I could see the stars on the sidewalks—the only place you might see stars in Hollywood proper these days. Seeing those stars at an oblique angle from the car made me think of Susan Karubian jumping from the Hollywood Sign. The stars must have blinded her, or maybe they blindsided her. I couldn't see the sign from here and that was just as well.

I turned onto Carlos' street, probably not the best place for a white male to go alone. I drove by the building and surveyed the neighborhood. It felt like another country. The signs were all in Spanish. The cars on the side streets old and gray for the most part, with a few spiffy new jobs, Beamers—drug dealers? And what did that assumption say about me?

There was no good place to park, so I pulled into the apartment's driveway. Carlos' once-white stucco courtyard apartment was a block and a half north of Hollywood Boulevard, nestled in the Hollywood hills. The hills, usually brown and dry, were green and lush now after weeks of rain. But even all this rain couldn't wash the grime from the walls. Cracks in the stucco might have been from the recent quake or they might just have been the cracking of the dreams of all the dreamers who had lived here over the decades. What was definitely from the quake were the piles of rubble along the street. Piles that had long been cleared away in other parts of the city, but not here.

The Firestar sat in my safari vest on the passenger seat. It might have been a photographer's vest, with large cargo pockets for extra film, camera accessories or a semi-auto pistol. It wasn't so safari that it had loops for shotgun shells or a padded shoulder to take the shotgun's recoil. It looked kind of ordinary and wouldn't draw suspicion. But it held my 9mm ball of fire with the outlawed Black Talon hollow points in the magazine. They were no different than any other hollow point round, but they had that nasty name and a black bullet and that was scary to folks who were scared of such things.

I put the vest on, felt the gun snuggled in the pocket, started to get out of the car. Ranchera music spilled from the building.

"Private parking, man," a young dude with a shaved do said. His oversized shirt hung low over the beltline of his baggy pants. Hiding a pistol?

"I'm only gonna be a minute."

The man moved closer.

"Don'chu understand English. *Quieres que lo diga en Español.*"

"*Yo hablo un poquito Español,*" I said in my best high school Spanish.

"*Bueno.*"

"But my English is better."

"What do you want?"

Should I trust him or not? He didn't have gang banger

tats, at least not visible ones. But he was putting on the tough act. Maybe he had something to do with Carlos' disappearance. What the hell, I was here—and so was he.

Another man spilled out of the nearest door on the side of the building.

"*Qué pasa?*"

"I'm looking into the death of Carlos Rivera for his sister." I had started to say it before the second man came out, so I finished it, wondering again if he was someone I should be talking to.

"Who are you?" the first man said.

"Hey, Chico, I seen him—haven't I seen you?"

"I don't know, have you?"

"On TV. This dude's some famous detective."

"No shit."

My fame had even followed me into the barrio. And my seven and a half minutes of it was turning into a full eight. I still hated being famous, but sometimes it worked for you.

"He's okay, man. He helped find the killer of that actress, what was her name—Teddie, Teddie Matson, *una muchacha muy bonita.*"

"Okay, man, you got five minutes," the second man said. He had short dark hair, slicked down on his round skull. No tats. A wisp of a moustache. Instead of baggy pants, he wore coveralls.

"Carlos lived here?" I said.

"*Sí.*"

"When was the last time you saw him?"

"You askin' 'cause you're curious or 'cause you wanna pin it on us?"

"I don't want to pin it on anyone. I just want to find out what happened."

"We don't know him too well. Like a lot of us he just needs a place to sleep at night, eat. We all chip in and—" His English was good when he wanted it to be.

"And it's very comfortable here, man. We sleep twenty to a small bedroom," the second man said. By now a crowd had gathered, but the two men still did the talking. "*El Sueño Americano.*"

My Spanish wasn't all that great, but he sounded sarcastic to me. Either way, I wasn't about to get into a debate with him. My eyes wandered to the green tag on Carlos' building, then to the red tag on the apartments next door. That little piece of paper wasn't stopping that building from being occupied. Children played, clothes hung from lines, and the smell of food cooking came from the windows. Someday an inspector would come and close it down, fine the owner. Until then it was business as usual.

"But we're comin' back, man. *Reconquista.* And then you'll be livin' forty to a room."

Jack would have loved that. *Reconquista* was the term for the Mexicans reconquering the Southwest United States. An emotionally charged word for both sides. I let it slide.

"If we let them stay," moustache said.

"Maybe we let them mow the lawn and clean the toilets."

"I think we're getting off track here," I said. It didn't look to me like they really believed what they were saying, but they were on a roll, trying to push and see if I'd push back. It wasn't the time or place to be debating immigration issues. "Did you hang out with Carlos?"

"Man, you can't help but hang out when you live like we do. Were we *amigos*? No."

"All we know is that he disappeared. His sister called— she's too good for us, she never comes down here, not even when he was alive—to ask us if we know anything. We don't know nuthin'."

"Who did he work for?" While talking with them my eyes kept scanning the perimeter. I didn't want any surprises.

"Anybody that would pay—day jobs mostly, I think. We don't keep tabs on each other."

"He do some work for the church, don't he?" one of the men said.

"The Catholic Church?"

He looked at me like I was an idiot—what other church was there?

"Do you know who he worked for at the church?" I said.

"There's some priest helped him and his sister when they first come here. I think he did some work for him sometimes."

"Do you know the priest's name? Or his parish?"

He shrugged.

"Can I see his room, his things?" I motioned toward the courtyard.

They looked at each other, nodded, then led me under an archway, across the cracked terra cotta tiles of the courtyard. At one time this must have been the height of L.A. chic, something Nathanael West's Tod Hackett or the Fitzgeralds might have been at home in. Now, with its decaying black-water swimming pool, dead plants, and people hanging out of every nook and cranny, it was anything but. Well, not all the plants were dead, a couple of hearty yuccas looked like they were hoping the rain would give them a comeback.

They led me inside. The walls were painted bright green and red and white—the colors of the Mexican flag. The house smelled of sweat and tamales. The fragrance of stale marijuana smoke seemed as if it was trying to mask the other odors the way some people might use one of those jellied room deodorizers. It wasn't winning. Mostly tired—maybe defeated—eyes stared at me as we walked through the house to a back bedroom. People were warehoused here like cattle or indentured servants, and many of them probably were indentured to the *coyotes* who'd brought them across the border. Packed in here like human sardines, twenty people to a room, forty or sixty to a house. Was this the American Dream they'd risked their lives coming here for? Blank eyes followed me through each room. A white man was a curiosity here. But that was me, a curiosity.

The back bedroom was maybe twelve by fifteen feet. It looked like twenty people slept here. And I wondered why Carlos, who'd been in the States awhile, wasn't living in better circumstances. The furnishings in Carlos' pad made Motel 6 look like the Four Seasons. People like to move when there's a murder, but not Carlos' people—they couldn't. Instead they sat vacant-eyed, staring at KMEX channel thirty-four on the TV, zoning out, until the next morning when they'd go stand on a street corner, hoping for work.

Carlos' death hadn't made the news. Unlike Susan Karubian he hadn't gone out in spectacular fashion. He wasn't a pretty young starlet with disenchanted stars in her eyes. People like Carlos died every day. It was like Stalin said, "One death is a tragedy; a million is a statistic." Carlos was just another statistic, though like Karubian he, too, had come here to fulfill his version of *El Sueño Americano*.

They showed me an olive drab bedroll under a fourteen-inch mahogany crucifix.

"This was his," the first man said, pointing to a rolled up sleeping bag. "We wrap all his stuff in it, thinking his sister might want it. But she don't come for it."

"She's afraid of us—her own people."

"Did the police come?"

"Sure, man, they come, for five minutes. Then they're outta here. We smell bad to them, even the Mexican cops."

"They're the worst, man. They got something to prove. Nobody kicks us harder."

"They don't give a shit about some dead *inmigrante ilegal*. And I don't give a shit about all the money in America either."

I didn't think it would make a difference if I told him that the American Dream was about more than money. "Can I take it?" I said, referring to the bedroll and Carlos' things wrapped up in it.

"We know some people who could use it."

"I'll bring it back. It might help me find who killed him."

"*La policía* say it was *un* accident. You don't think so?"

"No."

That was good enough for them. They handed it to me with a look that said I'd never bring it back.

"Is there anything else?"

"No, all his stuff's in there."

"Thanks."

"*De nada.*"

I talked to several more of Carlos' roommates, some through a translator. But no one could tell me much. Then they walked me out to the Jeep. I got in, rolled the window down. The first young man leaned in close enough for me to smell the smoke on his breath.

"You find the man who did Carlos—we'll take care of him."

"I'll find him, if I can."

"Don't forget the last part of what I said."

I ignored that a second time.

"Find him and maybe we'll let you stay on after *La Reconquista.*" He smiled a wicked grin. Now I thought he really meant it. I drove off, heading down to Sunset, the romantic passions of Ranchera music fading into the background.

Sunset Boulevard is the snake that winds and twists its way from Downtown L.A. to the Pacific Ocean just south of the Santa Monica Mountains. Once, as a boy, my father and I walked from our house up to Sunset to its terminus at Union Station, across from Olvera Street, the original Mexican settlement of the City of Angels. We walked down the Strip, through East Hollywood, past Chavez Ravine, where Dodger Stadium is. I was scared as we passed through bad neighborhoods and by bad people. At least they looked bad. But no one bothered us and my father wasn't scared. And his strength gave me strength. It's one of the good memories I have of him.

I was feeling a little dejected. After all, Marisol hadn't jumped at my offer to help her find out what happened to her brother. I had insinuated myself into the case.

I decided to go out for a drink at my favorite watering hole, the Café Noir, at the far eastern border of the Strip, the not-so-good area. But that also meant real people and real drinks instead of Hollywood phonies or wannabes, each with a damn script under their arm or a laptop on their table. Some cool people also hung out, like Scotty, the lead singer from a new band called Big Bad Voodoo Daddy, who just came out with their first album. Neo-swing music, so the Noir was the perfect dive for them.

I drove past a billboard for *Ace Ventura: Pet Detective*, found a parking space under another billboard for Madonna's *Secret* album. Sunset was the place for billboards, artists' contracts specified it. I hoofed the block from the parking space to the café. I thought of that long ago walk. My father. My estranged brother. My mother who'd been gone for several years now. Where did it all go wrong?

"Yo, Duke." The man with the groovy Steven Seagal ponytail headed my way.

Keep walking. Was I talking to him or myself?

He was getting closer. Tall. Bulked-up. Looked like he could fight if he wanted to. You never knew. The ponytail was wimpy, but I knew someone who'd fought Seagal in competition. This was one big dude with several martial arts belts. He said Seagal was no pushover. I wondered if this guy was a pushover or just a wannabe action star.

Here was that fame stuff popping up again. It's damn hard being famous. Especially when you didn't go looking for it. I had been on TV in short bursts for about a week after catching up with Teddie Matson's killer. It's amazing what a few minutes on TV will do for you. Everyone recognized me. The checker in the grocery store, the bank teller, strangers on the street, like this guy. Some of them just wanted to say howdy. Others wanted to prove how tough they were and how not-tough I was. Which one was this guy?

We were within ten feet of each other now and closing fast. Keep an eye on his hands—always. Watch his eyes, watch his hands. The eyes could give a tell and I could be one jump ahead.

Five feet.

Three.

"My man," he said and put his fist out for some kind of fancy handshake or bump. I balled up my fingers, brushed them on his and was past him. I could hear his footsteps receding down the sidewalk.

That was an easy one. But I was sick of being famous. I never asked for it. Sick of working for the Hollywood crowd, who thought they owned you just because they paid you, late more often than not, pleading poverty as they lived in the mansions above Sunset and drove Jags and Lamborghinis. Who knows, maybe it was all rented? Most of them were as much façade as the sets they filmed on. Which made me wonder about Susan Karubian. Why pick the Hollywood Sign to jump off? Another disappointed actress who didn't know the ropes? Who didn't know what it would take to make it in this town? She should have gone home and slipped under the covers until the dream passed. Then she could have woken up one day with a smile and faced the world. After all, a new world's born at dawn.

I opened the Café Noir's door, a flood of velvet blackness enveloping me as I entered. The transition from daylight, even overcast daylight, to the Noir's dimness made me close my eyes for a few seconds. Nat King Cole's "The Blues Don't Care" sinuously threaded its way from the jukebox. The bartender nodded. I nodded back. I settled in a corner at the far end of the bar, hoping no one I knew would join me. It wasn't crowded at this hour, but you never knew. And right now I just wanted to get lost in a drink and the shadows, in the music and the anonymity of a dark corner.

"Hey, Duke," the bartender said. He knew me before I was famous.

The club was retro, not because they were trying, but because they had never updated. So since what goes around comes around, they were cool again. People came in here to be anonymous. If they wanted to be seen they'd go to the other end of the Strip. I stared at the neon pink flamingo over the bar and ordered a lemonade and gin, not the usual bar fare. The barkeep mixed the special drink for me, some of his homemade lemonade with two fingers of gin. My drink.

"Your usual," the barman said.

"Maybe they'll name it after me. That'd be cool—'gimme a Duke on the rocks, bartender.'"

Not quite time for the after-work crowd, folks who needed a stiff drink to fortify themselves before going home and facing a nagging wife, a yelling husband and a bunch of screamy, snot-nosed kids.

The door opened and a bright shaft of light pounced through it. A man entered. I knew him to say hello to. Larry Darrell, an LAPD detective, who worked out of their Metro Division. Which basically gave him free reign throughout L.A. He liked to come here in Sheriff's territory for a drink, off duty, or on. He sat a stool away from me at the bar.

"Hey, Duke."

"How's it going, Larry?"

"It's going. It's going. Things are pretty much back to normal." He was talking about the Rodney King riots of a couple years before. Maybe the earthquake of a few months ago. Or maybe both. There's always something shaking in L.A. "Except our hands get more tied every day. Do the people want a police department or not?"

I nodded as the bartender brought Larry his drink—no-brand bourbon. He didn't need to ask what it was. I put down money for Larry's drink. I guess he knew a question was coming. "Larry, do you know a Detective James Courval?"

"Heard of him. Don't know him personally. I think he works out of Rampart Division."

"Good man?"

"I couldn't really say. What's this about, Duke?"

"Oh, case I'm working. Carlos Rivera. Your guys found him in the L.A. River. They're calling it an accident."

"Accident. Code for we don't have time to deal with this or maybe just we don't give a damn."

"I was thinking the same thing. But it might be premature. I called Courval. Still waiting to hear back, but it hasn't been that long."

"Who're you working for?"

I could have given him that "You know I can't tell you that" shit. Didn't. "His sister, Marisol. She's a housekeeper down the block from me. Nice kid. Wants to know what really happened to her brother."

Larry nodded, took a swig.

"What do you guys think about this 187 shit?" I said.

"It's just another thing to have the city blow up over."

"I just drove through a 187 protest on Hollywood Boulevard."

"Our guys must've kept it under control," Larry said. "I didn't hear anything unusual on the squawk box." He downed his bourbon in one gulp. "This used to be a nice city."

The bartender poured him another shot of no-name.

CHAPTER 7

I threw Carlos' bedroll on the kitchen floor. Molly immediately dived into it. I wasn't happy about that. It might not have been evidence for the police since the *accident* had taken place somewhere other than Carlos' crib, but it was evidence for me. Besides, it was filthy. Maybe I should have left it outside. On the plus side, maybe it meant that Molly was feeling better. She started tearing at the fabric, ripping it apart, which wasn't hard considering how threadbare it was. I gently pushed Molly aside—hell, I bribed her with a Milk Bone, which placated her—and started my own examination of the rank material. I should probably have put gloves on like they do on all the TV shows these days, but I didn't want to take the time. I didn't do a search of the bedroll at Carlos' place because I didn't want anyone there to see if I found anything.

I unrolled the sleeping bag. Wrapped in its folds were all the detritus of a life lived on a small scale. A sun-faded picture of Carlos and Marisol. Another of the two kids and two world-weary parents. A few articles of clothing. A wallet. No ID. No money. I figured Carlos' housemates had made a cash withdrawal.

"It's time to *coupage* you." I walked to the guest bathroom to steam up the shower, leaving Molly to her Milk Bone. Instead she tore up Carlos' sleeping bag with a vengeance. By the time I got back, her head was jerking back and forth like a frenetic fan at a tennis match. Her little teeth sank into the material. Rip. Batting flew every which way. It was a done deal and I'd have a hell of a fun time cleaning up this mess. I brought her back to the shower, stepped in and started patting her rib cage. She seemed to like the ritual. We bonded, though I wish it had been for a better reason.

Done, she went to her favorite pillow to lie down and I went to clean up the mess in the kitchen. I picked up batting and stuffed it in a green trash bag. As I did, I sifted it slowly to make sure there was nothing I'd missed. If Carlos had hidden something anywhere in the bag it was bound to come out now. I thought I had been wrong when after several minutes nothing showed up. Finally something did—a small piece of paper with a phone number on it. Evidence? A clue? Or just a girlfriend's number? I put it in a baggie from the kitchen drawer—just like they do on TV. Hey, I was a pro, no doubt about it. I didn't find anything else and stuffed the remains of the bedroll into a trash bag, which I put in a corner of my garage. I wasn't ready to toss it yet.

Molly got another Milk Bone for her excellent detective work and I dialed the number on the phone. I got a recording saying it was no longer in service.

I wrote the number on a separate piece of paper and put the evidence bag in a safe place—my kitchen junk drawer. I stared at the phone on the kitchen counter. Put my finger on the button to dial. Two years later and I still remembered Rita's number by heart, assuming it hadn't changed. Even if it had, I could find her if I wanted to. Hell, I found her sister—and now she was dead. Maybe that's why I couldn't bring myself to call Rita. I felt like I had a curse on me. Then again, maybe I was just chickenshit.

I took my finger off the phone, walked out the door and up the block to the Goldsteins', hoping to find Marisol alone.

Mrs. Goldstein answered the door. She was an older woman who showed her age, but not in the sense of older women when I was a boy, who had obligatory blue hair and frumpy dresses. She had to be going on seventy, but her hair, though gray, was soft and not done in one of those lacquered looks so common to older women. She wore a tasteful pearl necklace and a thin, leather-banded, feminine watch. Her shoes had a slight heel, but not like nurse or orthopedic shoes. She looked her age, but she was still attractive. I'd seen her a few times to wave hello.

"Mr. Rogers," she said, without need of introduction.

"Hello, Mrs. Goldstein. I'm sorry to bother you, but I'd like to speak to Marisol."

"Marisol?" The surprise in her voice was clear, though her face maintained its pleasant smile. "Of course. Are you going to help her find out what happened to her brother?"

She led me through the house to the back patio and bid me sit at a redwood table. Maybe Mrs. Goldstein didn't think it proper for a man and woman to be alone in Marisol's room together. Mrs. G excused herself.

Marisol came out. We exchanged pleasantries. I gave her the receipt for her hundred, and got down to business. I filled her in on what I'd been doing and what I'd found out—there wasn't much to tell.

"I need to know who Carlos' friends were. Anyone you can think of and if you have phone numbers or addresses that would be good too."

"I don't really know anyone," she said.

"What about the priest?"

"Priest?"

"A priest who helped you and Carlos when you first came here."

"Yes, there was a priest. But I have not seen him in a long time."

"Do you think Carlos and him—"

"I, I don't know. Carlos and I are not close."

"Don't you want to find your brother's killer?"

"I did not ask you to do this for me." She stared across

the yard. "I did not want to employ you. I do not want your help. Let him rest in peace."

"What are you afraid of?" But she was right, I had insinuated myself into the case. And I still needed to assuage my guilt over Teddie Matson.

"I was upset when we talk on the pier. I should not have gotten you involved, but I do appreciate your efforts, *Señor* Duke. And I do not want to seem ungrateful. I know that you are trying to do good."

"But"—there's always a "but" that follows a sentence like that—"I thought you wanted to know who killed your brother."

"It will only cause trouble. I think he was mixed up with some bad people. Doing things illegal."

It didn't occur to her that just coming here the way they had was illegal. Jeez, now I was thinking like Jack.

"If you want me to back off I will. But I can help you."

"Can you protect me? Can you protect me for all my days?"

"What are you afraid of?"

She stared at the bougainvillea that ran along the wall.

"Who was Carlos working for?" I said. "What do you think happened to him?"

We sat in bloodless silence for several minutes. I could only imagine what was going through her mind, a fight between wanting to know what had really happened to her brother and simply wanting peace at any price. Clearly she was afraid. And maybe as Jack said it was best to let sleeping dogs lie. But if you do that the bad guys win.

"I want to know. But I am afraid."

"When I was in the Navy I was afraid. I worked through it." That's the difference between a coward and someone who isn't, I wanted to add—didn't. Part of me wondered if I was doing the right thing anyway, pushing her into it.

"Please do no more. I thank you, but do no more."

She offered me a cherry Pepsi; I declined. Started to get up.

"I give him a St. Christopher medallion," she said, toying with her own St. Christopher medal, hanging from a gold chain on her neck. "It doesn't work."

There wasn't much I could say to that.

I went home, gathered up Molly; we walked to Beverly Boulevard and the office. The leaded glass windows and brick exterior looked like a movie façade in the golden hour sun. I loved this building. I was waiting for some developer to come and chop it into little pieces to put up some mini-mall—Joni Mitchell was right: they're always paving over paradise to put up parking lots and hideous buildings. We trotted up to my office on the second floor. The building had escaped unscathed in the ninety-two riots, though they came close. The quake also missed it. Sometimes you just get lucky.

Molly set to exploring the office. Two rooms, the outer office-waiting room and the inner sanctum, where I held court, mostly with myself. Decorated with a couple Edward Hopper prints, *Chop Suey* and *Rooms by the Sea*. Someday I would retire to rooms by the sea. Some day.

I'd been away from the office for over a week now. Not really a problem since I could check messages from home or my cellular phone. And most of the mail I got there was bills, but also checks when people decided to pay me. Because of my newfound fame I had actually paid off all my bills and was sitting pretty.

I opened the window, letting in the scent of orange and lemon blossoms. Yellow sunlight streamed in the room.

The answering machine light flashed three times. Two telemarketers and Joseph (don't-call-him-Joe at risk of your life) Hartman, Hollywood Hotshot—the last two words were part of his name. He wanted a meeting at his house. Call him back ASAP. That's the way it was with Hollywood folks, when they wanted something they wanted it yesterday. When it came to giving you something, time or money, well, that could go on *Hollywood Time*—never-never time. I'd worked for him before. As Hollywood types went he was no better, no worse than the rest.

"Molly, this is our home away from home. What do you think?"

Molly barked once. I took it as a positive sign.

I sat at the desk, flipping through mail. Plenty of junk mail. Offers for credit cards, offers to reduce my mortgage, offers to pay off my credit cards—and all out of the goodness and kindness of their hearts. A couple of checks. A couple of bills—yin and yang. I could have hired an assistant, but I didn't need the hassle of dealing with someone else.

I wrote checks for the bills, signed the incoming checks and put them in my pocket for deposit. Molly lay in a sunny spot under the window. I dialed the number for Joseph-Hartman-Hollywood-Hotshot.

"Joseph Hartman, please."

"Who is this?" the disembodied voice on the other end of the line said. I wanted to respond Adolf Hitler, Ronald Reagan, Bill Clinton, Chucko the Clown. I knew how the game was played. If you had the right name your call would be put through. If you didn't have the right name the hotshot would be in an instant meeting. *Oh, I'm sorry, he's not in now. Can he call you back?*—Don't hold your breath on that call. Was I the right name?

"Duke Rogers." I almost added PI, but even my sense of humor and irony wouldn't let me.

"Hold the line, Mr. Rogers."

I guess I was the right name, at least this time. Joseph-Hartman-Hollywood-Hotshot got on the phone after only six minutes of keeping me on hold. He had a problem. He wanted to talk about it. At his home. Could I come by.

Above Sunset Plaza. Yes, that's a good time. See you then Mr. Hotshot.

I hung up feeling as if I needed to alcohol the phone and my ear. What was it about these Hollywood glitterati that got me so worked up? Or maybe another kind of alcohol would help, but I didn't have any handy. I usually had some gin-laced lemonade around in the little fridge. Since I hadn't been to the office in a while, no lacey lemonade.

The meeting with Hartman wasn't until tomorrow. I called El Coyote, the Mexican restaurant down the road, ordered a takeout Guacamole Dinner—cheese enchilada, chili relleno, rice and beans and extra hot sauce and a special treat, soft tacos for Molly—and picked it up on the way home. They knew me well, so they didn't say anything when Molly and I walked into the lobby to get our order. In fact, they all petted her and made all the right oohing and aahing sounds, as if she were a baby. I hate people who bring their dogs everywhere, don't you?

The night passed slowly. I caught up on paperwork, played with Molly. Turned on the eleven o'clock news so I could catch up on the gang killings, celebrity trials, celebrity hijinks, celebrity divorces, celebrity marriages, weather, and sports scores. L.A.'s a factory town and the factory is the Dream Factory. There was almost never any real news on the *news*, but it was fun to watch nonetheless.

About eleven-fifteen the doorbell rang. Couldn't be good news at that hour. I grabbed the Firestar, finger outside the trigger guard, and padded to the front door. Through the peephole I saw Marisol standing there. In the distortion of the small round glass, she looked very small. I opened the door.

"*Señor* Duke, I am sorry to bother you at this hour."

Molly nipped at her feet as we walked into the living room. She sat on the wing chair, I sat on the couch, offered her a drink, which she declined.

"I have been thinking about what you said, about being a coward and working through it. I do not want to be a coward, but it is hard to have courage. I have heard the phrase 'a coward dies a thousand deaths'—I do not want to die a thousand deaths."

"I think Shakespeare said that first, or something like it. Yes, a coward dies a thousand deaths, a hero only once."

"I want to pursue my brother's killer. I am afraid. But I must do it for him. And I must do it for myself." She pulled something out of her purse. Handed it to me. A picture of Carlos. Short black hair, piercing coal eyes. An open face that made him look like a dreamer.

"I'll help you if I can."

"You must be careful. These are very bad people."

"Who are they?"

"I am not sure by name. They help people come across the border."

"Coyotes." I thought she might know a name or two

"*Sí.* But that is not what makes them bad. What makes them bad is how they, how do you say, blackmail people. They ask for more money after the people are here. They make them work for them to pay it off. They hurt people who will tell on them." She wiped a tear.

The roar of a Harley broke our eardrums. A minute later, Jack joined us. Molly ran up to him, wagging her tail.

He looked at Marisol, then at me. I made introductions. Hard to see what Jack was thinking behind the shades. But I knew. Proposition 187 flashed through my mind and I knew it was in his.

Marisol clammed up.

"Don't let me keep you from your business," Jack said.

"You can talk in front of Jack. He's my partner." I filled him in on her situation.

She went on, "Carlos may have done something illegal, but I have not."

Jack turned to her, glaring. She stared him down. "Okay, I come across the border. I did what I must."

"Don't mind Jack. He's really not living in this century."

Jack didn't crack a smile. Molly lay on her back in his lap as he scratched her belly.

"Molly likes him. He must be a good man."

She smiled. So did he. The ice was broken, for now.

"Do you know who Carlos might have been working for? The name of the coyote?" Jack said. It was his way of trying to show her he was okay with her.

"Miguel, that is all I know."

She responded to Jack's question, but not mine earlier. What did that mean, if anything?

"Do you know how to reach him?"

"No. I get away from him as soon as I can. And Carlos made the arrangements for us to cross the border with him."

She didn't have much more to offer.

CHAPTER 8

Eric picked up the ringing phone, trembling with expectation. A response to his ad? The girl from the book bin? In his former office he used to have a sign on the wall that read: "No Expectations—No Disappointments." Those were the days when most of his expectations had been met. Good college, great job, trophy wife. A house to die for. Great kids. He needed that sign and that attitude more than ever now.

"Hello. This is Eric."

"Hey, man, we wanna hire you, man. I'll pay you to suck my dick."

Eric heard laughing in the background. Kids. Fuck 'em. He slammed down the receiver. The phone rang again almost before the receiver was fully cradled.

"Yeah," expecting the kids again.

"Is this Eric?"

"Yes."

"I got a job for you. Why don't we meet and talk about it?" The man's voice was soft, almost to the point of being inaudible. It sounded as if he had an accent, or had had one at some point. Eric couldn't tell where from.

"Any time. Any place." A shot of adrenalin scorched through him, hands shaking.

The caller said to meet him at the arcade on the pier and gave him a time. Hung up.

Eric grabbed his things. His eyes fell on the Harvard Law diploma on the wall. Was it really his? Not anymore? He couldn't practice law ever again.

CHAPTER 9

I was glad to have something else—even low-paying—to work on besides Hollywood hanky panky and spying on the other guy's film projects, like this was important stuff that would lead to the downfall of the union. I became a PI because, corny as it sounds, I wanted to be the knight in shining armor. I found out quickly that it was mostly sifting through records and divorce work or sitting in cars on stakeout in the rain, while the armor rusted. You would have thought by the nineteen nineties that there wouldn't be a lot of need for PIs in divorce cases. Not so. There might even have been more—it was all about the money, who got what, who could hide what, who had the bigger gunslinger lawyer. Sometimes it was about who got the dog. That seemed more important than the kids in a lot of cases.

Marisol had given me the names, but no phone numbers or addresses, of a couple of Carlos' friends, and the name of the priest—Father Carrigan, at San Fernando Mission—who had helped them. Carlos' friends had common Hispanic surnames and first names. Without any more to go on, that was low on my to-do list. Besides, how do you find people who are living below the radar? It wouldn't be easy. Maybe I'd go back to Carlos' apartment and ask around some more, but it was like looking for the proverbial needle in the haystack. She hadn't been close to Carlos lately, but she knew he sometimes hung out with the day laborers who waited for work on the corner of Sunset and Western. He had a couple friends there, Manny and Jose. I'd have to check all of that out. First, I was having lunch with Tom Bond, my bud in the L.A. County Sheriff's Department. I told him I'd buy lunch if he ran the phone number I'd found in the sleeping bag. It was as good as done.

It pays to have friends all over when you're a PI I cultivated relationships wherever I could. Tom was my man in the Sheriff's Department. My friend Lou Waters worked at the DMV. She was good for a myriad of information, though like everything else it was a two-edged sword. It was through Lou that I tracked down Teddie Matson and gave her address to the Weasel, my client—Teddie's murderer. That case had tested our friendship, but it survived. Mary Kopeck was my forensics buddy. I had a few more. Kept in touch regularly. It sounds mercenary, like I only talk to them for the favors they could do me, but I actually liked these people and I think they liked me. And I did them favors on occasion too. I had done things for Tom that he could get in a shitstorm of trouble for as a sworn police officer. But it helped bring down the bad guys, and that's what mattered.

"*Hola Señor* Rogers," the hostess in the huge red and green Mexican flounce skirt said. She wore enough makeup to supply the Clown College for a year. Her skirts circled her legs at a diameter of about ten feet and I'm hardly exaggerating. "I have your regular table ready." El Coyote, my favorite dive, didn't take reservations, didn't have "regular" tables for patrons. But they had one for me. I had done them some favors in the past. Found an employee who was skimming money. Scared off a waitress' boyfriend who hung around threatening customers, thinking he was tough. He wasn't nearly as tough as he thought. El Coyote catered to an eclectic clientele of gays, straights, families, Hollywooders, and today Tom Bond and myself, the two squarest people in the joint, no doubt.

Tom entered the lobby right behind me. "Duke." He put

his hand out. We shook. The only person I knew who had a harder grip than him was Jack. Damn, I'd be rubbing my hand the rest of the afternoon.

The hostess led us to our table, past the lovely seashell décor, artworks made of shells and painted in garish colors. The lunch crowd filled the place, but my table was in a relatively quiet back corner, where I could sit with my back to the wall—an old habit. The hostess asked if we wanted drinks. Tom ordered a Coke, me a lemonade. He was in full Sheriff's uniform, it wouldn't do for him to be seen drinking a margarita. And I had a full day ahead. I didn't need one either.

We talked over old times, then got to the crux of things.

"I need to know who this number used to belong to. It's out of service at the moment." I gave him the phone number I found in Carlos' sleeping bag, which he wrote in his official notebook. "I can't get the LAPD dick on the case to call me back."

"What're you working on?"

"There's a housekeeper down the street. Her brother was killed."

"Murdered?"

I knew my conversation with Tom was off the books, as he knew anything he said to me was.

"I don't know. The LAPD's calling it an accident, but I don't think they're pursuing it with any vigor. She thinks he was murdered and that they don't care."

"Nobody believes they're loved ones are killed in accidents if there's no witnesses."

"Humor me on this one, Tom."

"Housekeeper—illegal?"

"*Sí.*"

The waitress, in her own multi-colored flounce skirt, took our orders and brought us a bowl of chips with a *grande* bowl of hot sauce. It used to be impossible to get a large bowl of hot sauce at El Coyote, until I talked to the owner. Before then they'd give you this little eyedropper's worth that contained a dollop of sauce—and I liked their sauce. It was an argument every time to get more. I talked to the owner and suggested they were being penny-wise and pound foolish. After that the policy changed and he asked that favor of me.

As we waited for our meals, I thought about the Last Supper. Not Leonardo's, but another last supper that was held in this restaurant. On Friday, August 8, 1969, four people sat down here for their last supper. Of course, they didn't know it at the time. After dinner they went home to Cielo Drive, off Benedict Canyon in Beverly Hills. That's where Jay Sebring, Wojciech Frykowski, Abigail Folger, and Sharon Tate met "Tex" Watson, Patricia Krenwinkel, Susan Atkins, and Linda Kasabian, acolytes of Charles Manson. And the rest, as they say, is history. Every time I eat at El Coyote I wonder which table was theirs, but I never ask.

Tom and I didn't talk anymore about Marisol or Carlos. He had the number and he'd do me the favor, that was all that needed to be said.

I left a nice tip for the waitress, paid at the register, and Tom and I walked out to the whir of Beverly Boulevard traffic.

"I'll have that info for you this afternoon," he said. "I'll try your mobile phone or leave it on your answering machine."

We shook hands again. Tom headed for his car, me for home or the office. I wasn't sure yet. As I stepped into the glaring sun I put on my Jack-Junior shades and slowly let my eyes adjust. They fell on the Original Spanish Kitchen just across Beverly Boulevard and I swear I saw a ghost flitting about inside the large glass window. There were all kinds of urban legends about the place and the owners having met untimely deaths. But the strangest thing was that from its closing in 1961 until now you could look in the window and see all of the original place settings, as if it had just closed up the night before. And if you looked hard enough, you just might see that ghost.

* * *

One p.m. Would there still be day laborers outside the market on Sunset and Western? Or would they figure it's too late in the afternoon for a job today? It was about a twenty-minute ride in good traffic—if there is such a thing in L.A.—from El Coyote. What the hell?

I headed east on Beverly Boulevard, the street morphing from business to residential. KROQ poured from the radio. "I'll Stand by You" by the Pretenders was on. The radio made the drive a little smoother.

I drove past the Beverly Theatre revival house, playing *Double Indemnity*, and on through Hancock Park. Old money. In the *good old days*, the nineteen fifties, Nat King Cole had bought a house here. The local white folks formed a committee to keep him out, not wanting any "undesirables" in their community. "If any move in," Mr. Cole said, "I'll let you know." I drove past Muirfield, his street. I didn't see any pedestrians, black or white. That was L.A. I did see a lot of security company signs and burglar bars on windows—that was also L.A. Cole's song, "The Blues Don't Care," popped into my head. I'd heard it the other day on the juke in the Café Noir.

I turned up Western. The supermarket parking lot was nearly as big as Disneyland's. And just as filled. I squeezed the Jeep into a place on the far side, headed for the corner where a few stray laborers still loitered. This was the site of the original Fox studio, before they moved to West L.A. Almost anywhere you look in L.A. there's some kind of movie history. But is that real history?

"Hey, buddy, can you spare a buck?" I smelled him before I heard or saw him.

I tossed him a quarter.

"That's all? You can't hardly buy coffee with that these days."

"You don't have to get your coffee at Starbucks."

"Gimme more. I'll pay you back, I swear."

"You will? When?"

"Aw fuck off! You rich fucks are all the same. Don't want to help a down and out vet."

"You're a dog doctor?"

"Vee-et Nam, man."

"You were a dog doctor in Viet Nam?"

"Fuck you."

"I gave at the office." And I did. I figured it was better to give money to the Union Rescue Mission and others like it rather than give to people on the street. At least that's what I'd heard.

"Well, I didn't get my share."

"I'll deposit it to your Swiss bank account."

"I work hard."

"I can see that." And maybe he did. Some bums make a few hundred dollars a day panhandling. He didn't look like one of them. Didn't smell like it either.

"Fuck you."

"You should be writing Hollywood movies. They're in love with the F word."

He walked off, mumbling to himself.

I reached the corner. With the bum gone, I was the only white face in a sea of brown. Several men approached me. So they hadn't lost hope for this day at least. Though I figured there would have been a whole lot more of them here earlier in the day.

"You gotta job, man. I'll do anything you need," the man said in heavily accented English.

"No job. No *trabajo*."

The men headed back to their posts near the curb. I followed them.

"I'm looking for Jose Rodriguez and Manny Gutierrez." The names Marisol had given me.

"Jeeesusss, man, you might as well be lookin' for John Smith. Don'chu know every Mexican's name is Jose." He said something in Spanish to the others.

The whole group of them laughed, then turned away, heading back to the bus bench that served as their office.

I pulled out the photo of Carlos and flashed it at them. "Do you know this man?

"*No hablo Inglés.*"

"*Ustedes conocen a este hombre?*" I said. That took them aback.

They shook their heads, no, but I could see recognition in some of their faces.

"I have some questions—*tengo preguntas. Y dinero* for the right answers, I guess that's a job." I showed the photo again. "This man was murdered, *asesinado.* I'm trying to help his family—*ayuda*, help."

"Who are you?"

"I'm a private detective." I handed him my card. He glanced at it, slipped it into a pocket.

Nobody said anything. Finally, the skinny one with the wiry arms said, "Yeah, I know him—Carlos. We haven't seen him in many days. *Está muerto?* He is dead?"

A young man, who looked barely old enough to shave, said something in Spanish under the brim of a bright green Fanta baseball cap. He had a bag of Vero Watermelon with Chile candy that he kept dipping into. His Spanish was a little too advanced for me.

"He says, 'You got *cojones* coming here, asking about this shit,'" the skinny man translated. "You think one of us done him?"

"You tell me."

"*Tu estás loco,*" said the man in the Fanta cap. But that I understood.

"Are any of you Manny or Jose?"

"I am Manny," said the skinny but tough-looking dude.

"*Danos el dinero*," Fanta cap said.

"He says, 'Give us some money,'" Manny said.

"Answers first. I said money for the right answers." I looked at the jail tats up and down those ropy arms. I knew how to fight. I also knew how to escape and evade when necessary. I didn't want to have to do either here.

We walked up the street, away from the others. I felt their eyes on my back, especially Fanta cap's. Some people said they just came here for a better life for their families. Working jobs Americans wouldn't. Others said they were destroying the country. They weren't our kind of people. None of that concerned me right now.

"Gotta smoke?" Manny asked.

"Don't smoke."

"You Americans. You all think you gonna live forever."

I didn't know if we all thought we'd live forever. I guess we hoped so.

"These guys," he waved his arm toward the day laborers at the bus bench. "They're just country kids. Just wanna make a day's wages."

"And Carlos?"

"He had bigger dreams. *Ojos muy abiertos*—wide eyes, you know."

"Like you?"

"Yeah, man, like me. But I don't do him."

"You know who did?"

He shook his head. "No, man. Wish I did. Carlos *es mi amigo*."

"What can you tell me about Carlos' death?"

"Why do you think I know anything?"

"I don't. But I gotta start somewhere."

"How I know you won't turn me into *La Migra*."

"Why would I do that? I need your help and I'd lose all my leads. So, let's get down to business. He was a friend of yours. Help me find out what happened to him."

"I don't know a whole lot, you know. We hang on the corner here. But he's got big ideas. Wanted to move up fast."

"So what'd he do to 'move up fast'?"

"Anything he could. Workin' construction, odd jobs. Name it."

"Who'd he work for?"

"How the fuck would I know? We work for whoever picks us up on the corner. They don't give us their history, man. We're lucky if they give us all the money they promise."

"When was the last time you saw Carlos?"

"I don't remember how long, man. But some guy rolls up in a fancy car, don't know what kind. They all look the same. He only needs one guy. It wasn't even Carlos' turn, but he picks him anyway. Carlos gets in and they drive off. I don't see him again."

"White guy?"

"I don't know. Maybe. Mostly white guys hire us."

"Do you know someone named Miguel?"

"Miguel? Jesus, man, that all you got to go on?"

"A Miguel who Carlos would have known?"

"Can't say, man."

"You know why anyone would want to kill Carlos?"

"They don't like Mexicans."

"Who did Carlos hang with, anyone bad?"

"Bad—all Mexicans are bad, aren't they—aren't we?"

I could have come back at him. What was the point? I wanted info. I'd do what I had to to get it. If he wanted to be coy he was only hurting the chances of his friend's killer being caught.

"I didn't come here to argue with you. If you want to help, help." I pulled out a twenty and tried to give it to him. He wouldn't take it.

* * *

The ride home was slow and tedious. I took out my cell phone—it was as big as a brick, almost requiring two hands to hold it. The signal was weak but good enough. I checked my answering machine. One message. Tom Bond: "You're not gonna believe this, buddy. The number you gave me is a dead end. But when it wasn't it belonged to Jeremy Birch. Name ring a bell? Probably not. But how's this—he's one of the Cardinal's assistants. Now what would your street corner guy have to do with them?" I wondered.

No message from Detective Courval.

When I called Tom back he already had current work and home numbers for Birch, addresses, DOB, and just about anything else I might want.

"I knew you'd ask," he said.

I hung up, dialed again. I was on the road, maybe I could drop by Birch on the way home. No answer. I didn't leave a message. Birch's home was in Hancock Park. I could do a *drive-by* on the way home.

CHAPTER 10

Eric's heart made a jackhammer seem tame as it pounded powerfully against his chest wall. He hadn't been this scared and nervous since taking the bar exam, and that was nothing compared to this. It shouldn't be doing this. He was a tough guy now, living in Venice, wearing tattered jeans—and not those strategically tattered jeans Hollywood stars liked to wear to get down with the People. Yeah, he was a tough guy all right, as tough as a bowl of soggy cereal. He might have made a claim to a kind of toughness some day in the past, when he was working out at the exclusive Sports Bar and Gym every day and going up against self-righteous prosecutors in court. But even then he didn't know how to fight, regardless of the size of his muscles. Oh, he could fight in court all right, but take him outside of the courtroom and he was afraid of his own shadow.

You would have thought he'd be afraid of some of the people he defended, especially those whose cases he'd lost. But he didn't lose many. And most of them knew he did the best he could for them. He didn't worry about his clients, scum though many of them were. He worried about the cops. His name had gotten around the various southern California PDs. He worried that if he got stopped for a traffic violation they would turn it into something more. So he always drove the speed limit which, of course, made everyone behind him insane. It might even be illegal to drive the speed limit in southern California, especially on the freeways. He never got a ticket. He never jaywalked. Tried to do everything right. So how the hell did he lose his law license? He knew the answer to that one. And it was his fault, all his fault. The question was, would he do it again?

He headed north along the Pacific and toward Santa Monica. Sitting in the endless traffic, he thought what it might be like to keep on driving, straight out into the ocean. Not a half bad idea. He drove past the gang graffiti that some called art. That he might have called art at one time. He didn't anymore. Not when you have to live with it every day. He came to the Santa Monica Pier, found a place to park, leaned on the headrest and took several deep breaths. Got out of his car.

He stood in the parking lot, looking up to the pier. The sun, bright, yellow, no golden, was on the far side, making its way around so it could set in the Pacific. The sun pushed the Ferris wheel and roller coaster into silhouette. Eric squinted up at them, wishing for a pair of sunglasses.

What the hell was he doing here? Why not get a real job? He tried. He was either overqualified or underqualified. He'd worked at a car rental place, but after a few weeks he was let go. He even tried McDonald's, but was turned down by a manager younger than his thirty-four years in favor of an immigrant, who could speak Spanish. "They work cheaper and expect less," the manager said. Even high school kids didn't seem to work at McDonald's anymore. Dejected, he gave up after the McDonald's experience. He'd considered suicide, but that took courage. Courage he didn't have. Besides, if he could get a job maybe he could afford a little better neighborhood. Aw, what the hell. For the kind of money he could make now there were no better neighborhoods. Besides, he had to live here. It was part of his "rehabilitation," as he called it.

"Calm down," he said to himself over and over, trying to remember his mantra from headier days. It wouldn't come to him. "Breathe. Breathe deep." Maybe the person who'd called him was legit, or maybe it was a setup. What could they do to him, he had nothing to steal and nothing to lose. He'd always been anti-gun—had even belonged to Handgun Control, Inc. He wished he had one now. He walked to the pier and up the stairs.

The sun beat through the cloud cover, illuminating the day with a bright blanket of light.

Bright as this, Eric thought, *and I'm scared shitless. Terror of daylight. I wish it would fuckin' rain again. This is just like the fucking movies. Maybe I should have worn a fedora and a white carnation in my pinstriped suit.*

His hand involuntarily patted his side. No gat there.

The sun beat down on his back. It felt good after days and days of rain and his damp apartment. Looked like everyone was taking advantage of a sunny day. Moms and kids and teens all ambled up and down the pier. The Ferris wheel spun. The merry-go-round horses, stars of a dozen movies, circled round, ultimately going nowhere. Other rides whizzed and whooshed and Eric looked for the man he was supposed to meet.

The pier used to be kind of dumpy. Eric had stopped coming after graduating high school. Then the city had remodeled it: slick new rides, fancy restaurants, a great place to come for burgers and to do drunken shooters at frat parties. Hell, those frat parties continued while he was a lawyer, drunken lawyer parties. He loved it. He missed it. Now it was a great new place and he couldn't afford it anymore.

Jennifer's face flickered across his mind like an old black-and-white movie. Slowly the movie dissolved to full Technicolor. Her eyes as green as the sea a few yards away. Her smile disarming. He wished he could melt into her arms once more. He wished he could take their children, Dylan and Samantha, here, go on the coaster, hear his children scream with delight. Push into him for safety. They had thought he was the King of the Universe. That he could do no wrong.

He had thought so too, until that day when he had to make a decision. Most lawyers wouldn't have even considered it. A few months before he wouldn't have either. So what was different on that day? And was he sorry?

Of course he was sorry about how things had turned out, losing his family, his house. But was he really sorry? He didn't think so. He hadn't liked himself much up to that day. Sure, he was a good lawyer, but not a good person. He followed the law, but not justice. And he had lost a lot, just about everything. But he had gained one thing. A new friend: himself. That didn't take away the pain of not seeing his kids, but at least he could live with himself, even if he had to live with the cockroaches as well. Would he do it again? Make the same choice knowing what he knew now? It would never come up, so why worry about it?

He walked to the arcade—the meet place—scanning for a man who would be scanning for him. The man wouldn't tell Eric what he looked like, said he'd recognize Eric.

A sinewy man in a crisp white guayabera shirt headed his way. Blazing dark eyes. A moustache brushed his upper lip. Hair neat, short. He looked like an extra in a Hollywood movie, some casting director's idea of a guy you might meet on a pier, in an eruption of sun blasting through the cloud cover, on a day between rains. The man seemed so dapper in a casual way, so elegant, Eric could almost see the vanity behind his eyes.

"Eric," the man said. A statement, not a question. "My name is Mike." His hand stretched for Eric to shake. The skin felt smooth to the touch. Not a working man—that's probably why Eric was here.

The area was open enough, Eric's jackhammering heart went into slow motion, still pounding, though not as rapidly. Eric took the man in, something he was used to doing from his lawyering days, assessing people quickly, based on their clothes, their attitude, their expressions. The look in their eyes. He always felt good about his ability to read people.

"Let's go have a soda or something."

A trip to the food court—Eric couldn't wait. God, what he wouldn't give for a Cowabunga Burger right now. And the place that sold those even had Pam Anderson's bikini on display. What a great place. The court's sterile spotlessness glared up at them in the intense sunlight. Why did the sun always seem brighter after a rain? Just the contrast to the dark, gray skies? Or did it really blaze brighter? They bought fruit smoothies, Eric a Tropical Berry Supreme, the other man Mango Tango. He paid.

"Let's walk," Mike said.

They headed out on the pier, away from the amusement park. Santa Monica was an interesting place, a contrast of rich and poor and homeless. The city council let the homeless sleep in the parks and pretty much anywhere they wanted. But they got them off the pier when they refurbished it. Now it was a money-making venture and that took precedence over it being a place for the homeless to go.

"I liked your ad. It's ballsy."

"I thought it was more like desperate." In his lawyer days, Eric wouldn't have been so forthcoming. He'd have played it closer to the vest. Maybe he should have now. But he needed the money and he wanted to get down to business.

"Desperation makes people ballsy, no?"

"In my case it does."

"You are not ballsy to begin with?"

Eric tried to place the man's accent. Couldn't.

"And a little nervous, so let's get to it." As a lawyer Eric would never have admitted to being nervous. He was out of his element here and just wanted to get it over with. Find out what Mike wanted, do it, and get the money. "What do you want me to do?"

"Nothing out of the ordinary. Run some errands, pick things up, deliver them, that kind of thing," Mike said, with a slight grin. "But first I must know a little about you."

Eric debated whether to tell Mike that he had been a criminal defense lawyer. Or how much to tell him in general. He decided to not say anything that wasn't a response to a direct question from Mike.

Mike asked questions. Eric responded. He was down on his luck. Drinking problem—he didn't bother telling Mike it had started after he lost his job. And he didn't tell him what the job was, other than that he was a cubicle worker, not quite true. Mike's face remained expressionless. He let Eric finish his story. When Eric was done, Mike said, "Sounds like you've had a rough time and some bad luck. I'm willing to give you a break but if you drink on the job or fuck it up, it'll be worse than being fired."

"So exactly what is your business?"

"It's nothing illegal, though to be honest it shades the law." Mike's grin returned.

Eric nodded. "So what's the gig?"

"For starters, I just want you to drive a car from one location to another. Simple. You do have a valid driver's license?"

Eric nodded, thought it over. Probably a stolen car. He could ask Mike, but he preferred the don't-ask-don't-tell policy here, then if he got caught he could honestly play dumb with the police. He could do that, drive a car from here to there. It wasn't anywhere near as bad as he had imagined, carrying drugs over the border, kidnap or kill someone. After all, when you place an ad saying you'll do anything for money you don't know what you're going to get in response. And it fit in with his hair shirt idea of his life these days.

"For this I am willing to pay two hundred dollars for what will amount to about a day's work. I am not open to negotiation."

"Okay." Right now, two hundred in cash—Eric assumed it would be in cash—was a fortune to him.

"One hundred now, one hundred on completion. Plus I

will reimburse your gas, so keep receipts and records of mileage. You did say you had a car, yes? So you can get to the spot where our car is located."

"Yes." He needed the money and didn't want to question his good fortune.

"Let me see your arms," Mike said.

"What?"

"Pull up your sleeves."

Eric did. Mike ran his silky finger up and down Eric's arms. "Good. No tracks. You ever use drugs?"

"No."

"Never?"

"I might have done some recreational coke at one time. I don't have the money now."

"I could check other places on your body for tracks."

"Do I seem stoned to you?" He had made a point not to have a buzz on before going to this meeting.

"I'll let it go. For now."

The way Mike said it was ominous and sent a chill down Eric's back. What was he getting into? Or maybe it was a good thing—Mike didn't want any druggies working for him. Eric decided that was a good sign.

They talked a few more minutes. Mike said he'd be in touch, shook Eric's hand. Mike's hands may have been soft, but they were strong. Then Mike told Eric to leave. Eric walked down the pier. He wanted to look back and see if Mike was watching him, but didn't.

Most of the money would go to rent, staples. And presents for his kids. But maybe he'd treat himself to dinner at a real restaurant. Nothing fancy. But a step above McDonald's. Maybe come back here for a Cowabunga Burger. And with his unemployment gone, he had fallen through the cracks. It felt good to have a job again, even if he wasn't quite sure what it was.

Maybe he'd even ask Lindsay to come along. The future looked bright. Or brighter than it had in some time.

CHAPTER 11

I figured Jeremy Birch would live on the outskirts of Hancock Park or as the Realtors like to put it Hancock Park Adjacent, the not quite as expensive area. Wrong. The house was on June Street, right in the heart of the old money enclave. Two story Tudor. Lush landscaping. I didn't think an assistant to the Cardinal would be living so high on the hog. I pulled in front of a house across the street—took in the neighborhood. Birch's house. At least four Bel Air Patrol security signs on his front lawn.

I walked up the path to the front door, expecting to see a piranha-filled moat and Claymore mines with the endearing instruction: "Front Toward Enemy." Hancock Park was an island of money and security in the middle of Los Angeles, surrounded on the east and south by, well, not-so-good neighborhoods. The house was green tagged—safe to enter. A house a couple doors up was yellow tagged and it was obvious work was being done on it. Other than that, no sign of quake damage here. These people wouldn't let things slide and they had the money and the power to get them taken care of in a timely manner.

Nice digs, if you liked living in a fortress. Working for the Cardinal paid well. Or maybe he was a silver spoon baby. Had a rich wife. Richer boyfriend. Who knew?

A housekeeper answered the door. She wore jeans and tennis shoes—they rarely wore uniforms these days. It made their employers feel better, you know one-on-one. We're all the same. All that jazz. I could have been wrong about him; I didn't think so.

"Hi, is Jeremy Birch here?"

"*Señor* Birch?"

"Yes, is he in?"

"Do you have an appointment?"

Most detective work is a lot of pavement pounding, schmoozing, and luck. And the art of BS, which is similar to schmoozing, but a little more finessed.

"I found something that belongs to your boss."

"I can take it for you."

"No thank you. I want to give it to him."

After a few more minutes of that she told me to wait on the front porch and closed the door on me. No telling who I might be—some maniacal killer, speed demon, car chase refugee; some nut she saw on the local news the night before. I smelled something familiar, honeysuckle. That sweet scent seemed to fill these old Los Angeles neighborhoods.

The door opened again. A tall, lanky man filled the frame. Three days' growth of beard—Hollywood cool, or in this case *Holy*-wood cool. White shirt, no tie, slacks, no jacket. Loafers, no socks—I hate people who wear loafers without socks. It says something about them—something I don't like, like how cool they think they are. Looked like he just got home and hadn't had time to change.

"Isabel said you found something of mine. But you look like a salesman to me." Only he pronounced her name Eees-sa-bell—very sensitive. He wouldn't step outside the house, standing ready to slam the door in my face.

"The only thing I sell is security."

"I don't need any of that."

"I thought you might. I also thought you might be selling redemption since you work for the church."

"And who are you?"

I handed him my card—the one without the street address,

not even for my office. "Duke Rogers. I'm investigating the murder of a man named Carlos Rivera."

"Who?"

"Your number was found with his things." I read the number off to him.

"I haven't had that number in months."

"No, but it's yours."

"His name isn't familiar."

"He had your number, only your number."

"Well, I don't know, I come across a lot of people in my work for the church. He might have called me."

His lips pulled tight. He stopped looking at me, only for a second. I thought it was a tell, one of those little mannerisms, shifts of the eyes, anxious habits, that give away the person's real intent.

"What do you do for the Cardinal?"

"I'm not sure why I should tell you anything."

"Mr. Birch, I'm looking into Mr. Rivera's death, his murder. You don't have to talk to me, I'm not a cop. I have no official standing. But I can easily forward all my info to the cops."

"Who're you working for?"

"You've seen enough movies to know I can't answer that." I loved being able to say that. And when I did, a look of defeat slid down his face. He didn't have to talk to me, but he would.

"I'm the Cardinal's liaison with the immigrant community."

"Illegal immigrants?" I said to dig at him, see what response I'd get. I wondered if this whole business of Carlos' death had something to do with immigrants, smuggling them, hiding them, getting them jobs. Something else? Sometimes diplomacy is the best way. And sometimes the best way to get someone to open up is to stick a needle in their eye.

"That's a crude term. Immigrants. Any kind of immigrants."

"I'm sorry—undocumented workers."

"Look I don't need your attitude. Please leave." He looked around, as if playing to an audience. He was. The maid was standing a few feet behind him, pretending to dust. When I didn't move, he said, "Get the hell out of here."

"Is that any way for a man of God to talk?"

"I'm not—the Cardinal is. Now go before I call the cops."

"We'll see each other again, I'm sure."

"Is that a threat?"

I didn't respond, headed back along the path to my car, wondering who all that Bel Air Patrol security was supposed to keep out. He gave me less than I thought he would and the little he gave, that he was the church's liaison with the immigrant community, I could have found out on my own. Still, it was worth the trip, just in terms of shaking things up. I tried using my cellular phone to call my bud, Tiny. But, for a change, it didn't get a signal, so I stopped at a pay phone. Like most Tinies, Tiny was humungous. During the Rodney King riots a couple years back, he had helped me get through South Central in one piece while I was working on the Teddie Matson case. For his trouble he got a gun shoved down his throat and landed in the hospital. It's not like we went to the movies all the time, but every once in a while we'd chat on the phone or get a bite to eat. That's what I had in mind now.

Roscoe's Chicken and Waffles—I never really understood how that combo came to be—lived on Gower, off of Sunset Boulevard. The décor was nondescript, but the food was out of this world. The food, jammed with butter and grease, made your mouth water, your stomach ask for more, and was considered by some to be a heart attack on a plate. What the hell, you only live once. If you drink green liquid mashed down in a blender from a variety of vegetables, you might live to be a hundred, but you won't enjoy it nearly as much. Besides, you could end up like Jim Fixx, the running guru who died running at age fifty-two. So you might as well have a good time while you're here.

No matter the time of day or day of the week, there's always a line at Roscoe's. Tiny joined me in line—he had farther to come. He greeted me with a bear hug that almost knocked the wind out of me.

"How you been, Duke?"

We caught up on things, Tiny's truck rental business, ball scores, how good the food was, how lousy the city was getting. The one thing we didn't talk about was Rita or her family, though Tiny knew them well. I wanted to ask how Rita and her mom were doing. I couldn't. I wondered if Tiny felt the same constraints. We never talked about that when we got together and we got together at least once a month.

"Hey, Duke, you hear 'bout that girl jumped from the Hollywood Sign?"

I nodded.

"Tragedy. Man, they all come here lookin' for sidewalks paved with gold and what do they find?"

"Tarnished tinsel."

"Right on, man, tarnished tinsel. And no amount of polishing is gonna make it shine."

I knew that for sure. And Tiny must have seen the faraway expression on my face.

"What's the matter, bro?"

I didn't respond.

After a long minute or two, he said, "I saw Rita the other day."

My heart raced. I tried not to show it. But Rita was always the unspoken elephant in the room in any conversation with Tiny. I didn't think he knew about my involvement with The Weasel. But maybe he suspected. Or maybe she'd told him. No, I don't think she would have done that. "How is she?"

"She's doing great. Gonna get her architecture degree in the spring."

I smiled, happy for her. She had been a draftsman, but I knew she wanted to become a full-fledged architect. I guess she was on her way. I wanted to ask him if she brought me up. He beat me to it.

"She asked if I ever saw you. Told her I have lunch with you sometimes. Said you're doing fine."

If only.

I waited for him to go on. To say she asked for my number or wanted me to call her. I could have brought it up. Didn't.

We both ordered seconds of our chicken and waffles. Somehow that would take the sting off trying to make this tarnished City of Angels shine.

Before going home, I turned up Sunset Plaza, heading into the hills above the Sunset Strip. Greenery shouted from every house, every corner. The rains had made everything bloom. And when they stopped and everything dried out just in time for summer, just in time for the Santa Ana winds and the fire season, the previously lush plants would make great kindling for the kind of cleansing fire that Nathanael West might have envisioned. But right now everything looked like a Mediterranean paradise above Sunset, except for a couple of red tags here and there. And Joseph Hartman's home, probably about eight thousand square feet, modest by Hollywood standards, loomed on a lookout point above the Strip. He had offices at Paramount in Hollywood, the only studio left in Hollywood proper, but often worked from home.

Two Jags in the circular driveway of the Spanish colonial revival cum craftsman home, with a little bit of ranch style, with turrets—true nineteen twenties Hollywood Hodgepodge, like something out of a B movie. I parked on the street, not wanting to block anyone in, though the driveway was certainly wide enough for me.

The door looked like something out of a Disney cartoon from the old days. Something that might have been on Sleeping Beauty's castle. Black iron knocker and hinges. A four-by-six-inch stained glass window at eye height for people to see out of—or into.

A man answered the door. Shellacked hair. Glasses that must have cost five hundred dollars, even though they wouldn't help him see any better than a pair from Lenscrafters. Armani suit jacket with pre-faded jeans, no tie. Regulation Gucci loafers, no socks, a la Birch. Two things that bug the shit out of me: men who wear shoes without socks and men and women who wear sandals with them. These little things say a lot about a person.

He was twenty-five or so, judging by the way he dressed. The standard three days' growth of beard. And he looked like the standard Hollywood D boy—development boy.

I started to talk—he cut me off: "I'm Barry Meltzer, Joseph's assistant. And you are Marion 'Duke' Rogers."

He had me there. I'd worked for Hartman before and he went through assistants like water through the proverbial sieve. I didn't know Meltzer. And figured there wasn't much point in doing so.

He invited me in. The entry hall dwarfed us. But the living room was cozy, like a great hall King Arthur would have felt at home in. The furniture and knick-knacks looked like props from a movie set, and probably were.

I cooled my heels. Joseph-Hartman-Hollywood-Hotshot only kept me waiting twenty minutes. I could hear him in the other room, on the phone I figured, since his was the only voice I heard.

For all I knew he was talking to himself, trying to impress me. Hollywood people always played a power game of keeping you waiting. But only twenty minutes must have meant I was somewhat important to him.

Meltzer returned. "Mr. Hartman will see you now."

Hartman walked in the room like he owned the place. I'm sure that's how he walked into every room. Tall and ugly as sin. But I'd seen pictures of him with every beautiful starlet on his arm. Men want pretty women, women want powerful men. He wore faded sweats, not the kind you see at Sports Club/L.A., but what you'd find at Target, ten years ago. Untied tennis shoes—another Hollywood uniform, mostly affected by writers. The epitome of cool. So cool he didn't have to dress to impress.

"Hey, Duke, give it up," Hartman said in a low, radio announcer's voice, putting his hand out to shake. Everything about him grated on me. Was that voice real—could it be? "Drink?"

"You have gin...and lemonade?"

He looked at me like I was from another planet. "How 'bout gin and tonic?"

"I'll just have an orange juice." Meltzer got the drinks from a gorgeous art deco martini bar-liquor cabinet with a swirled walnut finish. Great curves. If it was a studio repro they'd done a great job, but I didn't think this was a prop, at least it hadn't been originally made as one.

"Sorry to keep you waiting, Duke. I was on the phone with my bookie. Whadda you think of those Lakers? And what about this whiz-bang guy on the Orlando Magic, Shaquille O'Neal? If only the Lakers could get him."

I nodded. I didn't mind talking sports, Tiny and I had done it. But I wanted to get down to business now and get home. "So, what is it this time, Mr. Hartman?" Deference. I can be that way sometimes.

"Call me Joseph, Duke. We're old friends."

Friends wasn't the word I would have used, but I guessed I could call him Joseph.

"This is all on the QT, private eye and client privilege, right?"

I nodded. I didn't bother to tell him that that wouldn't hold up in court.

"I'm developing a property called *Kidder*, about a man who wakes up in a kid's body. And I heard a rumor that Universal has something similar in the works. I've tried my contacts, but no one's talking. I know you can find out for me."

"I'll do what I can." I had some contacts too. In the PI business you made them everywhere, even in Hollywood. People did favors for you, you did favors for them. I wasn't sure why Hartman's contacts were so close-mouthed, but it didn't matter.

We agreed on the usual price. I finished my orange juice and headed out: Duke Rogers—Hollywood Spy.

CHAPTER 12

I walked in the door, Molly jumped up to greet me, tail wagging. She seemed to be doing better. I grabbed her leash and out we went for a short walk. I didn't notice any new burglar bars on any of the houses. And still no rain, what was that two, three days. A record for this wet year. More was expected but it was in a holding pattern off the coast.

I thought about knocking on the Goldsteins' door, asking for Marisol. It was probably their dinner time, so I didn't. Molly and I ate our dinners together. Neither one looked very appetizing, though her kibble looked as good as my frozen dinner. I thought about who I would call first on the Hartman case. I was bored with all this Hollywood stuff, more so with the Hollywood people, but I needed to earn a living. I felt at loose ends with Carlos' murder. Nowhere to turn. No call from Courval. I tried him again. He wasn't in. Maybe I'd talk to Larry Darrell again, he might be able to find something out. I would definitely talk to Marisol again. She and Carlos hadn't been close, but she might know something without realizing it. She might even be holding back, but I didn't want to go there.

A book was sitting on the kitchen counter, Shakespeare's *The Tempest*, in a gold leaf faux leather edition. It was part of my father's complete Shakespeare collection. Even though it was faux leather he never let me touch it—it was his pride and joy. He never read it either, just liked the way the collection looked on the shelf. He loved Shakespeare and would read from a beat-up single volume collection of all his plays. I'm surprised that book hasn't turn to dust. When he moved to the retirement home and I moved back into the family house, I asked him if he wanted to take the leather set with him. He wanted me to have it.

"Don't be like me," he said. "Enjoy it."

I'd blown off Shakespeare in high school and college, faking my way through English and lit courses with Cliffs Notes and old Laurence Olivier movies. But after my dad moved out, I picked up his gold leaf *Hamlet*, isn't that one of the biggies? Wasn't bad. And I've been making my way through the plays ever since, in no particular order. Seems like Shakespeare said pretty much everything before anyone else.

Picking up the book reminded me that I should go see my dad, take him down to the pier or something. I wanted to get him a new volume of Shakespeare, but I knew it would go unread. He loved that beat-up old paperback he kept on his nightstand.

I didn't appreciate my dad when I was a kid; he was a harsh taskmaster. Not always wrong in what he thought, but almost always wrong in the way he expressed it, humiliating me when I didn't do something right—right being his way. But as I got older, I started to see some of the good in him and some of it even rubbed off. He liked the classics and classical music and swing. He could talk to Jack about that stuff for hours. It made me jealous. But maybe one of these days, after I'd read enough Shakespeare, that would give me and my dad something to talk about too.

But for now, Jack had his classical music and I had my shaky Shakespeare. What a pair of Navy SEALs.

Forbidden Planet flickered in the background. Molly's bark startled me out of a television haze. Ten p.m. What the hell was she barking at? And running to the front door. I grabbed the Firestar, walked to the Venetian blinds in the dining room, from where I could peek out and see the front of the house. Someone was coming up the walk.

Molly kept at it—a loud dissonant symphony of baby dog barks—while I crept down the hall and out the back door. The man slammed the knocker.

"Hold it!" I said, stealing around the bush at the edge of the driveway, Firestar pointed square at his center mass. Am I paranoid? Maybe. But this is L.A. And nobody comes knocking at ten p.m., at least not in my neighborhood.

"Mr. Rogers?"

I walked closer. In the dull yellow flicker from the porch light I saw Jeremy Birch.

"Can we go inside?"

"Come around here."

He joined me in the driveway. We walked toward the back door, he a few steps in front of me. His bomber jacket might conceal a gun. I didn't think so, but I patted him down anyway. His hands shook, as did his voice. He kept looking back. I didn't think it was at me. More out to the street, as if someone might be following him. I scanned the bushes, the street—no sign of anyone.

"Stop. Shh," I said. We listened to the still night. I didn't hear anything out of the ordinary. We walked up the stairs to the back door.

We squeezed into the cramped den. There was just about enough room for the two of us, the desk and computer, stereo receiver and a ton of books and papers. He didn't take off the bomber jacket. His fingers danced over each other in a nervous jitterbug.

"How did you find my home address, Mr. Birch?"

"Is that really necessary? I came to tell you—"

I cut him off. I might have cared about what he came to tell me. Time would tell on that. Right now I was concerned with how he found my house. I knew it wasn't that hard, but

I wanted to know how he had done it.

"I work for the Catholic Church, remember. We have friends. It wasn't hard."

"Specifically."

"I had a friend in the DMV pull your driver's license."

He used the same methods I used. I wondered if he used the same people. But I didn't think my friend Lou would give out my info. And after what had happened to Teddie Matson I doubted she gave out info to anyone. I hadn't asked her since then and didn't know what she would do if I did ask. I made a mental note to have the address on my license changed to the office.

"Okay, now what can I do for you? Something so important you had to track me down and come to my house at ten o'clock at night. And why are you so nervous?"

"Look, I love the church, don't get me wrong. But it's like any other organization. Good people, bad people. Good policies, not so good policies." He scoped out my house—what was he looking for?

"What are you getting at, Mr. Birch."

"I couldn't talk to you earlier today. Didn't want to be seen with you at my house."

"You sound a little paranoid."

"Are you paranoid if someone is actually following you?"

"Are you saying someone followed you here?"

"I don't know—I don't think so. That is, if they were I think I shook them. I drove around for over an hour."

"Well, if you had someone look up my home address, they might not have needed to follow you."

"I never thought of that," he said.

"What is this all about? What're you getting at?"

Birch hesitated, his fingers flipping over each other, like a swing dancer throwing his partner over his shoulder.

"Look, you came to me. Either tell me what you came for or leave."

"The church, you know, we have a sanctuary program," he said.

"For criminals? I thought that ended in the Middle Ages."

He shook his head.

"Illegals?"

"Yes, undocumented immigrants. Once they're here we do what we can to help them and help them stay."

"You break the law," I said.

"There's a higher law. But you wanted to know about Carlos Rivera when you came to my house."

"And you said you didn't know him."

"I did know Carlos. I met him when he and his sister came here, we helped them get settled." Birch drummed his fingers. "A few weeks ago he came to me saying he had some concerns about a coyote named Miguel."

"What did you do?"

"I didn't think it was anything. All these coyotes are scary. I thought Carlos was being paranoid. That's all I know." The nervous tick in his eye said there was more here than he was letting on. I decided not to press him, at least for the moment. Maybe the Good Cop would get more from him down the road than if the Bad Cop made an enemy tonight.

"And now you're being paranoid."

"Carlos is dead, isn't he?"

"Why are you telling me this? Why the change of heart?"

"Carlos." He stood up, made his way out of the room, to the entry hall. "He didn't deserve to die."

"And you think it was this coyote Miguel?"

His silence was response enough.

"Sounds like a dangerous business, coming into contact with all these coyotes. Why do you do it?"

"Why do anything? I work in an office. Have nothing to do with the dangerous stuff. At first I kidded myself into thinking I was doing it to help immigrants, but I don't have those illusions anymore—it was the money that appealed to me. I got paid off."

At least he didn't try to justify his actions with lofty phrases and ideals. His honesty made me like him.

"I've told you what I can. Maybe you can help Carlos now."

"I thought that's what the church was for."

I had the feeling he wanted to tell me more, but he opened the door and disappeared into the night.

I didn't know what to make about Birch's appearance at my door. He wanted to tell me something and he did, but not all of it. I'd give him a day or two to stew on it then I'd brace him again, maybe catch him off guard, get the rest of the story. He'd told me something and he'd told me nothing.

Molly and I went for our late night *coupage* and a quick walk around the block. I let the dark night seep into me. It was better than thinking about it—thinking about a young man, legal, illegal, it didn't matter, killed for what seemed like no good reason. I guess to the killers there's always a reason.

The pounding in my head went on and on until I realized it wasn't in my head, but at the front door. I sat up in bed, watching the dust mites dance on the shafts of sun sneaking in through the blinds.

It wasn't the knock of a letter carrier with something to sign for. No this was a cop knock. They must all learn it in Police Academy 101. Molly's incessant barking wouldn't allow me to pull the covers over my head and pretend there was no one there. I threw on a pair of faded jeans, put the Firestar in the rear waist band, threw a loose retro bowling shirt over that and left it untucked, covering the pistol. It sounded like cops—and answering the door to cops with a pistol in my waist probably wasn't the wisest thing—but it might not be the cops.

I opened the door.

"Marion Rogers?" the larger of the two said. I was surprised at how good his clothes were. Expensive shoes, with socks, and suit. But hey, this was Hollywood too.

"Who wants to know?" I said after wincing at my given name. No one who knew me ever called me that.

"Detective Sergeant Haskell and Detective Chandler."

Detective Chandler was the prettier of the two. A young woman of about thirty I guessed. Pale hair, natural, not out of a bottle, pulled back in a ponytail. Perfect skin. Was I being sexist in my assessment of her? Did I care? She was hot. If I saw her on the street in a dress I would have looked twice. Haskell was more nondescript. Just another schlub in a fancy suit, though one he filled out quite well. Everybody in Hollywood is a star, even the cops.

"Can we come in?" They proffered ID, two detective shields with that arresting—no pun intended—embossing of Los Angeles City Hall. Of course they could have bought it down on Alvarado like everyone else. I figured they were legit.

"Not yet. What's this about?"

"You know Jeremy Birch." A statement, not a question.

"I've met him." I hoped it would rain on their parade, since they were standing on the porch.

"When did you see him last?"

"Either tell me what this is about or I'll call my lawyer." I didn't have a lawyer, at least not a criminal lawyer, but it sounded good. It's what everyone on every cop show on TV says.

"Jeremy Birch is dead. Killed last night."

"Killed? How?"

"That's what we're trying to ascertain? Can we come in now?"

I let them in. We sat in the living room, which was only a few feet off the front door. I had fucked up again. I should have braced Birch harder last night. Well, how the hell could I know? My blood boiled. I tried not to let my face get red.

"Do you think he was murdered?" I said.

"We thought you might be able to tell us." Haskell looked like he thought he was being smart. Chandler looked noncommittal, while Haskell asked most of the questions.

"You think I had something to do with it?"

"We thought you could answer that too."

"I had nothing to do with it." The rage seeped out of my voice.

"You seem upset. Were you close?"

"I hardly knew him."

"When did you see him last?"

"Last night. He showed up at my door."

"Someone you hardly knew?" Haskell kept his eyes on my hands, while Chandler drifted down the hall, looking in doorways, but not going into the rooms.

"I was surprised too."

"What was your relationship?"

"We didn't have one. I'm working a case, I'm a private—"

"We know. You're very famous. Famous-Duke-Rogers." Haskell said it as if it was one word. "And I don't give a shit—not impressed."

I ignored the insult. What could I do? Blow him away? If I did respond it would only make my life more difficult.

"I questioned him peripherally on a case." I knew they'd ask, so I filled them in. Not everything. But I did tell them that I was double checking on Carlos Rivera's death. Detective Chandler wandered back, took out a notebook, began jotting things down. In the movies they always claim some kind of PI privilege. There isn't any. And why antagonize the cops? I didn't know much so I couldn't tell them much. "Birch was scared, I could see that."

"Of what?"

"He wouldn't say."

"It doesn't sound like he said much," Haskell said.

"He didn't."

"Well, he was scared," Chandler said. It was the first time she spoke. I figured maybe she was a new detective or maybe they were playing Good Cop-Bad Cop and she was the Good Cop.

"Then why did he come?" Anything Haskell said sounded like an interrogation and accusatory.

"I've been trying to figure that out myself. I think he wanted to say more. Changed his mind."

"Do you mind if we walk your house? We won't open any drawers or cabinets." Chandler again.

"You already did, but feel free." What were they looking for? Blood spatter? Torn up carpet where I'd killed and dismembered him? Did it matter? They were here. Besides, if I didn't let them, they'd get a warrant and really make my life hell.

They got up. "Where did you meet with him? In here?" she said.

"No, in my little office. You can't miss it, unless you blink."

They started out of the living room. "Do you want to accompany us? Make sure we don't—" The Good Cop, solicitous. Caring.

"I trust you."

"Come with us." The Bad Cop, Haskell, barking orders.

And I did. I didn't think they'd plant anything and I didn't have anything to hide. I was sandwiched between Haskell and Chandler as we walked the house. Molly followed, dogging their every move. She'd keep them honest.

We returned to the living room about three minutes later. It doesn't take long to walk my house. They each gave me a card and said to call if I learned anything, then left. I went into the office to check on things. The light on my answering machine winked at me. One message. Rita? Too much to hope for. I pressed the button, heard the tape rewind.

Jeremy Birch's voice came on.

CHAPTER 13

Eric fanned the five twenties Mike had given him out on the beat-up desk, over and over. More money than he'd seen in a long time. Mike said he'd call when he was ready for Eric to get to work. Eric knew it was too soon for that. In the meantime, maybe someone else would respond to his ad. Maybe he could make a living at this, being a glorified gopher. It was a far cry from the legal towers in Century City and Downtown, but it might be something he could make a go of.

He slipped three of the twenties under a loose floorboard, pocketed the other two, and felt like a rich man for the first time in a long time. Forty bucks—that would buy a half-way decent meal for him and Lindsay. He hoped she would call. She didn't have a phone, but he had given her his number so she could call from a pay phone. He wished he could call her.

He tried reading the Goodis book; couldn't concentrate. He wanted to celebrate. Wanted to see Lindsay. The twenties snug in his pocket, he locked up the apartment, headed down to the boardwalk.

Sun hacked through the cloud cover. Eric was surprised to see the boardwalk brimming with people on this gloomy day. He walked down the road, bought himself a cherry Sno Cone, without breaking the twenties. He looked for Lindsay at Small World Books, at the book cart where he'd met her, up and down the boardwalk. She said she was always there. But not now. Eric knew always never really meant always, but he was hoping she'd be there.

He broke one of the twenties, bought a kite for his son and a stuffed bear for his daughter. They were cheap toys, but it was the thought, wasn't it?

Eric looked up and down the boardwalk.

"Hey, do you know a girl named Lindsay?" he asked a girl with brown hair and a nose ring. She didn't bother responding, just walked by Eric as if he was invisible. He asked several more kids. Nobody knew anything.

Finally, a white boy with cornrows seemed to know her. "If it's the girl I'm thinkin' of," he said, "she hangs at a squat in the alley off Windward."

"Thank you." Eric thought about giving the boy a buck or two, decided he needed every penny right now.

"Don't know if I'd go there, if I was you."

"Why not?"

"I's a crack house, man. You might not come out."

Eric handed the boy a dollar bill. He walked up the boardwalk, turning onto Windward. The crack house was an old apartment building. Most of the windows on the first two floors were gone and many of them above that. He hesitated before going inside. A young girl was crashed out in the doorway. She couldn't have been more than fourteen. He wondered what had brought her here. And images of Samantha and Dylan flooded across his eyes. If he went inside this building, would he ever see them again? If he didn't, would he ever see Lindsay again? It was a Sophie's Choice he didn't want to make, but he was here now. And if Lindsay was here he wanted to help her. Besides, what were the odds something would happen if he went inside?

Eric walked past the red tag and rubble into the lobby of the old building. Splintered shafts of light slithered through the broken windows and cracks in the walls. The lobby was empty, no hint of its one-time elegance, not even any leftover furniture and barely any plaster on the walls. An odor of feces and urine and vomit emanated from the upper floors. Eric gagged. He swallowed down the bile that retched up his throat. He almost turned back. Instead he made his way past an elevator shaft with no doors and no elevator, to the stairs, or what was left of them. Testing the first stair with his foot, and every stair above it, he slowly made his way to the second floor, crunching needles and candy wrappers underfoot.

A noise, music, came from a room down the hall. Eric cautiously made his way. He recognized "What's My Name" by Snoop Doggy Dogg spilling from a boombox in a room that at one time might have been a nice apartment. Now it was a mess of plaster and exposed pipes going nowhere. Through a door Eric could see that the porcelain in the bathroom was smashed to bits. He could hardly stand the stink. At least eight people were in there, grooving to the music, having sex. One was reading a book in the corner.

Everybody looked stoned. Or if not they had the glassy-eyed look of people who hadn't eaten in days. Eric wanted to turn and leave.

"Hey, man, got any H?" a kid with spiked hair and a crack pipe said.

"No. I'm looking for someone. Girl named Lindsay? Any of you know her?"

"Lindsay who?" said a well-endowed girl half in and half out of her shirt, lying in the corner. Eric wasn't sure of Lindsay's last name. He described her. "Yeah, that's her," the girl said. "She's not here."

Eric's heart sank.

"You her father or something?"

Eric didn't think he looked that old. Maybe living down here had taken its toll.

"Does he look like a father?" the girl in the corner with the book said.

"I guess not. I saw her down on the beach a couple hours ago. In front of the restrooms where we go to wash."

"Thanks," Eric said. He laid his remaining twenty on the

floor and cautiously made his way down the hall, down the stairs and out of the building. He sucked in as much fresh air as he could and headed for the beach.

Not too many people on the sand today, but being L.A., there's always a few about. Eric trudged across the small sand dunes. He checked in front of the cement block restroom building. No sign of Lindsay. He walked several yards in either direction. Nothing. He made his way back to the restrooms. Checked the men's side first, then anxiously made his way to the women's side. He glanced around and darted inside. No one at the sinks and it didn't appear that there was anyone in the stalls, but he checked anyway. No one. He dashed out of there.

He walked toward a small clump of palm trees on the beach and there he found her, sprawled out between two trees, a needle and a blackened spoon carelessly tossed in the sand next to her. He didn't like to think of her being a junkie, but he saw no other answer.

"Lindsay."

She lolled her head so she could see him through glazed eyes. Strings of greasy hair fell across her face. Her clothes reeked, as if they hadn't been washed in days. As if they'd been vomited on. The wind blew papers over her chest and face, she did nothing to remove them. She looked like she needed rescuing. Eric's rescuing days were over. Still, he couldn't leave her. And he knew that by helping her he would be helping himself.

"Hey, Eric," she slurred.

"Are you okay?"

"Never better."

He bent toward her, took her hand. Clammy. Cold. "Maybe I should get you to a doctor, the free clinic."

"I'm okay. I'm just chipping."

"Chipping?"

"I only use occasionally. I guess you found me on one of

my occasional days." She tried to smile. It went slack. She forced herself to sit up. "How you been? Read the book yet?"

"I tried to. I was too nervous. I got a job."

"That's great. Doing what?"

"Just sort of an errand boy, but I thought we might celebrate. I got money for a nice dinner." Change from the remaining twenty bucks wouldn't have bought coffee at the restaurants Eric had been used to not so long ago. After buying the toys for his kids, there were only a few dollars left. Enough to get some food somewhere. He thought about the other twenty he'd left at the crack house. Now he wasn't sure it was such a good idea. He had left it as a gesture of gratitude for them telling him where to find Lindsay. He wondered if, instead of buying food, they'd buy more crack. "Come to my place. You can shower and put on some clean clothes. And we can get something to eat." He didn't know if it was a good idea to move her right now. But he couldn't leave her here either. Besides, maybe she'd come to his place and sleep it off. Does one sleep off a drug high—he didn't know.

She didn't want to go, so he scooped her up with little resistance on her part, and helped her back to his place. He ran the tub's shower, gingerly undressed her and put her in the tub, letting the water revive her. She slid to the bottom, legs splayed in front of her. He let her soak, keeping an eye on her, then helped her into a towel and walked her to the bed platform. She couldn't make her way up the ladder, collapsing instead on the floor. While she was crashed out he took her clothes to the laundromat and washed them, hoping she'd still be there when he returned. She was still on the floor, her eyes glued to something interesting on the ceiling.

"I brought your clothes back. They're clean."

"You don't have to do all this for me."

He knew that. And he wasn't sure why he was doing so much for her. He hardly knew her. He was lonely, sure, and she was the first person he'd met down here as a friend, the first person he'd allowed himself to meet. There was something about her, young as she was. A certain vulnerability behind the tough exterior. He didn't want to save her. Did he want her to save him? That was more likely. In the meantime, he just wanted a friend.

He gave her her clothes and turned his back so she could dress. Ironic, he thought. They didn't go out, instead ordering in Chinese, Kung Pao chicken, eggrolls, hot and sour soup, and plenty of rice. A feast for royalty.

She was finally able to climb the ladder, but they didn't have sex; they just laid in bed all day, munching Chinese, listening to the cheap radio Eric had. They didn't talk much. They held each other tight until the sun went down. Eric liked the warmth of her next to him. Was it her or would any warm body do? He didn't know. He didn't care. He was just damn glad not to be alone tonight. Holding her tight, he could close his eyes and he was in the Ritz in Paris instead of his crappy apartment in Venice, CA. He liked this Ritz, and it was as much an escape for him as her drugs had been for her.

CHAPTER 14

I was still reeling from Birch's message. Two words: "Marc Beltran."

L.A. city councilman. Republican. With much higher political aspirations. I felt like I'd stepped into quicksand and each time I tried to work my way out I got sucked in deeper and deeper. First the Catholic Church, now a councilman. Birch dead. And I hadn't even brushed my teeth yet.

And sooner or later the cops would get around to checking Birch's phone and they'd find that he'd called me. And there'd be another pounding on my front door.

"I wouldn't tell the cops till they call on you, buddy," Jack said. He'd come over to check on Molly. She still seemed to like him better. He'd brought eggs, white cheddar, green onions, and tomato and stood at the counter whipping it into batter.

I didn't know what Marc Beltran would have to do with Birch and even less so how Carlos might be involved. But it seemed that Marisol's brother traveled in headier circles than she might have been aware.

"If I wait they'll accuse me of hindering an investigation."

"If you tell them too soon you'll hinder your own investigation."

"Can't win."

"Ain't that the way, bro." He poured the batter into a

115

frying pan. "So what do you think Carlos and Beltran have in common?"

"Maybe he helped Carlos with an immigration issue."

"Maybe. Beltran's a Hispanic name, isn't it? Most people don't recognize it as one, but it is." Jack would think of that.

"So how do I get to Beltran? Just call him up and say, 'hey, man, I'm a constituent. Talk to me.'"

"Tell him you've got money for his campaign."

Marisol or Beltran, the fork in the road. Which one to approach first? I wondered if Marisol knew more than she'd told me.

Marisol was the easier of the two. I still had to figure out a way into Beltran's office. I mean just 'cause I was a taxpaying citizen that certainly wouldn't open any doors, literally or figuratively.

I thought about taking Molly with me. Instead I went alone to the Goldsteins'. I heard the vacuum cleaner in some distant part of the house. Most people vacuum using the start-and-stop method, at least I did, so I waited till the sound died down then rang the doorbell.

"Mr. Duke," Marisol said, letting me in. We passed a few pleasantries back and forth and she settled on the living room sofa. I sat in a huge wingback chair with a floral pattern that looked like a bad acid trip—not that I've ever experienced one first hand. The Goldsteins must have been at work or I guessed we'd have been out on the back patio again.

"Do you have any news?"

"I'm making some headway, nothing substantial to report." I filled her in on my trip to the corner of Sunset and Western and Carlos' crib. "I do have some questions for you."

She saw a speck on an end table, dusted nervously.

"You said your brother was a day laborer."

"*Sí.*"

"What did he do for Miguel?"

I watched her eyes, her face for any kind of tell. But I did it as covertly as I could. Looking beyond her, but looking at her at the same time.

"I don't know."

"Do you know how to get in touch with Miguel?"

"*No sé.*"

I couldn't see anything. Maybe I just wasn't any good at this end of it.

"He wanted to be rich. But he wanted to do it fast. How do you say, get rich quick."

"That's how you say it." The question was how you made it happen.

"When you were at his house, you found nothing?" she said.

"Not much. That's why I was hoping you could help out. Anything you remember, friends' names, where he hung out. Anything like that."

"We are not close."

Did she realize she was talking as if he was still alive? It's hard to reconcile someone's passing, especially a premature death.

I looked into her deep brown eyes. As brown as the California landscape. In another time, another place I might have looked at her differently. As it was, I had no designs on her. And she had nothing substantial to add in the way of information.

I went home. Pulled out the card Myra Chandler had given me. Sooner or later the cops would be onto Birch's call to me. I wanted to deal with Chandler rather than Haskell. She might turn out to be a bitch on wheels, but she was the prettier one, and I was a man. Take it for what it's worth.

After being put on hold for a near eternity, someone in

the Hollywood station detective bay answered the phone. "Beaumont," he said.

"Is Detective Chandler there?"

"Not here."

"Can you take a message?"

"Am I her personal secretary?"

I thought about giving him the "I'm a taxpayer so you're sort of working for me" routine. Decided against it.

"Tell her Duke Rogers called. I'm going to have lunch at Roscoe's Chicken and Waffles, one p.m. I have something to tell her if she wants to meet me."

"What are you, some kind of royalty, Duke? Are you in line to become king?"

Maybe you'd like to join us? I think you'd like a knuckle sandwich—I could have said it out loud, but why ask for trouble?

"Tell her I'll be there at one." I hung up.

I got to Roscoe's way early, so by the time Detective Chandler arrived, if she came, I'd already have a table. At one-fifteen I was seated; she still hadn't shown up. I had bought a copy of the *Times* and was scouring it for any news on Birch's death. There was a small story in the Metro section, but nothing in it jumped out at me. Just another La-La Land murder. There was a quote from Father Carrigan, who spoke on behalf of the Cardinal. He said, "It is a tragedy of our times that such things happen." I wondered if this was the same Father Carrigan that Marisol had mentioned.

At one-thirty the waitress was looking annoyed that I hadn't ordered. At one-thirty-seven Detective Chandler showed.

"Mr. Rogers."

I motioned for her to sit. I thought about standing up, but you never knew these days if a woman would appreciate some old-fashioned chivalry or cut your balls off, verbally anyway, if you showed some. A paperback toppled out of her purse as she set it on an empty chair. I picked it up—*How To Be a Private Detective*—at least she had a sense of humor.

"Have you ordered?"

"I was waiting for you. And I don't think the waitress is any too happy about it."

"How'd you know I'd show?"

"I didn't."

That elicited the slightest upturn of lips. Maybe you could call it a smile. We both ordered the chicken and waffles— what else would you get at Roscoe's Chicken and Waffles?

"Why did you call me?"

"I have something to tell you. Though after talking to the detective who answered the phone, I wasn't sure you'd get the message."

"I didn't mean that. Why'd you call *me* instead of Sergeant Haskell?"

Hmm, now what to tell her? "I thought you'd make a better lunch companion."

"I can't fraternize with you, you're a possible suspect."

"Can't fraternize with the enemy?" I said. She laughed. "And only a possible suspect?"

"This meeting is on the record, you know."

"That's fine, I want it that way."

The waitress brought our food. We ate in silence for a few minutes. She looked up at me, expectantly.

"I got a phone call, message actually. From Jeremy Birch." I was hoping if I told her up front that maybe there'd be a *quid pro quo* down the line. Something she might give up to me. "'Marc Beltran,' that's all it said."

"The councilman?"

"I assume so."

"What did Birch mean?"

"I haven't figured that out yet."

She took a forkful of waffles. "You know, all the years I've worked in Hollywood, I've never eaten here. Everybody talks about it, but I seemed to have missed the boat every time."

"Ah, so that's why you agreed to have lunch with me."

"Of course." But that hint of smile was back. "Marc Beltran. Jeremy Birch. And you're investigating the death of Carlos Rivera. Where's the tie?"

I had been thinking about that. "When I met with Birch, we didn't talk about much. I think after getting to my house, he sort of chickened out. But he did mention the church's sanctuary movement for illegals."

"Undocumented workers."

"Illegals. As far as the government is concerned, Carlos Rivera was *illegal*." I watched a group of Hispanic workers enter Roscoe's, wondering if they were legal. What did that say about me?

"Birch was the Cardinal's deputy for sanctuary. Makes sense. Now what about Beltran?"

"He's Hispanic, isn't he?"

"Yes. But he's a Republican. Conservative Republican at that." Chandler washed a bite down with a glass of orange juice.

"Cheap labor."

She mulled it over.

"It's beginning to make more and more sense. I don't have all the connecting wires, but think about it. Carlos is the wild card here," I said. "Birch and Beltran both have their hands in the cookie jar for whatever their respective reasons."

"Strange bedfellows."

Strange indeed.

Her fingers drummed the table. She saw me watching. "Sorry. I quit smoking a month ago. Still get the cravings. Gotta do something with my hands."

I looked at her face, her eyes, for the first time really.

"What?" she said.

"I was just picturing you with a fedora and trenchcoat, cigarette dangling from your lips. Female Bogie." I nodded toward the book she had laid on the table.

"Oh, the book. I'm not reading it to become a PI I'm reading it to understand what makes people like you tick." That brought a full smile.

We agreed to stay in touch. She picked up the tab, expensing it to the city. So I guess in a way I still paid for it. You know what they say, no free lunch.

We walked to our cars. She looked at me in a hungry way.

"I'll need to get that tape from you," she said.

It wasn't what I was expecting. No free lunches.

Chandler followed me back to my house. She visited with Molly a few minutes.

"A guy with a dog like that can't be a murderer?" I said.

"You'd be surprised."

I couldn't tell if there was a smile in her voice, so I changed subjects. "I have a couple of questions for you. Why haven't I heard more about Birch in the news?"

"We're trying to keep a lid on it."

"Okay, I get it. And why isn't Metro or Robbery-Homicide handling it?"

"I better get that evidence now."

"Okay, I know, you're keeping it under wraps."

She borrowed my answering machine tape, still with the Birch message on it, slipping it into an evidence bag she pulled from her purse. After she left I wasn't sure what to make of her visit. I thought there was some attraction, but ultimately she was all cop. I dug out an old answering machine tape from the garage, stuck it in, hoping it still worked, at least until I could buy a new one. I didn't expect the one Chandler had borrowed to be returned any time soon.

* * *

She wasn't gone long when Jack stopped by to criticize my choice in music again. This time Philip Glass' *Songs from Liquid Days*. He never used to come by this often, not until the day he left Molly here. Should my feelings have been hurt? I filled him in on my morning as he rolled a green tennis ball across the floor for Molly to chase.

"Birch and Beltran," Jack said.

"And Carlos."

"What's the connection?"

"Smuggling."

"Drugs?"

"People. That's the tie. Cheap labor. More parishioners. More voters."

"So how does Carlos fit in?"

"He worked for them. With a coyote named Miguel." I threw the ball for Molly. She grabbed it and brought it back to Jack. "I guess my next step is Beltran."

"If you think someone won't kill him. Birch got hit after talking to you."

"He probably wouldn't take a call from me anyway."

"Why should he? You're only a constituent, not a contributor."

"Guess I'll have to have a private talk with him."

"You'll never get to him at city hall. Can Lou get you his home address?"

"She's been kind of shy about that since getting me Teddie Matson's address. Tom Bond got me Birch's, but I don't think he'd be up for getting me a councilman's."

"Well, then you have to take more drastic measures."

"I could stake him out."

"Waste of time and if you get caught how you gonna explain it. Leave it to me. I'll find out where he lives."

I didn't want to ask him how. He had his ways. I had mine. I'd wait and see what he turned up.

CHAPTER 15

While waiting to hear back from Jack, I decided it couldn't hurt to call Beltran's office to see if I could get in. The officious-sounding receptionist asked who I was.

"Duke, Duke Rogers. Is Councilman Beltran in?"

"He's in a meeting. And what is this about?"

"I'd like an appointment to see Councilman Beltran."

"And your business is?"

"I'm a constituent. I'd like to see my representative."

"Do you live in the district?"

"Can you please just set up an appointment for me?"

"The councilman is very busy. He can't meet with every constituent."

"I'll leave my number. Can he call me?" I gave her my number without much hope of hearing back.

I *coupaged* Molly and we went for a walk. While we were out Jack had left a message with Beltran's info.

Beltran lived in what might be considered Hancock Park or on the border at any rate. A little east of where Birch lived. In a classic craftsman bungalow that was probably seventeen hundred square feet and going for a million bucks. Not bad for a councilman. I parked a few houses up on the opposite side of the street and waited. If you don't like waiting, the PI game isn't for you. He drove up in his Jeep Grand Cherokee. Alone. No bodyguard. I was glad for that. He pulled down the driveway. I got out, jogged for his house. One good thing about these old houses, the garages weren't attached. So he'd have to walk some distance between house and garage. I was there waiting for him.

"Councilman Beltran—"

"Can I help you?" he said, more imperious than his secretary. His eyes darted to the back door, several feet away, a minor obstacle between him and it. Me.

"Look, if this is about council business you'll need to—"

"We need to talk councilman." I moved close to him, close enough to feel the mist of his breath. He was taller than me, but my money was on he couldn't or wouldn't fight. You could tell the type. "We can talk here or inside."

He started to walk past me. I moved in line with him.

"Look, if this is a shakedown."

"It's not the kind of shakedown you think. My name is Duke Rogers."

He eyed me. "Yes, I think I recognize you. Private investigator. What then?" Fear seeped from his face as sweat spilled from every pore. I was waiting for him to start shaking or pee his pants. He couldn't know what I was here about. Or did he tie it to Birch—some connection? Of course, if I was a city councilman in Los Angeles I'd be scared of every shadow too, especially my constituents.

"I just want to talk."

"Make an appointment." His jaw jutted. He spread his feet apart. His attempt to be tough, maybe dangerous. It was laughable. I watched his hands. They stayed by his sides, twitching nervously. I moved a foot closer to him. He held his ground. He'd rather have died than show cowardice, I guess.

"Do you really think that would have gotten me anywhere?"

"So what is this about?"

"Why don't we go inside and have a little chat?"

"You are not coming into my house."

I moved another foot closer. Now we were two feet apart. He stood taller. He also stood shakier. I reached inside my windbreaker.

"If you're going for a gun—"

"I just want to talk." I handed him my business card. "We don't have to go into the house, let's go in the backyard."

Knowing he had no choice, he ushered me through a flimsy wooden gate into a backyard, a lush green tropical paradise, complete with pool. Now, when we were having a lot of rain, a yard like this made sense. Most of the time it didn't. And hadn't I heard him on the radio preaching water conservation as L.A. is a desert? We sat at a small round table by the pool that should have had an umbrella, but didn't. Real L.A. He sat as far to the other side of the table as he could. Didn't matter, I could grab him before he finished blinking if I wanted to. And I would if I had to. The table was false security.

"Carlos Rivera," I said.

"Who?"

"Jeremy Birch."

"What are you getting at?"

"You knew them."

"I knew Jeremy." Fright popped on in his eyes. I knew what he was thinking—was he sitting across the table from Birch's killer? I could have assuaged his fear. Why bother? It would work for me.

"And Rivera." I shoved a picture of Carlos in his face.

"Don't know him." But he did. That much was obvious from the look of recognition on his face.

"We can play games. Or you can be straight with me and I can get out of your face." My mind should have been on him, but I was on autopilot. I was thinking about Rita. Strange place to be thinking about her, but I was. I pictured us lounging in this tropical garden, with a couple of piña coladas. I had a pool, but no tropical paradise like this. Rita would look damn good in a bathing suit. And then Detective Chandler's face crossed my mind. I blinked to get rid of all that and get back with Beltran.

He got up. "This meeting is over."

He saw I wasn't going anywhere, not even getting up from the table.

"Mr. Rogers, it might do you well to remember that there is no one who isn't dangerous to someone some time."

"What the hell is that supposed to mean?"

"Who are you working for, Mr. Rogers?"

"I'm just checking into Carlos Rivera's death."

"Haven't the police closed the book on that?" His voice trembled.

"The book's not closed for everyone."

"You don't want to get into this," he said. He was expecting me to say something. I waited for him to go on. He wasn't exactly an open book, but he talked. I guess he couldn't stand the silence—*horror vacui*—which is what I was hoping for. "I should never have gotten involved in this shit. What was I thinking? But I'm nobody. I just took some contributions—"

"—to throw your vote their way."

His lack of response expressed more than anything he could have said.

"And Birch?"

"He was a nobody too."

"Nobody."

"Yes."

"Okay, you're all nobodies." I was getting tired of the political rope-a-dope.

"Carlos—I didn't know him, but I know who you're talking about."

"Another nobody?" I said and he nodded. "What are all you nobodies doing?"

He glared at me, trying to be tough. He wasn't. I moved a foot closer, crowding him. That's all it took.

"Smuggling immigrants over the border," he said in a voice so soft the breeze almost carried it away before it got to my ears. He looked around, as if to make sure no one was watching, listening.

"Birch?"

"A cog. He helped hide them out until we could place them, get them papers." The tremble from his voice now reached his hands. He clearly didn't like talking about Birch.

"Sanctuary."

"Something like that."

"But not as noble."

He shook his head.

"And Carlos?"

"He was a runner, I think."

"A runner?"

"Like a junior coyote. He worked for the real coyote, maybe as a driver, driving the immigrants up to Los Angeles." Like a virus, the tremble spread. His foot tapped violently on the floor.

"Why was he killed?"

"I don't know. Maybe he saw something he shouldn't have. Maybe he was going to talk to INS. I don't know, Jesus. That's all I know. I thought you might be from them."

"The coyote or the INS?"

"Does it matter?" "But I don't know why they would kill Birch."

"How'd you get involved?"

"Through Birch. He came to see me one day." It looked like he was thinking about shutting up. But he went on. It was the fear talking, but also the truth. "Promised me campaign money if I helped out with some legislation."

"How could you do that? You're an anti-immigration Republican."

"I can BS with the best of them. I'd argue it on humanitarian grounds."

"Yeah, and in the process maybe they'd throw some votes your way. A good thing for a Republican in a Democratic town."

His eyes shot down.

"Birch said all I had to do was vote pro immigrants on humanitarian grounds, and help get some local legislation passed to make L.A. a sanctuary city," Beltran said. "He only came to see me the one time. Understand no one wants this out in the open."

"Who was Birch's boss?"

"I don't know."

"Birch came to see me, too." I wasn't sure if I should say it or not. I figured maybe it would scare him—thinking I'd killed Birch—then again maybe it would scare him too much.

"I think you might have stirred up a hornet's nest."

"I've barely begun. I don't see how anyone—"

"They keep close reins. They might have been keeping tabs on Jeremy." Beltran's eyes darted back and forth nervously.

"Who is they?"

"I don't know."

"What do you mean you 'don't know'?" I stared him down. "They pay you, they give you instructions."

"Another runner pays me. I never meet the big people. They helped me get elected."

"And now you're going to help me find out who they are."

"The only name I know is Miguel." Beltran got up, turned on the hose faucet, dipped his hand under, and splashed his face.

"He's the coyote?"

"Yes. But he's not the boss."

"Maybe not, but he's a place to start. I want to meet him."

The only way that I can describe the look that washed across Beltran's face is utter fear. He hid it quickly and probably thought I hadn't seen it.

"Set something up," I said.

"I'll see what I can do." He looked at the gate, his only means of escape. "All I wanted was some votes to stay in office."

"Power."

"You know it's hard to get by in L.A. A councilman doesn't make that much. All I wanted to do was make a buck."

"That's all Carlos wanted too." I walked off.

I called Jack, while sitting at the kitchen table. Molly slept at my feet. As I dialed, I thought about taking her to the vet to see if she was doing better. I filled Jack in.

"You're gettin' into quicksand," he said.

"Yeah." I stroked Molly's back.

"What're you going to do?"

"I don't know. Seems like a lot of tangled webs."

"And you think this councilman is okay?"

"No, and he's scared shitless, but what else do I have to go on?"

"He's a politician, they're always scared."

"No, he's really scared."

"But he said he'd help?"

"Said he would."

"He might have second thoughts. He might go to them, tell 'em everything. Watch your back, pal."

"That's your job."

"Yeah, like I could ever forget. Why don't you move on, man? Tell this maid down the block her brother was killed by coyotes—the two-legged kind—and it's better to leave it alone." Jack's voice twisted around itself, frustration and anger intertwining.

"I can't leave it alone."

"Why not? You got no stake in this."

"Broken windows."

I needed exercise. So did Molly, but I needed something more strenuous than a walk with the dog. The sky was clouding up again. And the pool wasn't heated. But I put on a pair of khaki trunks from my old Navy days and dove in the pool. Swam one hundred laps, each stroke working out the kinks and tightness in my neck and shoulders. The cold water slapped at me like a wake-up call.

Rita's face floated around the edge of my consciousness until finally it came into full view. Coffee-colored skin with chestnut eyes.

Jack's voice echoed, "A faint heart never won a lady."

A shiver went through me as I toweled off and headed inside. The light on the answering machine was blinking. But there was no message—a hang-up. I still had Rita's number in my head. My hand reached for the phone. Before I could grab it, it rang. Maybe someone was trying to tell me I shouldn't be calling Rita. I picked up.

"Hello."

"Mr. Rogers."

Beltran.

"Yes."

"I think I can help you. But only if you promise not to leak any of this to the press. I'm cutting off ties and you keep my name out of it." It sounded like his voice was shaking, though it was hard to tell over the phone connection.

"I can't guarantee anything, but I'll try." It wasn't exactly a lie. But it also wasn't the truth. In most cases my word was my bond. To a rat like Beltran, well, time would tell. My response was good enough for him.

"My contact wants to meet with you," he said.

"That's very generous of him."

"He's serious. He hopes maybe you two can get things cleared up."

I agreed to the meet. Beltran said he'd call back with the particulars. I called Jack to let him know about it.

"It's a setup."

"Maybe," I said. "But what else do we have to go on?"

CHAPTER 16

A man named Eddie drove Eric to Will Rogers Park in Beverly Hills, across from the pink and green Beverly Hills Hotel with its famous star hangout, the Polo Lounge.

"All I have to do is drive the car to this address?" Eric said, looking at a piece of paper with an address on Pico near Alvarado. The only thing Eric knew about Alvarado was that it was a scary place and a good place to get phony documents, green cards, birth certificates and the like. The paper shook in his hands.

"Don't be so nervous, man," Eddie said with a slight accent. "I been working for Mike forever. No sweat."

This was the third job Eric was doing for Mike. He would have thought he'd be less nervous by now. He still wasn't sure if the cars were hot; they probably were. But it wasn't like it was a capital crime.

Eddie pointed; Eric got out and walked to a silver Infinity. Using the master key Eddie had given him, he opened the door, got in, and started the engine. Eddie waited until Eric drove off, then drove off himself. He didn't follow Eric, but turned at the first corner and Eric was on his own.

He drove within five miles of the speed limit, made sure not to run any lights. But he delivered the car on time to a man who looked out of place on Alvarado with his oversized Rolex. Eric took the bus back to Venice. In a couple days he'd have another envelope of cash from Mike and maybe over time it would get easier and his heart would race less.

* * *

The rain pelted the pier. To Eric it looked like it threatened to wash it into the sea. A couple piers up the coast had been lost. He walked up the steps from the parking lot. No one was here today. The amusement center was closed, but the restaurants were open. He met Mike by the smoothie shop. He noticed the man's immaculate fingernails and barber-shop-close shave. The Burberry slicker. This was a man with good taste, who clearly cared for himself.

"Good job, Eric."

"Thanks."

They walked to the end of the pier, past a lone fisherman, his line dangling into the sea, leaning on the railing as the rain came down. Mike had an umbrella; he didn't bother covering both of them, just himself. Eric thought he'd buy a coat for Lindsay with the money Mike would give him today.

"I think I'll try giving you a little more responsibility," Mike said.

"Good. That's good."

Mike pulled a number ten envelope from his pocket and shoved it into Eric's coat pocket. Who would notice on a day like this, even if there were anyone here to see? The fisherman certainly didn't seem interested in them.

"You ought to get an umbrella," Mike said, heading back down the pier. "I'll call you when I'm ready for you."

Mike walked off as rain trickled off Eric's face. He fingered the envelope in his pocket. Maybe he'd buy that coat and umbrella. And pay the rent and utilities. But in the more immediate future, he would take Lindsay to dinner.

"This is a nice place," Lindsay said.

Schaffel's on the boardwalk was at best a two-star restaurant. A notch below Applebee's, a notch above Denny's, but they offered decent portions of decent food in a decent if nondescript atmosphere of fishnets and mass-produced, paint-by-numbers, seascapes. In the old days, Eric would have considered it passable, but not very. But these weren't the old days. "Yes, yes it is."

They ordered the seafood platter, shrimp, crab, calamari, bits of lobster.

"So is this where you ask me how a nice girl like me wound up in a place—a life—like this?"

"No, this is where I look into your big saucer eyes and tell you how pretty you are."

She rolled her eyes.

"I wasn't being ironic."

"I am." She stirred her finger in her ice water. "I don't blush easily, but I think I'm blushing now."

"You are." He smiled.

"Well, then I guess it's my turn. You drive a nice car and though you look a little rough around the edges, you don't look like you were born to the streets."

"And you don't talk like you were either."

"I wasn't. But the ball's in your court now."

Eric debated what to tell her. He liked the idea of making up a romantic past. Instead, he told her the truth. "I used to be a lawyer, got disbarred and my life, I mean my wife left me."

"So when you get, uh, disbarred, that means you can't be a lawyer anymore?"

"Yes." Eric wondered if she could hear the wistfulness in that one syllable. All he'd ever wanted to be was a lawyer. And he had been damn good at it. Too good in some ways, or at least with too much of a conscience.

"What kind of lawyer were you?"

"Criminal law mostly—a defense lawyer."

"So you're used to all the people down here?"

"Yeah," he smiled sourly.

She stuck a crab-filled fork in her mouth. "I'll bet you look at them differently now."

He sure did.

"So what do you plan to do? How are you getting by, on savings?"

Was she just being friendly or trying to feel him out as a mark? Was he being paranoid? He knew how his clients manipulated people. He didn't want to be that cynical about her. "I've got nothing. Just the car. Living hand to mouth. But I did another job for that guy a couple days ago. Maybe he'll want me for something else."

"What kind of job?"

"Just sort of odd jobs, whatever he needs."

"Legal?"

"See no evil, hear no evil."

"But you're a smart guy, you must have some sort of plan for the future," she said. "I'm not very smart. My mother kept telling me so. In fact, every day she'd tell me just how stupid I was. She'd tell me I was no good and that I'd grow up to be a whore."

He looked at her.

"You're wondering if I am a whore."

He didn't respond. But she was right. He also wanted to ask about her drug chipping. Decided against that too.

"Don't ask. I'm not saying I am, or was, but just don't ask."

"Okay."

"I guess she was right though, at least in some senses. If I was smart I wouldn't be out here on the streets, whore or no whore."

"Where're you from?"

"Milwaukee. I came out here like everyone else—to be a *stah*," she vamped, gliding her backhand across her forehead. "Never even got one audition. Not for the real stuff anyway."

"Real stuff?"

"UnPorn." She thrust her chest out, what there was of it. "Boy that Hollywood Sign sure glitters, but when you get up close to it there's graffiti and dirt all over it."

"You ever think about going home?"

"I am home."

"I guess we both are."

"Here's to home." She picked up her glass of root beer, so did he, and they clinked. "At least it doesn't get to twenty below here in the winter."

Eric entered his apartment feeling lighter than air. Better than he'd felt in months. He now saw the dingy walls and ragged carpet as a project to be done rather than a rat's nest to endure. For the first time in all these months he felt hopeful.

He noticed the light on his answering machine blinking. Hit playback: "Yo, Eric, Mike here. Got another gig for you if you're interested. I'll try back later."

Mike still hadn't given Eric his number. The first couple of jobs had been a breeze. Maybe after Mike got to trust Eric he'd also trust him with his phone number.

Eric stuck his head out the window and listened for the ocean. He felt a droplet of water on his face. It was starting to rain again.

CHAPTER 17

I fed Molly while waiting for Beltran to call back. The phone rang.

"Rogers?" the caller said.

"Yeah."

"You know who this is?"

"I think so." It sounded like Beltran. I was sure he didn't want his name said, and I was also sure that if I could have traced the call, it would have gone back to a phone booth.

"I've made some calls. Here's the deal about the meeting."

I didn't say anything, thinking about what that might mean.

"You there?" he said. "Are you still interested?"

"Yeah, I'm interested."

"The meet is at Rocky Point in Smuggler's Gulch, south of San Diego. Know it?"

"Yeah, sort of. We used to train near there."

"Rocky Point. Thursday. Two p.m. There's a big flat rock there. You can't miss it."

"Who's the meet with?"

"Miguel."

"How will I know him?"

"He'll know you. Now leave me alone. I'm out of it." He hung up.

* * *

Jack's five-plex was another typical L.A. Spanish colonial job. His was the only unit on the second floor—the *penthouse*, he called it. I hadn't seen a For Rent sign in front and I also hadn't seen seventy-seven illegals packed into one apartment, like at Carlos', so maybe he had been exaggerating. Beethoven's *Eroica* blared from the speakers. A bust of the maestro, looking his most wild, sat on top of the stereo.

"Like I told you, it's a setup, man. An ambush," Jack said.

"Maybe, but what else can I do? I don't have any other leads."

"Where is it?"

"Smuggler's Gulch."

"Smuggler's Gulch? Sounds like something from a pirate movie," Jack said.

"You remember it?"

"Yeah, I do. And that whole stretch of border just gets nastier and more polluted every day. But it'll be a nice vacation."

"You're not coming," I said knowing he'd be there come hell or high water.

"Hell I'm not. Somebody needs to watch your back, remember."

I followed Jack through his workshop, with all his carpentry tools neatly laid out, and into his office. When things were slow in the PI biz, he restored old furniture. The office closet had been converted into a larder or more precisely an armory, complete with steel security door, but with a crappy wood veneer finish so it wouldn't stand out. He opened the door, pulled out several packets of MREs, his Doc Martens steel tocs, compass. Night vision goggles. He pulled out a sleek black Mossberg 590 shotgun and a box of buck and ball shells, usually a brush hunting load that contains a large ball as well as buckshot. Good for jungle combat or other combat in thick growth. You don't want to be on the receiving end of that.

"You're not taking the shotgun?"

"Might, at least for backup."

He pulled a CAR-15 from the closet, sort of a cut down version of the military's M-16. His had an infrared scope and was ready for action. "No, this is what I'm taking for my main weapon."

"I hope you won't have to use it."

He just grinned.

I went home to feed Molly, get her settled, and get some things for my trip. I knocked on the Goldsteins' door. Marisol answered.

"Hi, Marisol, I have a favor to ask."

"Of course." She stepped outside on the front porch. The Goldsteins must have been home. I felt like saying, "We have to stop meeting like this." Didn't. "What may I help you with?"

"I'm going away, not for long, maybe a day. I'd like you to look in on my dog. Make sure she's okay, has enough food and water."

"I would be happy to." She hesitated, but finally came out with it. "Does this trip have to do with Carlos?"

"Yes." I knew she'd press so I went on. "I'm meeting someone who might know something about his death."

"I want to come."

"You can't. It might be dangerous."

"He was my brother." She promised her friend from down the block would look in on Molly. Mrs. Goldstein came out.

"I couldn't help overhearing," she said. I thought she was going to take my side, say it was too dangerous for Marisol to join me or that she couldn't have the time off. "I think Marisol needs to go with you. I don't mind giving her the time off, with pay, and my husband and I will look in on your dog."

I didn't want Marisol to come, but I knew if I was in her position, I wouldn't take no for an answer. And with Mrs. Goldstein backing her up, it was a losing battle, so I reluctantly agreed to let her come. I knew Jack would blow a gasket, so I didn't tell him. Besides, he'd already left for the mission. He'd be there a day early, scouting, checking it out. Finding a place to hide. Working without Jack was like working without a net. I could do it, but it was better to have that extra security.

When I bought the Jeep after my classic sixty-eight Firebird was destroyed in the ninety-two Rodney King riots, I thought I'd use the four-wheel drive and extra heavy-duty suspension to go off-roading. Never got around to it. Now, as Marisol and I bumped and bounced through the arroyos near the border, I knew why I had gotten it. The chili pepper red wasn't very good camouflage, but then I hadn't bought the car with that in mind. Jack was already down at Smuggler's Gulch and in place. He would find a spot near Rocky Point and blend into the bush. You could be standing two feet from him, taking a leak, and not know he was there. He was expert at making Ghillie suits—a camouflage outfit that makes it almost impossible to see someone.

Bullets of rain caromed off the windshield as the Jeep's torque helped it through the mud. I still didn't want Marisol there with me. It could be a dangerous mission or it could go smooth as pie. Beltran might have set me up or maybe Jack and I were just being paranoid. Still, better safe than sorry and with no other leads, I had to take the chance. But even if he hadn't set me up—and I didn't put it past him, the coyotes and the drug runners were dangerous in themselves.

The brush glowed green and vibrant after all the rain. The usually dry gulleys ran with water. The normally stingy Tijuana River might have been the Mighty Mississip now. We jostled our way through mud flats, that earned their name today, in four-wheel-drive glory, and parked by a twisted tree silhouetted against an angry blue-black sky that would have made a good advertisement for a horror movie.

"You're going to stay in the car."

"Alone?"

Since I'd let her come, against my better judgment, Marisol would be safer in the Jeep than hitting the bush with me. I picked up the binoculars that sat on the dash, scanned the countryside. Even in the rain, people were everywhere, my bet that none of them were legal US citizens. Coyotes and runners sat just inside the US border, no Border Patrol in sight. People moved back and forth like ants. *Neither snow, nor rain, nor heat, nor gloom of night stays these couriers from the swift completion of their appointed rounds*—and I was damn sure that if it ever should snow here, it wouldn't stop the coyotes and their prey from dodging across the border.

"Right now I wish I had a CAR-15."

"What kind of car is that?" Marisol asked. I thought I had mumbled it, but not enough. I didn't want to tell her that it was a cut down, carbine version of the M-16. Though I guess she knew I was armed to the teeth, the Firestar in an ankle holster. One of Jack's Sigs in a shoulder holster under my jacket. KaBar knife taped to my shoulder under the jacket. And extra mags for the pistols. None of it was as good as a CAR or an Uzi or an H&K-MP5 submachine gun. But I couldn't let them know I was expecting trouble, or could I? Too late now. But I was showing good faith by not having a long gun with me.

I wondered what Molly was up to now. I figured we'd be gone a day, day and a half at the most, so Mr. & Mrs. Goldstein were looking in on her, *coupaging* her even.

* * *

The walk from the Jeep to the meet point was uneventful. No snakes in the grass. No booby traps. I carried my old Navy poncho and wore the old camo boonie hat. The rain stopped and the sun beat down, giving no warmth. The wind off the ocean chilled me inside and out. I scanned the horizon for someone who might be Miguel or one of his people. In the distance below, human ants scurried back and forth, most coming this way, into the U.S., but some, amazingly, heading the other way. I found the flat rock by the meet point—didn't look like great cover. Scanned three hundred sixty degrees. I like to be aware of my surroundings and old habits die hard. Some people go through life oblivious. They walk off curbs into oncoming traffic. They don't notice when lights change. They don't notice when their husbands or wives give them yellow caution signals that say, watch out. I was like that once. I try not to be anymore. I try to bring out the old training in all aspects of my life. Make it work. I sat there wishing there was some part of that training that could get me to figure things out with Rita. Where women were concerned, I was my own worst enemy. I wanted to call her. I hoped she'd call me. But wanting and wishing doesn't make it so. I knew that. And still I did nothing.

Doing this thing for Marisol was still doing penance for the damage I had done to Rita and her family, if inadvertently. How much penance could I do? How much should I do? My father had always said I was a fuck-up. Maybe I wanted to be one; whenever people back me into corners with their wrong assumptions about me, I don't like to disappoint them for some reason. And maybe if I could pull this off, I could get a little justice for Marisol; maybe then I could find it in me to dial Rita's number. Maybe.

Time slowed, as I sat on the rock Beltran had described as the meet point, watching the river of people flow by. I felt exposed, but what could I do? This is what Miguel wanted. This is what he got. I tried to spot Jack—couldn't.

Broad daylight and hundreds, maybe thousands of people dashed over the border and up the trails. Coyotes leading the way. Was Miguel one of the coyotes down there? And where the hell was he? I had been early, but now he was late.

The sun disappeared behind a leaded gray cloud that looked pregnant with water. It didn't take long till the sky began to drip again like a leaky faucet. My old Navy poncho and boonie hat kept me fairly dry as I sat on the damp rock waiting for the meet.

I had a hinky feeling about the whole setup and that's what I was beginning to think: setup. Jack was right: ambush. These thoughts had crossed my mind earlier, but I had pushed them aside, hoping the meet would go as planned, the way my mother used to hope that my father wouldn't yell at her or hit her sons for no good reason, as if wishing it made it so.

I slid down the rock, using it for cover as best I could, but it wouldn't cover me from all sides. Leaning back I kept my eyes mostly on the human parade, scanning this way and that and listening for any sounds that didn't seem quite right for this off-the-beaten-path location. The traffic in people didn't come by here, at least not this day.

And there it was, a quick rustling in the nearby brush. It sounded small and light, a rabbit maybe. I never saw it, but I was sure it wasn't human. The old training.

Rain beat a steady tattoo on the boonie hat. The rhythm hypnotized me. And the rain didn't stop the rush across the border and up the gulleys into the U.S.

Cha-cha-cha-cha-cha.

I knew that sound too well. The rapid fire of a fully auto AK-47.

Tuck and roll.

Hit the deck.

Reach for the Star.

As if it would do any good.

Damn—pain shoots down my arm.

Shot.
Scan the horizon.
Visibility poor in the rain.
Flatten down.
Lay chilly.
Scan with eyes only.
Head down.
Try not to move.
Another burst:
Cha-cha-cha.
Like the dance.
Pinging off the rock.
Ricocheting.
Bullet reports echoing.
Caroming this way and that.
Hard to tell which direction they're coming from.
Watch for movement.
Water spilling over the hat brim.
Hard to see in the damn rain.
Hard to hear with the rain.
Hard to tell where the shots are coming from.
Gotta look up.
Gotta roll.
Shoulder up.
Cha-Cha-Cha.
Hit.
Damn.
Boom!
A single loud report.
Echoes.
The cha-cha stops.
Suddenly—very suddenly.
Jack must have popped from his spider hole.
Snapped one off at the AK.
Jack doesn't miss. Ever.
Images flood my mind's eye.

The old cowboy movies I watched on TV as a kid.
The ambush.
Was it over?
Sloshing footsteps.
Marisol.
"Go, get down. Go back to the Jeep."
But she didn't stop coming.
"I hear shots. Are you okay?" She saw the blood on my shoulder. "You are shot. *Dios mio.*"
"Firefight."
"What? What is that?"
"I never even fired a shot."
"They are gone?"
"I hope so."
Jack probably knew I was hit. And I knew he wouldn't want to break cover. He'd be waiting to see if any more bad guys showed up. Waiting to take them out. More fun than shooting ducks in a gallery. He might wait here for a day or more, waiting, just waiting to see if Miguel showed up looking for his man. He might move around. He could stay up for three days straight and hardly show the effects. When we were younger it was five days. But hey, we all get old.
"Damn, hurts like a son-of-a-bitch."
"I must get you to a doctor."
"Can't do that. They have to report all gunshot wounds." It sounded so clichéd, like something out of a bad a movie. That didn't make it any less true.
"I will take care of you." She reached for me, to help me up. I yanked her down.
"I'm sorry. There might be more of them out there. We have to stay low."
I listened. Tried to listen above and below the rain. Behind it. For anything. Any sound. Nothing. Just rain. I had one last thought before passing out: Setup.

CHAPTER 18

"Beltran." The first thing I muttered after waking, still next to the rock. Marisol had dressed my wound as best she could with what she had at hand. I wasn't out long. A few minutes at most. But for those few minutes I was in a black hole.

I'd been wounded before. Passing out is a funny feeling as your world begins to spin and you lose control and down you go. I didn't have far down to go since I was already on the ground, but it might as well have been the biggest dip on the tallest roller coaster in the country. Down and out. The first sensation I noticed on regaining consciousness was teardrops of water hitting my eyelids. I opened them and a splotch of water filled my right eye.

"How long have I been out?"

"Maybe five minutes. Maybe ten. Everything is so slow."

"Were there anymore shots?"

"I don't hear anything."

I reached for the Star, which had slipped out of my hand and was now sticking out of the mud. Reholstered it. She helped me to my feet. I was doing better than I had expected. Maybe the wound looked worse than it was. Or maybe she'd stopped the blood in time. You never knew with wounds. Sometimes the ones that looked the worst weren't. And the ones that seemed benign were just the opposite.

"We have to get out of here."

"I will help you walk."

She put her arms under my shoulders and helped me stand

up. Then everything went gray as I slid from her. My face hit the ground and all was black.

My eyes half opened to see Marisol driving the Jeep.

"How did I get here?" I leaned my head against the rest. Forced my eyes to stay open. Saw a tourniquet on my arm. Marisol didn't respond. I don't know if she heard me and I was too weak to repeat it.

Marisol had a little trouble driving, but did pretty good. We bounced over the dirt road, making our way over the ruts and through the brush until we hit paved road. The sky never really opened up. In fact, the sun came out and baked the ground.

I dropped in and out of consciousness as we made our way up the coast, deeper into the U.S., though not very deep. She pulled into a gravel lot in front of the *Mi Casa es su Casa* motel. It looked like it hadn't rained here at all. The ground was dry. The hotel looked parched, paint flaking off the walls.

"We have to get back to L.A."

"You say no doctor. Okay, no doctor. But you need to rest. You wait here. I will get a room."

She came back a few minutes later, helped me from the car, though I didn't want help. Walked me across the parking lot. People hanging out. Talking Spanish. Not a word of English. Kids running everywhere, kicking up gravel dust. I could taste the dust, dry and corrosive on my tongue, as it tastes only in southern California.

Marisol opened the door to the room with a key with a plastic orange diamond attached to it. No magnetic key cards here. The darkness blurted out at us as we stepped inside.

I fell onto one of the twin beds and more darkness surrounded me. Children's voices echoing in the distance— voices of hope and the future. I closed my eyes.

* * *

"Hello," Marisol said.

I must have been out for at least an hour. I didn't know if it was day or night. Shades down, blinds drawn. "How did I get here?"

"Jack helped get you to Jeep." She must have seen the look of surprise on my face. "He comes from nowhere."

He broke cover for me. "Where is he now?"

"He stay behind."

To clean things up, no doubt. "Where are we?"

"A motel, up the highway."

"Something smells good."

"Albondigas soup." Marisol snapped the light on so I could see the sad and sagging room even better than I had in the twilight streaming through the drawn blinds. She helped me sit up. Brought me a cup of soup she'd been simmering on the hotplate. "From a can, I am sorry. I like to make fresh, but not here."

I wondered where she got the can. Maybe she was a mind reader.

"From people in the next room."

My thoughts wandered: Miguel. Beltran. An unseen shooter? Pain streaked down my arm, waking me out of my daydream. I looked at my shoulder, Marisol had changed the bandage while I slept.

"I don't think it is a serious wound, but we must make sure it does not become *infectado*—you must rest, you have lost blood."

I didn't think the bullet was lodged inside me. There seemed to be an entrance and exit wound. I got lucky—not for the first time.

I fell into a black hole that swallowed me completely. A bottomless pit. I was falling. There seemed to be no end to it. Parachute. Where the hell's my parachute?

Vague images flashed through my mind. Not of recent events, Smuggler's Gulch or Marisol and her brother. But of ancient history. Another battle. Another war.

Abrasive sand and desert heat ate you alive and you couldn't carry enough water to make you happy if you had a tanker truck following you.

The drop on the ravine was twenty feet, maybe thirty. Hard to tell in the haze and smoke. The acrid sting of cordite singed my nostrils. And the deadweight on my shoulders was pounding me into the ground. But what could I do? I wasn't going to leave the son-of-a-bitch behind.

How the hell was I going to get him down the face of that jagged wall?

I'll tell you one thing—it was a hell of lot easier in the dream than it had been in real life.

Somehow, some way, we got the hell out of there. I got my sat phone working again and called for dustoff.

"Now you owe me," he said, before passing out. And I knew just what he meant.

Because, before I saved his life, he had saved mine.

My regulator stopped. Just stopped working.

I'd been in the ocean a million times, but never with SCUBA apparatus. We'd had pool dives, but this was our first ocean dive. And though we were familiar with the gear, I still didn't know what to do. I wanted to shoot to the surface, but I knew that could cause problems. I looked around. My dive buddy was nowhere to be seen. Somehow he'd drifted off—a real screw-up, he wasn't long for the program.

We were all a little nervous that day. All except for that racist, son-of-a-bitch blowhard—well, blowhard's not the right word, as he was generally quiet. A quiet, taciturn blowhard, if there is such a thing. He wasn't nervous. He was never nervous. And he did everything well. Jesus, where the hell did he come from?

He never talked about his family, his past. He just railed

on about how the country was going to hell in so many ways.

"Hey, shorty," he had said to me on the first day of BUD/S.

I was one of the shorter guys trying out. But hell, I was over the minimum height requirement. Fuck you, buddy.

Luckily we were on different boat crews, each crew consisting of men of relatively the same height.

That day in the water he swam over to me, beating the instructor. I was panicked. He yanked the mouthpiece out of my mouth, jammed his in my face. Motioned me to breathe. And slowly we ascended, taking turns breathing through his mouthpiece.

Our heads broke the surface.

"I guess you're my responsibility now," he said

Yeah, right. He was going to be my protector for life because he believed, actually believed in some ancient code that if you save someone's life you're responsible for them forever. But he did believe in that code—and he expected me to believe in it too. And he did become my friend and my backup. And I learned to see through the macho bullshit to the real guy underneath. A guy who most often said the wrong thing but always—always—did the right thing.

I must have drifted off again. When I looked up Jack's blazing eyes stared intently at me, while his fingers, gloved in latex, felt around my wound. I winced.

"How'd you find us?"

"Took a bit of doing, but it wasn't hard." He rewrapped my bandage, went to the window and peeked out through a crack in the curtain. "The shooter waited for the rain. I buried him."

"How many?"

"Just the one. I waited three hours. Figured that was it."

I didn't ask Jack where he had hit the would-be assassin—

probably the forehead, right between the eyes—he was that good.

"Miguel?"

"I don't know," he said. "I doubt it. No ID. Clean. I even looked in his shoes and socks. No car nearby. No way to trace him. Serial number was filed off his rifle. Probably just some flunky Miguel sent down here to get rid of a pest."

The pest was me, of course.

"We got a problem now," he said.

"I know."

"Maybe you should stop. We know bad people have killed my brother. There will be no stopping them." Marisol's fear was palpable and I wondered again if she was telling me everything.

"We can't stop now."

"I think you're clean." Jack stripped off the latex gloves. He wasn't a doctor, but he'd had some training, like we all did. He looked at Marisol. "She did a good job patching you up. But we gotta have somebody who knows something take a look, don't want it to become infected. I know just the guy, Jerry Larchmont."

The name sounded familiar. "Corpsman, from the old days?"

Jack nodded. Jerry had been a Navy Hospital Corpsman, a medic. I didn't know if he was still in the service or not; maybe Jack knew. He gathered me up, put me in the Jeep's back seat. He sat with me to make sure I didn't bleed out or something like that, while Marisol drove. The Hummer was bigger, but she couldn't have handled it. They talked, looking at each other via the rearview mirror, while I drifted in and out.

"...He will be okay?"

"He's a tough mother, uh, guy. He'll make it..."

"...It is all my fault." Marisol's eyes stared at Jack via the rearview mirror. "...You do not like Mexicans."

"I don't like illegals."

"So why do you help me? Or you help *solamente por tu amigo Señor* Duke."

"I do it for him. Maybe for you, too." His voice softened.

"Because you see me close up. You see we are human beings too."

"You're definitely human. Hey, keep your eyes on the road."

"You like me?"

"I don't like anyone."

"You like *Señor* Duke."

I woke to see that we were pulling up the driveway to a small stucco house. Not the nice kind of Spanish colonial that populated my neighborhood in L.A., but one of those small cracker boxes built in the sixties and seventies. No personality and you're happy if it just keeps the rain out.

Jack helped me from the car to the back door. A familiar face greeted us. Jerry's face had aged—I suppose all of ours had. There were smile lines around his eyes and he wore a full beard, red pocked with gray. The hair on top wasn't so full. Jack passed me off to Jerry.

"Duke, you're looking good."

Humor.

He took me into the master bedroom and put me on the bed. The bedroom was all hearts and flowers, pinks and deeper pinks. "When you called," he said to Jack, "I sent the wife and kids to Chuck E. Cheese. Now let's have a look."

He pulled out a small medical bag.

"How long you been separated?" Jack said.

"'Bout a year. Did my twenty. Now I work as a nurse, can you believe it?" Jerry looked me over, took my blood pressure, probed here and there. "It looks like a clean wound. We'll antiseptic it and bandage—couple stitches maybe—and it should be okay. But you should see a doctor when you get back to L.A."

With all my contacts in various fields, I didn't know a shady doctor who would check me out without informing the police. So unless gangrene set in or some other complication, I wouldn't be seeing a doctor.

After leaving Jerry, we picked up Jack's Hummer at the motel. Marisol drove the Jeep, following Jack and me back to L.A. Neither Jack nor I offered any money to Jerry, not even for the price of the pizza at Chuck's. And Jerry didn't ask for any. That's the way it was with old swabbies. Maybe someday we'd be able to do him a solid.

Marisol and Jack helped me into the house. Molly greeted us and Marisol made tea, but didn't have any. She asked how I like it.

"Just a little honey."

"How do you like your tea?" she asked Jack.

He walked to the far side of the room, stared out the window. Was something going on between them? Still half out of it, I couldn't tell. But after thanking us and saying how grateful she was I wasn't hurt any worse, she went back to the Goldsteins'.

I looked at Jack as if to say "What's going on?" He didn't bite.

"We have to go after Beltran," Jack said. "He's our only link right now. He set you up. And we have to assume he knows you're not dead since there was no body and their guy didn't return." He sat down at the kitchen table; Molly jumped into his lap.

"How do we get to him? I already braced him for the good it did."

"Everyone has something they're trying to hide. Everyone has three lives, a public life, a private life, and a secret life." Jack grinned. "Their families might know about their private life, maybe they drink, but not always their secret life and sometimes their secret life can be bad stuff that seeps into their real lives, like serial killers."

Jack had a way of putting things that you just couldn't argue with.

"So I guess we need to find out what his secret life is," I said.

"Probably not our good fortune that he's a serial killer."

"Probably not, so I guess we have some homework to do." I shifted, trying to keep my arm elevated.

"I know it's too late—it's always too late—but why the hell did you get involved in this mess in the first place? I mean, jeez, you're making good money—"

"—Chasing down arm candy so those rich bastards, who always have a hard time paying me for some reason, can get out of their prenups and pay even less than they promised. Great job."

"You still haven't answered my question. You're still do-ing penance for Teddie Matson."

"When I'm seventy, if I make it that far, I want to look back and see that I've lived a good life. Be proud of it."

"And you think saving expendable people will give you an E ticket to heaven. Go to the front of the line or put you in the VIP line."

"You think they're expendable?"

"They're not worth dying over."

"They're desperate, Jack. For money. Work. They get used and then they get killed or just die the death of a thou-sand cuts. Besides, I don't exactly see you running away from helping Marisol."

Man of few words that he is, Jack flipped me off. I guess he figured a picture, so to speak, is worth a thousand words.

"You're just a bleeding heart after all," I said as he split out the back door.

CHAPTER 19

The rain had stopped again. I cracked open the window in my home office to let in the cool night air. My arm burned like a phosphorus grenade. I popped three Extra Strength Bufferin. The oldies station played the Eagles' "Hotel California." The lyrics struck a chord, especially when they sang about how you can check out, but you can never really leave. That's how I felt in more ways than one.

The computer booted up and stared back at me, as if to say "your wish is my command." If only it were so. Damn thing often seemed to have a mind of its own.

I logged onto the Writers Guild of America, west computer bulletin board system. I was a lucky boy to be in the WGAw. After my celebrated capture of Teddie Matson's killer, I was approached by at least a dozen producers who wanted the rights to my story. I optioned them to one whose specialty was action flicks, after he promised that Harrison Ford would play me. But I optioned them on condition that I would get to cowrite the screenplay; he didn't like it but he agreed. And I had to join the Guild—no choice in the matter. So every once in a while I diddled on their BBS, though mostly I couldn't stand it. They put down anyone who liked Beethoven's "Moonlight Sonata" and Pachelbel's "Canon" as being too trite. No, they preferred things that even I thought were unlistenable. But, as they say on the American Express commercials, membership has its privileges. And one of them was being able to tap into the Lexis-Nexis database through the Writers Guild for a nominal fee. And that's what I was doing now, searching for anything I could find on Beltran. Maybe a hint of his secret life.

Mostly a lot of PR flack, how wonderful it is that Councilman Beltran did this or that. Opening a new school in his district, creating a program to add cameras at stoplights to catch scofflaws. Articles about Beltran at various functions, charity events, movie premiers. Face time. Then I came across something interesting. A picture of Beltran and a young woman at some Hollywood charity event. The people who attended were divided into three groups. The first group ate lobster and other extravagant dishes at elegantly set tables, the next group ate sandwiches while standing around, the third group ate rice while sitting on the floor. All of this to let them know how it feels to be in a classist society. As if. When they gave away ninety percent of their highly inflated incomes, I would believe their concern.

But that's not what interested me. No, it was the young woman in the photo. Her name didn't appear in the caption or the article. But she looked familiar. I went to the service porch and dug through the newspaper recycling pile and there it was. The same young woman who had jumped from the Hollywood Sign a few days ago. Susan Karubian. She stood just behind Beltran. I'm not sure why I recognized her face. Maybe when the second person in history jumps from the Hollywood Sign, you remember. But there she was. Coincidence?

It might have been making too much of a leap to conclude he or his pals had anything to do with her death. After all, it was labeled a suicide. That aside, he probably didn't want to be hooked up with someone publicly who had died the way she had. That would be our wedge into Beltran.

But even without knowing more about that wedge, Jack and I decided to brace Beltran again. We headed for his house and waited. No sign of activity in the house and after three hours he didn't show. We tried four times over two days.

"Looks like he rabbited," Jack said.

"He's scared. He knows they didn't take me out."

"In hiding."

"But a councilman can't be in hiding forever."

"Whadda you mean, they're always hiding." Typical Jack.

Since we couldn't find Beltran, Jack and I delved a little deeper into Ms. Karubian. The more we knew about her and her relationship with him, the more we'd have to hold over him. I had a database of famous Hollywood names and some not so famous. And about half of them would probably still take my calls.

I thought about calling Joseph Hartman, put him on my list. But I decided to start with a woman named Fawn Farmer, a one-time typical Hollywood Hopeful. She had been dating a bankable actor, even had his kid. Then suspected he was cheating on her, hired me to find out. Now she and he don't speak, but she magically has a major producing career.

We met on the patio at Joe Allen's—Hollywood hangout—on Melrose during another lull in the rain. Nice patio right off the street, shielded from view but not from the exhaust. The building next door was yellow tagged, but Joe's was open and crowded.

"Good to see you again, Duke," Fawn said. She took off her sunglasses revealing large ocean-blue eyes framed by a blonde Jennifer Aniston-Rachel cut. She couldn't have been much more than thirty, over the hill in terms of Hollywood. But those eyes were the most beautiful I'd ever seen. And, if I were a producer, I'd have kept her in front of the camera instead of behind it.

I tried not to let the pain in my arm show. It was doing better. I didn't need to see a doctor. But it still hurt like a son-of-a-bitch. We hashed out old times. Decided it would be better to talk business after lunch. So we got out of there and walked down Melrose.

"Susan Karubian?" she said, after I told her who I was interested in. "The one who jumped off the Hollywood Sign?"

"The same."

"Yeah, I knew her, slightly. I think she auditioned for me a couple of times. Hung around at some parties."

"How'd she get invited?"

"I'm not sure, but you know, it's not hard for a pretty girl. Maybe someone brought her."

"Any idea who?"

"Can't say."

"Do you think she might have shown up anywhere with Marc Beltran?"

"The councilman?" she said.

"Keep it under your hat, please."

"Detective-client privilege?"

"Something like that." We walked under a sign that said "No cruising." Boy, Melrose had changed from when I was a kid.

"Is that what you're working on, something with Susan Karubian and Beltran?"

I didn't say anything.

"I know," she said. "You can't talk about it. But I'd love to see that Beltran brought down. He's a real slimeball."

Takes one to know one, I thought. I was, however, discreet. On the other hand, maybe I was being too tough on her. In a town of slimeballs, why not blackmail your former lover into bankrolling your producing career. More power to her.

"I don't think Susan got much work. Not legit anyway."

"Legit?"

"She worked in porns, I think."

"That's what I get for not going to the movies much these days."

"You don't have to go. You can rent them and bring them home."

And that's what I did. I drove to a store called Circus of Books on Santa Monica Boulevard in West Hollywood. Old building that looked like it was about to fall down, but green tagged. Hey, the county's overseers know what's important to keep open to the public. Trying to find a place to park on Santa Monica was next to impossible. And every street I turned down had restricted parking and signs that said "No Right Turn" after nine p.m. This area was a major gay cruise and the homeowners, straight and gay, were fed up with the open solicitations and sex on their front lawns, and finding used condoms there the next day. So the parking was even more of a mess than it would have been. I finally found a spot.

"Because the Night" by 10,000 Maniacs surged from the store's speakers as I entered. The front half of Circus of Books was a regular bookstore, selling Time and Newsweek, Hemingway classics, and the latest Toni Morrison novels. But behind a swinging saloon door was another store. And that's where I headed. You had to be eighteen to go back there, but nobody stopped me. I guess I stopped looking eighteen a while ago.

The back store was about one-third gay porn magazines and movies and two-thirds straight, though the latter included various subcategories like bondage and other fetishes. I didn't think Susan Karubian would have used her real name in the movies, so I just started browsing until I found some boxes with her picture on them. I found one by a company called Eros Dei, actually several from them, but I figured I only needed one. I kept looking till I found her picture on the box of another company called Cupid's Rat. Since I didn't have an account at the store, I had to leave a credit card imprint, as well as enough cash to cover the rental fee.

I thought about stopping to get popcorn, decided it was a bad idea, and headed home to watch my new rentals.

* * *

Susan Karubian didn't have the hard look that so many porn actresses have, or get. And she didn't look comfortable doing the things she was doing. But she probably thought of it as acting and a door into Hollywood, not realizing that almost no one makes the move from porn to the big time.

I hadn't seen a skin flick in a long time. The production values had definitely gotten better and it did seem as if they were trying to incorporate a story of some sort into the plot. But I didn't think that's why people bought or rented them. Still, the plot of *Forrest Hump*, sounded intriguing. It wasn't. In fact, there was nothing special about the videos. And even though they were from different companies, the stories, people, and sex in them seemed largely interchangeable. I forced myself to watch them both all the way through, torture though it was. They bored Molly, who slept next to me on the couch. When it was over we did our *coupaging* and went to bed at ten o'clock, early for us.

Pounding on the door woke me up...again.

Chandler? Haskell? Jehovah's Witnesses?

I stumbled into a Smurf Suit—blue sweats—held the Firestar behind my back and made my way to the front door.

Marisol.

"I'm sorry if I wake you. I want to make sure you are all right."

"I'm fine. Do you want to come in?"

"I think not. I have to work." She handed me a covered pot. "I make you some *menudo*. To keep up your strength."

I took the pot from her and thanked her, knowing I wouldn't eat it. I love Mexican food, but bovine stomach linings didn't appeal to me, no matter that they were a delicacy for some.

"I am glad you are okay." She started to turn, turned back. "Mr. Duke, maybe you should no longer pursue my brother's killer."

I looked her in the eye. "Listen, Marisol, if you want me to stop, I'll stop. But as far as I'm concerned I'm on the case."

"But you get shot."

"It's part of the job." I was redlining and didn't want to stop now.

"But I cannot pay you anymore than I have already."

"You're paying me in ways you can't imagine." I could see she didn't quite get what I was saying. "So, do you want me to continue?"

"I do. I want my brother's killer, how you say, brought to justice. But I do not want to see you getting hurt."

"I'll be more careful. Believe me." She smiled and headed back to the Goldsteins'. I closed the door behind her, just as glad she didn't come inside as I had left out the porn videos with their lurid covers.

"More rain is on the way. And more rain means more problems," the radio newscaster said. I knew there'd be more problems on the road we were traveling. I didn't know if the rain would cause them.

"Deep," Jack said. "And that's the award-winning news."

"You can imagine what the non-award-winning news is like."

Even in this day and age, the porn companies kept a fairly low profile. So it was nearly impossible to find out where Cupid's Rat hung his hat. Same for Eros Dei. Enter Joseph-Hartman-Hollywood-Hotshot.

Actually, Jack and I entered the fabled Paramount Studio gates. Only it wasn't the original gate. It was the faux gate recently built to look like the original gate. Oh well. Nothing in this town sticks around forever.

We parked and walked to Hartman's offices. Meltzer and Hartman greeted us under more posters of his great works. Pictures of him with Ronald Reagan and Bill Clinton. An equal opportunity ass-kisser.

Hartman looked Jack up and down. In Hollywood that could mean a lot of things.

"Duke, you find out *Kidder's* competition?"

"Still working on it. Lips are tight on this one."

"Must mean Universal's doing something. Can you speed it up?"

"I'll do my best." I didn't bother to tell him I had other priorities.

"Good, now what can I do for you?"

I filled him in, told him I was checking into Karubian and needed to know where these companies worked out of. He told Meltzer to make some calls. Meltzer went to another room.

"Barry's a good kid. He should have the info in a few minutes." He looked thoughtful. "I think I might have crossed paths with her at some point."

I didn't want to prompt him, just let him keep on talking.

"At a couple parties. You know those Hollywood political things, fundraiser, something like that," he said, tenting his fingers.

"Do you know who she might have been with?"

"That, uh, councilman. But I'm not sure how much he wanted it known. What's his name?"

His name was Beltran—all roads led to Beltran. A few minutes later Barry Meltzer came in, handed me a piece of paper.

"That what you need?" Hartman said.

"Yes. Thank you and I'll keep plugging on the *Kidder* stuff."

"Good deal."

I nodded. Jack and I headed for the door. Hartman got up, put his hand on Jack's arm—not the smartest thing. I waited for Jack to deck him. Nothing. Hartman finally said. "You should be in pictures."

Jack shook his head and we exited, stage left.

We headed to the Valley in my Jeep, per the notes from Meltzer. Laurel Canyon, the closest way to the Valley, was closed for quake repair so we drove west and headed over Coldwater Canyon, where rumor had it the burning of Atlanta in *Gone with the Wind* had been filmed. A dribble of rain hit the windshield so I didn't think there'd be much burning in the canyon today.

The Valley really boomed after World War II, when all those servicemen who'd passed through L.A. during the war decided to come back and make it their home. It was white-bread, ticky-tacky houses for the most part. But nice, if you liked the burbs.

We pulled up to a nondescript business mall in Chatsworth at the far end of the Valley. Several low-lying, sludgy beige buildings surrounded by asphalt parking lot. Could have been widget factories or clothing outlets. All green-tagged, which was saying something as this was close to the epicenter in Northridge.

"Who would ever know?" I said.

"Hell, the whole Valley is honeycombed with porn shoots in disguised warehouses."

"It's Spielberg Country."

"Spielberg Country is porn behind the doors."

We got out of the Jeep and headed to the door of the building on the far left. A bronze sign next to the door read: "Cupid's Rat Productions" and under it, "Eros Dei." Seemed like they were the same company under the covers, so to speak.

CHAPTER 20

We didn't knock, instead trying the door. It was unlocked so we invited ourselves inside. No receptionist in the small lobby that, with its cheesy *art porn* paintings and posters on the wall, and cheap motel furniture, looked like it could have been a set for a porn movie. Probably was.

"I don't hear any moaning or groaning," Jack said, as we made our way deeper into the bowels of the studio. No one paid us any mind. The usual crew types milled about, camera, lighting, grips. Three women sat on a cot in a *dungeon*. They had most of their clothes on. The dungeon walls were wood, painted to look like huge stones in some old castle. Another set looked like a doctor's office, complete with gynecological examining table.

"Looks like it's gonna be a good one," I said.

A woman with straight blonde hair and a navel ring under her cropped tank top came up to us.

"Can I help you?" she said.

I looked at my notebook. "Is Dick Johnson here?"

She looked at me, uncomprehending.

"He's the producer of *Hot Tails*." I had gotten his name off one of the video boxes.

She thought a moment, "Oh, you mean Dick Steel."

I didn't think I did, but I'd take whatever was offered. She walked off, returned a moment later with a man in a maroon Speedo, and nothing else. I tried to avoid looking at the Speedo, concentrating on his face, which was average in every way, so I figured his assets lay elsewhere.

"Gentlemen. You are?"

"—looking for Dick Johnson."

"Your business?"

I looked at Jack. His expression remained, and I hesitate to use the word, *steely*. He was going to be no help here, but I had a feeling he was enjoying my discomfort. I started to pull out a card, when Mr. Johnson erupted:

"Hey, don't I know you? You're that detective—Teddie Matson."

I handed him the card, confirming his suspicions. People love to brush shoulders with the famous, whether they're Michael Jackson, a serial killer, or an infamous detective. Hey, fame is fame in America these days. Better currency than greenbacks.

"Famous," Jack muttered under his breath, barely moving his lips. His expression not changing at all. I couldn't really see his face from where I was standing, but I knew.

Steel Dick, I mean Dick Steel ushered us into an office, a buff-colored cinder block cubicle. And like every producer's office it had posters of his latest and greatest triumphs on the wall, *Wee Willie Kinky*, *Forrest Hump*, *Pulp Porno*, *Four Weddings and an Orgy*, *The Shawshank Rejection*, *Little Women and Big Men*, *Hot Dogs and Wine*—a true cornucopia of titles to be proud of. I was sure the posters didn't do the actual movies justice.

He put on a robe, which made me think there really was a God, and sat behind a battered wooden desk, the kind my father used to have in his office at work. He motioned for us to sit on a couch. Jack moved to a corner of the room, where he could keep an eye on things—he clearly didn't want to sit on *this* couch. Neither did I, but I took my chances and sat down on the very edge of the couch, though I doubted it would make a difference.

"You think you're going to catch cooties?" Steel said.

"Uh, cooties wasn't what I was thinking."

"And you think this couch is any worse than most couch-es in most homes? Or hotels? Did you know they did a study for one of those TV magazine shows and found semen and urine all over the beds in most motels, even good hotels. Even on the doorknobs."

Jack's mouth twitched the slightest bit. I remembered my stay in the Mi Casa es su Casa motel. I sat back on the couch. Jack didn't move and the twitch was gone before most people would have noticed.

"I take it you're not here to audition." He turned to Jack. "Though you'd make a great star. Of course, we'd have to check your—"

I wanted to interject before Jack launched himself across the room. I couldn't think of anything to say.

"—personal die-mensions." And that's just how he pro-nounced it: *die-mensions*.

"Uh, we're here to see Dick Johnson."

"You're looking at him. And Dick Steel too. Johnson's my producer's hat, Steel is my actor's hat."

I worried that he'd lose his enthusiasm for talking to a famous detective once we brought up Karubian. But there's no time like the present. "We're here to talk about Susan Karubian."

"Who?"

"The girl who jumped from the Hollywood Sign. She's in some of your movies."

His jaw clenched. "You mean Susan Downy."

I didn't want to ask where they'd gotten that name. I pulled out one of the video boxes I'd rented, pointed to her picture.

"Yeah, Downy. You think I had something to do with her death? Maybe I better call my lawyer." His tone, his de-meanor, his body language all tightened up as he battened down the hatches. "And who's he anyway? Your bodyguard." He said, thrusting his jaw at Jack.

"He's my enforcer. You don't want to piss him off."

"Hell, I got five guys here. Can he, can both of you, take them all on?"

"Try us." I said it so nonchalantly he knew we didn't have any fear. "We didn't come here to bust your balls." Man, I hated all the puns that came to mind in this place. "We just want to find out a little about her."

"I don't know much. It's not like I do a background check on these people." His tone had gone business. "I'm sorry she's dead. I don't think any of my people had anything to do with it. I know I didn't."

"Who did she hang with?"

"I could get in trouble if I talk to you. You're not even cops."

"True. But if you like we could put the cops onto you."

"I don't want any hassles."

"Neither do we. We just want to find out a little about her."

"I, I don't know much. Nice kid. Came here with big dreams like all the rest of 'em, but she had to eat."

I thought of another pun, didn't say it.

He went on about what a good actress she was—sure—how everyone liked her, that kind of thing. How come every time someone's killed in the news they're nice, wonderful people, who would have contributed greatly to the world if they hadn't been cut down in their prime? Hell, that's even how they talk about gang bangers with multiple kills to their credits. No bad guys ever get killed.

I interrupted, "Do you know where she lived, who she hung with?" I'd tried, but couldn't find info on her, at least not yet.

"She lived in one of those apartments just north of Hollywood Boulevard. You know, the places that used to be ritzy, but are now sort of decayed. Still nice to a degree and big.

She lived there."

He looked up her address in a computer, wrote it on a scratch piece of paper with some kind of oily stain. I didn't want to think what that might be.

"I don't know who she hung with outside of the office."

The office?

"I think she was homesick. Lonely," Steel said.

I looked at the posters on the wall.

"Who could be lonely amid all this warm flesh?" His eyes lit up.

Who indeed?

He told us to feel free to question anyone who was hanging around and we did. They couldn't tell us much. Seems Susan kept to herself when not on camera. No one took her under their wing, no one explained the ropes to her. They were all too busy trying to keep their own heads above water.

Jack and I didn't talk much as we headed up De Soto to the Ventura Freeway. We hit the freeway, heading away from Ventura and back toward L.A. We switched to the Hollywood Freeway, got off at Highland. Sat in the perpetual traffic jam that is Highland, finally crawled past the Hollywood Bowl, closed for the winter season or traffic would have been worse. We turned left on Hollywood Boulevard, heading east, past the dingy brass and terrazzo stars embedded in the sidewalk. I wondered if ninety percent of the people stepping over Bette Davis or Rudolph Valentino even knew who they were today. After all, if it didn't happen during their lifetimes, it didn't happen.

Susan Karubian had lived about a block off the boulevard. We knew that parking would be impossible, so when a space opened up on the boulevard, we took it, jammed in some quarters, and walked off.

The Carvelle Arms still looked like a nice place. Well

maintained. Clean modern lines. About eight stories high. Palms graced the front, along with a piece of concrete that had fallen off the building. Still, it had only been decorative and the building was green tagged. We walked to the front door. No fancy stars embedded in the sidewalk here.

"Security door," Jack said.

"I didn't think of that."

"Pretty fancy for this part of Hollywood."

"Probably need it here more than most places."

We rang the buzzer for Karubian's apartment, hoping she might have had a roommate. Hoping, too, that it hadn't been released by the police yet and re-rented. While we waited for a response, I watched Jack's face screw into a grimace. "How the hell does it get on doorknobs?" he finally said. I didn't have a good answer for that, at least not one I wanted to think about.

No response. Nobody answered the manager's buzzer either.

"We could make our own way in." Jack grinned.

"Not important enough to do in broad daylight."

We turned to head back toward the street. A scrawny man with wire-rimmed glasses perched on a pug nose below a head of straw-colored hair approached us.

"Can I help you?" He shifted the grocery bag he carried from one arm to the other.

"We wanted to talk to someone about Susan Karubian."

His eyes widened. He shifted the bag again. I could see inside it now. Papers. Not groceries. Eight-and-a-half-by-eleven paper, three-hole punched. A screenwriter! Though I doubted he was a success at it or he wouldn't be living here. Now his uniform of blue jeans, pristine untied tennis shoes, and sport coat made sense.

"And who are you? I already talked to the police."

I handed him a card. He perused it. "The Teddie Matson detective. Didn't you sell your rights to Hollywood?"

169

"Yes."

"So you're in the Writers Guild?"

"I plead guilty to that too."

"My name's Derek Futterman. I manage this building. Just got back from Xeroxing a script I'm working on. Maybe you can take a look at it. It's a thriller, you might be able to give me some pointers."

Behind Futterman's back, Jack lifted his shades and rolled his eyes. I recognized the name from the radio news story about Karubian's suicide.

"Come in." He led the way to his first-floor apartment, set his script down, and offered us a drink. "All I have is Jack-Black."

I thought it might be a good idea to be collegial and take the drink, but I didn't really want to be drinking at this time of day and I knew Jack wouldn't. We declined. We also declined water. We didn't want what came out of the tap here, though it was probably the same stuff that came out of the tap at either of our places.

"Did you know Ms. Karubian well?"

"Not as well as I would have liked." I could almost see him salivating. "She kept to herself pretty much."

"Have you re-rented her apartment?"

"Not yet. The police said I could, but to tell the truth, I've been so busy on my screenplay the apartment's been on the backburner." He looked forlorn, as did most would-be screenwriters.

"Maybe we could take a look."

He started to smile, until he realized I was talking about the apartment, not his script.

"Is the police tape still up?"

"No. And they did return all the stuff they took from it. I guess there's no harm in taking you up there."

Karubian's apartment was bigger than Futterman's. Two bedrooms. Both with beds and vanities and the like. I wondered what she used the second bedroom for. But basically, another faceless apartment for a faceless person with a faceless life in the city of faces.

The air hung heavy, as if the windows hadn't been opened in ages. The faint lingering smell of a fruity perfume.

Futterman seemed to know what I was thinking. "Stuffy, I know. But with all the rain, no point airing it out till I'm ready to rent. I'd probably forget to close the windows then I'd be in real shit. The owners'd take the damages out of my salary."

An envelope of Susan's things the police had taken and returned lay on the dining room table. It included her phone book. While I flipped through it, Jack rummaged through the envelope. I wondered why her family hadn't come for her things yet. But you never know how people will respond or why they really do what they do.

I turned to the Bs—no Beltran. There weren't a lot of names in it at any rate. I copied down a couple of them and the phone numbers and addresses that went with them. Seemed like most of them were people we talked to at the porn studio. Jack slipped out.

"How well did the police search this place?"

"Not very since it was a suicide. I think they were mostly looking for her family info."

"You couldn't give it to them."

"She didn't list any on her app. But someone called, said she was Susan's mother. Said she'd continue paying the rent for a while until they could come by and get her things, but didn't know when that would be. I think they're out of state. Maybe you can get this stuff back to them?"

I nodded.

Jack came back in the dining room, a small cherry wood box in his hands. "Look what I found."

He handed me a memory box that held a photo album, letters from Beltran, other personal mementos.

"The police never looked at this?"

"I don't know," Futterman said.

"It was hidden. This might explain why." Jack handed me a letter from Beltran that said that as much as he loved her, they had to keep their relationship a secret until she segued out of the porn business 'cause even in this day and age it wouldn't look good for him to be with a porn actress. She must have taken him literally.

"Can we take this?"

"I, I don't know."

"You said the police are done here."

"Yeah, I guess they are." He shrugged. "Besides, I know who you are from the TV."

"Did you ever see Ms. Karubian with Councilman Beltran?"

He looked puzzled. "I don't think so. But I don't keep track of people's comings and goings."

I handed the letter and memory box back to Jack.

"You read my script, maybe turn it over to some people you know in Hollywood and I'll let you take the stuff." Almost breathless—ah, the stuff dreams are made of.

"Okay."

Jack closed the box; we headed for the door. On our way out, Futterman stopped at his apartment, brought me a bound copy of his script.

"How do I know you'll honor your word."

I leaned into him, glaring into his eyes. "I may be a fuck-up in some ways, kid, but my word is good," I said in my best Bogey accent, which wasn't saying much.

CHAPTER 21

Jack looked through the memory box as we drove south on Highland, heading for Hancock Park. "Lots of nice pictures of our man with the young *actress*." The way he said actress you could clearly tell he wasn't impressed. "Good for blackmail, since he doesn't seem to want any of it to get out."

"I can't wait to have a return engagement with Beltran," I said.

"He'll be surprised to see you."

"The walking dead."

"You think word got back to Beltran yet that things didn't exactly go as planned down in Smuggler's Gulch?"

"I guess we better be careful."

We cruised by Beltran's house—no car in the driveway. I parked the Jeep across the street and a couple doors up. We sat in the car watching, waiting. To paraphrase one of the famous lines from *Casablanca*, as a PI you wait and wait and wait. And then you wait some more. Most of the time it pays off. And it did now, as Beltran cruised his gas guzzling Grand Cherokee into his driveway, not a care in the world.

"At least he drives American."

"Hell, what does that mean anymore? Half the parts are made overseas." Jack being Jack.

We were out of the car and down Beltran's driveway before he could gather his stuff together and get out of the car. When he did, we were there to greet him, me behind the driver's door, Jack behind the car, standing lookout. No one had seen us dash across the street from my car. After all, this was L.A., nobody was on the street.

He still didn't know we were there, he was so intent on gathering up his junk. He opened the Grand Cherokee's door; I grabbed it and slammed it open so hard there was a cracking sound. I winced in pain—my wounded arm. I tried not to show it. He looked up. A streak of terror crossed his face—he dropped all the stuff he'd spent so much time gathering.

"Don't piss your pants, Councilman," I said.

He tried for a look of calm. The nervous fingers and twitching eyelid said otherwise. "You startled me."

"In more ways than one, I'm sure." I scanned the neighboring houses, making sure no one was watching our little drama.

"What're you talking about? How did your meeting go?"

"It was raining. I don't think they found the mark, I mean the spot."

He tried closing the car door. It wouldn't budge. "You broke the damn door, you broke the spring."

"Why don't you call the cops, Councilman?"

"My battery'll die," he said so faintly I could barely hear him.

"You've never said a truer thing."

Beltran looked for a way out. He was trapped between his open car door and me.

"Let's go into your yard. We just want to talk."

Relief colored Beltran's face. After all, if we wanted to kill him wouldn't that be better done inside the house? He didn't know us. But we didn't want to kill him, at least not today.

We walked into his pool area.

"Have a seat," Jack said in his best monosyllabic delivery.

He didn't sit, just looked from me to Jack, clearly scared. This was a man who had his dirty work, whatever it was, done by underlings, a man who was used to being treated with deference and respect. He was getting neither from us and now he was having to take orders. On top of that he had tried to have me killed, yet here I was. He had reason to be scared.

"What're you going to do?"

"What do you mean? Why should I do anything?" I moved closer to him. The eye twitch grew more pronounced. He stepped back a couple feet. I shoved him down with my good arm into one of the patio chairs. The chair tottered as he landed in it. "Have a seat, Councilman."

"It's not my fault."

"What're you talking about? I know you really wanted to help."

"I did. I couldn't help it," Beltran pleaded.

"You know some nice people, Councilman. Politicians. Fundraisers."

"Assassins," Jack piped in. "I didn't think Miguel would try to kill you, just scare you off. That was the plan."

"Apparently it wasn't Miguel's plan," I said.

Beltran looked to the sky. I guess he hoped some *deus ex machina* would swoop down and rescue him.

"Susan Karubian." I let that one hang in the air a while.

"What do you want?" Beltran said. "Just a friendly visit with one of our duly elected representatives. What do you think I want?" My eyes darted to Jack. I didn't think Beltran noticed the tell.

"Coast is clear," Jack said, scanning around, not that there was much to see from inside the fenced off pool area. "No neighbors around. 'Course that's the kind of neighborhood this is. Nobody knows their neighbors. No kids playing on the streets. Bars on the windows."

"Yeah, a good neighborhood. The kind Mr. Beltran and his pals have made for us. Not like the L.A. I grew up in where you could go just about anywhere and feel safe."

Jack walked over to Beltran. "Put your hand out."

"What?"

"Do it." Jack was the prototypical man of few words, but when he talked people listened. Or cowered.

Beltran put out his right hand, palm up. Jack dropped something small, metallic, and deformed into it. Beltran stared at it.

"That's the bullet that slashed through Duke's arm. I dug it out of a tree in Smuggler's Gulch."

Beltran's hand shook noticeably. Jack dropped another piece of jagged metal into it.

"And that's the bullet I pulled out of the assassin you sent to kill my friend here. It was a little tricky since it was right between his eyes and I didn't want to mess up his good looks, but, hey, we can't all live fast, die young, and leave a good-looking corpse. Your friend only got one out of three, he died young." Jack took off his shades and looked Beltran in the eyes in the cold-blooded way only Jack could. Beltran scrunched back into the chair as if there was some escape there. "Now don't bother lying to us."

"I don't need this. I'm a Los Angeles City Councilman." He got up, started to walk around the pool, away from Jack.

Before he could make another move, I darted a foot under his and he went for a swim in his nice L.A. pool. His head popped up. "You son-of-a-bitch." Water dripped from his mouth. His hair. I smiled warmly at him. He waded to the steps, started climbing. When he got to the top step I shoved my boot into his chest and pushed him back. The thrill of a lifetime, dunking a glad-handing, flesh-pressing, baby-kissing worm of a politico. How many people would have traded places with me right then? I didn't think about any future consequences. It just felt damn good.

"There is no one who isn't dangerous to someone some time, Councilman," I said, echoing what the councilman had told me earlier.

"It's cold in here. The heater's not on."

"Then you might want to start talking quickly. 'Cause you're not getting out until I get what I want." I kept my voice calm and even, remembering what Teddy Roosevelt had said, "Speak softly and carry a big stick."

Beltran's lips trembled. He sat on the second step. I had to walk around the edge of the pool to see his face now. It was a hangdog face.

"I, I didn't know. They said they were going to talk to you, I swear." His voice quivered with the cold as he sat there. Looking at the color of the sparkling blue water I couldn't help but think of Fawn Farmer's eyes.

"They didn't talk to me, but you will." I pulled out three pictures of him and Susan Karubian that we'd gotten from her memory box, one of them in bed naked together. "How'd you take this one? Timer?"

"Okay, yes."

"Yes what?"

"I'll talk to you."

"And if I think anything you say isn't the whole truth and nothing but the truth—you've heard that before—you won't be a happy camper." I smiled at him ever so slightly.

"I'm not a happy camper now."

"At least you're a live one," Jack said—love that Jack. Beltran nodded.

"I want it all, every bit of info you have."

"You can't release the stuff about Susan—it would wreck my career. She was a porn actress."

"We know. And we'll see about releasing it or not. Now, I want it all."

"I'll tell you. But first, it's like I told you before, you don't want to get into this. It's like an iceberg. You only see the tip. Why can't you just leave it alone?"

"I don't leave people alone who shoot at me. But I have other reasons as well."

"My question was rhetorical. I see that you're not the

kind of man who will leave it alone."

"Is there really a Miguel? Is he the head man?"

"Yes. No."

I could see the wheels in his mind spinning, trying to decide what to say. How much truth. How much diversion. "What do you mean?"

"He sort of runs things day to day. Like a foreman, but he works for someone else."

"Who? Do you know how to get in touch with him?"

"He'll kill me."

I let that slide too. I'd get it from him before we left.

"So why'd you give me his name?"

"I was just trying to get rid of you," he said, biting his lip.

"But then you talked to your buddies and they set me up?"

"I didn't know they were going to try to kill you. I swear."

"So who do you work with? For? Who's Miguel's boss?"

Beltran hesitated. His lips were turning purple and trembling. Maybe from the cold, maybe from fear. "I'I can't tell you. They'll kill me."

Jack took one short step closer, a sly grin on his face. His eyes once again hidden behind the reflective shades.

"And I guess you'll kill me if I don't tell you." He looked at Jack, whose expression remained pointedly noncommittal. "It's all of them. They're all in it."

"Who?" I said.

He hesitated, then blurted out, "All of them. You don't want to get into this." He was expecting me to say something. I waited for him to go on and he gushed like Niagara Falls. Nothing like a little cold water to motivate you. "I should never have gotten involved in this shit. What was I thinking? But I'm nobody. It goes way up. Carlos Rivera, he was even more nobody than me. And Birch, he was our face to the public, sort of a PR guy. It's like the roots of a tree, they go everywhere, they reach down and choke off the pipes and the water. And me. I just wanted some clout, to play with the big boys. I just wanted to be somebody."

"A *contenduh*," Jack muttered, mimicking the famous Brando line.

I wanted Beltran to get to the point and stop talking circles around it. I still didn't say anything. You never know what little tidbit might spill once someone opens up.

"It's a network, everyone's involved. Jesus," Beltran sank down onto the pool steps.

"A conspiracy?"

He nodded.

"Who?"

"The church. The government. The political parties. Business. Everyone."

"Names," I said.

"And once they have you they won't let go. It's like the fucking Mafia. Once you're in, you're in for life. Everyone talks about undocumented workers, how they should do this or shouldn't do that, but no one really cares. Hell, even Reagan gave them amnesty. And now there's this Proposition 187. Jesus. Everybody complains, but everyone wants them here. Who would do the gardening, clean the shit off our babies. Jesus. But then you try to bring them across and you're the bad guy. I mean, Jesus, it's Santos and Wilkman."

"Assemblywoman Santos and Congressman Wilkman. Democrat and Republican." It started to come together and I could see a picture forming in my mind.

"I told you, it's everyone."

"And the church? The Catholic Church."

"Jesus. Birch knew. The Cardinal knows, Birch was his man." He didn't come up for air as he sat on the pool steps shivering. "Carlos. I didn't know him. But I knew he was working for them, doing something, running maybe. Working for Miguel. I don't know why they killed him. Or Birch. Probably saw something they shouldn't have. Maybe they were going to the INS. I don't know. Jesus. That's all I know.

They'll kill me if they knew I talked."

"They wouldn't kill a councilman—too high profile."
Even I thought I was being naïve.

"They might. They could. They'd make it look like an accident. Sounds like a goddamn movie, doesn't it?"

"Maybe you can ask *Him* to help you." I looked to the sky.

"I doubt *He* could help me with him." He nodded toward
Jack. Jack remained impassive, but I knew he was enjoying
Beltran's distress."

"Lie down with dogs," Jack said. "Santos? Isn't she the
one who got elected with the illegal alien vote?"

"That's what they say," Beltran said, resignedly.

"Tell us what you know," I said.

"Let's just say everything wasn't kosher."

"But you're a Republican. She's a Dem—"

"It doesn't matter, everyone wants something from the
undocumented. Cheap labor, votes, parishioners. You name
it," Beltran said.

"All wolves under the skin," Jack said.

"What do Santos and Wilkman have to do with it?"

"You don't get it, do you?" Beltran said.

"Enlighten me."

"Santos. Wilkman. The Cardinal. They're all in it—they
all smuggle undocumented workers over the border."

"What do they all get out of it? I can't see them working
together."

"Don't be so naïve." It seemed as if Beltran thought he'd
zinged us with that one.

"Everybody gets a cut," Jack said.

I thought about it a moment. "The Dems get votes. The
Republicans and business get cheap labor. The church, parishioners and power."

Beltran flashed the thumbs up sign.

"So they're all working together to get their piece of the
pie. And Miguel is sort of their muscle and the guy who brings

people over." I tried to hold his gaze. He turned away. "And Birch got people settled once they got here. But why get rid of him? 'Cause he talked to me?"

"I think so."

"But why Carlos?"

"I don't know," Beltran said with a shiver. I almost felt sorry for him shaking in the cold water. "He must have gotten in the way somehow."

"This is big stuff for these people."

"And big money," Jack threw in. "One way or another it comes down to money and power for all of them."

"And you, what's your part?"

"I voted to make L.A. a sanctuary city on the council. Other pro-immigration things they want."

"They bought your vote? Do you get paid in cash?"

"Only in soft dollars, but mostly in connections for the future," Beltran said.

"Where does the money come from?"

Beltran hemmed. He finally said, "The church. Business. The two political parties. I sort of funnel it to Miguel. He paid Carlos. I don't know why he killed him, really. He probably just got in the way somehow."

"What about Karubian?"

Beltran's eyes closed. He looked genuinely sorry, though what's genuine for a politician in an ice water pool is hard to say. "She knew Miguel. I met her through him. He's the one who got her into the porn flicks. She was a nice kid. Really got screwed, no pun intended. I dumped her."

"Why?"

"Can't you let anything be private to me? It has nothing to do with anything else. I just needed a cleaner life."

"So you could go on fooling everyone?"

"I think the only person I really fooled was myself."

"You're going to help us." There was no wiggle room in my voice. No way out for him and he knew it.

"Do I have a choice?"

"And no tricks, no funny business."

"I told you, I didn't know they were going to try to kill you."

"You don't let on to them—don't let them know you've talked to us. We'll come up with a plan. What's Miguel's number? Don't fuck up."

"He'll kill me," he said, looking straight at Jack, but only for a second. Then he had to turn away from Jack's detached gaze.

Beltran finally gave up Miguel's phone number; I wrote it down. Jack and I headed for the gate.

"What about the photos?" Beltran said.

"Be a good boy," I said, "and maybe you'll get them back when this is all over."

Jack turned around. "Watch your back."

As we headed up the driveway, we could hear him sloshing out of the pool and shaking off like a dog.

I pointed the Jeep in the direction of home and lit off to enjoy the traffic.

"Lorraine Santos. She got elected with the illegal vote. And now she's a congresswoman," Jack said. "And Wilkman. He talks a good game. They're all a bunch of liars and phonies."

"That's news?" I nodded. "Seems like this Miguel is the key. He does their dirty work, then the church hides the undocumenteds till they can be moved on and get jobs."

"Wilkman probably helps in that department."

"Beltran's scared shitless."

"He's a politician," Jack said. "They're gutless."

"Said he'd help."

"Said he would. He might have second thoughts. Go to them, tell them everything." He rolled the window down, as if wanting to air out more than the car.

CHAPTER 22

The rain drummed Eric's apartment window. The apartment didn't seem so small and dingy right now as he lay in bed, looking at Lindsay. The swell of her chest rising and falling in front of him. Someday, he thought, he might be able to get out of this dump. Though it did have its charms, if you lived life at a certain level.

"I think I can hear the ocean," Lindsay said.

Eric didn't think so, not with the rain and the window closed. But he didn't want to burst her bubble. Besides, it was like one of those shells you bought where you could *hear* the ocean when you put them to your ear. You heard what you wanted to hear. And that was fine right now. Everything was fine for Eric right now.

"You can almost see it from the window." Almost, he thought. "Especially if you have a good imagination."

"So what do you plan to do now?"

"Keep on doing my gopher job. It's not glamorous, but right now it's as good as being president of Exxon."

"Do you want to go back to practicing law?"

"I think about it, but I don't think I can." He knew he couldn't. It was hard to say it directly. It had too much of a final sound to it.

"Won't they forgive you, or whatever it's called, legally?"

"I can petition to have my license reinstated, but I don't think they'd do it. I'm a pariah."

"Well, then, you're my pariah—whatever that is. It sounds

kind of cool."

"If that's what you want it to be, then that's what it is."
In the good old days, he would have scoffed at someone who
didn't know the meaning of the word. His superior scoffing
days were over.

"So then, what do you plan to do?"

He ignored the question, wasn't sure why she was asking.
Did she have designs on him, especially if he might be successful again? Could he be successful working for Mike? Did
Mike have enough things for him to do to make any decent
money?

"My pariah," she said. "I like the sound of that." She
leaned over and kissed him on the lips. The phone rang. He
debated whether to pick it up.

"Hello," he said.

"Eric, Mike."

At least there'd be some more work for him now. Maybe
he and Lindsay could drive up to Santa Barbara for the
weekend the way he and Jennifer used to. Of course, they
wouldn't stay at the Biltmore on the beach, but at a cheap
motel. But it would be a nice getaway. And there was something he liked about Lindsay. In one sense she was very
smart, street smart. But in another she was very naïve and
innocent. It was a captivating combination.

CHAPTER 23

Jack and I grabbed a bite to eat at El Coyote—where our conversation was at a minimum—before heading back to my place for him to pick up his bike.

The rain had started again. I like rain, I love it, but it was getting to be a bit much even for me. Good thing we had those couple days to dry out a little. 'Cause we knew from the award-winning newscaster that more rain meant more problems. We came in the back door to be greeted by Molly. Maybe it was only my imagination, but she still seemed to favor Jack.

"The question is, how best to attack the problem? Do we go after the assemblyman—"

"—Assembly*person*. Santos is an assembly*person*," Jack said, Molly playing at his feet.

"Right. Or the congressman. Or is Wilkman a congress-*person* too?"

"I don't think he's any kind of person. Just a political putz who wants Hispanic votes."

"So what do we have here? A Republican councilman. A Democratic assemblyperson."

"And let's not forget the church," Jack said.

"This is getting to be bigger than the Kennedy conspiracies."

"One difference, this one looks like it's real."

"So who's the kingpin? Santos? Wilkman? The Cardinal?

"Now you're talking," Jack said, bending down to pet

Molly.

"Yeah, but we can't go after the church."

"No?"

I gave him my best skeptical look. "So where do we begin? Back at the border? Miguel? Our duly bona fide representatives, Santos and Wilkman?"

"Why don't you have your deputy friend do a reverse directory check on our pal Miguel and we'll pay him a visit." Jack looked fed up. "Maybe we should just kill him?"

"My friend's not going to like that."

"Cross that bridge when we come to it."

"If we try to get in touch with our duly elected reps, we'll just get the runaround. Or worse. So what does that leave us?"

"Miguel," Jack said. "The infamous Miguel."

He pulled out the bullet that he put into Miguel's man at Rocky Point. The bullet he had intimidated Beltran with and that he'd retrieved before we left him. He twisted it between his thumb and forefinger.

Marisol knocked on the door a few minutes later. Jack slid the bullet into his pocket, as I let her in.

"I want to be more involved," she said, joining us in the kitchen.

"You're already too involved," Jack said, harshly.

"What do you mean?"

"It's dangerous." Jack hesitated. "You'll get in the way."

He didn't seem to want her involved. I thought maybe he liked her. Maybe he was just protesting too much.

Marisol was determined. "I feel like it is my fault *Señor* Duke gets shot."

"It's not. I want to help you," I said.

Jack's face softened, "The best thing you can do is just give us any information you have but otherwise stay out of it."

"But it is my brother that gets you into this in the first

place. I want to help. You cannot talk me out of it, this time."

"There's not much you can do. And it really is danger-ous," Jack said, his tone much softer now. "It's late. You should go home. It's not safe here at Duke's. I'll walk you."

After he and Marisol left I sat in my small office, lit only by the light of the computer monitor. Molly sat in there with me. I stared at the rain falling on the window. It never quite looks like it does in the movies, but there were streams of water sliding down the glass, landing somewhere unseen in the dark night.

I had plenty to think about: Marisol, Carlos, Birch, and Beltran. Wilkman, Santos, and the church. And the mysteri-ous Miguel. I pushed them all to the periphery. Put on the song "In the Wee Wee Hours" from Chuck Berry's *Greatest Hits*.

Not typical Berry. And all of Berry was before my time, but good rock 'n' roll is good rock 'n' roll. And I liked Berry. And I liked "In the Wee Wee Hours," more of a bluesy bal-lad than the typical Berry rocker.

And I thought about Rita. It was too late to call her—I wondered if it was too late in more ways than one. Too much time passed. I wondered if I would ever call her as I hit the repeat button and heard the song play again and again.

In a wee little room,
I sit alone and think of you,
I wonder if you still remember,
All the things we used to do.

I figured Jack wouldn't be back and I knew I wouldn't be able to sleep so I packed Molly in the Jeep and hit the free-ways. Southern California's become one long rush hour for the most part, but at that time of night, traffic moved at a good clip. We drove south, toward the border. Landed back at Smuggler's Gulch. Rocky Point. I surveyed the area with night-vision binoculars, making sure no cops, Border Patrol, or even some of Miguel's friends were there. I knew Jack had hidden the body well, but you can't be too careful. When I knew the coast was clear, we walked to the rock. I sat there with Molly on the same spot where I'd been shot. She'd been getting stronger by the day and I thought she might enjoy getting out of the house.

The rain hadn't migrated down here yet and the moon broke through the cloud cover, illuminating the scurrying immigrant ants heading to our side of the border. I watched them through the binoculars that made the world green. From this distance they were all interchangeable. And I wondered if that's how Wilkman, Santos, and the Cardinal saw them—as interchangeable cogs in whatever wheels they were turning. Maybe that's why Carlos was expendable. And even Birch. Just another interchangeable part and when that part wears out—or wears out its welcome—it's dumped in the trash like so much else in our expendable society.

I wasn't sure why I went back to Smuggler's Gulch. When I started out I didn't have a destination in mind. I needed time to think and it was as good a destination as any. I didn't know what brought me here—but something pulled me back.

I knew a little more about Susan Karubian now. I knew she was a Hollywood wanna-be porn actress. I knew she had a thing with Beltran. I still didn't know why she was dead. I had my doubts about suicide. I'd have to chat up Beltran on that one again.

Meanwhile, Molly and I watched the gathering multitudes stream across the border until a knife edge of sun started rearing its head. Then the onslaught slowed. By the time the sun was full up, the river had slowed to a trickle.

Molly and I walked several yards in the direction of the sun. Then I saw it. A spot where the grass was flattened, as if a man had sat there waiting. Waiting for his target to appear. No sign of the man or his weapon. Jack had done a good job. And wherever he buried the man I was sure no one would find him. Jack wouldn't dig a shallow grave, he would dig deep. And he would camouflage it. No, that man was lost to the world forever.

And maybe that's why I ended up down here. To feel closer to Miguel somehow. I knew it was all voodoo. I couldn't really get any vibes about him. But when someone wants you dead, it creates a connection.

Molly and I had spent the night watching the green sea of people heading over the border. All with one-way tickets. No one was leaving the U.S. I thought about the reasons people might want to come here as we drove across the Coronado Bay Bridge, heading toward the island. Were they coming for freedom and liberty, the Bill of Rights, or were they only coming for economic reasons? Did it matter? Why did our grandparents come? And did that matter?

Some of the new immigrants considered this their land—Aztlan. To them the whole Southwest U.S. They said we stole it from them. But didn't they steal it from the Indians? And who did they steal it from? And what if the Mexicans stole it back? Did any of that matter?

We hit land—Coronado Island, off the coast of San Diego. I'd been there before.

I drove past the California bungalows and Victorian houses, the ocean luminous in the distance. We headed toward the legendary Hotel del Coronado. When I was a kid my family had vacationed there for a long weekend. I was looking for girls, but didn't find any. But I did see soldiers—I thought they were soldiers at the time, not realizing they were in the Navy—running along the beach in fatigue green T-shirts and heavy boots, never realizing I'd be one of them someday.

We drove past the Hotel del, down the Silver Strand, to the Naval Special Warfare Center, a nondescript compound. I parked my car, opened the windows, and listened. Above the pounding surf I could hear yelling, though I couldn't make out the words. But I knew what that yelling was. I had been here too—for BUDS and SEAL training. Oh, yeah, I'd been here. So had Jack. In fact, this is where we met.

And once I got here, I realized those soldiers I had seen all those years ago weren't soldiers, but sailors. And I'd never make that mistake again.

I could have gotten out of the car, gone in, said hello. I probably still knew some people here. I thought about it. Instead, I turned the key in the ignition, headed back over the bridge, and north up the 5, back to L.A.

Once I hit Long Beach, traffic came to a dead stop, just as the radio played Missing Persons' "Nobody Walks in L.A." Sitting in this traffic, I figured nobody drove either. If anyone did walk, it was the immigrants coming across the border.

CHAPTER 24

I drove home feeling frustrated at not having a way to go after Miguel. I was torn between that and which to follow up first: Carlos' death or Karubian-Beltran. All these people's paths had crossed, which meant they may or may not have been connected. Beltran tied them together, but if it was any more than that I couldn't say. I refreshed Molly's food and water and hit the sack. It was the middle of the day, but I'd been up all night and I was ready for some down time.

I woke around five-thirty p.m., showered. I was about to head out when there was a knock on the door.

"Mrs. Goldstein?"

"Oh hi, Mr. Rogers. I was wondering if Marisol was here?" Her eyes were red. Tired? Worried?

"No. Is something wrong?"

"She took the day off, but she said she'd be home by four, so I was just a little concerned. I know I'm being overprotective, but she's like part of the family."

"Maybe she's just running late. I'm sure she'll call you. But if I hear from her I'll let you know."

"Thank you."

After Mrs. Goldstein left, I put on a jacket and drove up to Sunset and the Café Noir. If Larry Darrell wasn't there yet, he would be soon.

I doubted there really was anything to worry about, but I couldn't help thinking Marisol wasn't quite telling me everything. And I was frustrated. I wanted to go after Miguel. When someone takes a shot at you, or hires someone else to, you go after them. But I didn't want to bother Tom Bond again just yet. I could wear out my welcome and I didn't want that.

The darkness of the street was nothing compared to the wall of black that hit me when I opened the door to the Noir. It took a second for my eyes to adjust. The bar was cool and dark. Not too many people, still early. But Larry was there.

It dawned on me in that darkness that I could have called Chandler. Maybe I should have. But I was here now and Larry Darrell seemed more old school cop, the kind willing to bend the rules a little. I couldn't say that for sure, just a feeling I had. He sat at the bar. I sat down next to him.

"I'm buying," I said, by way of a greeting. "Refill for my friend here, and the usual for me."

The bartender nodded.

"I have a feeling this isn't a social visit," Larry said.

"Is that what you hear all the time from people you're bracing?"

"You know, I'm here in the heart of Hollywood. You'd think I'd have a better scriptwriter."

"Why should you be any different from any of the other scriptwriters out there?"

I looked around the sparsely populated bar. No hordes of wanna-be screenwriters here.

"You're saying we're all hacks?"

I felt a little incredulous. Was he really writing a script? Maybe I shouldn't have been surprised. "Don't tell me you're actually writing a script."

"I don't have to write one. I live one every day. I did try

my hand at it a few years ago," he said, sheepishly, especially for a cop. "Figured, you know, I work Metro, sometimes in Hollywood, come across these folks from time to time. Why not? I could give them the real skinny. But they didn't want the real thing. They'd rather rehash *Kojak* or some other crap from the past. *Dragnet—just the facts, ma'am. Just the facts.*"

The bartender brought our drinks. I didn't know how many Larry had had before I got there, but the bitterness of being a cop in L.A. was already seeping out. Seemed like almost everyone in L.A. was bitter about something. You'd think those people with the golden tans and platinum bank accounts, those people who really did make it in Hollywood, wouldn't have anything to bitch about. But they did and that's almost all they did, at least the ones I ran into. Writers bitched about agents, agents bitched about producers, producers about directors and the money men, actors bitched about the script, even though most of them had barely graduated high school. The craft service people bitched about the extras eating too much and the extras bitched that they weren't stars. Then it came full circle, the producers and stars bitched about their maids and nannies and gardeners, most of whom were illegal, er, undocumented, many of whom couldn't speak English. Yeah, L.A. was a great town. Land of milk and honey, golden boys and gorgeous girls. Of Carloses and Marisols. And everything in between.

I had met enough of those golden girls. They didn't interest me 'cause they had nothing to say. Oh, they thought they were smart, but have you ever met someone who thought they were smart and weren't? So you know what I'm talking about. No, I wanted Rita Matson—she really was smart. Maybe too smart to call me. And I was too dumb to call her. Was she going through the same thing I was, thinking about it, dialing and hanging up? Or was she over it, moved on, married, with child? Tiny never said anything. And he would know. Her brother Warren, who I still kept in touch with on occasion, never said anything either. And he would know even better.

Tom Bond was my man in the L.A. Sheriff's. I was hoping Larry Darrell would be my man on the LAPD. I thought about cultivating Chandler, but every time I did Rita crept into my mind.

Larry took a sip of his drink, then, "So, what can I do for you, Duke?"

"You know anything about that Susan Karubian thing?"

"Girl who swan dived to her swan song off the Hollywood Sign?"

"You should be a writer. Yeah, that's the one."

"Thanks. Mrs. Hazelton will be pleased to know." Larry dived into his drink again.

"Who?"

"My first grade teacher. Anyway, what about Karubian?"

"Was it suicide?"

"You doubt the word of the LAPD?" he said, with a sharp faux incredulity. "That's what they're saying."

"Do you believe what they're saying?"

"I wasn't the detective assigned, but I can check into it for you. 'Specially if it means another drink."

I didn't know much about Larry. Just that we'd had drinks on occasion in the Noir. If he had a life outside that dark place I didn't know 'cause we never talked about it. I figured he had no one to go home to and bought him the extra drink, hoping he wouldn't forget to check into Karubian for me after he got out of his alcoholic haze. I was about to get up when I decided to ask him another question.

"Do you know detectives Haskell and Chandler?" I purposely put Haskell's name first, so he wouldn't think I had a thing for Chandler. I probably also wanted to convince myself of that, especially as I had just been pining for Rita. It's no wonder women have the opinion of men they do.

"I've come across them. I used to work out of Hollywood Station before moving to Metro. Haskell's a putz. Chandler's okay. Thinks she's Nancy Drew. You got something going with them too?"

"They showed up at my door, wanting to know about Jeremy Birch. He'd come to see me the night he was murdered."

"You get around, Duke."

"Just a man-about-town."

"Watch your back. Haskell doesn't like your kind."

"Which kind is that? I'm lots of kinds."

"All of them."

CHAPTER 25

To paraphrase Gertrude Stein, even in the fading light of day, a narc car is a narc car is a narc car. And there was a narc car in all its turd-colored glory sitting across the street from my house as I pulled into the driveway. Haskell? Chandler? Both? By the time I opened the door and got out of the Jeep, the cop was standing by the rear bumper and Molly was barking from inside the house.

"Detective Chandler."

"Can I come in?" Chandler said.

"I suppose I don't have a whole lot of choice. And you'll probably come in and find something to bust me for."

"Got that right," she said in her hard-cop voice. But she was smiling as she said it. "Am I going to be safe from that vicious barking dog?"

"Well, if not you can bust me for barking dog nuisance." I opened the back door of the house. Molly bounded out, right past me and up to Detective Chandler. She picked Molly up, cuddling and petting her.

"Hello, baby," she cooed. "What's his, her name?"

"Molly. After the Unsinkable Molly Brown."

"That's cute. I loved that movie as a kid. Watched it over and over."

"My last dog died. We figured the name would be a good omen, even though he didn't drown."

Something dawned on her. "We? Are you married?"

It took me a second to figure out what she was talking

about. "Oh, no. My friend Jack. He actually found Molly but figured it was time for me to have a new dog." I wasn't sure, but I thought I saw a sign of relief in her eyes. I had a pang of loss for Baron, my dog who'd died—who'd been murdered by someone. I still wasn't sure who killed him, though I had an idea who it was.

"I'm sorry about your other dog. I love dogs."

"I couldn't tell. But aren't you putting yourself in a dangerous position? I mean, here you are, no free hands to go for your gun if I decide to pull on you?"

"Molly will protect me," she said.

Detective Chandler, wearing a brighter shade of lipstick than I'd seen her in before, followed me into the house. Molly followed her in and sat on her lap in the living room. We sat in the same positions we had the night she and Haskell had come. On our way to the living room I had noticed the light on my answering machine was blinking. Too soon for Larry Darrell to have any info. I wanted to play it back but didn't want Chandler to hear it.

"Molly likes you," I said.

"I like her, too."

"But aren't you fraternizing with the enemy? Suspect dog?"

"I suppose she could be an accessory."

We bantered a couple more minutes, till I finally said, "I just came from talking to one of L.A.'s finest."

"Who?"

"Larry Darrell, he used to work out of your station." I figured I'd tell her before she found out on her own. And these things always have a way of coming out and around. I didn't have to tell her it was more than a social visit.

"Larry."

I couldn't tell what she was thinking—Larry: good guy—or Larry: bad guy. "You know him?"

"Like you said, we worked out of the same squad. He's a good man. Though lately a little distracted."

"I guess Metro can do that to you."

"What's your business with him?"

"Scotch and soda, well that's his, mine is gin, in a variety of ways. With tonic, in lemonade, straight. I like diversity you know." I looked to see if she cracked a smile. I thought there was a small one. "We hang out at the same bar sometimes."

"I know the place." She thought a moment, "The Café Noir, up on Sunset."

I nodded.

"So you weren't talking business with him?"

I shook my head, then said, "Shop talk creeps in sometimes. You know, cop-PI We share stories."

"I bet you do."

"Not to be rude, Detective, but what can I do for you? Dinner maybe. I make a mean lasagna or we can go out. Unless you don't want to be seen around town with a shady gumshoe."

"Again."

"That's right, we did have lunch once."

She was staring at me, but not at my eyes, at my arm. I'd forgotten about my wound. It still hurt sometimes, but not bad. I'd also forgotten that once I had taken off my jacket coming in the house, I had a short-sleeved shirt on underneath.

"What happened to your arm?" she said.

What could I tell her, the truth? That wouldn't work. A lie? I didn't want to get caught in it. So I said, "You don't want to know."

"You're right, I probably don't." She flashed me a knowing cop look. Maybe she already knew.

"So, Detective, shall we get down to cases?" Since she hadn't exactly jumped at my dinner invitation, I figured why not bring it around to business again. Besides, I wanted to change the subject from my wound. "Beltran."

"What about him?"

"When we met at Roscoe's you thought he might be involved in Birch's death. Any new thoughts or info?"

I couldn't give away what I knew to her. I didn't want the cops spoiling our plans and rounding up the wrong people before we got to the right people or the low echelon slug before we got to the high echelon slugs. In other words, now I really couldn't tell her the truth, so I said, "Not much. I'm working on it."

"I'm sure you are." She looked pointedly at my arm. "Well, we've had a little chat with Beltran. Asked him about—"

Here it comes.

"—Birch," she said. "He seemed mighty nervous."

"Politicians are always nervous. Always looking over their shoulders."

"I thought you might know something about that."

Still the cop. I felt like giving her that stupid *moi* thing that everyone was doing these days. Didn't. "I went to see him, asked about Birch." I was dancing on the head of a pin. "He claimed he didn't know anything about his death. Didn't know why Birch would have left his name on my answering machine."

"Uh huh." She glanced at my bandaged arm.

I wasn't about to tell her about our little trip to the border, where I got my wound and someone else got a bullet between the eyes. That wouldn't do.

"You know," she said, "I've been checking into this and that Carlos Rivera thing too. Do you think they could be connected?"

"Maybe. Birch worked helping get undocumenteds sanctuary. Carlos may have run into him at some point. Still, the connection might only be tangential."

"Big word. They teach you that in Private Eye 101?" she said.

"You're the one reading *How To Be a Private Detective*."

I made my fingers and thumb into a gun, pretended to fire in the air. "C'mon Chandler, now you're sounding more like Haskell. If you wanted to sound like him you should have brought him along."

She got up. Any trace of a smile disappeared from her face. "Next time I might."

"And here I thought this was a friendly visit. But it's just another cop routine. Good cop-bad cop. I guess you're the good cop and the bad cop today. But still a cop."

"Always a cop." She headed for the door.

"You sure you can walk in front of me? What if I jump you like I did Birch?"

Her back spoke to me, then, "Haskell knows where I am. And I wouldn't be talking like that about Birch. Someone just might believe you."

I didn't think she did. But you never knew. A few minutes later she was gone and I wasn't sure what I was feeling. She'd caught me off guard coming here alone and all, buddying up to Molly. I really thought there might be more to it than cop shop stuff. Maybe there was, but for now I couldn't take any chances. And for all I knew, Haskell was parked in his own shit-brown or mint-green narc car a few doors up, just waiting for some sort of signal. I decided to stop thinking about Chandler the way I had been.

I hit the answering machine button, a goddamn telemarketer. All day and all night. Couldn't have been Larry Darrell or someone else related to the case. Or maybe they'd tried and gotten a busy signal 'cause of the goddamn telemarketer.

I fed Molly and headed for the Jeep.

The Firestar sat under my thigh. The riots were over, but the mental smoke in South Central lingered on. I wasn't sure why I was here, but when I got in the Jeep after Detective

Chandler left, I headed straight here. It had nothing to do with my cases, nothing to do with Beltran or Birch or Carlos.

I drove by the house, went down a block, and turned around. Slightly nervous at being the only white face here. Maybe at night no one would notice. Or maybe they would and wouldn't care.

I drove by again, this time on the opposite side of the street, and got a better a view. The lights in the living room and kitchen were on. Mrs. Matson was probably inside reading or watching TV. She didn't like to go out at night.

Rita didn't live here anymore. And I didn't see her car in the driveway. But I'd never found out exactly where she did live, though I supposed one of my contacts, Tom Bond or Lou Waters, could have found her easily enough. For some reason I never asked them to.

I slowed in front of the house, remembering the first time I met Rita—a mirror image of her sister Teddie, minus the Hollywood flash, though even prettier in some ways.

Damn! Why couldn't I bring myself to call her?

No, this little drive-by had nothing to do with any of my cases. It just had to do with my life.

CHAPTER 26

Eric turned the dirt-encrusted Beamer down a familiar street, Sunset Boulevard. Winding down the road. Snaking in and out of cars. With a wash his car would fit in pretty good here and maybe now he could afford to have it washed and detailed. More than ever, he was glad he kept it. Mike wanted him for another job. Good news. But it was still a day off. So Eric and Lindsay were going to Santa Barbara for the afternoon.

What the hell was he doing? She was just a kid, but seemed pretty street-wise. Street living will do that for you—if it doesn't kill you first. He wondered if he'd become street-wise? When he was growing up, when he was in college, when he was at the firm, he had considered himself street-wise. Yeah, bourgeois white boy, you didn't know jack about street-wise or much else for that matter. But you knew how to get the bad guys off, even when they were guilty. Even when you knew, or highly suspected, they were. You were just doing your job, defending your clients with the vigor required. And collecting hefty bills for the company, getting a good salary, the Beamer, nice house in Pacific Palisades, and that hideous diamond you gave Jennifer as an engagement ring.

He had a couple hours to kill before picking Lindsay up. As if her calendar was full. What the hell was she doing that she couldn't leave earlier? Oh well, don't be controlling.

He turned off Sunset onto Anita in Brentwood. Drove a

block and a half south of Sunset and slowed. His foot twitched on the gas pedal. He eased it off, letting the car drift.

Had he made a mistake? What the hell was he doing here?

He slowed to a stop across the street and one house down from the blue-gray Cape Cod cottage plopped here in the middle of L.A. Well, it wasn't exactly a purebred Cape Cod. Nothing in L.A. is pure. Everything has a little of this and a little of that architectural style thrown in. His old house was Cape Cod with a smidgen of California bungalow-arts and crafts-traditional. Did it make sense? It must have to whoever designed it. And it did to Eric and Jenn when they bought it. They loved that house. They spent months fixing it up, getting it just right. Nothing from Levitz or Wickes. A top flight interior designer. Their furniture was top of the line, their knickknacks one of a kind. Their wine collection impeccable and their art originals from hot up and comers. That neither of them was really interested in furniture or wine or art didn't matter. He didn't see it then. But he saw it now; they were both dilettantes.

Then Tom Hanks moved in next door, just renting, while he and his wife built a real house in Malibu. They said hello but kept to themselves. But that's the kind of neighborhood it was. Eric had arrived.

From where he sat he couldn't see down the driveway, so he didn't know if Jenn's Jag was there. What would he do if she came out? Duck down in the seat, like in some bad movie. He couldn't let her see him.

Why the hell not?

He gave her everything. He bought the house. The cars. The stupid knickknacks. Screw her—now there's a thought. And what had she done? As soon as he was in trouble, as soon as it looked like he'd be asked to leave the firm, as soon as it looked like he would lose his law license, she bolted.

She had wiped him out financially. Even when he got a

job she garnished his wages for alimony and child support, even though she was still a high-powered lawyer and on her way to being a partner in a Century City firm. She got full custody and a restraining order. He couldn't even see his kids if he wanted to. And what'd he do to deserve this? He embarrassed her, even though he'd done the right thing. Maybe not legally, but morally. His depression kept him from fighting her anymore.

Whatever happened to for better or worse? The hell with her.

He looked around to see if anybody was out on the street. No one was. He grabbed the presents he'd bought for Sam and Dylan from the passenger seat and dashed across the street and down the driveway. He no longer had a key to the house. Jenn had changed the locks. He left the presents on the back stoop, rang the bell, and ran back to his car. He hoped the kids would be home and get them right away. But he didn't want them to see him as he was now.

He jammed it into drive, slammed the gas pedal to the floor, and flew the hell out of there, burning rubber, leaving his mark for her and anyone else to see. It felt good to piss on her tree.

Lindsay's smile, as she got into the Beamer, made him forget about Jenn. Though he still wondered why she couldn't meet him earlier. He decided not to press it now.

They kissed and he put the car in gear, headed for Pacific Coast Highway and Santa Barbara. They wouldn't be staying at the Biltmore, like he used to with Jenn, instead he took her there for lunch. They ate on the patio overlooking the ocean. He always liked the food there, especially considering it was a hotel restaurant.

After lunch, they walked down the beach, not saying much. Just enjoying the clash of the waves, the seagulls, and each other.

"Did you do time?" Lindsay said, out of the blue.

"Not the way you're thinking about it."

She didn't ask any more questions about it. He debated if he should tell her the whole story, but it might ruin the moment. She took his hand and they walked off down the beach.

"Why couldn't you leave earlier this morning?" he said. "No, wait, I guess you don't owe me any explanations."

"It's okay." She squeezed his hand, as if, he thought, hoping this would keep them connected. "I had an appointment at the methadone clinic. I was afraid to tell you."

"Afraid?"

"Junkie and all that. I guess I do more than chip, you know."

He knew. That much was obvious when he found her on the beach. "You're doing the right thing," he said and squeezed back.

Eric and Lindsay made love that night when they got back to his apartment. She spent the night, but she was gone now. He didn't know where. And they had no plans to hook up again, though he thought they would. Right now he had a job to do for Mike. He didn't really know anything about Mike or what his business was. He was just a gopher for the man, but it paid the rent and paid for lunch at the Biltmore. And he hoped that one day Mike might take him more into his confidence and he could move up in the organization.

Right now he had to pick up plane tickets for Mike, but the tickets were in Eric's name. And he thought it was better not to ask why. Piece of cake.

CHAPTER 27

The Trieste Hotel, petite though it was, screamed exclusivity with its doorman and red carpeted entry, nestled between the high rises of the Wilshire Corridor in Westwood. Four stories of marble and luxury. The restaurant served exquisite food at extravagant prices on Irish linen tablecloths they claimed had originally been used on the Orient Express. So if you liked used tablecloths and chamber music, this was your place.

Arkam and Dalita Karubian were an Armani-outfitted, well-groomed couple who greeted me with a calm reserve. He had a thin white moustache and his hair was going gray at the temples. Her hair was big and swept back and black as night. Her diamond as big as Gibraltar. I had learned from Larry Darrell that they were in town to pick up their daughter's remains and I had called them to see about a meeting. So here we were. Unfortunately, Larry didn't have any new info on Susan Karubian's suicide yet.

After introductions I ordered a Campari and soda with a twist. Seemed like the place for that kind of drink instead of gin.

"So Mr. Rogers, you wished to talk with us," Mr. Karubian said, with the softest trace of an accent. "You said something about our daughter. You are a private detective?"

"Yes."

"And you are working on our daughter's case?" said Mrs. Karubian, with no accent at all.

"Not directly. I've crossed paths with it on another case I'm working."

"What is this other case?" Mr. Karubian toyed with his food, but didn't eat any.

"I'm not at liberty to say."

"But you have questions for us," he said.

"If you don't mind, yes."

"Why should we answer your questions when you won't answer ours?"

"I can answer some of your questions," I said. "I can't answer everything, nothing of a confidential nature."

They were quiet a moment. I sipped my Campari, which the waiter had just brought. It was good—like a Shirley Temple for grown-ups.

"Well, let us see where we can get from here." He stared at me with intense dark eyes. I had done some research on them. He came to this country from Armenia thirty years ago, began a diamond importing business, and did very well. Mrs. Karubian came here when she was three, went to college at Smith, and now worked with her husband. Self-made people. They lived on Long Island.

"I'd like to know more about Susan. When she came here, why? Her friends. Anything."

"Why does anyone come to Los Angeles?" he said.

I could think of a lot of reasons, but I knew what he was getting at.

"To be in the movies. She wants to be a star," Karubian said.

"We told her not to come," Mrs. Karubian said. "She was too young. She could take acting lessons on the East Coast, and stay close to home. Maybe even try Broadway. But she had her own mind."

"She is too American," Susan's father said.

"She had stars in her eyes," Mrs. K said.

"So she came out here to be an actress. Did she get any

207

work?"

"She told us she had gotten a few jobs, was taking some classes." Mrs. K held back a tear. "But she would not tell us what these jobs are. Do you know?"

I did, but I wasn't about to say. "No, I'm sorry."

"She tells us she is making friends with important people. Connections."

I knew who one of those people was. I wasn't about to tell them that either. When it was all over, I'd give them a report, gratis. Right now I didn't want them mucking up the waters for me. And it seemed like I knew more about Susan's time in L.A. than they did, and I hardly knew anything.

"Do you know who her friends were. Her connections?"

"She never tells us. She just keeps telling us that everything is okay. She did not need to come here. We could have provided everything for her." Karubian slammed one fist into the other. Mrs. Karubian put a gloved hand over her husband's. Her eyes were glassy, but no tears rolled down her cheeks.

"We know a little about you, Mr. Rogers," Mrs. K said. "You are a very well-known private investigator."

My seven minutes of fame had spread far and wide, or they had done some background research on me? The investigator being investigated.

"Perhaps you can do some research for us on our daughter's death."

"The police are saying it's suicide," I said.

They were silent again, then Mrs. Karubian said, "My daughter would not commit suicide."

"I don't want to sound cruel and with all due respect, but many parents think that, but they don't really know."

"I know my daughter. Will you help us? We can afford you."

It almost sounded like she was saying "we can buy you." I gave them my rates and they almost laughed. But they hired me anyway.

"I'll do what I can. Is there anything you can give me? Anything at all?"

They thought, then Mrs. K said, "Her best friend is a girl named Ashley Fitchner."

"Is she out here?"

"She was. We don't know what happened to her."

"I'll try to find her." I didn't remember seeing Ashley's name in Susan's phone book. But that didn't mean anything. "What about a boyfriend?"

A quick but knowing glance passed between them. "Brett Yazejian, he came out here with her."

"Against our wishes," Karubian said.

"Is he still here?"

"We haven't been in touch with him, though we've certainly tried. He doesn't return our calls."

Two of her friends out of touch made me wonder. Beltran's face floated across my mind. And a giant question mark for the enigmatic Miguel. Was it all tied together or just coincidence?

We talked for a few minutes more. They gave me pictures of Susan alone and with Ashley and Brett, also the name of Haig Saroyan, Dalita's brother who lived in Glendale, a suburb of L.A., in case I needed to talk to him. They thought he might know more than they did since he lived out here and she was close to him. And they offered a retainer; I said I'd bill them, then, "I'll do what I can. Don't worry if you don't hear from me for a while. These things take time."

"Susan has all the time in the world," said Mrs. K.

"But we do not." Her husband looked at her pointedly, then at me.

I got home to find Marisol, Jack, and Molly playing catch on the front lawn. Jack had used his key to the house to let

Molly out. "I go away for a couple hours and the neighborhood goes to hell."

I was surprised, though not unhappy, to see Jack and
Marisol on the friendly side. He still had the shades on,
didn't matter how overcast it was. And she was in her usual
uniform of jeans, nice T-shirt, and tennis shoes.

Molly ran up to me. She actually ran from Jack to me.

"We both came by to see how you were doing," Jack
said.

"I thought you came to see Molly."

"How is your arm?" Marisol said

"Better."

"And how's the case coming?" Jack said, sitting on the
front steps.

I felt like I was being played. Nobody brought up that
Marisol had gone missing. Had they talked about it and now
I was out of the loop? I turned to Marisol, "Does Mrs.
Goldstein know you're home?"

"Sí, yes, she is glad to see me."

"So am I, but where were you?"

"Why don't you lay off the third degree?" Jack said.

"I didn't think it was the third degree. But I need to know
where she was." I thought I saw a look pass between Marisol and Jack. I wasn't sure what it meant, if anything.

"I just need time to think. To gather my thoughts, as you
say here."

I wasn't sure I bought that. I decided to let it drop for
now. I didn't want to give her any new info, nothing about
the Karubians or Brett. I'd fill Jack in on that later.

"I made enchiladas, brought you some," Marisol said,
picking up a Pyrex dish that was sitting on a planter ledge
and covered in aluminum foil.

"You really didn't have to do that."

"You need your strength."

"Marisol, you shouldn't be coming around here. The people who shot me might still be after me."

"I am not afraid of them. Besides, it is my fault you are shot."

"It's not your fault. But if I need any information, I'll call you."

"Please tell me what have you learned?"

"Not much. We're still in the very early stages of investigation." I didn't want to involve her any more than I had to. I wanted to find her brother's killers. But the maze that was Carlos' case was just the beginning. It could only get her hurt.

Her eyes turned dark. "You are working on my case. You cannot keep me from it."

"If there was anything to tell you I would."

She turned on her heel and huffed toward the Goldsteins' house.

"You fraternizing with the enemy?" I hoped Jack knew I was kidding him.

"She's got spunk," Jack said. I knew he was starting to like her despite her illegal status and despite himself.

I filled him in on the meeting with the Karubians.

"Everybody's in show biz," he said. "Everybody wants to be a star. Get their fifteen minutes of fame, like you got, Duke."

"I'd gladly trade it in for a different model."

"Well, let's go talk to these people."

CHAPTER 28

Haig Saroyan lived in a two-story traditional American co-
lonial-clapboard style home, complete with green shutters, in
Glendale. Clean white paint and crisp lawn greeted us as we
pulled up in Jack's Hummer. I didn't really need Jack on this
mission, but I didn't mind the company and he didn't seem
to have anything else that needed immediate attention.

Mr. Saroyan answered the door. A stout man, dressed in
a starched white shirt with sharp creases. As sharp as the
lines on his face. A rep tie. Slacks and highly burnished black
wingtips. Clean shaven. Neatly brushed back silver hair. It
was the middle of the day and as far as I knew he was retired
from his job as a small newspaper editor. I always find it interesting how many older people dress with a sense of pride.
No casual options here. And if he was working when they
invented casual Fridays, he probably still wore a suit and tie.
Or maybe to be truly casual a sport coat and tie. He looked
a lot older than his sister, but that wasn't going to be one of
the questions I asked.

We hadn't called ahead, though it probably would have
been smarter. I introduced Jack and myself; he knew who I
was, having received a call from his sister after my meeting
with her and Mr. Karubian. He took us to the living room,
decorated in warm colors and filled with pictures of people I
assumed were his wife and kids and grandchildren. Offered
us tea from a samovar, which I always thought of as a Rus-
sian accoutrement.

"I've been expecting you," he said, as a way of easing into the difficult conversation, and with only a hint of accent. "I believe I've heard of you."

I felt my face flushing. Jack remained impassive, trying his best to look comfortable on the too-soft sofa.

Mr. Saroyan offered us biscuits. "I'm afraid I'm not a very good host. Ever since my wife died—" his voice trailed off. "I was very fond of my niece. My sister said you are looking into Susan's death. You're thinking it's not a suicide."

"It's a suspicion. But right now I have nothing to back it up."

"And Dalita also said that you were working on this peripherally to another case you're working."

"She filled you in pretty good. But now I'm also working for her and her husband."

"Anything I can do to be of help, just ask."

"Some of the questions might be tough."

"Ask."

"How often did you see Susan?"

"When she first moved to Los Angeles I would see her constantly. In fact, she lived with me the first three months she was here."

"Then where did she go?"

"Her and that boyfriend of hers moved to some dumpy place in the Valley. Stars in their eyes. They were going to be big movie stars. Like all you had to do was get off the plane and walk into a studio and there you were. They weren't no Lana Turners I can tell you, getting discovered at a soda fountain."

"So they had little success?"

"They had no success. Do you know how many of these kids make it?"

I knew. I also knew what Susan ended up doing to make ends meet, but I wanted to see if he knew or would tell.

"What about the boyfriend?"

"Good kid, for a kid today. Not like when I grew up, here or in the old country. Good looking. Tall, dark, and handsome, as we used to say. Not much ambition. I think it was Susan's drive to come out here, to be in the movies. He just went along, to be with her."

"Do you know where he lives?"

"Yes, sir. His name is Brett Yazejian and he's back home on Long Island."

"They break up?"

"As far as I know. She moved to Hollywood after the Valley dump. I don't think he went with her."

That was an interesting tidbit. I wondered why. And the apartment we'd seen in Hollywood was a pretty nice place, refurbished. Couldn't have been too cheap. "Do you have Brett Yazejian's phone number?"

"No, but I think his people are in the book."

"Do you know Ashley Fitchner?"

"Susan's friend."

I nodded.

"She's still out here somewhere, I think. I'm not sure where." He stared out the window, looking beyond the lawn and street in front of his house.

I made a mental note to follow up on that, saw Jack nod almost imperceptibly. No one else would have noticed.

Saroyan turned to Jack. "Does he talk?"

"Only if you feed him Milk Bones."

"I see, he does tricks."

And in a way Saroyan was right. Jack didn't react to Saroyan's words about him.

"Mr. Saroyan, do you know why Susan committed suicide?"

"Susan did not commit suicide."

"The police—"

"—The police don't know what they're talking about. And this is not just an uncle in denial talking."

"Then tell me why she wouldn't have done so."

"She had too much to live for."

I didn't want to tell him that a lot of people who commit suicide have a lot to live for. They just can't see it at the moment.

"She, uh, she would have said something to me. We were very close."

Despite what he said, I had the feeling he was holding back. Not sure whether to fully trust me.

"How often did you see her once she moved out?"

"About once a month. We would go to dinner somewhere. She would take me to the new hip places and I would take her to Armenian restaurants. We would alternate."

I got a list of those hip places from him. It was a long shot, but someone there might know something. The names were *très* cool: Zebra, Tourniquet, and Lashes. There were some others, but he couldn't remember their names. I hoped we might run into Ashley Fitchner at one of them, if we couldn't find her another way.

We were about to leave. I turned back to Mr. Saroyan, Columbo style. "Do you know how she made ends meet?"

"What are you implying?"

He wouldn't have asked the question that way if he didn't know. "I'm not implying anything."

His shoulders slumped; his face sagged. He gained ten years in ten seconds. He looked as if he was about to fall into the sofa when he straightened himself up and seemed to get a new lease on life or at least a second wind. "She was an actress," he said. "Just not the kind she wanted to be."

He wouldn't tell us much more than that and abruptly changed the subject. We left and I pictured him sagging again only this time no second wind to puff him up.

* * *

"Not a lot of great info there," Jack said as we took off from Saroyan's in the Hummer.

"Maybe it's all he knows."

"Maybe."

From Glendale, we headed over the hill to Silverlake, where two of the restaurants were. No good info at either Zebra or Lashes. Tourniquet would have to wait.

Jack dropped me off at the office. I picked up the mail and checked the answering machine. There was a message from Haig Saroyan. I called him back; he answered on the first ring. "I wasn't totally truthful with you, Mr. Rogers," he said after I identified myself. "Susan worked in pornography. It's hard for me to admit, let alone say. I don't know for who or any of the details, but I hope it helps. And I still don't think she killed herself."

It all gushed out. He wanted to help more than he wanted to protect his niece's reputation. And he gave me Brett Yazejian's phone number. I'd figured as a newspaperman he might have done a little digging on his own.

"Call any time," he said. And I think he meant it. We hung up.

I went home to Molly to escape the crazy world. Was it just my world that was crazy or the whole damn world? Either way, I went home to shut it out, at least temporarily.

That didn't last long as I decided to call Brett Yazejian before it was too late East Coast time. Of course he wasn't home so I left a message for him to call collect. Molly was doing much better, almost back to her puppy self. We did our thing, ate, *coupaged*, checked out the newspaper. Watched a little TV, a *Twin Peaks* rerun. Then I showered and put on a black T-shirt with black stovepipe jeans, biker boots. Did I look hip? Cool? Bad? I hoped so. Around nine I drove over to Tourniquet on Melrose. One of those hipper-than-thou places. I wondered if the name had anything to do with shooting heroin and why they didn't just call the place

Horse. Or maybe that was already taken. And black was definitely the order of the day, or night, as the case might be.

There was a wait to get a table, but I headed to the bar. The bartenders were all retro punk chicks with electric hair and pieces of metal in their eyes, noses, lips, oh and ears too. They'd never get through the metal detectors at the airport.

I ordered a Sam Adams, asked the bartender if she knew Ashley. She didn't recognize the picture. I checked out the scene, which was mostly men and women checking out each other. They probably wore three-piece suits and sensible business dresses and shoes during the day and came here to let their hair down, so to speak. Though there were probably a lot of real punk types too. I always wondered how they could afford such places. 'Cause this was the kind of place where you'd pay a huge amount of money for a tiny amount of food, but it would be very nicely arranged on your plate.

A young gothed-out woman wearing all black, with black lipstick, and a geisha-white face came up to me. "Don't I know you?"

I looked at her and if I knew her I sure as hell couldn't tell under all that makeup. "I don't think so."

"Wait! You're that PI—the one who found Teddie's killer." She talked as if she knew Teddie personally. But a lot of people did that.

"Did you know her?"

"We took some acting classes together once upon a time. But she hit the big time and I'm still doing extra work when I can get it."

I could barely hear her over the din. There was a small patio and we ended up out there with the smokers, not my favorite people. But at least you could hear a conversation.

"Teddie was good people. She got me work on her shows. Extra work mostly, but a couple bits here and there."

Talking about Teddie made the beer turn sour in my stomach. It also brought up images of Rita and my paralysis about calling her. I hoped my uneasiness didn't show.

"So you took care of her killer. I should buy you the next round."

"That's okay. I'm not a starving artist."

We talked a little about the biz. She'd heard that I'd co-written a screenplay based on my exploits. "Is there a part in it for me?"

I couldn't really tell with all that makeup. But with it, she could play the punk girl in the motel scene. She'd even get some lines. "I don't know, maybe. But right now it's in development hell."

"Development hell. Where all good scripts go to die."

We talked a little more about the biz, then I asked her if she knew Susan Karubian or Ashley Fitchner. I showed her pictures.

"Karubian, that's the one who took a dive off the Hollywood Sign. I didn't know her." She looked at both pictures again. She looked around the patio. Smokers and talkers and drinkers under heat lamps. All hip, young, and cool. "No, I don't think I know either of them." Her voice had become staccato. It could have been ordinary nerves or it could have meant she knew more than she was telling. Maybe I was suspicious since I thought everyone knew more than they told me. She stood up. I supposed that meant the interview was over. We'd been talking, but I hadn't gotten her name. I asked.

"Janet, can you believe that? No one is named Janet anymore. Call me Jan, but sometimes I go by Janine, nicer huh. That's my professional name when I get parts. Janine Radnor."

I gave her a card and she disappeared into the crowd inside. I sat on the patio a few minutes, not finishing my beer, then headed inside. It was pointless to try to talk to everyone here, though I did ask a couple people on the way out. No one claimed to know either Susan or Ashley.

I drove home and the skies opened up. I wondered if it put out the fires of the people smoking on the patio.

CHAPTER 29

It might have been raining hard enough for Noah to start gathering the animals, but that didn't stop the party-hearty crowd from clogging the streets. I flipped the car radio on: "A Lynwood mortuary is being laid to rest. Owners think there's another reason it's being buried," the news yenta said, her voice full of cheer at the clever pun she'd made—everything's a pun to these people, no matter how serious it is. As soon as she was done an announcer came on proclaiming the station's in-depth-award-winning news yet again.

Molly was glad to see me as I dripped my way into the back door. Still no message from Larry Darrell. The case was going nowhere fast. I once read a book about L.A. called *The Nowhere City* by Alison Lurie—that's how I was starting to feel—nowhere. I wasn't any closer to finding Carlos' killer than I had been days ago. That's how it went sometimes, but I never liked it like that. I'm not a go-with-the-flow type, though more so than Jack. And someone had shot at me and hit. That requires a response. Granted, the shooter was dead, but I needed to get the person who sent him or I'd be looking over my shoulder the rest of my life.

Midnight. Restless. A lull in the rain. Molly and I went for a walk, past the sleeping houses. In the distance someone's bass thumped—NWA's *Straight Outta Compton* album. Some pimply white boy trying to be black, upping his street cred, no doubt. *Neighborly.* I rounded the corner, saw a silhouette in the distance. Getting closer. Heard yapping.

Marisol with Guillermo and Hillary.

"I could not sleep," she said.

"Me either."

Molly and the two Yorkies sniffed each other. Marisol turned around and walked with us. We didn't say much at first.

"All of this, so much trouble," she finally said. "But I owe it to my brother, to Carlos, to find his murderer, no? Even if he then comes after me."

"Where'd you go when you went missing that day?"

"I need time to think. Everything is so crazy."

"Have you told me everything?"

"We come here to live the good life," she said. "But at every turn there is someone or something that makes it difficult. Even impossible. Always somebody who wants something. We cannot get papers. We cannot afford good housing. And just to come here we must make company with some very bad people."

"You're not out trying to investigate on your own, Marisol?"

She shook her head. "Even our own people, how do you say, exploit us. They charge money and more money and we are in their debt. They do not let us go. It is like the web of a spider."

"Please tell me what you're talking about."

"There is nothing to tell."

But I knew there was. I just didn't know how to get it out of her. I didn't want to take the gloves off.

"You are a good man, *Señor* Duke. You want to help. But some things one must do for themselves."

"What must you do for yourself?"

She didn't respond. We kept walking until the skies opened up again.

* * *

The phone was ringing off the hook when Molly and I got home. It was the middle of the night, who the hell was calling? I picked it up, nearly knocking it off the table.

"Hello, Mr. Rogers, this is Janine Radnor."

"Janet. Hello."

"Yeah, Janet," she slurred that two-syllable word to four, maybe five. Stoned? Drunk?

"Are you all right?"

"I don't think I should be driving."

I wondered when I'd turned from a PI to a chauffeur. Ah, fame.

"Can you come get me?"

It was two a.m., closing time for the bars.

"Where are you?"

"Same place. I'll be waiting in front."

Well, I had just gotten back from my walk with Marisol and Molly. Still dressed. What the hell? I picked Janet up in front of Tourniquet a few minutes later. A young man with bleached blonde razor cut hair, dressed in black with silver B&D studs and slave bracelets, gave her a look like "what's your daddy doing picking you up?" I didn't think I was old enough to be her daddy and it hurt. She scooted in.

"Can we get something to eat? I need something."

"Munchies."

"You're cool."

I drove to the Tail O' the Pup on San Vicente—a hot dog stand that looked like a giant hot dog on a bun. With mustard, of course. Always a line, even at two a.m., especially at two a.m.—munchies. And if you hit it right, you might see some movie stars, big stars, the ones who hadn't gone vegan yet. We ordered a couple of chili dogs and soft drinks and found a table in the back. The wood was scarred so deep you could almost lose your hot dog in it. She didn't talk much while eating.

"Ah, that's better. I needed to get straight before driving

home," she said when she finished. "Thank you." She pulled
out a five and pushed it toward me. I pushed it back. "Chivalry." She smiled coyly and seemed to have sobered up a bit.

"I didn't call you just to pick me up," she said.

"No?"

"I was thinking about it and maybe I have some information you can use. I should have told you when you were
at Tourniquet, but my generation has a thing about snitching
people out. Even when we should. And I didn't want anyone
to hear me telling you."

"Who could have heard in that place?"

"You do have a point. You were asking about Susan
Karubian and Ashley Fitchner. I lied about not knowing
them. I didn't want to get in trouble or get them in trouble.
Though I guess Susan can't be in any more trouble than being dead." She caught herself talking a little too loud and
lowered the volume. "I knew Susan and Ashley. If you knew
one you knew the other."

"Where'd you know them from?"

"Acting classes, hanging out, maybe we did a couple extra jobs together. You hang around and you get familiar
with faces."

"So you weren't close friends."

She looked away, avoiding looking me in the eye. "I knew
them. Do you think Susan's death wasn't really suicide?"

"What do you think?"

"She had so much talent. Why would she?"

"She made pornos, not Hollywood movies."

"She had a *joi de vivre*. And she had that big shot boyfriend, the councilman. He said he'd help her get real parts
in real movies."

"Do you know him?"

"Only what I heard from her. She liked him okay. But I
think she was using him. Lot of good it did. Like all politicians, all hot air."

"So why do you think she didn't kill herself?"

"She believed in God. I think she said she belonged to some Armenian church—I'd never heard of it before. I know, that doesn't jibe with doing porn. But there's a big difference between that and offending God by committing suicide, something I don't think her religion approves of. I know mine doesn't. I'm Catholic."

We talked a few more minutes and I was about to suggest that I'd drive her back to her car, follow her home if she wanted me to. But then she said, "There's one more thing. I think I know where Ash is."

"Where?"

"She wanted to get away," she said.

"From what?"

"I think she was tired of the scene."

I tried to read subtext into what she said. "Scared?"

She nodded. "I'm not sure. I think it has something to do with the people she and Susan hung with in the porn biz. Maybe not."

"Where can I find her?"

"I'm not sure I should tell. Though I guess I can trust you, you found Teddie's killer."

There was that double-edged sword again. "Where is she?"

"I think she works at a market in Bonita Vista. At least she was a few days ago."

See what a hot dog will buy you these days.

I hit the freeways the next morning, taking the 405 north through the smog belt of the Valley to the 14. Every time I put on the radio news there was another accident on the 14. Only two lanes in some places, three in others, it was a bottleneck everywhere and accidents waiting to happen. I flipped radio stations till I found a song I liked, Prince's "When Doves Cry," already ten years old, which made me feel old.

Developments sprouted along the freeway in Santa Clarita and Canyon Country like weeds after a rain. But after Canyon Country it was wide open spaces. It reminded me of the Old West, or at least the Old West of a thousand cowboy movies, as many of them were shot here. I passed the jagged moonscape of Vasquez Rocks. I didn't want to think about anything, just the drive and the jerky drivers.

The town of Bonita Vista is a semi-rural oasis in northern L.A. County that was once considered as a candidate for the state capital. Many of the homes there are on well water; everyone's on a septic system. They run the gamut from trailers to million dollar-plus homes. It's close enough to Los Angeles that people can drive in or take a commuter train. And remote enough that for the people who live there it's like coming home to a completely different environment, horse country. In the summer the high desert is steaming hot; in the winter it snows. Four seasons in L.A. County. Not a bad place to live.

Not a bad place to hide.

I got off at Desert Rose Canyon Drive. Drove a mile or so down into the town of Bonita Vista, such as it is. A few ramshackle buildings that look like a western movie set. Post office, real estate office, restaurant, feed and tack business, general store. I was headed to the last one. I didn't want to call ahead, scare her off. Figured I'd take my chances on the hour-long drive—in good traffic—and just show up and hope Ashley'd be working today.

Before leaving the house, I had tried Brett Yazejian again. Still no answer. I didn't leave a message. And I still hadn't heard from Detective Courval or Larry Darrell.

The Jeep settled nicely into a parking place right in front of the general store. Before going in, I tried Courval again. Still out, or at least not in for me. I went inside, just another customer. I was hoping to come out something else. Small, the store was packed from floor to ceiling with everything you might need. No supermarkets in Bonita Vista. No chain drugstores. Only a handful of restaurants. Not even a stoplight. So this was the place if you needed anything and didn't want to drive twenty miles to get it.

From the picture of Ashley and Susan that Susan's parents had given me I knew the woman at the register wasn't her. I explored the store. Could hear a couple voices in the backroom.

"Take your break now," one of them said.

I bought a Three Musketeers bar, went outside, and around the back, hoping the breakee would be there. She was, sitting on a stoop, lighting a Benson and Hedges. The hair was jet black, unlike the blonde in the photo. But it was her, blonde roots showing—time for a touch up. She nodded slightly as I took the candy bar from its wrapper, walked over to a dumpster. Her whole body pulled in on itself as I got closer. Arms, legs, head just tightened up, as if she were curling into a ball. She got up, started to head back inside.

"Ashley."

She turned. Her jade eyes glowered. Behind the angry stare was fear. She wasn't sure what to do, cut and run or try to go inside for help.

"I'm working for Susan's parents. My name's Duke Rogers. I'm not one of the bad guys."

She stared at me. A flash of recognition shot through her.

"I've heard of you." The fury subsided. The fear didn't. "How did you find me?"

"I'm a detective."

That seemed to satisfy her for now, though it couldn't have been very reassuring.

"What do you want?"

"I want to find out some things."

She looked around. No one there. A car whizzed by on Desert Rose Canyon. Didn't slow. "I can't."

"If I can find you, whoever you're afraid of can too. And

it wasn't hard to find you."

"It would have been easier for them to find me if I'd gone home. Susan hung with some pretty nasty people. I don't think they'd come after me, but you never know."

"So you don't think she killed herself."

"Why would she? She had what she wanted."

"Let's go somewhere. Talk. You want to go to Sutter's Mill?" That was the restaurant next to the general store.

"No, let's just walk."

The wind blew up as we headed up Desert Rose Canyon. The wind is always blowing in Bonita Vista. Two people rode by on horses. There are no sidewalks here and where they would be has to be kept horse-friendly.

"You saw Susan's parents?"

"A couple days ago. They came out to claim her body."

"Why'd they hire you if it was suicide?"

"Why are you in hiding?" It was a dance. Back and forth, hitting the same subjects again and again, until hopefully she'd open up.

"I'm not really hiding. Just need to get away."

"From what?"

She looked around to see if anyone was coming. "I don't think she killed herself like the papers said."

"Even if that's true, why would they be after you and who is 'they'?"

"I was her friend. I don't know. Maybe I'm just being paranoid, seen too many movies." She leaned against a pepper tree. "We came out here, to L.A., the three of us."

"You, Brett, and Susan?"

She nodded. "We were gonna make it in Hollywood, you know, overnight successes. Susan and I would be great actresses. Brett would be a great director. Our parents didn't want us to. Told us how hard it would be, especially without connections. Told us all the horror stories about kids coming here. But we weren't kids. We were adults—or so we thought.

We thought we knew it all. We didn't know shit."

"I don't think you're alone."

"Brett gave up before Susan or I. He wasn't really into it. Couldn't get his foot in any studio or production company door. We didn't know what we were doing. We didn't know about *Dramalogue* or *Variety* or *The Hollywood Reporter.* We didn't know anything."

"He came out for Susan?"

"I think so, yeah. He would have been happy staying in Long Island. Maybe going to college. Is he back there now?"

"I think so. I haven't been able to reach him."

"I'm sure you know, but things didn't go our way. Susan was the one who really wanted to be here, at any cost—and look at the price she paid. We couldn't get work as real actresses, so she started doing the porns."

"It seems out of character from what I know about her."

"It was, at first. But you have to realize how badly she wanted to be in the movies. It was her life."

"Her parents didn't seem to like her coming out here."

"They're very old-fashioned. Even her mother, even though she came here as a kid. But her father is from the *old country*—that's what Susan always called it. And he's living in another century. He didn't approve her coming out here to be a legit actress, let alone what she ended up doing."

She looked off down the road, following the horses and riders as they trailed off. "It started out as just soft porn stuff, you know, simulated sex, but then she realized how much money she could make if she did the real thing—but what she didn't know is how far they would push her—rape scenes, B&D, even scat, really hardcore stuff. It was like they broke her in like a horse—tamed her spirit so she just didn't care anymore."

"They broke her?"

"She let herself be broken. How many casting calls can you go on with nothing to show for it before you give up?"

"What about you?"

"I wouldn't do it. I just did clerking, like I'm doing here, in a couple hip shops on Melrose. It sucked; not as much as porn." She realized what she'd said, added: "No pun intended. I tried to talk her out of it, but she was seduced, by the money, by the idea of being a star."

"Even a porn star."

"People recognize you. She liked that." Ashley pulled some leaves off the pepper tree. "It went to her head. She thought she was someone. She turned from a nice, sweet, even naïve girl, into a porn star. All she cared about was the star part."

"Did she turn her back on you and Brett?"

"Not completely, but yeah, for the most part. She had exciting new friends. Half of them might have had AIDS but they could get into all the clubs, didn't have to stand in line. They were known. That's all she ever wanted."

"So Brett went back to New York early?"

"Well, yes and no. He stuck it out for a while. He was madly in love with Susan, though I'm not sure why, she treated him like dirt. I think in her mind he was just another fan, her biggest fan. And then she started doing the porns and he still stuck it out. But then she started seeing that city councilman—"

"—Beltran."

"Yeah. That's what did Brett in." She caught herself. "Maybe I shouldn't be talking like that after what happened to Susan. Anyway, Brett couldn't stand that. She wouldn't break it off with him, just kept leading him on, giving him hope for the future."

"Even with the porn stuff?"

"He was *in love*. He didn't like it, but he tolerated it. He thought she'd give it up. I knew she wouldn't. I shouldn't be talking this way about her."

"Keep going. What did she see in Beltran? Middle-aged

guy. Average looking."

"He's a councilman. By definition that means power, right? And he's got that power in Los Angeles, that means Hollywood. She thought he'd be her entrée into real movies. He told her he had the connections." She squinted, following the riders as they grew smaller and smaller in the distance, cowboy hats silhouetted by the sun. "She thought he'd make her his wife, take her away from porn and introduce her to Mel Gibson and Harrison Ford. He said he knew them."

He might have known them, I didn't know.

"He led her on, with all kinds of stories," she said. "Even *took* her to a couple real Hollywood premiers and stuff, but he got her an extra ticket. He wouldn't even sit with her. Then they'd sneak off for a quickie or something. Really gross."

They say the truth will set you free. Ashley didn't look free and it didn't appear she was living free.

"I'm probably saying too much."

"Talk the truth. If we're going to find out what really happened—"

"She'd go out with Brett when that Beltran guy was busy. He wouldn't take her to most of his social affairs. I mean, a porn actress and all. But he sure liked to spend time alone with her if you know what I mean. But Brett, puppy dog loyal as he was, finally got tired of it. He was willing to live off the crumbs for a while, but when he finally saw it was hopeless, he split town."

"Seems like he got out just in time."

Her eyes searched the steel gray sky. "I know you're working for her parents, but you want the truth. Susan, and I loved her, we grew up together, was a very self-centered person. Her world revolved around her. I guess all our worlds revolve around us, but with her it was—"

"—I know what you mean."

"A person like that would never commit suicide. I knew her too well. She loved life. Loved what she could get."

"Maybe she wasn't getting what she wanted."

"She wasn't getting it all, but she was getting some. And she was young and hopeful—"

"—And maybe naïve."

"Maybe. She thought she'd have the world on a string in another year or two. Maybe it was unrealistic, but that's what she believed."

"You're right, she doesn't sound like the type. So what do you think happened?"

"I think she wanted more than Beltran could give her. Would give her. And not being like Brett, she wasn't willing to let go."

"You think Beltran killed her?"

"I only met him a couple times, but I don't think he has the guts. He's a weasely little slime." She shivered just thinking about him. "But he knew people."

Miguel? "Who?"

"I don't know who they are. But she'd tell me stories. He'd have a couple drinks and start showing off to her, dropping names. Saying things like he knew people who could put her in a movie or a music video, legit stuff. Or even kill someone and get away with it."

"Nice thing to show off about." But, rubbing the still-healing wound on my arm, I knew she was right.

"There was one time. We were at Beltran's house, nice place in Hancock Park. There was another guy there, very cool. Looked like he was some movie bad guy, even had mirrored sunglasses. He scared me."

"Why? Did he do anything to you?"

"No. Didn't even threaten us. He just gave me the creeps."

"Do you remember his name?"

"Mickey maybe?"

"Miguel—"

"Miguel, that was it."

Hadn't Beltran told Jack and me that he'd never met Miguel face to face?

"And now you're in hiding?"

"I don't think anyone's after me, if that's what you think. I just don't want that life anymore. I don't want to get mixed up in Susan's mess. Sometimes I worry that Beltran will think that Susan told me things. I don't know if she knew anything, but I don't want to stick around to find out. Better safe than sorry."

"Are you sure you don't know why he would want to get rid of Susan?"

She thought for several minutes, as if debating whether to tell me something. "She told me she'd blackmail him with some pictures of them together if he wouldn't help her break into Hollywood. But I knew, from what she'd said previously, that he wouldn't. He didn't want to cloud his career."

"So you think she blackmailed him?"

"I don't think she would have gone through with it—it was just insurance for her. I think she really liked Beltran. I think she actually was in love with him. I don't know. Maybe. I thought she was kidding about blackmailing him, but maybe she wasn't, why else take her out?"

"The police say it's suicide."

"I'm sure I don't have to tell you that Beltran has clout."

And a friend named Miguel who had a friend with a rifle.

"But how did they make it look like suicide?" she said. "It's not like 'taking poison' where you can stuff it down their throat or even how you could fake a gunshot."

"I guess there are ways if you're good at what you do."

"That's all I know. I don't want him to get away with it. I don't want to spend the rest of my life looking over my shoulder."

I figured if Beltran or Miguel wanted to get her, they would have by now.

"I have to go now." But she didn't head back inside the

store. She took her apron off, folded it nicely, and walked to a mid-eighties Corolla, got in and laid rubber out onto Desert Rose Canyon toward the freeway, heading for who knows where.

CHAPTER 30

"I don't know anything. Don't call me again," the message from Brett Yazejian said on my office answering machine. I picked up the mail. Couple-a checks for services rendered. Plenty of junk mail. I skimmed through the computer catalogs, and the Victoria's Secret catalog too. It was a nice break. Done, I thought about Ashley Fitchner and wished her luck; and dialed Brett Y's number.

"I told you not to call," the whiny boy's voice said, after I introduced myself. I knew he was about to hang up.

"Don't hang up!"

Too late. Dial tone. I called back. Answering machine. "Listen Brett, I know you're there. I also know something else, you're going to talk to me. Now we can do it on the phone or I can fly out there and we can have a little face time. Doesn't matter to me. I wouldn't mind an expensed trip to New York. I'll try you again or you can call me. Let's talk soon." I left my number again. He'd left the scene early on and I didn't really think he'd offer much, but you gotta cover all the bases. I'd try him again later.

I dialed Courval again, with the attitude that it was better to be proactive than sit around waiting for him to call me back. But it didn't matter. He still wasn't in, for me.

I met Jack at El Coyote for a late lunch. Filled him in.

"It's looking more and more like Beltran is tied to everything," Jack said.

"Or his henchman, the ever-present Miguel. The girl said

Beltran's a wuss."

"Time to see him again?" Jack said.

"I want to see Marisol first. See if she's remembered anything more."

"Okay with me."

I shot him a knowing smile.

"Hey, bud, it's not what you're thinking."

We left it at that.

I had walked to El Coyote and Jack had ridden his bike, so I hopped on the back and we headed up to the Goldsteins' house. Got off and rang the doorbell. No answer. The Goldsteins were probably at work, but Marisol should have been there.

"Day off?" Jack said.

"Maybe." I looked down the driveway. Both Goldstein cars were gone. They worked together, drove together. Maybe one had an appointment so they'd taken both cars.

Señora Goldstein's white Lexus was easier to drive than Duke Rogers' Jeep. And it was much more comfortable. Marisol concentrated on the road—no radio, no CD—and on the directions she clutched in one hand next to the steering wheel. The hammering rain made it harder to drive and she went slowly, annoying many other drivers, who showed their irritation with loud horn honks and extended fingers. That made Marisol's heart pound faster and her car go slower.

The winding road over Laurel Canyon in the rain was something else for an inexperienced driver. Water sloshing down the curbs at breakneck speed, carrying everything from mud and small tree branches to little animals. Marisol's hand jerked off the wheel as she crossed herself.

"*Dios mio*," she said out loud.

She slowly made her way through the leafy green canyon,

emerging on the Valley side, where she picked up the Ventura Freeway, heading west. She connected to the San Diego Freeway north. Traffic flowed at a steady fifty miles per hour. Not bad.

She drove north until she came to San Fernando Mission Boulevard. Exited the freeway. The mission—the seventeenth of the twenty-one California missions built by Father Lausen, Father Serra's successor in the seventeen hundreds, and rebuilt after the 1971 earthquake—would pop up shortly. She'd been there before, though she never drove herself. The mission's architecture and landscaping were comforting and reminded her of home. She had been to Tridentine Mass here, the traditional Latin Mass, with Father Carrigan.

She had been surprised, but happy, when the telephone rang and Father Carrigan was on the other end. She didn't think he'd remembered her. He had helped her and Carlos when they first came across and got settled. And now he wanted to meet at the mission. He said he'd heard about Carlos and wanted to console her. He also said he wanted to have Carlos' body moved to the mission. He deserved *un sepultura sagrado*—a decent burial. But that she had to come right away, even in the rain, before Father Carrigan left town on sabbatical. She borrowed Mrs. G's car, took off for the mission. She didn't feel good about *borrowing* the car. Hoped Mrs. G. would understand.

The rain broke. She parked the car and walked toward the fountain, where Father Carrigan wanted to meet. There was no sign of him. She stared at the overflowing fountain, wondering if tossing in a penny and wishing might really work. She fished in her purse when she heard a noise. Turning around she saw him.

"You."

"It's good of you to meet me," the man said, with the slightest of smiles. Even that miniscule smile was evil.

"Miguel? Where is Father Carrigan?" She looked around.

No one there. Not the priest, nor a nun, nor children on a field trip. But who would come outside on this wretched day?

"He got tied up with church business. Asked me to meet you so your trip would not be a waste of time. I'm sorry our other meeting didn't happen, but I saw you talking to someone on the pier and—" He smiled at her, but she knew him well enough to know it was only a mask. "If you'd kept that meeting, I could have helped you with Carlos."

"It was just a neighbor I bumped into." She thought back to the day she had met *Señor* Duke on the pier. She had been waiting for this man. She had agreed to the meeting against her better judgment. But he said he could help get Carlos buried in hallowed ground. She didn't want to meet him. He was a bad man. And then when *Señor* Duke had shown up, the man had obviously seen him and not kept the meeting. And now why was he here instead of Father Carrigan? The thought sent a shiver down her back.

"Ah. I thought maybe you had a boyfriend." The slender smile returned.

"Me, no." She felt her face flush as a vision of Jack flashed through her mind, gone in an instant. She knew better than to tell this man about Duke and Jack working on Carlos' death. She knew this man. He had helped her and Carlos and many others get across the border. Carlos said he was a dangerous man. So why had Carlos gone to work for him? And why hadn't she told *Señor* Duke she was going to see Father Carrigan? He was trying to help her and at least he would know where she is.

"*Cómo estás?*"

"How can I be? My brother is dead, no one knows what happened to him." She looked pointedly at the man.

"You think I know something about his death?"

"He worked for you, no?"

"Sometimes. He did odd jobs. But I was not his keeper."

He moved to put his arm around her. "I am sorry about Carlos. Truly. I considered him a friend. I am your friend, too. And I would like to help you. Let's put this behind us and it will all be over."

But she knew it would never really be over. "Was Carlos working for you when he was killed?"

"I hadn't seen him for maybe two weeks. He only worked for me on occasion."

"What kind of work did he do?"

"You think I hurt him?"

"I think the work you do is dangerous." She looked around, still alone with him.

"Nothing dangerous. I simply gave him errands to run to help him make some money. Carlos wasn't one for standing on street corners day after day to wait for a job from some gringo."

"Sometimes I think we should never have come to *los Estados Unidos*."

"Someday our people won't have to come here, this will be our land once again."

"I want to know what happened to my brother."

"And you have been doing some investigating to that end?"

"No. The *policía* do not seem to care," she said.

"And you've talked with no one else about it?"

"Who do I have to talk to? I have no friends here." She wanted to protect *Señor* Duke and Jack.

He thought a moment. "You know, maybe I can show you where he worked, some of the places he went. Maybe I can help you find his killer."

She wasn't quite sure she could trust him, less sure how she found herself in the passenger seat of his Mercedes. She wanted to find out what happened to Carlos, but now she was sure she shouldn't have gotten in the car with him. They had slithered down the San Diego Freeway and were now heading east on the Ventura Freeway toward Pasadena. The rain had begun again, slicing down the windshield. He kept pumping her for information on who might know something about Carlos' murder. She kept evading. And she was feeling uneasy, looking for a place she might jump out. But she couldn't. He pulled to the curb on the Colorado Street bridge in Pasadena. A beautiful structure of sweeping arches from another time that spanned the Arroyo Seco. There was no traffic on the bridge at this time of day and in this rain.

"Why are we stopping here?" she said.

"Don't you want to see where your brother died?" There was a glint of smile in his eyes.

Her hand slipped onto the door handle. She tried it. Locked. She couldn't figure out how to unlock it.

"I think you know more than you're telling me," he said. "I think you're working with that man you met on the pier. I know who he is. He's a well-known detective."

"He's a neighbor. I did not even know what he does. I see him walking his dog when I walk my employers' dogs."

"So you met him by accident?"

"*Sí.*"

The man's face remained an impassive slab. His right arm slid around her throat. He pulled her close enough that she felt the moistness of his breath on her face. "You are a liar. But you will not bring me down."

He looked around, as if making sure there was no traffic on the bridge. Then he unlocked the door, pulled her out, around the front of the car, never letting go. His arm a steel bar across her neck. Her breath grew shorter. She tried to get her bearings, tried to figure which way to run. It was futile. She couldn't escape that arm. And still his face remained impassive as he dragged her to the side of the bridge.

The powerful hand gripped her neck harder than she knew any man could.

Her hands went for his throat. He slapped them down.

She flung again, scratching his face. Blood trickled from his eye to his mouth.

"*Puta.*" Spittle fired onto her cheek.

He crushed his right hand around her throat. Her windpipe shut down. She flailed her arms at him and he pushed her toward the suicide railing. She stared into the violent eyes. Nothing else there, just hate and brutality, while the rest of his face remained unemotional. Her right hand jerked free, driving toward his left eye again, nails forward like claws.

"Fuck!" the man screamed as a nail drove into his eye. "Fucking *puta.*" He pulled her hand free, pushed her toward the rail. She let out a screech of terror as he picked her up and threw her over. She went flying down into the gorge, one thought in mind: stay alive long enough. She knew she'd be joining Carlos soon. She just had to stay alive long enough.

Molly, Jack, and I sat in the breakfast room, watching the rain pelt down. We weren't saying much. That's the way it was between us. A couple of beers sat on the table. But neither of us had gone for seconds. I couldn't imagine what he was thinking. I was still trying to put all the pieces together, but it was like a jigsaw puzzle that was missing a couple of major pieces.

The doorbell rang. Then loud knocking. Molly and I went to the front door. Jack hung back, ready to back me up if need be. I opened the door to a dripping Mrs. Goldstein. Let her in.

"She stole my car."

She must have read the look of incomprehension on my face.

"Marisol. She took my car."

"She can barely drive. Do you know where she went?"

"No."

Jack came in, stood behind me. I couldn't see him, but I felt his presence even though I hadn't heard him.

"How do you know it was Marisol?" he said. "How do you know it wasn't stolen by someone else?"

"I can't say for sure. But it's not there. The keys are gone and she's not supposed to be off today. No note, nothing. I wanted to come to you before going to the police."

"I'm sure she'll be back soon. Marisol wouldn't steal your car," I said.

"Should I call the police?"

I looked to Jack. Noncommittal.

"Yes, you probably should."

"All this rain. Why would she take the car? Why today?"

Good question. Mrs. Goldstein went home to call the police.

"What do you think?"

"Must've been important since she can barely drive." Jack looked worried—Jack never looked worried. "I don't think she was going shopping."

"Shopping for a killer maybe."

We walked down to Mrs. Goldstein's house. She told us she'd had a tense discussion with her husband and had notified the cops, who were on their way to take a report. I didn't tell her that it could take six hours for them to show up, literally. She let us into Marisol's room. The same posters, the same everything as the first time I'd been there. Nothing looked new or different.

We did a thorough search. Found nothing that might help us figure out where she went or if her disappearance was tied in with the case.

"Too bad she didn't leave a trail of breadcrumbs."

"The rain would've washed them away." So Jack.

CHAPTER 31

Larry Darrell was waiting in front of my house in his un-marked as Jack and I waded back through the rain. He toot-ed his horn, signaled us to come to the car.

"Get in."

We did. A dry slicker sat on the back seat. His jacket and hair dripped water. Must've gone to my door and decided to wait in the car when no one answered.

"Larry, what's up?"

"Official business."

Jack closed the door and Larry pulled out or maybe float-ed out onto the street.

"It can't be too bad if you didn't cuff us."

"It's not a joke, Duke."

"Okay. What's it about?"

"A woman was found in the L.A. River."

I was sitting in the front seat, glanced in the rearview mir-ror to see Jack's face. No expression.

Nobody said anything until we reached the coroner's build-ing on North Mission Road. Larry parked the unmarked in a space reserved for the police. We headed inside. It reeked of disinfectant and God knows what else.

We went into the freezer, as Larry called it. Jack brought up the rear. I turned to look at him and I could see the tensed muscles in his neck. His face looked like stone. An assistant coroner recognized Larry, walked us over to a large wall of stacked stainless steel drawers and opened one. It slid out.

Marisol, white as a ghost, blankly stared up at the ceiling. Jack walked to the far side of the room. He'd seen dead bodies. In worse shape than hers. But this one meant something to him.

"Know her?" Larry said.

"Marisol Rivera."

Larry nodded at the coroner, who slid the body back in place. We started out of the room. The coroner called after us. "What do you want us to do with her when we're done, Detective?"

Larry hesitated.

"I'll take her. I'll pay for the burial," Jack said. We walked out of the room, past the L.A. County Coroner's store, where you can buy body outline beach towels, skeleton key chains, coroner travel mugs, so you'll have a memento of your visit. Even zippered travel bags called body bags—cute. And body-shaped Post-It pads. Something for everyone. And only in L.A.

We walked down the sterile hall, into the harsh knifelike slashes of rain coming down outside. We stood under an overhang. Better than hanging inside that place.

"What happened?" Jack said to Larry. To most people Jack would have seemed calm. But I could see the seething river of rage beneath the surface. Before this he was helping me out on a case. Now it was personal for him and that meant trouble for someone.

"Fished her out of the L.A. River. We think she went in at Arroyo Seco, floated down."

The Arroyo Seco passes through Pasadena and drains water from the San Gabriel Mountains, just northeast of Los Angeles. Its channels are beautiful but treacherous and at some point it connects up with the Los Angeles River.

"Any leads?" I said

"Nothing," Larry said. "I heard the call on the squawk box. Thought you might know something." He searched his pockets, as if looking for a cigarette, though I'd never seen him smoke. Old habits?

"Any idea if she was still alive when she was in the river? Or was she already dead?" I knew it was a stupid question, but sometimes you just reach.

"No, sorry. But it looks like she put up a good fight," Larry said. "She had defensive wounds, skin under her nails."

Jack smiled slightly. And I knew he admired Marisol's feistiness.

The ride home was silent, interrupted now and then by bursts of information. We filled Larry in on Carlos and how we thought his death might tie to Karubian. He said he still hadn't learned if Karubian was anything more than a suicide and added, "Now it's looking more interesting."

"Can you take it?"

"Karubian's a Hollywood case. I can talk to the dicks. But I can ease myself onto it now since Marisol's mine. I took it from the division dicks."

"Haskell and Chandler're in on it too, at least peripherally," I said. With Larry on the case, he had to know about them, so he'd know what to say or not say in front of them. I still wasn't totally sure whose team he was really on, ours or the LAPD Blue.

"How so?"

"Birch."

"The guy from the Catholic Church? What's he got to do with it?"

"Somehow I think it all ties together. Birch's tied to Beltran. Karubian's tied to Beltran."

"But not Marisol?"

"Maybe. Maybe not. It all comes back to Beltran. And maybe a couple other pols. And this guy Miguel, who seems to be their muscle."

"Suicide's sounding less and less real to me," Larry said.

"But how do you get someone to climb the Hollywood Sign and jump off?"

"Good question."

Eric walked into the apartment door, dripping water from his face and shoulders. His heart beat a fast tattoo. His left eye twitched nonstop. Is this what he had to look forward to from now on? A dingy apartment. Doing odd jobs for shady characters like Mike. He thought he'd be making more money from Mike, moving up the ladder. Maybe it was too soon. He'd never been known for his patience. Since losing everything, he'd had to learn patience. He almost saw his life flashing before him. Then Lindsay came up to him, threw her arms around his shoulders. Caressed his neck with her delicate fingers. The tension started to slip away and it wasn't long before Eric and Lindsay lay in each other's arms, naked, on his bed, listening to the rain come down.

"When it rains this hard," she whispered, "I sometimes think it can wash away all the ugliness in the world."

"It can. It can wash it all away." He knew it was bullshit, but it sounded good—made him feel good for the moment. Hoped it made her feel good too. He leaned over and kissed her deeply. She sighed, rolling onto her back.

He looked at her. Young and pretty. He should have been able to add innocent. She wasn't. She'd been on the streets awhile. But she hadn't been totally corrupted by them yet. It was only a matter of time. When he was practicing law he'd seen it many times. Sometimes he'd have the same client over and over. The first time they were young and almost innocent. Had done something wrong and he thought he could help them. Maybe even save them. The next time he saw them they were older, more street-wise. And if he saw them after that, they were lost causes.

He looked at Lindsay, praying she wasn't a lost cause.

His thoughts were interrupted by the harsh ringing of the phone.

"I'm gonna break Beltran's neck." The muscles and veins in Jack's neck stood out. Not a good sign.

"You better let me handle it. We want to get them all."

He slammed his fist into the wall. Plaster cracked and fell to the floor. I was sure his hand was okay. I walked down the block and told Mrs. Goldstein that Marisol wouldn't be coming back. Tears formed in her eyes. "She came here for a better life," is all Mrs. Goldstein said.

I searched Marisol's room again. More thoroughly.

The police hadn't yet recovered Mrs. Goldstein's car and they'd found nothing on Marisol, no indication of who she was meeting. I hoped maybe there'd be something in her room that we had overlooked. I was striking out.

As I was leaving the house, Mrs. Goldstein came up to me. She handed me a scratch pad without writing on it. Blank.

My expression must have been blank too.

"You rub pencil on it, then you can see what was written there. Like in the movies."

"Where'd you get this?"

"I keep it next to the phone in the hallway alcove."

"It wouldn't be something you wrote?"

"I never use that phone or that pad. Neither does my husband."

Jack stood staring at the rain sliding down the windows, Molly yapping at his feet. He ignored her and I knew he was in overdrive, put a hand on his shoulder.

"We can't go off half-cocked. We have to have a plan."

"I have a plan," he said, with his Jack Nicholson grin. Never a good sign.

"Not that kind of plan."

I took off my coat, took out the pad of paper that Mrs. Goldstein had given me. Jack watched as I started lightly rubbing a number two pencil on it.

"What're you doing?"

"I'm a detective. I'm detecting." Then I told him about the paper. A one appeared, then a five, until I could make it out: 15151 San Fernando Mission Blvd. I knew that was in the Valley, but I didn't know what it was. I kept rubbing. An F emerged, then an A, and on, until the word "Father" showed up. I couldn't get anymore.

"Father?" Jack said.

"You think it could be her father?"

"I thought she had no family."

"So what's next?" Jack said.

The rain continued pounding, which didn't help the swarming traffic on the San Diego Freeway. But hey, we could use the carpool lane. It didn't help.

"Just add water," Jack said.

"Huh?"

"And you get instant rush hour any time of day."

He was right. Though you almost didn't need the water. L.A. traffic is always a nightmare. The drive to San Fernando Mission Boulevard should have taken about forty-five minutes. It took us ninety-five. Double your pleasure—double your fun.

We got off the freeway in Mission Hills at the north end of the Valley.

"This is where people used to go to escape the city," Jack said. "Now they're heading even farther north, to Santa Clarita."

"Or out of state altogether."

We followed the boulevard to 15151.

"The mission," I said. Green tagged. Somebody must've been looking out for it.

"*Father*—like a priest," Jack said. I nodded, parked the car.

The mission, low-slung, almost squat, with saffron colored arches and Spanish tile, looked like so much of the Los Angeles I had grown up in. This is where the architects had borrowed from. A fountain overflowed. We rushed to the portico, dodging the rain as best we could.

"You think anyone's home?"

The place looked deserted. No cars in the lot. The chapel locked. The rectory also. We rang the rectory bell. A peep hole slid open, revealing a pair of blue eyes.

"May I help you," said the overly solicitous voice.

"Father?" Jack said.

"Yes."

"Can we talk to you?"

The eyes peered at us, questioning. The fear was visible. Who could blame him though? Two men come to your door on a rainy day. Even if you're a priest you'd have good reason to be worried. This was Los Angeles.

I was surprised he answered the door himself, but he agreed to meet us in the chapel. We headed back there.

"Maybe he thinks the Lord will protect him there," Jack said.

"Hold your horses."

The chapel door opened from the inside. "Come in, gentleman," the man said. He wore a beatific smile that couldn't hide the lingering fear in his eyes, below the balding head. We followed him in. He kneeled and made the sign of the cross. We stood respectfully. Then he sat in one row of pews, we sat in the row behind.

"I'm Father Timothy Carrigan. How may I be of service?"

"Father, my name is Duke Rogers. This is Jack Riggs." I handed him a card.

"Ah, private detectives. Has one of our flock gone missing?"

"I'm not sure, Father. Do you know a Marisol Rivera?"

His eyes narrowed. "No, I don't believe that name is familiar. Though I can't remember everyone, so many come through here. Is she missing?"

I could see Jack squint out of the corner of my eye—we both knew Father Carrigan was lying. "She's dead, Father."

"I shall pray for her soul." He made the sign of the cross.

"I'm afraid I don't know much about that, Father. But I'm out to get her killer."

"Why come to me?"

"We have reason to believe she met someone here."

"Hmm, I don't know who that could be."

"Are there any other priests here?"

"Father McMartin. But he's not here today."

"Was he here yesterday?"

"Yes, yes I think so."

"And you're sure you don't know this girl?" Jack said, thrusting the morgue shot of Marisol in his face. He blanched. The fear in the eyes increased. I put a hand on Jack's arm. I could almost feel the blood coursing through his veins. "And you didn't have an appointment to meet her?"

"I've already told you I don't know her, so why would I have an appointment to meet her?"

"Thank you, Father," I said. "You have my card if you think of anything."

He nodded, walked to the front of the chapel, knelt, and crossed himself again. He stayed there praying as we walked into the rain.

"He's a lying son-of-a-bitch." Jack's voice was a razor blade, ready to slit a throat. "Marisol told you she knew him, he helped them get settled. Told me, too."

248

"I know. But if he's hooked in with this Miguel or who-ever, maybe our visit here will help smoke him out."

We got in the Jeep, I turned over the ignition.

"Can we hit Beltran now?" Jack said.

CHAPTER 32

Mulholland Drive cuts across the mountains that divide Los Angeles proper from the Valley, Beverly Hills from Sherman Oaks, like a scar. With views of both L.A. and the Valley, it's one of the city's best-known lovers' lanes. Named after William Mulholland, the inspiration for the Mulwray character in *Chinatown*, it's a long, windy road, with plenty of places to turn out and do your thing.

I'd set up the meet here because it was fairly remote and quiet. Beltran didn't want to do it. I told him either here or I'd come back to his house, with Jack.

The turnout we were headed for was about fifty yards up the road. I pulled over to the Valley side, stopped the car. If you like views of smog-shrouded suburbs, this was your place. Though today, after a rain, it was pretty clear. Jack got out—Sig pistol concealed under his coat. No rifle this time, couldn't chance it here in the heart of the city. The LAPD just wouldn't understand.

I was concerned that Jack might blow Beltran away just on principle. But I trusted him. Almost one hundred percent.

I drove on alone, pulling into the turnout next to Beltran's Grand Cherokee. I got out, walked to the edge of the cliff, and looked out. I remember hearing stories about how the Valley was all orange groves when my grandmother was a kid. No more of those today. Today the cash crop was people, millions of them, busy little beavers all, hiring people like me to clean up their messes and immigrants, documented and undocumented, to clean up their houses.

I knew he was there, in the car. I wasn't about to go to him. I wanted him in the open so Jack could take a good shot if he had to. I hoped it wouldn't come to that. And I hoped Jack could maintain his cool. I knew he could. But there's always a little *but*, isn't there?

I walked to the edge of the cliff, staring out over the Valley. It was a long way down. Beltran walked up next to me. I could hear him breathing hard before I saw him.

"I thought you'd come sit in my car, so we wouldn't be seen," he said.

"Who's going to see us up here?" I knew one person who was watching us. I hoped there weren't any others. I thought I heard a click. Jack's camera? Hopefully not his Sig.

"The city is beautiful from up here. So clean."

"Yeah, you can hardly see the corruption from this distance." I looked at Beltran. He couldn't hold it, turned away.

"I'm trying to help you."

"Yeah, you tried to help me when you sicced Miguel on me."

No reaction. Of course, that meant he didn't deny it either.

"And on Marisol," I said, not taking my eyes off him.

"Who?"

"Ever heard of a Father Carrigan?"

"I don't think so."

Yeah, sure.

"You have Miguel's phone number?"

Beltran shuffled his feet, kicking up dust. The rain had been gone for less than a day and already the sun-baked soil was a dust bowl. "I could be ruining my career."

"Like you ruined Karubian's. Look at it as karma," I said. "Maybe you've got someone here in the bushes like down at the border."

"No. There's no one. I came alone. I want a clean break." His voice broke. His breath came in short bursts. "Where's your psycho friend? How do I know you came alone?"

"You don't."

His eyes darted back and forth. Nothing for him to see.

He yanked a piece of paper with a phone number out of his pocket. I looked at it quickly. He hadn't wanted to talk about Miguel on the phone and he sure as hell didn't want to be giving out the man's number where it might be over-heard. That's how we ended up here, on top of the world.

"You wouldn't warn Miguel, would you?"

He scanned the brush again. "I'm not crazy. I just want out of this, all of it. I'm sorry I got involved in the first place."

"That's what they all say."

"And keep my name out of it."

"I know, you have your good reputation to protect. Okay, I'll try." I lied. We wanted to bring down Beltran and Santos, Wilkman, and the church, all of them, everyone breaking the law, bringing in illegals for whatever purpose and killing anyone who got in their way. The hell with keep-ing his name out of the news. If I could, I'd skywrite what a scumbag he was all over the L.A. skies. Nobody had kept Susan Karubian's name out of the paper.

I headed for my car.

"Why are you doing this?" he said.

"What?"

"Who are you working for? Why are you doing this? All of this for an illegal alien and her brother, who nobody misses?"

I hoped Jack couldn't hear that. I got up in his face. "His sister missed him—now she's dead too."

The look on his face said it all. He hadn't known. Things were going on and he was out of the loop. Nothing worse than being out of the loop in L.A.

"Another wetback," he said, by way of recovering, "no doubt."

"No doubt." I got up closer on him. Nose to nose. He wasn't backing down, because that wouldn't fit with his machismo image of himself. But he was shaking. His eyes twitched and he couldn't hide that behind a façade of machismo. I pushed myself into him. He lurched backwards, almost flying over the edge of the cliff. It reminded me of when I had fought the Weasel at the Griffith Park Observatory and we went flying over the side. I made it; he didn't.

Beltran caught his balance. I didn't back off, but he sidestepped and was out of his precarious situation.

"And what about you?"

"I'm an American citizen."

"One generation removed from the wetback experience yourself." I probably shouldn't have said it. But my temper got the better of me.

"My people came here legally."

"A gold star for you."

"I don't get you, Rogers. You've got a big private detective practice and you waste your time on this pissant shit and pissant people that nobody gives a damn about."

"Sometimes I don't get me either." I walked off.

I got in my car, sped away. Picked up Jack down the road.

"Is the son-of-a-bitch good to go?" he said.

"Good to go to hell. Got the phone number though."

I tried using my cellular phone to call Miguel—no signal. We stopped at a pay phone by the fire station and called the number. I turned to Jack: "Out of service message."

He didn't have to say anything—homicide was in his eyes. He jammed to the driver's side of the Jeep before I could get there, started it up—the keys were in the ignition. I got in and he tore out of there and down the mountain.

Beltran's house seemed lifeless, his car nowhere in sight. He must have stopped off somewhere on the way home. We cruised the block slowly. No one around. We parked several houses up and sauntered down the block. Walked down his driveway, checking to see if anyone might be watching from behind the blinds. Didn't notice anything.

Breaking in the back door was a cinch, disabling the Mickey Mouse alarm even more of a cinch. We closed the door and reset the alarm. And waited.

Half an hour later we heard a car pull down the drive. Then whistling.

"Happy man," Jack whispered as the back door opened and the alarm beeped as Beltran disabled it. We were on him before he had a chance to close the door. Jack body slammed him to the floor; the Taco Bell bag in his hand flew out, smashing against the wall. His eyes read scared. More than scared—scared shitless. Scared of a maniac named Jack bearing down on him. Jack picked him up by the suit collar, flung him into the Sub Zero fridge. A flying fist to the gut knocked the wind out of him.

I picked up the bag of Taco Bell, pulled a burrito out, nibbled it. "Authentic Mexican food."

"What do you want?" he huffed, with what little breath he had. "I gave you the number."

I yanked him out of Jack's hands, shoving him toward the kitchen phone. I shoved the paper he'd given me at the lookout point into his face.

"Dial."

Beltran dialed the number. We could hear the no-longer-in-service message with no forwarding number. His face deflated like a balloon that had lost its air.

"I didn't know. I swear. That's the number I had for him. He must have changed it after you had your run in with his, uh, associate at Smuggler's Gulch."

I held him with my left hand, shoved the Taco Bell burrito into his face with the right. Jack watched in amusement, though I was sure he'd rather be having the fun. Beltran looked toward him and knew that, despite what I was doing to him, Jack was the one to really watch out for.

"Want some hot sauce with that?" Jack said.

"You can look in my computer." Beltran picked pieces of burrito from his politician's face. "Look anywhere you want. That's the only number I have for him."

"Who else do you deal with on this stuff?" I said.

"Birch and Miguel. That's it. I'm not really involved."

"You *vere* only following orders," I said in my best German accent.

Beltran smoothed down his hair. Tried to regain his dignity. Some semblance of control. He had none, whether he knew it or not. "I told you, it's all about bodies."

"Bodies?" That was a loaded word.

"Votes. Cheap labor. That's all." He tore a paper towel off the roll, wiped his face. "We, the Republicans, want votes and cheap labor. The Dems want votes."

"And the church wants—"

"Parishioners," Jack said.

"The unions want the bodies too. Their membership is down. They see it as a boon. They'll support me big time if I help, so I help. Bodies. That's all any of us want."

Jack glared at him. "So you sell your country down the river for thirty pieces of silver."

"I never got even that much. More like *treinta centavos*."

"Now let's try again—ever heard of Father Carrigan?" I said.

"Yes."

"You mean you lied to me at the lookout point?" He was so scared my sarcasm flew over his head.

"He, he's a priest at the Mission San Fernando."

"How does he tie in?"

"He hides people there," Beltran said.

"Bodies."

"Yes." He shifted his weight from one foot to the other

and back.

"Illegals?"

"Yes, until they can move them out into the work stream."

"And Miguel?"

"He's more than a coyote. He brings the illegals in for the others and has a whole network of coyotes working for him. But when they need some strong-arm shit, he's their man. He keeps it all running smoothly."

Before we split, we checked his computer for more Miguel info. Nothing. Just the same dead-end phone number.

We started to go, I turned back. "What really happened to Susan Karubian?"

"She committed suicide."

"Yeah? Or did Miguel have a hand in it—you know, your go-to guy."

"I swear, I didn't have anything to do with her death. Far as I know, neither did he."

Stepping out the back door, I said, "If you're lying to us about Miguel this time, we'll be back. If you talk to them and tell them about us, we'll be back. If you breathe wrong, we'll be back."

"And you don't want us coming back," Jack said, as we left him with his authentic Mexican dinner.

Jack still had the keys. He drove us to Sunset, found a place to park. We went inside the Café Noir. The ride over was a silent dirge.

We sat at a table in a dark corner, darker than the rest of the bar. Ordered a couple Coors beers.

"We have to go after all of them," Jack said. "Hit hard. Hit fast. Wilkman. Santos. The Cardinal. And that fucking worm Beltran."

He swigged beer.

"That's asking for real trouble," I said.

"Trouble? Trouble is my middle name," he laughed, swigged again.

"You're talking about people with real power."

"We have to bring them down. They're just like Beltran. Take away their power and their Armani suits and they stand naked like the rest of us. And just as scared. Goin' after their bodyguards'll be fun too."

"Why don't you take on the 101st Airborne while you're at it? You wanna go after both a Republican and Democrat."

"Don't forget the church."

"Suicide mission."

"You're not sounding like yourself, Duke. You're usually more gung ho."

"I am gung ho. Also practical."

"We have to act. Let's not screw it up."

"Now you're sounding like my father." Just the thought of my father sent my blood pressure soaring. My dad and I were on a better footing these days, but the old barbs still reverberated whenever I thought about him.

He finished his beer, signaled for another.

A wash of white light peeled into the room. A man walked through the front door, looking like he was on fire in the flood of backlight from outside. He removed his shades, let his eyes adjust to the dark interior as the door swung closed behind him.

Larry Darrell.

Headed our way.

"Buy me a drink." He sat down.

"You find something out?"

"Not much, but worth a drink at least. Nobody's talking, but officially Karubian's a suicide and that's that. Unofficially, well, there's some doubt. And the case is closed. Heat's coming from somewhere."

Jack and I passed a look that said one thing: Beltran.

"I thought the LAPD was cleaning up its act. No more

covering up."

"You haven't had enough to drink, have you?" Larry said.

The bartender brought Larry his usual. I paid.

"Any news on Marisol?"

"We still don't have the car. Not much to go on at this point." Larry toyed with his glass.

"Marisol went to the San Fernando Mission," I said. That brought a raised eyebrow from Larry. "Mrs. Goldstein, her employer, gave me a scratch pad that we got an address from. It was the mission. We talked to a Father Carrigan. He claimed to know nothing of her. But Beltran knew who Carrigan was. Said he hid illegals out until they could move them on."

"He's the same priest who helped Marisol and her brother when they first came to this country," Jack said.

"So why do you think she went to see this Carrigan?"

"I think it was a setup for her to meet Miguel. I have no way to prove that right now, but he's their muscle. I think Carrigan may have set it up—he's safe. At least she would have thought so. Then when she gets there it's Miguel instead of the priest."

"And somehow she ends up in the river."

I nodded.

"He sounds like a real piece of work."

"He sounds like a stone-cold killer," Jack said.

"I can check into it, but right now he's out of my purview," Larry said.

"It all ties together. It all comes back to this Miguel, at least on the killing end. And from what Beltran says, Miguel works for Wilkman, Santos, and the church.

"Jee-zus!"

"Maybe you can help us."

"I guess this is the 'serving' part of 'To Protect and Serve.'"

"We have an out-of-service phone number for Miguel. And we'd like to know all the incoming calls to the Goldsteins for the last week or two."

"Can do. I can get all of that from the phone company. People don't realize how well tracked they are these days."

I gave him the number Beltran had given us. We left Larry nursing his drink, headed back to my place. I was driving now.

"Call me as soon as you hear from Darrell," Jack said.

"What's this interest in Marisol? She was *illegal*, remember."

"She was an innocent. I don't like seeing innocents get hurt by scum. Broken windows, remember. Einstein's thing about people who do nothing."

I couldn't argue with that logic.

CHAPTER 33

I dropped Jack off, headed up the driveway to the back
door. Molly did her squeaky yelping that passed for barking.
Turning the key, I heard something, turned to see Chandler
behind me, at the bottom of the steps. Her hair was hanging
to her shoulders instead of being in her usual cop ponytail.

"You came up pretty quietly."

"You don't seem surprised," she said.

"I thought I saw your narcmobile out there."

"Can't keep anything from you."

The tension was thicker than the smog on a normal Los
Angeles day. A few days ago I thought she could be a friend.
Now I didn't know what to think and I didn't feel like flirt-
ing.

"I'm not the enemy," she said.

"I know, with friends like you I'll be cut down by friendly
fire."

"I have to do my job."

"It's not you doing your job that's the problem. It's how
you do it. You sandbagged me."

"I didn't mean it to come off that way."

"Nonetheless, I'm a suspect in Birch's homicide. So don't
get too close. Do you want to pat me down?" I lifted my
shirt to show her: no gun. Having seen her car when I pulled
up, I left the Firestar under my seat. "You should have
brought Haskell."

"I'll send him next time. You'll like that. Especially getting frisked by him. He's very gentle."

"At least I'll know if he's friend or foe."

"What's the point?" She turned to leave.

"What'd you come for?"

"Never mind."

"You have your job to do."

"I didn't come for the job."

That stunned me to silence. "Do you want to come in?"

But she was already halfway down the driveway. If she heard me she didn't show it; kept on walking.

"Hey, Molly," I said, closing the door on the outside world. I bent down to pet her and a car engine roared to life, then tires squealed. Then silence. "Let's go *coupage*. Another fun night together."

I had blown it with Chandler. My anger at being sandbagged got in the way. I could only hope that she realized her part in my response at seeing her again. It was probably better this way since I knew I was a suspect and she probably shouldn't be fraternizing with me.

But I still had a case to consider. And I was letting a couple of Hollywood cases slide. You know, those lousy cases that made me the money to keep me in the style to which I'd become accustomed. I rationalized, saying I was on a Hollywood case—Susan Karubian. It doesn't get much more Hollywood than dying on the Hollywood Sign. The plot thickened, as they say, when Larry Darrell hinted that unofficially her suicide wasn't. What the hell did that mean? Did someone kill her, then push her from the sign to make it look like suicide? Had they dragged her up there dead? Alive?

And Beltran was tied into her. Was she tied in with Wilkman and Santos too? How deep did it go?

He claimed to be helping us now. I wondered if he really was. After all, he'd sent us to meet Miguel, given us a dead-end phone number. And now where the hell was this Miguel? Here? Back in Mexico? At the end of an out-of-service-no-referral number. Who the hell knew?

We could have dealt with Beltran. But he was still our best link to people pulling the strings. If not for that, Jack would have given him a *civics lesson.*

Done *coupaging,* I sat at my desk, such as it was, radio on softly, pulled out a legal pad. Put Carlos' name at the top of the page. From there I drew a line down the page, adding Birch and Marisol. Another down arrow to Miguel. From him to Beltran and Karubian. And finally the big fish at the bottom, Wilkman, Santos, and the church. I went back and added a question mark after Birch, as I wasn't one hundred percent sure that Miguel had gotten him. But I was pretty sure. And I was sure it was Miguel who got Carlos.

Carlos
↓
Birch(?)←→Marisol
↓
Miguel
↓
Beltran←→Karubian
↓ ↓ ↓
Wilkman←→Santos←→Church/Cardinal/Carrigan

The top two rows were the dead. The third row, the killer. Then the middleman, Beltran, and Karubian, another victim. Though I still wasn't sure how she fit. The bottom row, the Powers That Be. A Republican. A Democrat. And the church. That pretty much covered everyone.

If I was right, Miguel was at the center of it all—the enforcer, to use an old-fashioned term. And Beltran was right there with him. I was sure the people on the bottom row tried to keep their hands clean. Could they all really be involved?

I thought we could get a line on Miguel from the dead-end number. At least it was a place to start. I considered calling Larry Darrell, but figured he'd call when he found something out.

Then there was Santos and Wilkman—the big fish. A state assemblyperson and a congressman—Democrat, Republican. And the Cardinal, the church. Now that Birch was gone who was their front man on the sanctuary issue? Oh, the tangled webs we weave.

Ah, the life of a PI in Los Angeles verging on the millennium. Glamorous. Just like in the movies. Hell no! Just a work-a-day job. Lots of tailing people, following up on minute bits of info. Divorce or financial work. Hollywood scandal. This case was different. More like in the movies and definitely more at stake. Like Marisol's life. Carlos' life. Birch's life. Karubian's life. And how many other nameless, faceless lives?

My life.

I was only a pawn in the game. And Miguel had missed his chance. Wishful thinking? But now I was onto him, or hoped to be soon.

Santos and Wilkman.

Strange bedfellows.

On the surface, in public, they hated each other. Her left-liberal, he right-conservative. They agreed on almost nothing. On the surface.

Santos and Wilkman and the church.

Even stranger bedfellows.

Like Jack, I wanted to get them all.

The radio hummed. The Clash sang: *Somebody got murdered, His name cannot be found, A small stain on the pavement, They'll scrub it off the ground.*

CHAPTER 34

The Café Noir was its usual self of shadow and innuendo. Larry Darrell sat at a table in the darkest back corner, thrumming a spiral notebook.

"Glad you could make it," he said.

I sat across the booth from him. A glass of lemonade and gin was waiting for me.

"Hope it's not too waterlogged," Larry said.

I took a sip. "It's fine."

"I found out some info on Miguel Gonzalvo."

"Good."

"But I can't give it to you. It's part of a case now."

"Okay." It seemed odd that he would invite me for a drink and give me nothing. Though he had given me Miguel's last name. Accidentally-on purpose?

"But I thought you should know. We're going to move on it this afternoon. I didn't want you to think I was shafting you, going behind your back. After all, you gave me the lead." He rifled the pages of the notebook again. Slapped it down on the table. Stood up. "I have to go to the can."

He walked into the dark recesses of the bar. He'd *forgotten* the notebook on the table. I looked around, slid it toward me, and thumbed through it. On the last page with writing was Miguel Gonzalvo's address in Venice, with "2 p.m." written next to it. I figured that was the time the cops would pay him a visit. I memorized the info. I also looked to see if Larry had the info on the phone numbers that had been dialed from the Goldsteins' phone. I didn't see them and he was on his way back. I slid the notebook back. I didn't think it had to be in the exact spot Larry'd left it in. It was eleven in the morning. He wasn't drinking. He invited me here to tell me nothing, but show me everything.

He returned, picked up the notebook and thrummed some more.

"I owe you one," I said.

"For the lemonade. Forget it."

The cops were going to Miguel's this afternoon. I still had time to get there before them.

When Abbott Kinney founded Venice, California, south of Santa Monica, in the early nineteen hundreds, he had big dreams for it. Modeled after Venice, Italy, complete with canals and gondoliers, it was supposed to be a place of high-minded culture. Maybe it was, a hundred years ago. I don't think so. And certainly not today. Now it was divided between the Hollywood Haves, who filled many of the little, but exceptionally expensive homes along the canals, and the low-rent people a few blocks away, whose *homes* were the gangs they belonged to more than the houses they lived in. Los Angeles Schizoid Dream.

I decided not to call Jack. Maybe I should have—maybe I needed backup. But his rage was spilling over the top and I figured it was better to go it alone.

I drove south to Venice Boulevard, then headed west toward the community of Venice. I managed to find a place to park, squeezing between a hunter green Jag and a silver Beamer in a tight space that would have pissed me off if they'd done it to me. The Firestar was under my shirt and I was ready to go for it as I walked up to the small, clapboard house. A man, with a shock of gray hair in a checkered shirt and faded blue jeans two sizes too small, stood in front. He wore old tire-tread sandals with thick white socks.

"Hi."

"Hi. You coming to rent?"

"Nice place," I said, ignoring his question.

"It was. And it will be again."

"Bad tenant?"

The man looked at me suspiciously. Turned his back. But turned around again.

"Navy?" he said.

"What?"

He glared at me, at my T shirt. Then I remembered I had thrown on a T shirt that read SEAL Team I. "Yes."

"I'm an old swabbie myself, Frank Adami. I was just getting out when they were starting that stuff up." He eyed me up and down. "Kinda small, aren't you?"

"Porsche engine, Volkswagen body."

He laughed, walked up to me, leaned in conspiratorially. I could smell whiskey on his breath. "He was an all right tenant, mostly—but moved out without any notice. And I prob'ly shouldn't say this—I voted for Clinton, you know—Mexican. But you know I have to rent to him or get in trouble."

"Besides leaving without notice, was he a problem?" I looked around him, trying to see into the house.

"No more than the rest of them."

"Mexicans?"

"Who else? You know we try to keep the neighborhood up, but there's Mexican gangs everywhere. Of course, this is the good part of Venice, but just a few blocks over it's all graffiti and the like. And they come and do our houses—what the hell they call it?"

"Tagging."

"Yeah, tagging. They tag our houses and the bridges over the canals. And if we chase them off they threaten us. Friend of mine was killed by some gang banger asshole." His whole face soured. "I can't wait till we pass Prop 187. Not speaking English. Making us cater to them." His mouth stopped moving as if shut off by a switch. "I better shut up. You might turn me in."

"To who?"

"The Thought Police."

"I'm not going to turn you in."

"Since you're an old bluejacket too, you can take a look around the house."

What more could I ask for, being invited inside, though I could have lived without the adjective "old." He led me up the cracked concrete walk. Other than that the house looked in good shape. Paint wasn't cracked. No dry rot. Grass mowed.

"I take care-a the lawn, have a guy who comes once a week. Inside-a the house is the tenant's responsibility."

We entered the house. Dark. Cool. Polished wood floor. Built-in craftsman-style shelves. Nothing on them.

"Did he leave anything behind?"

"Nope, it's pretty clean. And what he did leave I threw out."

"Today?"

"Yeah."

"Can you describe him?"

"Who the hell are you anyway? You're not here to rent."

I figured the guy would be impressed with the truth so I told him. "I'm a private detective. I'm looking for your former tenant."

"He's gone with the wind."

"No forwarding address?"

"No nothing. Luckily I got the last month's rent up front."

"Where will you send his mail, his bills?"

"I guess he don't want 'em."

Sounded like a man who wanted to live under the radar. I figured Miguel for that kind of man. "Mind if I look through your trash?"

"Help yourself. You can look through the whole house. I'll just get on with my work." He was getting antsy. "I thought it was a little early for a prospective tenant. I haven't even put the ad in yet, but people hear about houses for rent through the grapevine. Didn't even know the guy had cleared out till a neighbor told me. No notice, no nothing. I guess he won't be getting his security deposit back. What're you looking for him for anyway?"

"Murder. Attempted murder."

"Jeez. Who was the victim?"

"Me."

I searched Miguel's house. Room to room. It had been picked clean, whether by Miguel or the owner I didn't know. I looked for loose floorboards and other niches where things could have been hidden or might have fallen into. Nothing. The owner came in after a few minutes.

"Trash is out back if you want to look through it," he said. "But he didn't leave much. And I been cleaning since early this morning. Wouldda left it dirty if I knew you were coming out so you could get a fingerprint or something."

"Did he pay by check?"

"Cash, always."

"So you wouldn't know where he banks?"

"Sorry. 'Sides, I think he got his mail at a post office box. All I ever saw here was junk mail."

"You went through his mail?"

"I didn't come in the house, but I admit, I looked in his mail box a couple times."

I went out back and looked through the trash. Nothing of use there. I was about to leave when I thought of something.

"Did he have a car?"

"Sure. Can't remember though."

"On your rental forms would you have that info? License or something?"

"Matter of fact—"

But he didn't have it with him.

"Tell me what he looked like."

"Moustache. Clean cut. Very fastidious."

"And his last name?" I wanted to see if it was the same as what I'd gotten from Larry.

"Gonzalvo. If he wasn't lying on the app."

I got his number, handed him a card. He said he'd call me with the info as soon as he got home. I headed for the street.

"I'm a good person," he said. "Been a Democrat all my life. I don't like hating people. But I just do."

I hadn't found out much, but at least I got there before the police came in and really muddied things up. Speaking of the police, Chandler, Haskell, Larry Darrell, a couple other plainclothes guys, and a couple uniforms were walking up the driveway as I was walking out.

"What're you doing here?" Haskell said.

"Just visiting."

"This is a crime scene."

"Well, it wasn't when I got here." I studiously avoided looking at Larry. Chandler studiously avoided looking at me. Frank Adami came out.

"And who are you?" one of the plainclothes detectives said. Adami identified himself and the detective said he was Art Velasquez from Pacific Division. I figured he was in charge since this was his area.

The uniformed cops rolled out the yellow crime scene tape, while Haskell and Velasquez grilled me. I had nothing to tell them and after half an hour they let me go.

Chandler and I hadn't said a word. Neither had Larry Darrell and I. I got to the Jeep and sped off, burning rubber. Not easy for a Jeep. I almost thought Haskell would come running after me, a handheld lightbar flashing in his hands.

* * *

It was out of the way, but I drove by Beltran's on the way home. Made sure Jack's car or bike wasn't anywhere near there. He was champing at the bit to get Beltran. I didn't think he would, but couldn't be one hundred percent sure. I stopped at a pay phone, tried his apartment. No answer.

"Hello Brett. This is Duke Rogers again. If I don't hear back from you within twenty-four hours, I'll see you a few hours after that." I had barely walked in the door and said hello to Molly when I dialed Brett's number in New York. I was about to hang up when I heard the tentative voice pick up and the answering machine cut out.

"Hello."

"Brett?"

"Yes."

"Thank you for picking up."

"Look, I just want to get this over with. I don't want you showing up at my parents' door. Besides, Mr. Saroyan called and asked me to help. So let's just do it."

"What are you hiding from?"

Silence. Then, "Listen, dude, how do I know this isn't some sort of test? That if I answer one way, you'll leave me alone, if I answer another, well—"

"Tell me about you and Susan."

"Susan, Ashley, and I. We all headed to Hollywood together. What did we know? We had big ideas and little plans on how to make them happen." He filled me in on a lot of the same things that Ashley had. I asked him to skip to the part about why he left. "Susan was changing. We, I wasn't good enough for her anymore. She wanted to be a star— famous, that's the only thing that mattered to her. Oh, maybe if I could have been a director we could have made a go of it. But I guess I didn't have the drive. Anyway, she was willing to do anything to get ahead. Bed anyone."

"Like who?"

"That councilman, Beltran. She thought he could help her, thought he had connections, you know."

"She thought he'd help her get out of the porn films?"

"You know about that. I guess you would. Yeah, she saw that as a stepping stone. I told her almost no one makes the transition from those to legit Hollywood movies. She didn't care. She liked being under the lights, with a camera rolling. I guess she didn't care what she did for the camera." His voice was tired, defeated.

"Took a toll on your relationship."

"I thought I could handle it, you know, her being with those other guys. We made a go of it for a while. But I knew it wouldn't work."

I wanted to tell him to hang in there, that he'd find someone else. But I didn't want to come across as a soppy nanny. "How'd she meet Beltran, do you know?"

"Through a guy in the porns."

"His name?"

"Miguel, I think."

Miguel.

"What was his involvement?"

"I'm not really sure. I think he did security for some of the sets, maybe for the actors too."

"Do you know anything about his other business interests?"

"I'm not sure what that has to do with anything. I don't even think he was that involved in the porns, just sort of there sometimes, you know. But no, I don't know anything about him except that he weirded me out."

"Anything else?"

"Her only interest in Miguel was the promises he made to get her connected. But the only one he ever did that with was

Beltran as far as I know. And that went nowhere."

"Are you hiding from Miguel?"

"He's one scary dude. Like he runs with the Mexican Mafia or something." More silence. I decided to let him think on it, hoping he wouldn't hang up. "He told me to stay away from Susan. Jesus Christ, she was my fucking girlfriend." There were tears choking his voice. He sniffled.

"Is there anything else you can tell me?"

"No, I don't think so."

"Well, hang in there. You'll find someone else. Maybe you'll even get a shot at coming back here and directing."

"I don't think so. I found out a few weeks ago. I have AIDS. Man, that's a death sentence."

That hung in the air like the silent hangman's noose that it was.

"Did Susan give it to you?"

"Who else? I've never done it with anyone else. We both got tested after she found out that a porn actor she was with had it."

"You think that's why she killed herself?"

"I, I don't know." His voice broke.

"I'm sorry."

"Yeah, me too." There was a quiet click as he hung up the phone. No slam down. No yelling. Just the hushed sound of hopelessness and defeat.

CHAPTER 35

Eric hadn't seen Lindsay all day. Where the hell did she go? Scoring drugs, or maybe the methadone clinic. He liked her, but didn't like that about her. Besides just caring for her, it gave him a feeling of impermanence in their relationship.

He showered, put on his best, cleanest pants and shirt. Combed his hair and was out the door, heading for the pier. For some reason Mike liked to meet there. Maybe the anonymity of the crowds and since the sun was in the sky today there would be crowds.

"Good of you to see me, Eric," Mike said. The wind whipping off the ocean blowing his hair over his eyes. He brushed it with his hand. "I have another gig for you. Your car's still in running order?"

"Yes."

"It's a tail job. You up for that?"

"Tail job?"

"Like in the movies. And a big step up in my organization."

"Who am I tailing and how will I find them?"

"Oh, he's easy enough to find. You just have to log his movements. I want to know where he goes, who he hangs with. That type of thing. He's not on the run or anything so it should be easy. And I'll pay you a two-grand bonus if you tail him twelve hours a day—at least twelve—for two weeks."

"Two weeks."

"It might not come to that, probably won't. But I want you to commit that much time just in case."

"I've never done this kind of thing before."

"Expand your repertoire. It's not hard."

"What if he spots me?"

"Make sure he doesn't. Hang back enough to follow him, but not enough to lose him. You've seen how they do it in the movies. So, you'll do it?"

"Yes." Eric knew Mike had other people working for him. Why choose Eric to do this job? It seemed important. Maybe he was really moving up the ladder. Eric thought about asking Mike why he wanted the man tailed. Decided it was better not to ask and not to know. He wanted the money. And he wanted to regain some of the respect he'd lost. So he wouldn't question Mike. Besides, he was afraid to ask.

Mike gave Eric a piece of paper with the man's name, home and office addresses and type of car he drove. He also gave him a Xeroxed photo of the man. A little blurry, but he could make out the features well enough.

"The name sounds familiar," Eric said. "But I can't quite place it."

"Don't worry about it. Report in every night. I've changed my cellular phone number. The new one's here." He handed Eric a fresh paper. Then Mike gave him a thousand dollars cash on account. The most money Eric had seen, touched, or smelled in a damn long time.

Eric stopped at a gas station. Gassed up, bought a map of Los Angeles, another of the West Side. Drew red Sharpie circles around the mark's home and business addresses. He drove to a Big 5 sporting goods store and bought the cheapest pair of binoculars he could, thinking they might come in handy. He stopped at a drugstore, picked up a pad of lined yellow paper, a couple pens and pencils, to make notes of the target's movements, and headed toward his business on Beverly Boulevard.

Deserted.

He parked across the street, put quarters in the parking meter, and watched the man's office for an hour. Nothing. The office building was a gorgeous old red brick building with leaded glass windows, not too far from El Coyote, a restaurant Eric used to frequent before he started making good money as a lawyer.

The man's home was close by. He drove there—a single-story Spanish colonial, with a low wall in front. Gate centered between the driveway on the left and what appeared to be the living room on the right. Small courtyard in front sporting the requisite palm tree. Driving by, he saw no car in the driveway and no car on the street that matched Mike's description of the guy's red Jeep Cherokee. He parked a few doors up, slid down in his seat. This was a middle-class residential neighborhood. Not as nice as the one he'd been banished from, but nice. And though few people were about, he didn't relish someone seeing him loitering in the car and calling the cops on him. He slid farther down, wishing he had stopped to take a leak before coming here.

An hour later, the red Jeep pulled into the driveway. From his vantage point, Eric couldn't see him, but he assumed the mark was driving. He hunkered down further, continued to watch. For an hour. Two. Three. Five. At midnight, he decided the man was in for the night and headed back to the apartment in Venice.

CHAPTER 36

I had hoped to wake up to a message from Frank Adami. No such luck. When I tried him I got his answering machine. Left a message, but I wasn't sure I'd hear back. And I hadn't seen or heard from Jack in two days. Now I was getting antsy to make a move on Beltran and his pals. There was one place left to check. I fired up the Jeep, jammed it up to Sunset, heading for the beach. Sunset Boulevard is like a microcosm of L.A. It starts or ends, depending on how you look at it, at the Pacific Ocean, and winds up at Union Station Downtown. In between is everything from the ritzy Beverly Hills and Bel Air, to the Strip in West Hollywood, Silverlake, and Echo Park.

Just before Sunset's terminus at Pacific Coast Highway, I turned left across traffic into the Self Realization Fellowship Center. Founded by Paramahansa Yogananda in the twenties, it covered several acres in a little green valley near the ocean. Jack's bike was in the parking lot. This is where he often came to think or get away. And after what had happened to Marisol, I figured he might be here. He didn't talk much about his feelings, but like all of us, he had them. At least here he could come to deal with them.

I found him standing by the lake shrine, steel-rimmed shades in place, staring out. Still as the water in front of him.

I didn't want to sneak up on him—that could be dangerous—so I made a scuffling noise.

"You found me," he said, without turning around.

"I figured either here or the beach somewhere, but too much coastline to check out."

"I like it here. But I don't subscribe to their religion."

"You don't 'subscribe' to any religion."

"But it's peaceful. And mostly very few people." He continued staring at the lake shrine. "I said a prayer."

"For Marisol?"

"She was all right, Duke. Saved your ass."

"You both did."

"I already bought a plot, saw a funeral director."

"Catholic?"

"Even talked to a priest. Don't look so shocked. Everything's taken care of. I'm moving her brother there too. So they can both be together in a nicer place. One that'll be taken care of, lawn mowed. Green. Trees. Quiet." He slid the shades off.

"She'd like that." A glint of something hit my eye. I looked closer at him. Something shiny around his neck. "What's that?" But I knew.

"Let's get going."

"You're not getting out of it so easy," I said.

He looked like he was ready to pounce. Then the fierceness in his eyes dissipated. "It's a St. Christopher medal."

"Marisol's?"

He nodded. "She gave it to me that day she got home late, remember? You were pissed off. But she was with me. We cruised up the coast on the Harley."

"I'm surprised you're wearing it. You don't believe in that stuff."

"But she did. She was stand-up."

That meant everything to Jack.

We were silent for several minutes, and I wondered if there was more to their relationship than simply being friends. But I knew he wouldn't tell me either way. He said, "I thought maybe—" His voice trailed off. He never finished the thought and I knew better than to try to get him to. For Jack, this was as emotional as it got.

We moved to a bench. Could hear praying from one of the chapels. It sounded like a Gregorian Chant to my ears, but what did I know? The sun danced on the gently rippling waters of the pond.

I filled him in on my trip to Venice. He wasn't happy but I told a little white lie and said I'd tried to contact him. That was enough. Told him I hadn't heard back from the Venice homeowner yet. If I didn't soon, I'd give him a call.

I filled him in on Brett Yazejian.

"Bummer." He twirled the shades in his fingers.

I knew his response came off colder than what he felt. But that was Jack.

"I feel like we're back to square one. In fact, I'm not sure we ever stepped out of it."

"It still comes down to Wilkman and Santos," he said. "They're obviously running this Miguel guy."

"Why not Beltran?"

"Look at him. He's scared. He couldn't put this all together."

"Yeah, but he's like their ground-level guy."

"Don't worry, bud, we'll net him too."

A group of robed monks walked by, not a sound out of them. A couple strolled in the distance. And a single man in a gray sport coat watched the sundial, which might have been like waiting for water to boil. Do you ever really see it move?

"And the church?" I said.

"And the church."

We split, hit Frisco's on San Vicente in Brentwood. There's a hip little strip of restaurants and stores along here, not too far from where O.J. did—*didn't*—do his thing.

We both ordered Frisco *Grandé* Margaritas and nachos in *molé* sauce. *Molé*, a sort of spicy chocolate sauce, is an acquired taste. I had acquired it a long time ago. As we walked back to the Jeep and Jack's bike, I noticed a man in a gray sport coat drinking Starbucks coffee a couple doors up.

"Wasn't that guy at the Self Realization center?"

"Don't know. Don't remember him."

That was unusual for Jack, who saw and remembered everything. I guess his mind was elsewhere at the moment.

"There's a prop 187 rally tomorrow at the La Brea Tar Pits. Wanna go?"

"Not really," I said.

"Wilkman's speaking."

We made plans to be there. I wanted to give him a hug. Thought he could use one. But I knew better.

"I gotta go apartment hunting," he said, swinging his leg over the bike. And he was out of there.

I went home, *coupaged* Molly and took her for a walk. I half-expected to run into Marisol with Guillermo and Hillary. I ran into no one. But I couldn't help feeling as if I wasn't alone. Being watched. I scanned the street subtly. Didn't see anyone or anything out of place. Chalked it up to paranoia about Miguel.

I'm not big on crowds. The one place I actually enjoy them is the Farmer's Market, on Third at Fairfax, not far from the La Brea Tar Pits. Old, white clapboard buildings. Plenty of food stalls of all kinds. Other gimcrack stores. Restaurants. Even my favorite toy store as a child was there. And it's still there today.

Jack and I ate muffuletta sandwiches at the Gumbo Pot, followed by a beignet and chicory coffee. There were hipper places where the glitterati went. But we liked the Cajun food. You could find it better elsewhere, but it wouldn't be in the Farmer's Market.

Always crowded, the tables and paths between the stalls

were wall-to-wall people today. Some probably doing what we were, having a snack before going to the 187 rally.

We drove to the tar pits in Jack's Hummer, got there early enough that we could park in the lot, and sauntered over to the roped off section of grass where the rally was. Already solid people. Already protestors marching, shouting and taunting the people going to the rally.

"This is *México*," one said as we passed inside the rope.

"*Hola*," Jack said. That only made the protestor angrier, but we were swallowed by the crowd and he lost us. American and Californian flags waved inside the rope lines, Mexican flags outside. A few yards away, tar bubbled up from the ground, the smell acrid. Statues of a saber-toothed tiger and a mastodon sat on the grass. They were still pulling ancient bones from the sticky mess. I wondered if someday someone would be pulling our bones from the same mess.

After the usual preliminaries, Congressman Dan Wilkman was introduced. The applause sounded like a sonic boom and I half-expected the stage to collapse. Wilkman, Republican congressman, looking like Buffalo Bill with his long yellow-turning-to-gray hair and goatee waved to the crowd. And waved. And waved. His speech began slowly, winding up as he went along.

Jack and I scanned the security measures, while Wilkman spoke over the loudspeakers: "We must obey the laws of our great state and our nation. We cannot have people coming over our borders willy-nilly, which by its very nature is a crime."

Applause from those inside the ropes.

Boos and jeers from the protesters. A man waving a Mexican flag shoved a woman who looked old enough to be my grandmother. Jack started toward them. The crowd slowed him down; security got there first.

"Talks a good game, doesn't he?" Jack said.

"Out of both sides of his mouth. Or do you think maybe

Beltran's BSing us about Wilkman?"

"He's a politician."

That sort of said it all. Jack scanned the crowd. Said, "One. That's all I see is one bodyguard. There's other security, of course, but just one that looks like a personal bodyguard. Should be a cinch to get to him."

"You think it's a twenty-four-seven thing?"

"I think these politicians would like to sleep with their bodyguards if they could."

"That can be taken a couple different ways."

"Yeah, it can."

Wilkman kept going, "State Senator Art Torres says that Proposition 187 is the last gasp of white California. Were I to say something like that I would be called a racist. Is Senator Torres called a racist?"

"No!" the crowd bellowed.

More Mexican flags hovered around the edges of the rally, separated from the ralliers by only a single strand rope barricade. They tried to out shout Wilkman. They tried to drown out the ralliers. A uniformed police officer stepped to the stage.

"Ladies and gentleman, we must ask that you put away your flags," she said.

"What's she talking about?"

"Yeah, put those Mexican flags away. This is the USA," another crowd member shouted.

"I'm sorry, but I'm asking this crowd to furl your American flags. For your own safety," the officer continued.

The crowd booed. Seethed, as more uniformed officers arrived. They posted themselves around the perimeter of the rope line, trying to keep the two sides separate.

"Ladies and gentlemen, please," Wilkman said, "for your own safety, do as the officer asks."

"Traitor." The crowd began chanting traitor as their mantra.

On the edges, more skirmishes between the pro 187 ralli-ers and the anti-protesters.

"Let's get out of here," Jack said. "We've seen what we came for."

"Emotional issue."

We threaded our way through the throngs, outside the rope, toward the car in another part of the parking lot. Two men, both wearing green, white, and red bandanas blocked our path between two cars.

"I guess this is what we call a Mexican standoff," one of them sneered.

I could see the muscles in Jack's neck tensing. I knew what would happen next. I put my hand through his belt and pulled him back, so we could go around the cars. I knew he'd hate me for it, but it wouldn't last. And sometimes dis-cretion *is* the better part of valor. We had bigger fish to fry.

They followed us to his Hummer, kept taunting. We got in. He turned the ignition. One of them got in front of the truck, started rocking the hood up and down. The other one joined him. Jack revved the engine a couple times, put the Hummer in gear and drove right through them. They were lucky to get out of the way before being run down. We were headed for the lot's exit. The two protesters had righted themselves. They now had another man by the arms. He looked vaguely familiar, though I couldn't place him. Jack screeched to a halt, put the Hummer in park. He jumped out. I followed, what else could I do?

Jack held a pipe that he carried under the seat of his car for just such moments. I had the Firestar under my shirt, but wasn't prepared to use it. We headed for the protesters.

"Get the fuck out of here!" Jack erupted.

"You get the fuck out of our country," one of the men said.

Jack walked right up to his face. "Listen Paco or Jose or whatever your name is, this isn't Aztlan, this isn't *your* coun-try."

"It used to be."

"Not anymore."

"It will be again."

"Fine, if you want to live in a third world hell you can have it. But why not just go down to Mexico and you can have it now."

"*Chinga tu madre!*"

"At least I know who she is."

Both men puffed themselves up, wanting to be brave. But they looked at Jack, saw death in his eyes. They spit, but let go of the man they were holding, walked off cursing in English and Spanish.

"Damn lucky they didn't hit us with their spit. I'd have killed them."

I turned to the other man, "Come with us. We'll take you to your car."

"Thanks," the man said. He told us where his car was.

We got in the Hummer and drove through the parking lot.

"I'm lucky you guys were there. No cops out here in this lot. Let me buy you a drink or something," the man said.

"No thanks."

He checked a loose thread on his gray sportcoat, then reached his arm over the seat to shake hands. I turned toward the back seat, reciprocated. "Duke, Duke Rogers."

"Jack Riggs."

"Eric," he said. No last name. I figured that's how he wanted it. He seemed genuinely glad to meet us. We dropped him at his car, a beat-up Beamer. He thanked us again and we watched him drive off, the way you'd watch to make sure your girlfriend got off okay. Then we headed back to my place, only a few minutes from the tar pits.

"This city's gonna blow," Jack said, turning right onto Sixth Street. "The whole state. Maybe the whole damn country. If not now, sometime in the relatively near future. You got people on one side and people on the other—it's like we're in a second Civil War. Just no shooting yet."

"Damn close to it."

"Incidents here and there. Like John Brown at Harper's Ferry. People aren't mad enough yet, but one of these days there'll be another Fort Sumter. Or Alamo."

"What about Wilkman?" I said, trying to get back to our immediate concerns.

"Anybody can be gotten to. We just have to figure out how."

"I hear Santos is going to be at a rally on the other side. You want to check it out?"

"You've got a date."

"Thanks, Jack."

CHAPTER 37

Black clouds smeared the sky, smudging the sun, like a child's finger painting. Eric and Lindsay walked along the Venice boardwalk. They hadn't spoken in ten minutes.

"You're very distant," she said, taking his limp hand in hers. "I feel like I'm with an eggplant."

"Eggplants are good."

"Not if they don't have cheese and tomato sauce on them. And that's what you're like, a plain old boring eggplant."

"I'm sorry. It's this job."

They sat on a bench, staring out to the choppy, white-capped Pacific. Few people were about. Everyone expected the skies to open up.

"I thought you liked it, said it was exciting."

"It is, but I wonder if I'm doing the right thing. You know this guy I work for—"

"—Mike."

"Yeah. You know he's kind of shady."

"That's what I thought was exciting."

"Yeah, but now I'm starting to get worried. I already have enough baggage what with my law license and all. Now he's got me tailing this guy."

"That sounds so...Hollywood. Why would he want someone 'tailed'?"

"I don't know. That's what worries me. I'm sure it can't be for any good purpose."

"Well, didn't you have people tailed when you were a

lawyer, to find out things about them?"

"Sure, but we hired licensed private detectives. What am I? A fallen lawyer."

"Well, you said his business isn't exactly legit."

Eric went quiet. More like numb.

"What is it?" she said.

"The weirdest thing happened. I was tailing him and he and his buddy went to this pro 187 rally at the La Brea Tar Pits. They left early, so I followed. In the parking lot I was hassled by some anti-187 guys and the guy I'm tailing and his buddy pulled my ass out of the fire."

"So you're feeling guilty."

"I guess you could say that."

"Why are you tailing him?"

"I don't know. 'Cause I'm being paid to." He stared across the Pacific.

"What are you looking for out there?"

"I don't know that either."

"'Cause you're certainly not here with me."

Several minutes passed. Eric finally said, "He saved my life."

"Who? Mike?"

"No, he gives me money for jobs, but he didn't save my life. This guy I'm tailing and his buddy saved my life. But that's not even it. Even before that I was thinking maybe I shouldn't be doing this, but I'm fucking desperate. I have to eat. Speaking of which, let's get some dinner. I'm flush with Mike's money." "What does this guy you're following do?"

"I think he's a private detective, Duke Rogers."

"Duke Rogers?"

"Yeah, you know him?"

"Of him. He's the guy who found Teddie Matson's killer. It was all over the news."

"I knew she was killed. Maybe that was when I was going through my legal dive. I'd never heard of him before."

His cell phone rang. He pulled it from his pocket.

"I didn't know you had a cell phone."

"Mike gave it to me." He figured out how to answer it; he had to do this every time it rang. "Hello, Mike." Mike was the only person who called him. "Yeah. He doesn't seem to stray too far afield. I'll write it all out and send you his schedule. Okay, great. Bye." Eric's face sank. He wished he could sink into Lindsay's arms and never come out, or hide from the world in a converted missile silo. He had been so damned happy when he got the gig with Mike. But he was beginning to realize that all that glitters isn't gold, and right now his golden dream was turning black. Cheap, fake gold, cheap dreams.

"I thought you were having second thoughts."

"I am, but I don't know how to get out of it. This Mike guy scares me."

"Has he done anything?"

"No. But you can tell. He's cold. I just don't think he gives a damn about anyone. He just likes being in control, having power over people. I know, I saw plenty of the type when I was a lawyer. Hell, I used to defend them, even when I knew they were guilty as sin." Eric had been confident then. Now he felt out of his depth. "And now on top of it all, I've probably blown my cover, though maybe that's not such a bad thing."

"What're you going to do?"

"I don't know."

CHAPTER 38

The Watts Towers was a strange place to have a pro-187 rally. Made from steel pipes wrapped in wire mesh and coated with mortar, embedded with tile and glass, they reach to the sky on a residential lot in South Central. Hardly big enough for a rally of any size, but I guess the symbolism is what mattered most.

We parked the Jeep three blocks away, as close as we could get, walked over. Lots of people heading there with us. I knew what we were there for, but at that moment my mind was on a house in the same relative vicinity: Rita's mother's. I wondered if I'd see her here. Doubted it. South Central was changing. Nearly all black, it was being re-populated with recent Hispanic immigrants. Tension was high. The black-Mexican alliance was faltering as blacks saw Mexican immigrants displacing them in their neighborhoods and *stealing* their jobs. This wasn't a good place for a rally today.

As we approached the towers, the streets were blocked. Mexican flags flew everywhere. Some, not many, white faces in the crowd. I guess we fit that bill.

State Assemblywoman Lorraine Santos took the stage to the strains of the Mexican National Anthem. The crowd roared.

"I know when I'm outnumbered," Jack said.

The song finished. I expected them to play the "Star Spangled Banner"—my expectations weren't met.

Jack went on, not as quietly or discreetly as he should

have. "I've heard that at soccer events—what the fuck kind of sissy game is that anyway—and some boxing matches that they sing the Mexican anthem and boo ours. Is this a great country or what? They're going to kill the goose that lays the golden eggs, then wonder what the hell happened."

He scanned the crowd, the stage, the security setup, as he talked. I did too. "Whadda you see?" I said.

"Similar layout. One, maybe two personal bodyguards. But this is a public thing. Lots of cops too. I wonder what kind of security they have at night at home."

"I wonder."

I couldn't shake the feeling that I was being followed or watched. But it was impossible to tell in this crowd.

A handful of pro-187, anti-immigrant protesters tried shouting. They were quickly shut up and hustled off by the police. Then a black woman, maybe in her seventies, stood up, shouting. The crowd quieted.

"Why should we pay for people who are here illegally to go to our schools?" she said. "Why should we pay for them to use our emergency rooms? Use them for the common cold so we can't get in them when we need them?"

"*Sí*, so you can't get in for your gang boys' gunshot wounds," shouted one of the anti-187 ralliers.

"We didn't cross the border. The border crossed us," an anti-187er shouted.

"These are our neighborhoods," the woman went on. "We marched for them. We fought for them. We died for them. These are our schools."

A rock hit her in the face. She fell to the ground. The crowd surged around her. Young blacks and Hispanics, charging each other. Fists flying, protest signs crashing. The police trying to keep them apart. Shouting, yelling. Cursing. English. Spanish. *Spanglish*.

A scream pierced the crowd. Jack and I turned. Several anti-187ers charged a middle-aged woman, holding an

American flag. Jack lurched in that direction. I grabbed his shirt tail.

"We can't. Not now," I said. "Remember the bigger picture."

"The cops aren't even breaking it up."

Jack broke free.

The last thing I wanted then was a fight. We had plenty of fights coming: with Congressman Wilkman and Assemblywoman Santos. The church. The shadowy Miguel. And with the country as a whole. This immigration thing wasn't going away. And while I wanted to help the woman, I also didn't want us to get thrown in jail and not be able to pursue our mission.

I grabbed Jack. Held him firmly. He probably could have broken away if he'd wanted to.

"I think we've seen enough," I said. We headed for the Jeep. "Hey, you see that?"

"What?"

"I don't know. Guy looked familiar. Like the guy from the tar pits."

"I didn't see him. But maybe he's here to protest the anti-187 people."

"Maybe." Maybe—but I didn't believe it.

The drive home was uneventful. I felt like we were making progress and going nowhere at the same time.

"I tell you, this city's gonna explode," Jack said. "Sooner or later. Hell, the whole country's gonna explode and it's gonna make the Rodney King riots and the sixties riots look like kids playing at war."

I didn't say anything. I didn't want to believe that Jack was right, but I feared that he was.

* * *

We hit the Café Noir. Dark. Quiet. Swing music on the juke. A bartender who knew us. As comfy as an old, worn in Navy peacoat. We sat in the corner again.

No Larry.

I thought about asking Jack about Marisol. But he wasn't the talkative type. If he wanted to talk, he knew I'd be here for him.

"Man, we're juggling a lot of balls."

"Just the church, Karubian, Marisol, Carlos, Beltran, Santos, Wilkman, Birch. Miguel." I took a deep breath. "Chandler and Haskell, who might want to tap me for Birch. That's not a lot."

"Don't forget Rita."

"That's a lot of balls. But I think I might have dropped the last one."

"Why don't you just call her."

I sipped the gin-soaked lemonade the bartender had brought. "I start to call her. I dial. I hang up. I can't go through with it. The other night I drove by her mother's house."

"Hoping you'd run into her. Like some moonstruck high school kid. Why didn't you just drive by her house?"

"Don't have the address."

"You're a damn detective."

"Not a very good one."

"I never met a happy coward. And you don't seem very happy to me lately."

"I'm not a coward." The words fell flat.

"You're being a coward about this Rita stuff. And you're no coward."

What could I say? I didn't have any good answers as to why I couldn't call Rita. Maybe it was the circumstances under which we met. Or the way we parted. Maybe it was that I had indirectly led to her sister being murdered. I had had the guts to tell her, but now I didn't have the guts to call her.

I kept hoping I'd pick up the phone one day and it would be her. But why should she call me? No, it was my task to call her. If I waited any longer it would be too late. Or had I waited too long already?

"And you're wearing a hair shirt about it too," Jack said, picking up his drink.

"What're you talking about?"

"This whole mess with Marisol, Beltran, Wilkman, et al. Why do you think you're doing it? Penance. For Teddie. For Rita. You feel you don't deserve her, but you do, buddy, you do."

"Segue, Jack." I downed my drink. "So where does that leave us? They aren't going away."

"Back with Beltran, Santos, Wilkman, the Cardinal, and our friend Miguel."

"The Five Horsemen of the Apocalypse."

"They might be the horsemen of your apocalypse, buddy, if we don't handle this right."

We left the Noir, pulled out into the river of Sunset Boulevard traffic that made the raging L.A. river look like a piddly stream.

Eric's legs, stiff from sitting in the Beamer for the hour Duke Rogers and his pal Jack were inside the Café Noir, fired up the engine, pulled out into traffic, four cars behind Duke's Jeep. He thought this kind of work would be exciting. Mostly it was excruciatingly boring. And it made him feel dirty. He had sometimes felt dirty when repping a client he knew to be less than innocent. But at least that was aboveboard, how the game was played. This made him feel like a trapped rat.

* * *

After dropping Jack off, I hit a pay phone. Dialed. Not Rita, but the Hollywood Police Station. Asked for Detective Chandler. Left another message for her—to meet at Roscoe's again. This time for dinner around seven p.m.

I hit Roscoe's and waited to see if Chandler would show. They wouldn't give me a table until my party joined me 'cause it was dinner hours. When she didn't show by eight, I grabbed some takeout and split.

Molly greeted me at the door. We *coupaged*, walked, ate, and settled in for the night. I was checking my e-mail, which I didn't get much of, mostly unsolicited ads for porn sites, when there was a loud knock on the front door. Cop knock. I grabbed the Star, headed for the door. Looked out the peep. Chandler. I looked harder, trying to see if Haskell or any other cops were with her. I opened the door, Molly yapping at my feet.

"You weren't expecting company," she said, obviously taking in my disheveled appearance. Light from a side window hit her so she stood half in light, half in shadow, like a Hurrell photo of some long forgotten Golden Age movie star.

"No, this is how I always dress for company?"

"Can I come in?" She inched forward. I was almost expecting her to stick her foot in the door.

"Jeez, the way you knocked, I thought it was a raid."

She looked down at the gun in my hand. "Habit. And you can put your *gat* away now."

"Habit," I said, referring to the gun. I put it on the entry hall table. We made our way to the living room, sat facing each other. Molly jumped into Chandler's lap. She was very at home there.

"Don't you know that guns can get you killed?" Chandler stroked Molly's back.

"Not if you shoot first."

"Then you go to jail."

"It really isn't fair, is it?"

She smiled a closed-lip smile.

"What can I do for you, Detective?" I let the officiousness seep back in. After all, our last visit was a little icy.

"I got a message that you wanted to meet me at Roscoe's," she said.

"Hold on, I'll go cook up some chicken and waffles."

"I got the message too late. I guess I could have called but I figured I'd see if you were home."

"In other words, you might stumble on me burying another body." Did she know I was joking? Some cops had no sense of humor.

"Well, you do answer the door armed," she said, no hint of irony.

"You never know who might be lurking. This is L.A."

"So now it's my turn," she said. "What can I do for you?"

I debated what to say. Figured on the truth.

"I just figured we parted kind of uncomfortably last time you were here. And our meeting in Venice was—"

"—Let's just say it was professional," she said in that *professional* cop voice.

"Yes, professional. Anyway, I don't need any more enemies."

"You have lots of enemies?" Cop question.

"Not that I know of and you know what I mean."

"I hate to change from such a convivial subject, but we do have some business between us," she said.

"Ever the cop."

"That's what my father says."

"Have you learned anymore about Birch's death?"

"I'm the cop, I'll ask the questions."

"Well, I don't know anything. I feel like a dog chasing his tail. I've got some pieces, I just can't put them together."

"Why don't you tell me? And don't leave out how you got to that house in Venice before us."

I filled her in on much of what we'd learned. That Birch's

death was part of the conspiracy. Somehow, we thought Marisol and Carlos, were tied into it, if only by Miguel. That maybe even Karubian was part of it. She looked at me incredulously. I mentioned Beltran, not Santos or Wilkman. She was already in disbelief mode, why give her more ammo?

"So now you're withholding evidence," she said, half joking, which meant also half not.

"Not evidence. Just hunches."

"Why don't you let me decide. Or maybe I should haul you in for withholding evidence."

It was one of those jokes that had a serious subtext.

"You wouldn't do that," I said.

"Why not?"

"You like me too much."

Stunned silence. "Okay, I like you," she finally said. "But I think we need to keep it professional. I don't like arresting people I like. So tell me what else you've got."

"There's no cop-suspect confidentiality. If I tell you, you might blow my plans."

"If your plans are criminal in nature I'll be doing you a favor."

"Then I'll be involving you in a criminal conspiracy and we'll both go to jail under RICO. Do they have co-ed jails these days," I joked. "Maybe you can help us."

"Help?"

"Chandler, this thing is bigger than you imagine."

"Now I'm intrigued."

The phone rang. I almost let the answering machine pick up.

"Hello," I said.

"It's time to go on the offensive," Jack said. "Time to rock 'n' roll."

My eyes shifted from the phone to Chandler. The rock and the hard place. I told Jack I'd call back and hung up.

"Anything important?" Chandler asked.

"No."

"So I guess we go back to my being intrigued."

Now I wasn't sure what to do. Jack wanted to move forward, but how much should I tell Chandler?

"So how are all these people you mentioned before tied together, Beltran, Birch, Carlos and Marisol Rivera, this Miguel? And Susan Karubian. Seems like a pretty disparate group," she said.

"Illegals."

"Illegal aliens?"

"Yes."

"Birch worked for the Catholic Church."

"They're all tied in. Smuggling," I said. "I don't know what each particular connection is. Miguel is the coyote. The church hides them out, finds them places to live. Carlos was working for Miguel. Beltran gives them some political muscle, maybe helps bury things. Karubian was Beltran's friend. Miguel introduced them, but I'm not sure how her death ties in."

"So what're you gonna do?"

"I'm not sure about that either." And I wasn't.

But I was sure that Jack was right. It was time to rock 'n' roll.

CHAPTER 39

The wind blew in off the ocean, tiny darts of salt water stinging Eric's cheeks. The Santa Monica Pier Ferris Wheel spun, the roller coaster flew. A Saturday without rain and the people came out of their houses looking for fun, a way to relieve the boredom.

"You like the pier, don't you, Mike?" Eric said.

"It's a happy place. I like happy places."

But Mike didn't look happy. He looked serious. As he always did. And Eric wondered if he saw some anger under the serious face. There were also scratches. He didn't want to know where they came from.

"And it's an anonymous place."

Mike didn't respond. "You're doing a good job, Eric," he said, after Eric had briefed him on Duke Rogers' movements. He pulled out a wad of hundreds. Handed a couple to Eric.

The bills, crisp and new, felt grungy in Eric's hands. He slid them into his pocket. He told himself to quit right now. The steel in Mike's eyes said maybe that was better accomplished on the phone. He knew Mike wasn't on the side of the angels, just as he had known that about most of his clients.

What had he done? What the fuck had he done to screw up his life so much that he found himself in this position? All he ever wanted to do was practice law. If Mike had come to him when he was a defense lawyer, he would gladly have taken his case, his money. This was different. Now Eric was on the other side. So far the things he'd done for Mike were minor offenses of the law. But why the hell was he having Eric tail Duke Rogers? He couldn't think of any good reasons.

"You go back, get on him again. Keep in touch with me on the cell phone. I want to know his every move." Mike slapped Eric on the back. "I see a future for you with me."

Mike might have. But Eric didn't see much of a future here.

Saturday had been uneventful. But the sun had broken through so I took Molly to Griffith Park, by the merry-go-round. Moms and dads and kids of all races ran and played and rode the colorful horses that floated up and down. We walked the park, up and down the trails. Molly was game and was definitely doing better than she had been. The one place we avoided was the Observatory. It would have been a hell of a hike up there, though I had done it when I was younger. But I didn't want to go there now. Memories of the Weasel plunging to his death didn't bother me. But it brought up the whole Teddie-Rita thing and I wanted a day off from my penance.

But that was yesterday. Now it was Zero Dark Thirty, Sunday morning and the clouds were back, though no rain. The sun was barely above the horizon as Jack and I sat on surfboards off the coast of Malibu. We weren't the only surfers out there, but there weren't many. I hadn't had a wetsuit on in some time and mine fit snugly. Had I gained a few pounds? Muscle, of course.

"I get the feeling I'm being followed," I said.

"Seen anyone?"

"No. Just a feeling."

"Keeps you on your toes."

"How'd you find out about Wilkman?"

"A little birdie told me." Jack grinned.

I thought I had good sources. Jack had the best. He wouldn't reveal them, even to me. Somehow he found out that Congressman Wilkman liked to surf the ocean near his beach house when he was in town. And he was in town. So here we sat, bobbing on our boards, hoping he'd show. We let a lot of good waves pass. People must have thought we were *kooks* or *gremlins or gremmies* or whatever they were calling wannabes these days.

Jack squinted toward shore. "That's his house. The one with the aqua-colored pipe railing."

"Very modern."

"Yeah, I guess when you're bringin' in illegals you can afford modern in Malibu as your second house."

A miniscule figure emerged from the house, insignificant in the distance. Clearly wearing a wet suit, electric blue so the whole world could see. Grabbed a long board from the house's deck and trotted toward the shore break. He paddled straight toward us.

"Bandit dead ahead," Jack said, with the slightest grin of satisfaction.

"And closing."

Wilkman paddled right out to us. He nodded. The three of us sat waiting for the perfect wave.

"You boys are like me," he said. "Not quite as young as most of 'em." His hand swept the ocean in the direction of some of the young boys waiting for waves. He had at least fifteen years on us.

"Yes, sir, Congressman."

His pol's smile lit up his face, happy to be recognized. Jack paddled around so we were on either side of him. The smile faded like a wave that had lost its energy. He made a show of looking for a wave, any wave.

"You just got here, Congressman. Don't be in such a hurry to leave."

"Who are you?" Still looking for a wave to catch. Jack paddled closer to him.

"We want to have a little chat," I said.

"Call my office for an appointment." Wilkman spoke in that officious voice politicians love and citizens love to hate.

"Haven't we heard that before?" Jack said.

"Think so. 'Sides, you know the Congressman would be too busy to see us."

"Threatening a federal official is a crime," Wilkman said.

"Have you been threatened?" I said. "Or do you just feel threatened?"

"What do you want?" Wilkman scanned for a wave. The water was glass. He was stuck with us for a while unless he wanted to paddle in.

"You're running a pretty little scam. Hustling illegals over the border."

"You're full of shit," Wilkman said.

"You and Santos and the Cardinal. And a little worm named Beltran."

"Don't forget Miguel," Jack said.

At that name Wilkman's jaw tightened, his eyes squinted down. "Never heard of him."

"You want cheap labor for your Republican friends, your business pals," I continued. "Santos wants votes—I guess you're in a safe district so you don't care about that. The church wants parishioners, and thus power. And you have your little friend Miguel help bring people across and when they balk at one thing or another Miguel takes care of them."

"You're crazy," Wilkman said.

"Like a man named Birch. A woman named Marisol Rivera. Her brother Carlos. And who knows how many others."

"Certifiable."

That was the perfect cue for Jack to pull his SEAL Pup knife from its leg sheath and start cleaning his fingernails. He preferred the sleek little blade to the KaBars and MK-3s.

Wilkman pretended not to notice, still scanning the horizon for a wave to get him the hell out of there. "Is there a point to all this?" he said.

"You've got a lot of blood on your hands. You and Santos and the Cardinal." I looked straight at him.

"I've never killed anyone," he said.

"You have others do your dirty work for you. That makes you worse."

"What the fuck do you want?"

"You have to own up," Jack said, still toying with the knife.

"You two sound like a cheap detective novel." But there was little conviction in Wilkman's voice.

"Maybe. But you, Santos, and the Cardinal, step down. Confess. Go to jail."

The smile that broadened Wilkman's face made the Cheshire Cat look depressed. It said, surely you jest, without words.

"Give it up, Mr. Rogers. You have no power. And no proof." Wilkman paddled forward, stood with grace and rode the perfect wave into shore in perfect form.

"He knows your name," Jack said.

We bungeed our boards onto the Jeep's luggage rack and hit the road.

"Any point in talking to Santos?"

"Can't hurt. Wilkman'll tell her and the Cardinal what they need to know. Better put your antenna up high," Jack said.

I looked in the rearview mirror in time to see a dirty Beamer pull out onto Pacific Coast Highway. Jack saw me looking.

"Watch the road," he said. "I'll keep track of that Beamer."

"Can you see the driver?"

"Nope. Guess you were right when you thought you were being followed."

We turned up Sunset, the Beamer still with us. Jack

watched him through the rearview and side mirrors.

"You think it's Miguel?"

"Hard to tell through the glare," Jack said.

We drove past the Self Realization Fellowship, through Brentwood and Bel Air, past UCLA.

"What the fuck, let's do it," Jack said. "Give the guy in the Beamer a run for his money."

"Do what?"

"Go to Santos'."

"Now?"

"Now."

"Where the hell does she live?"

He pulled out a piece of paper with an address scribbled on it. A house in Garden Grove—a bedroom community in Orange County. I should have known he'd have some info on her. It was a brutal drive from Malibu and even on a Sunday morning, L.A. traffic was a bitch.

"She stole the vote from B-1 Billy," Jack said. "Illegals voting and all."

"It was never proved."

"Nobody ever looked into it. It was covered up."

He was talking about Santos beating longtime Assembly-man Billy Draper for her seat. It was alleged that undocumented immigrants voted in mass numbers, thus her win. Never proven. Nobody really wanted to know the truth. Still, the rumors helped fuel the 187 debate.

We pulled up to her house. Quiet enough.

The house was yellow with white trim, one of those stucco ranch styles—only in SoCal—and, of course, it had fake half wagon wheels as the railings to the front porch. We walked to the front door, but before we even knocked some guy with a shaved head and a muscle shirt came out and made it clear we weren't welcome.

"We're constituents."

He clearly didn't care.

"I'm calling the police," a woman's voice shouted from inside the house. Santos?

I'm always up for a good fight, but you can't fight the cops. We got out before they showed, the Beamer still on our tail.

I dropped Jack at a coffee shop a few blocks from his place so the guy in the Beamer wouldn't know where he lived, then headed home. The Beamer stayed with me, trying to be discreet. I knew Jack wasn't going home, he didn't even bother to take his board off the Jeep. I wondered if the Beamer driver would notice or think anything of that.

I pulled in the driveway, jumped out of the car, and went into the house, wishing I had surveillance up and down the street. But why would I need that when I had Jack?

Ten minutes later the phone rang. Molly ran for it. But I picked it up.

"It's the guy from the tar pits," Jack said.

It didn't register. Then, "You mean the guy whose ass we saved?"

"The very."

"That's gratitude for you."

"He's parked four houses toward Beverly on the opposite side of the street." His voice crackled, breaking up on his cell phone. "I'll watch him for a while."

"And I'll just sit here like a sitting duck." I hung up.

The guy from the rally. What'd he say his name was? Eric. Could he really be Miguel?

Molly and I watched TV. What else can you do when you're bait?

At eleven-fifty-seven the doorbell rang. Not even noon yet and we had gone surfing, so to speak, had a *conference* with a congressman, a *pleasant* visit with Assemblywoman Santos, and now here I was in my domicile with my pup, ready to enjoy a relaxing day when the doorbell rang. I looked out the peephole to see Eric. I didn't know how this would go down, so I put Molly in the master bedroom and closed the door on her. Why would the guy tailing me come to the door?

"Rally-man," I said, opening the front door, Firestar in hand, to find Eric standing there in a beat-up blue parka. He shifted from foot to foot. His eyes wouldn't meet mine. I was standing to the side of the open doorway, good thing too. Eric came crashing into the house, propelled by a force of nature: Jack.

Eric landed on the Spanish tile entry hall floor, face down. Jack was on him, patting him down, leaving no parts untouched. He yanked Eric up. "Clean."

"Come in," I said. "Welcome to my home."

Eric looked ready to piss his pants. We went to the breakfast room. I pointed to a chair. Eric sat. I sat across the table from him. Jack stood, back to the wall, arms folded, like a Master at Arms—ready for anything.

"He's alone," Jack said.

Eric held his hands together, trying to keep them from drumming the table. He started to speak. I cut him off.

"I'm thinking our running into you at the 187 rally wasn't an accident." Who am I not to state the obvious?

Eric shook his head.

"Who are you?" There was no room for equivocation in my voice.

"Eric Davies."

"Nice to meet you—again—Eric Davies," Jack said, evenly, not an ounce of malice in his voice. He might as well have been a greeter at Walmart. But there was more menace in his soft-spokenness than if he'd let loose a stream of verbal threats at the top of his lungs.

"Look, I came here. I didn't have to. You didn't have to rough me up."

"You're not hurt," I said. "So why don't you tell us why you came."

Eric's fingers drummed. I guess he lost the battle. He hesitated. "My name is Eric Davies. Been down on my luck late-ly. So I put an ad in the *L.A. Weekly*, said I'd do anything for money. This guy calls and has me do some errands for him. Nothing too bad, but shady. I figure the less I know the better. And then a few days ago he has me start tailing you. Tells me I'm moving up in his operation."

"Why are you tailing Duke?" Jack said.

"I'm not really sure, but I don't think it's for any good reason. He called me last night and wanted me to send him my notes on your comings and goings. Said to keep at it and keep in touch on the phone." He reached for his parka cargo pocket, thought better of it. Looked at Jack. Jack nodded. Eric pulled out a cellular phone. "On this."

"So, what're you doing here?" I said.

"I already screwed up part of my life. I used to be a law-yer." He ran his hands up and down his shabby parka. "Now look at me."

I could relate to him screwing up his life. I knew that one inside out. It actually made me feel for him.

"So you came by for a nice social visit," Jack said. "Just a minute, I'll get the tea and watercress sandwiches. Sans crusts, of course."

"I sure as hell didn't come here to be ridiculed."

"And your employer's name?" I said.

"Mike."

"Miguel?"

"No, just Mike."

Jack and I passed a look. It was too similar. It had to be the same guy.

"What's his last name?" I said.

"I don't know. He never told me."

"You said you were a lawyer. Wouldn't a lawyer be more circumspect?"

"I'm not a lawyer anymore. I can't afford to be circum-spect, I need the money." The look of defeat on Eric's face said it all. He was telling the truth. "He pays me in cash. I always meet him somewhere, usually the Santa Monica Pier. So I don't know anything about him."

"But you have a current phone number?"

"Yeah."

"Did he change it recently?"

"Yes, how did you know?"

Jack walked over to Eric, leaned into him. An inch from his face. Eric scooched back, but there was nowhere to go. "Now I don't want to be politically incorrect here," Jack said. "But do you think Mike could also go by Miguel?"

"What?"

"Could Mike be Hispanic?" I said.

Eric thought a moment. "Yeah, I suppose he could."

"Does he speak with an accent?" Jack said.

"Not really. Well, come to think of it, there might be a trace of one. Do you know him?"

"No, but we'd like to," Jack said.

"He's a bad man, Mr. Eric Davies." I glared at him. "You've really gotten yourself into something."

"I figured as much."

"He shoots people," Jack said, pointing to my wounded arm.

"He shot you? Jeez, I just needed a job."

"He's a killer," I said. "Runs people across the border. Kills them when they get in the way or become useless."

"I think I'm on the road to being useless."

"What kind of lawyer were you?"

"Criminal defense."

"Figures," Jack said. "Well, you might need your legal skills before this all plays out."

"What'd I get myself into?" He cupped his head in his hands and let it fall to the table.

"You could help us," I said.

"Haven't I helped you just by coming here, telling you

what I know, telling you you're being followed and by who? I just want to get away."

"You don't have to help. But you could."

"What do you want me to do, set him up? That's it, right?"

"He needs to be taken down," Jack said.

"I thought I was just getting my life back together. Had a little money for the first time in a long time." His face caved in on itself with despair. "I'll think about it."

"And we'll think about you," Jack said. "Where can we reach you?"

Eric wrote a number down.

"You wouldn't do what some girls do, give us a wrong number, would you? 'Cause we'll find you again." Jack flipped him a piece of paper with the license number and description of the Beamer on it. Then he yanked a leather wallet out of Eric's pocket. Opened it, copied down Eric's driver's license info. Tossed the wallet across the table.

"Maybe your coming here is a setup," I said.

"Why would I come here and get bullied?"

"So, why *are* you doing this, coming to talk to us?"

"I already screwed up my life once. I don't want to do it again." He got up, paused a moment, as if waiting to see if either of us would stop him. "What do I do now?"

"Just keep doing what Mike wants you to do."

"We'll be in touch," Jack said.

We heard the front door open and close. Watched Eric walk out to the street from the breakfast room window.

"What do you think?" Jack said.

"Let me check up on him."

CHAPTER 40

It's amazing what a drink or two will buy you. Larry Darrell and I sat in the Café Noir, talking about old times. You know like suicides from the Hollywood Sign. Nat King Cole's "The Blues Don't Care" spilled from the jukebox again. I think it was Larry's favorite song.

"There's something else," I said. "I need to know why a lawyer named Eric Davies was disbarred."

"That's easy."

"You know him?"

"Of him. He's a hero in the department, at least to the grunts in the trenches."

"What'd he do?"

"He was a defense lawyer at one of the top firms. Real scumbag—hell, all defense lawyers are."

Except those who defend the police, I thought. Larry went on:

"All kinds of BS defenses for some major douchebags. Then I don't know what happened. Maybe he had an epiphany, maybe he drank too much one night. Maybe guilt seeped into his lawyer's heart and rusted it. Maybe he found God. I don't know. But he found out a client of his—Robert Troy was—surprise—actually guilty."

"I remember that case. Didn't they call Troy the Pied Piper? Rich game show host. He'd lure kids to his home when his family was out and molest them. He bought off the kids' families so nothing could be proved since they wouldn't testify."

"Yeah, a real scumbag. Fame and money, it'll take you a long ways. Anyway, Davies finds out and I guess even he couldn't stand it anymore. Sets Troy up to take a fall."

"What'd he do?"

"He kind of did it all. First, he finds out Troy is guilty. And even though he's a piece-of-shit defense lawyer he can't take it, knowing what the 'Pied Piper' did to those kids. So Troy has videos of all the stuff he's doing to the kids but the cops can't find them. Being the arrogant schmuck he is, he tells his lawyer—Davies—where they are, knowing that with lawyer-client privilege Davies can't do anything. Davies goes to the guy's house, finds the tapes. But he can't turn them in to the prosecution. He thinks about mailing them anonymously, but doesn't like that idea. So he's in court, in the phase of trial where he's having all these character wits come on say what a great guy Troy is. And one of them's going to show these home movies of Troy to show what a terrific father he is. They shove the tape in the machine and guess what, it ain't those home movies. It's stuff that makes two of the jurors throw up. Nobody knows where the tape came from, nobody but Troy who stupidly shouts it out, confirming his guilt but also frying Davies at the same time."

"They should have given him a medal. Instead they disbarred him," I said.

"Faster'n you can say habeas corpus. Anyway, he's a hero to the department. Whatever happened to Davies?"

"He's a bum, living in Venice."

"You know what they say about good deeds."

I knew.

Eric watched Duke leave the Café Noir. Duke didn't seem to notice him. But Eric knew better than that now. He had to wonder why he was still tailing Duke if he was going to side with him against Mike. Not an easy decision. But what choice did he have? Sure, he could make some money with Mike till Mike decided he'd outlived his usefulness. Even if that didn't happen, what kind of life would it be?

"Fuck this," he said loud enough for the woman standing near his car to hear. This was L.A.—she'd heard it before. He turned the key in the ignition, headed home. He was done tailing Duke for the day. He'd go home and make up a phony report for Miguel.

The usual traffic greeted his drive home. When he got there, he flopped on the bed, exhausted. Sun-drenched beaches, piña coladas and bikini babes filled his dreams. Not very original, but fun. The phone jangled. He looked up. This was no dream. This was a nightmare.

"Hello."

"Eric. Duke. We want to set up a meet. We need a picture of Mike-Miguel, whatever his name is. Next time you meet with him I want to be there, in the shadows."

That's where I'm living, Eric thought, in the shadows. He said he'd let Duke know about the meet.

Jack wore a brightly colored Hawaiian shirt, jeans, and motorcycle boots. And shades. I wore a T shirt, jeans, tennis shoes, and a ball cap. Tourists. We cruised the pier, waiting for Eric's meet time with Miguel.

"Maybe we can help him out when it's over," I said, then took a bite of my hot dog on a stick.

"What, get his law license back?"

"I have an idea."

"Even if you could, he'll just go back to being a scummy defense lawyer. He won't setup all his clients."

"Never know when we might need a scummy defense lawyer."

"Right now we have a lot of people to take down."

"Oh yeah," I said, finishing the dog. "We're gonna bring the church down."

"Or die trying."

"Or die trying." I thought it was more than just idle speculation. "We need more evidence. Right now all we have is our conjecture."

"I think it's pretty tight. We see how they're all tied together."

"We don't have enough for court."

"Who said anything about court?"

We walked into the pier's amusement area, found a place to sit near the Ferris wheel, but far enough away that we'd just be small faces in the distance. A few minutes later Eric came into view. He met a man in front of the wheel. The man wore a tropical white guayabera shirt. He was clean and crisp looking, just the way he'd been described to us. They sat in one of the wheel's cars and went for a ride. Jack snapped several pictures on his Nikon with a long lens.

"Got some good ones," he said.

Eric and Miguel's ride came to an end. They stayed on board for another.

"Must have a lot to talk about."

"I hope he's not giving us away." I didn't think Eric would. Just a feeling, but you have to go with those in this business. "You think he's nervous?"

"Like a turkey on Thanksgiving."

"What if Miguel doesn't come alone? What if he brings an army?"

"He won't. Too messy. He wants to clean this up and he doesn't want anyone else screwing it up like before."

The plan was to have Miguel think Eric was setting me up. That I'd spotted Eric, approached him, and wanted a meet with Miguel at the Hollywood Sign. I would meet him there whenever he wanted. As far as we knew, he didn't know about Jack, didn't know someone other than me had killed his man down at the border. Jack was my ace in the hole. As long as Eric didn't blow it.

We waylaid Beltran in his driveway again. It was getting to be a habit.

"What now?" But there wasn't much fire in his voice.

I put the photo of Miguel we'd shot at the pier in front of Beltran's eyes. They immediately dilated wide with fear.

"That's him." Beltran sank down on his back steps. "Keep him away from me."

"Politics. Strange bedfellows," Jack said.

"Did Miguel kill Susan Karubian?"

"I, I don't think so. She seemed pretty depressed lately," Beltran said. "Her career wasn't going the way she had hoped."

"Or maybe you asked Miguel to do you a favor and get her off your back?"

"No, that's not true. I actually cared for her."

I laughed. "You wouldn't even be seen with her."

"She would have been bad for my image. You might say she was my backstreet girl."

"You're a stand-up guy, Beltran," Jack said.

"I'm just trying to get by. Like you. Like everyone."

"We need proof that ties Wilkman, Santos, and the church to Miguel." I was going for menace in my voice; wasn't as good at it as Jack.

"I don't have anything. You think I keep records of this shit." Though he tried, there was no way to hide the fear in his eyes. "Christ, maybe you're wearing a wire."

"Maybe," I said, turned, and walked off. Jack waited a few seconds, glaring at him, then joined me.

CHAPTER 41

Miguel had agreed to the meet that Eric had set up. Supposedly it was to talk about a truce so we could all get on with our lives. I knew it wasn't that. I'm sure Miguel knew too. The meet was set for three a.m. I drove to the sign, getting there at two-thirty. I knew Miguel would already be there, so it had to look like I was just acting normal. I parked, scanned the area and headed for the edge of the road.

Until the late nineteen forties, the Hollywood Sign had said *Hollywoodland*. A come-on for a new real estate development. The "land" had fallen off and a state of mind was born. As a kid, I'd hiked up here a couple times.

Easing down the slope, I felt the Star in my belt, against my back, under an untucked long-sleeved shirt. I didn't think it would do me much good.

Jack had gotten to the area around eight p.m. I knew he'd scope out the best position to watch from. And I knew he had more than a pistol with him. Eric got to stay home, waiting for a phone call from either me or Miguel, whoever survived. We weren't planning on killing Miguel; we wanted to take him in and have him give up Wilkman's-Santos'-the church's scheme so they could be prosecuted. But you never know how these things will go down. And nothing ever went according to plan.

I continued climbing down the ridge in the dark, toward the actual sign, with only the moon to guide me. Even a penlight would have given me away. I planted myself behind the sign. That way, hopefully there'd be enough moonlight so I could see if someone was aiming from up above and the sign would block me from below. It wasn't perfect, there were still the sides. But it was all we had.

We had to make sure that the park rangers wouldn't see us. But at this hour of night that should be easy—notwithstanding the best laid plans and all of that—and they probably had better things to be doing, like sleeping.

I didn't know if Miguel would just try to kill me or want to talk this time. While waiting to find out, I peeked around the sign to the lights of L.A. below. The sparkling lights hid so much of the corruption and dirt. During the day, the smog hid it. But it was there. Just under the surface.

A coyote howled. I never could get used to their wail. Like nothing else.

Then it was silent again, except for the ambient sound of the city below. A low hum caused by cars and bodies hustling and other city sounds. No silence anywhere to be had around this city.

Metallic click.

I know that sound.

Bolt sliding.

Jesus!

The man from the Ferris wheel.

Miguel.

Aiming point blank at me.

Is Jack sighting on him?

Jack would already be cocked and locked.

I hunker close to the ground.

No time to draw the Star.

I have faith in Jack.

But you never know what might happen.

Miguel came toward me, automatic pistol aimed at my gut. I could see him in the light from the far side of the sign.

"Drop your gun," Miguel said.

I dropped the Firestar. He picked it up.

"You shot my man at Rocky Point. But I got the drop on you now." There was silence while he seemed to be reveling in how clever he was to have caught me.

"Why'd you kill Karubian? The others I can sort of understand. But why her?" My foot slipped on the scree. Not good when you're trying to make an impression.

Miguel debated a moment, then, "What'd'you think this is? Some stupid movie where I spill my guts, tell you everything?"

"I'd like to know what I'm gonna die for."

"You fucked up, man. You're gonna die for nothing. That's what we all die for in the end, isn't it?"

"I'd like to think I died for a good cause."

"Enough talk. It's poetic justice for you to die here, no?" He glanced up at the towering sign. When he looked down he saw the red pinpoint of a laser beam on his chest, right where his heart should be. Miguel didn't drop the gun right away. But after another few seconds of the laser sight on him, the gun fell to the ground.

Miguel looked around, as if expecting backup. But if I knew Jack, they were already taken care of.

"Looking for someone?" Jack emerged from the bush, grinning. "I don't think the cavalry's coming."

"*Chinga te.*"

"You're in no position to *chinga* anyone." Jack shoved him to the ground.

"I knew you couldn't have taken out Felipe in Smuggler's Gulch by yourself," Miguel said to me.

"You're not dealing with some poor wetbacks now. Your guys are amateurs, and easy to take down both times," Jack said.

"And now you've fucked up, too," I said.

"I'll kill that Eric son-of-a-bitch. He set me up."

"He didn't," I lied. "But either way, first you have to get

away. And where you're going, it'll be a long time till that happens."

"You never heard of the Mexican Mafia? I might be in jail but my homeboys will get him. And you too."

Miguel looked up at the sign.

"How many people have you killed?" I said.

"Enough."

"Couldn't kill us," Jack said.

Miguel looked down. "What do you want with me?"

"We want you to spill the beans on Beltran. Wilkman. Santos. Everyone," I said.

"And what do I get?"

"Maybe your life instead of the needle."

"Nobody's put to death in California. It's inhumane." He snorted.

"We still want to know why you killed Karubian. I can sort of figure out why you wanted to get rid of Marisol, her brother, and Birch. But why Karubian?"

He looked like he wanted to play tough. Maybe bluff his way out. The red laser danced across his chest. He was trying to look defiant. He knew that Jack had killed his man in Smuggler's Gulch so I would have thought he knew Jack wouldn't hesitate here. And he must have been wondering what happened to any troops he brought along tonight. I looked to his eyes for a sign of fear. Not much. This was a game of chicken to him. Maybe he thought we were bluffing.

"On your knees, hands behind your head," Jack said.

Miguel did as he was told. "Maybe we can negotiate—you let me go—and then I'll tell you what you want to know." He smiled at us, rubbed his scratched-up face. "Look what that bitch did to me."

Before I could open my mouth to respond, a steel-toed Doc Marten boot slashed through the air, smashing into Miguel's mouth. He spit a couple teeth out.

I wondered why Jack had used his foot instead of the rifle

butt, taking a chance that Miguel could grab it and trip him—as unlikely as that might be. Then I knew. In his own way, he was still reeling from Marisol's death and wanted that human connection with Miguel. He wanted to feel his boot crash into Miguel's face.

"You feel like talking now?" Jack said.

"Hard to talk without teeth." Blood shot from Miguel's mouth. He grinned a toothless grin. He glared up at Jack, a look of recognition crossing his eyes. "You had the hots for Marisol."

"I guess you called our bluff," I said, hoping to hold Jack off.

"*Maricón.*" Miguel wiped his bloody mouth on his sleeve.

"Beltran, Santos, Wilkman. The church. Tell me about them, the connections, what's going on." I didn't know who I needed to watch more, Jack or Miguel. I tried to keep an eye on both.

"Marisol," Jack said.

Finally, Miguel's eyes filled with fear. It was obvious he could see the fury inside Jack. What else might this crazy man do?

"And don't forget Susan Karubian."

"Sure, I'll tell you. That *puta*. I didn't kill her. She thought Beltran was gonna help her get a big break in Hollywood. And what'd he do, he just used her."

"I thought you did that."

"No, all I did was introduce her to Beltran. Anyway, she gave that *pendejo* boyfriend of hers AIDS. She was gonna die from it sooner or later. But that's not why she jumped. She felt bad about giving it to her boyfriend." He said the last part with a phony whine. "I wouldda killed her, though. That moron Beltran told her everything. He was in love. Then when he didn't help her become a big star—a movie star with AIDS, can you imagine?—she threatened to go public. I wouldda had no choice but to kill her if she went public on me. I guess she thought it would be dramatic to jump from the sign, eh."

"And you killed Birch for talking to me?"

"Birch was soft. We got big business going on here. He would have jeopardized the entire operation."

"And the operation is?"

"Bringing illegals over the border."

"For Wilkman, Santos, and the church."

"Yes, for all of them. But you have it backwards. I didn't go to them. They came to me to solve their problems."

"Looks like they only got worse." I wanted to keep him talking, hoping I'd get some more info.

"Because Beltran's *un pendejo*. He thought by playing their game he would become one of them. Big. Powerful. Rich. He doesn't know how the game is played."

"He's on your hit list?"

"Yeah. Right after you. Tonight even. With your gun."

"What about Marisol and her brother?"

He ran his fingers over the claw marks Marisol had left on his cheek. "Her brother didn't have the stomach for the job. He actually felt sorry for the people he was bringing across. When he lost a shipment in the desert to the heat, he wanted to quit. Nobody quits."

"Marisol?" Jack said. He trained the red laser beam right between Miguel's eyes.

"Loose end."

Jack didn't think of Marisol as a loose end. And neither did I.

"And Father Carrigan?" I said.

"He just helps out when we need it. Provides sanctuary. He's a man of God, doesn't want to get his hands dirty. But he does other things on occasion."

"Like setting up Marisol."

He nodded. "Can I stand up? I'm getting stiff. It's damp."

Before I can respond, he lurches up, throwing dirt in my

face.
Runs.
Dark.
Stumbles.
He doesn't know where to go.
Run this way, he hits me.
The other way, Jack.
Down, well he might take a tumble and break his neck.
So he goes up.
Scrambling up the sign's scaffolding.
It's never a good idea to go up, because sooner or later you run out of places to go. And where could Miguel go once he hits the top of the sign?
I start after him.
"Let him go," Jack says.
Up he goes.
Now he's at the top of the 'H'.
I go 'round to the front.
Jack stays in back.
The light from the full moon silhouettes him.
His foot catches in something up there.
He tumbles, head over heels.
Flies down the front of the sign.
I have to jump out of the way.
He hits the ground two feet from me.
Something cracks.
His neck?
His eyes pop open.

The news of Miguel's death hit the morning papers. Another person jumping off the Hollywood Sign in so short a period of time. It was a trend now. The local morning news shows were all over it. This would be good for another week's worth of leads, 'cause *if it bleeds it leads.* Unless something bloodier came along. And the news today will be the movies of tomorrow.

But this time the talking heads and scribblers didn't know what to make of it. No ID was found with the body. The police were running his prints. But we figured they'd come up empty.

Jack and I had covered our tracks pretty well, at least we thought so. Before leaving the sign, Jack had said, "Got one more thing to do."

"What?"

He walked a few paces, yanked Miguel's two homies from the bush. Pulled out his blade, sliced the plastic zip ties that he'd strapped on their wrists and ankles.

"Get the hell outta here."

They beat it down the hill, tumbling and rolling most of the way.

"Won't they—?"

"Nah, they're just punks. I don't think we have to worry about them."

But even though we covered our tracks, we still might have to worry about Wilkman and his pals. They'd probably figure out who it was sooner or later and they had power.

We hoped it would be later. For now it looked like the man had fallen or jumped from the sign. No signs of foul play, at least I hoped it would look that way after his fall from the Sign. No guns—we'd taken them. As far as anyone knew he was just a copycat jumper. An accident.

We decided to take a couple days off and try to come up with a plan on how to get Wilkman and his cronies. We wanted to bring them all down. But we didn't want to just take them out. They weren't worth our going to jail over. We wanted to hoist them on their own petards, get revenge the way the Count of Monte Cristo did, slamming each bad guy with the thing that would hurt them the most.

Molly, doing much better now, and I went to Poinsettia Park to play. She loved running in the grass, chasing a tennis ball, which barely fit in her mouth.

On the way home, I checked the office for bills and checks and anything else. I dropped Molly off and joined my friend Lou Waters at El Coyote for lunch.

CHAPTER 42

The next night that cop knock was back banging on my door.

Chandler.

And Haskell.

That couldn't be good.

"Mr. Rogers," Chandler said, putting on her cop face for Haskell. We might have had some rough edges to our relationship, but it wasn't formal. "Please come with us."

"What? Why?"

"We believe you're a material witness to a crime."

"What if I want to call my lawyer."

"That's your right."

I decided to go with them. Haskell frisked me, hard. He seemed to enjoy it and probably thought he was humiliating me. Maybe he was. They didn't cuff me. Didn't talk to me. They put me in the back of their car. Chandler drove. Haskell with me in the back seat, in case I tried something funny. They gave me that jazz about being a material witness, but we passed the cop shop on Wilcox, so where the hell were we going? To talk to the feds? Get busted for Miguel's death? Was I gonna lose my PI ticket? Would Molly be okay? The things that go through your mind in the back of a cop car.

We drove to Hollywood. To a low, nondescript beige brick building also on Wilcox, just off the boulevard, not too far from the Hollywood police station. They parked, walked me to the door. But didn't enter with me.

A man in a well cut dark suit, with the hard cut jaw of a Secret Service agent, led me to a small room. The drab wall color matched the outside of the building. No windows. No pictures. It looked like an interrogation cell, except the chairs and table weren't bolted down and it was better lit. Jack was already there. I figured they'd frisked him too. If he'd fought back I didn't think he'd be here, so his curiosity must have gotten him. The suit left us alone.

"What's this all about?" No easy way out of this one if we had to make a break.

Before Jack could respond, the door opened. Wilkman, Santos, and another man entered. They closed the door behind them. We didn't stand to greet them.

"Let's skip the prelims," Wilkman said. The three of them looked all business.

"Are you recording this?" I said.

"No." Wilkman leaned against the brick wall.

"I checked," Jack said. "Nothing obvious anyway."

"Should we check them?" Santos said.

"No need to do that." Wilkman took a seat, lit a cigarette. "We're all in this together, aren't we, gentlemen?"

I wondered what he meant by that, though I had an idea.

"Okay, what's it about?"

"This is Lorraine Santos, and Father Gregory Barger," Wilkman said. He looked at Jack and me. "And, of course, we've met."

Barger didn't look like a priest, at least not today. No clerical collar. In fact, he looked more Hollywood than Vatican in his faded blue jeans, polo shirt, and loafers without socks.

"I represent His Eminence, the Cardinal," he said.

"We have a proposition for you two. It's obvious that you had some part in this Miguel Gonzalvo's death," Santos said.

"Are you accusing—"

"Let's cut the crap," Wilkman said.

"We don't want to be looking over our shoulders for the rest of our lives." Santos adjusted herself in the uncomfortable metal chair. Shooed Wilkman's smoke away from her face.

Now it was Father Greg's turn, "As we're sure you don't."

"What does that mean?" I said.

"A Mexican standoff," Jack said. That quieted the room.

Another one, I thought. I finally said, "What's your proposition?"

"A truce. We leave you alone. You leave us alone." Wilkman dropped his cigarette on the concrete floor, crushed it under a shiny, alligator-looking shoe.

"Isn't that admitting guilt?" Jack said.

"We're not admitting anything. We're just playing what-ifs." Wilkman was all charm, all smarm.

"None of us, as I'm sure neither of you, want to worry that someone has the wrong idea and that they would do something that we'd all regret." Father Gregory fingered his open shirt, as if missing the security of his clerical collar.

"That's it?" I said. "Someone has to go down."

"Beltran," Father Gregory said.

"Small fry," Jack said.

"And Miguel. How many people did you have him kill?" I watched Wilkman light up again. Santos scooted her chair away from him.

"Miguel?" Santos said with a straight face.

I looked at her incredulously.

"You think you know what's going on here," Wilkman said. "You don't. But even if you do, you have nothing on us and we have a lot of power and friends and money between us. You will not win."

"The New World Order," Jack piped in.

"Beltran?" It looked like this was going to be a war we couldn't win. Maybe we could win a skirmish.

"He can take the fall." Wilkman exhaled a cloud of smoke.

"And the rest of you get out of the human smuggling business," I said.

"You're making a giant and unsubstantiated leap, Mr. Rogers. And should you do so in public, we would have to go after you with everything we've got." He crushed out his second unfinished cigarette with a vehemence I had suspected was lurking underneath the highly tailored Armani suit and red silk power tie.

It was a threat. But the sour truth was that we didn't have any real proof. On the other hand, would they even be here talking like this if we weren't damn close to it? Maybe just our knowing would get them to quit and we wouldn't have to die on this hill.

"In any event," Santos said, "Beltran did it all on his own. A special committee will deal with it."

I knew there'd be no special committee. But it sounded good at the moment. I also knew that we had been naïve earlier to think that there'd be any real justice.

"Deal?" Wilkman said.

I wasn't sure their collective word was worth much. "Give us a few minutes."

The three of them solemnly filed out of the room, closing the door.

"What do you think?"

Jack rocked back in his chair, arms behind his head. "You gotta know when to hold 'em and when to fold 'em. We don't really have anything on them."

"They're scared. That's what this meet is about. They think we killed Miguel and that we'll do them next." I paced the room. "It's clear they're guilty."

"As sin. But we don't have any proof. And he's right, they have power and money and friends. What do we have?"

"This isn't the Jack I know."

"We can't kill 'em or anything else if we're locked up in solitary up in Corcoran or Pelican Bay. Strategic retreat.

Marshall our forces for another day. Another battle."

The stark walls began closing in on me. "Why don't they just arrest us?"

"We'd open our mouths. They can either kill us or cut a deal. Killing us causes more problems for them." Jack always saw the clearest picture.

"So we take Beltran and skulk away."

"To fight another day."

Now that was the Jack I knew. "But if we make the deal with them—"

"We'll keep an eye out. If we hear anything that they might be back in the smuggling business, we'll reconsider our options."

"I hate to let them off the hook," I said.

"They'll always be looking over their shoulder. Wondering if we're gonna come up on 'em," Jack said, toying with the St. Christopher medal Marisol had given him.

"We might be doing the same."

"Their killer is gone."

"They can find another."

"I think they're scared. I think they want to back off." Jack sounded weary. As he'd said earlier, you have to know when to fold 'em. I thought he just wanted to go off alone somewhere and think about Marisol.

"And what about Miguel? He didn't act on his own."

"No way. But what else have we got right now? Without killing them all willy-nilly what else can we do?" Jack being practical.

We banged on the door, sent word via jagged jaw that we were ready to talk to them again. They took their sweet time coming back. Power play.

While we waited, I asked Jack, "So, did you find an apartment?"

"I'm not moving."

"I didn't think you would."

"Huh?"

Before I could respond the others came back. We all sat around the table as if it were a conference about what fancy name to give a new cereal or toothpaste.

"There's still the question of Miguel," Wilkman said.

"We didn't kill Miguel," I said.

"And we had no idea what Beltran was doing," Santos said, with a sanctimonious smile. "But we appreciate your bringing his transgressions to our attention."

Everybody BSing, trying to save their own asses.

"It doesn't matter anyway." Wilkman smirked. I got his meaning. They could make it look like we offed Miguel. We truly were in a Mexican standoff.

The deal was set. They would get out of the smuggling business. We wouldn't go after them. They wouldn't come after us, legally or otherwise. And Beltran would be thrown to the sharks.

"What if he talks?" I said.

"He's a small fish. He can't fight us. If he tries, we'll slam him so hard he won't know what hit him." Wilkman got up. Power smile on his face.

The rest of us stood up.

Wilkman said, "This meeting never happened."

Nobody shook hands. There was nothing to toast our new relationship with. Everyone filed out of the room.

"They got away with it," I said as Jack and I walked out.

"They always get away with it."

"Well, we get Beltran."

"Consolation prize," Jack said.

Jack's escort took him home. I got in the car with Chandler. Haskell had disappeared. I sat in front with her.

"Big doings," she said, pulling out into traffic. "We've been told that this event never occurred."

"What event?"

"Right."

We didn't have much else to say to each other. She pulled in my driveway.

"Maybe I'll see you around some time," she said.

"As long as you don't have your cuffs on you."

"Don't you mean on you?" She grinned and I smiled back at her. I got out and she drove off. I had no idea whether we'd see each other again or in what way.

Molly greeted me at the door and we did our usual routine. For some reason the house felt cold, empty. No case to work on, unless you include the Hollywood cases and I didn't. No Marisol down the block. I wasn't sure where Jack was. The resolution of the case not totally satisfactory. Wilkman, Santos, the church skated. Miguel and Beltran took the fall, Miguel literally. I guess it was something and sometimes you can't have it all. I didn't think we'd solved the problem either. Even if Wilkman and his pals really did stay out of the immigrant smuggling business, someone else would fill the gap. Regardless of your position on it, the issue wasn't going away.

I popped a Missing Persons CD in the player and "Destination Unknown" came on. It seemed appropriate in more ways than one.

While I was trying to figure out what to do with the rest of the night, someone knocked on the front door. Feeling like the immediate danger had passed, I didn't pick up the Star. It wasn't a cop knock, so I didn't think it was Chandler. Besides, she had just driven away a few minutes ago. I doubted she would come back so quickly. I looked through the peephole to see Beltran standing there. For a split second I wondered how he got my address, but that wouldn't have been hard.

"Councilman," I said, opening the door.

His face was twisted into a cross of rage and defeat. I figured someone had told him about the deal. I didn't particularly want to let him in, but the small automatic in his left hand said I didn't have a lot of choice. We settled in the living room, across from each other. Molly sat by my feet. Beltran kept the gun on me. I wondered if he'd remembered to take the safety off.

"You ruined me," he said. "I'm going to be the fall guy. I hardly had anything to do with it."

"Then I guess you can tell that to the court."

"I can bring them all down with me."

"Why don't you?" I hoped he would. That would make me feel better.

"I have to look over my shoulder all the time now. They'll send someone after me."

"Miguel's dead."

"You think he's the only one like that?"

"Then I guess I have to look over my shoulder too." I'd thought about that. And I didn't particularly trust Wilkman and his pals.

He put his arm out, the gun two feet closer to my belly now.

"It's a lot messier than on TV," I said.

"What is?"

"Shooting someone. Besides, I don't think your conscience could take it."

The gun shook in his hand. "I just wanted to be part of something. And now I'm finished and Susan's dead."

"She thought you were going to help her. And what'd you do, promised her the moon and gave her nothing."

"She committed suicide. I didn't do it."

I tended to agree—he didn't do it. Not completely anyway. I thought Susan Karubian committed Suicide-by-Hollywood. She'd come out here to be a star. When she couldn't get in, that and her depression over giving Brett AIDS led her to jump from the Hollywood Sign. Beltran and working in porns probably didn't help. But I'd known enough people like her to know how debilitating this town can be. I didn't say anything to him though; I didn't want to let him off the hook.

"She had AIDS," I said. "Did you know that?"

The gun hand fell to his knee. His face fell almost that far as he realized what that meant.

"That means I probably have it too. It's a death sentence."

I didn't respond. What was there to say? He walked to the front door, trailing the pistol at his side.

CHAPTER 43

I had bought Larry Darrell a drink at the Café Noir and stepped out into the electric Los Angeles sun. I wanted to thank him for his help on the case. Before heading home, I went to Carlos' apartment. His friends were surprised to see me. Even more surprised by the half dozen sleeping bags I'd brought. I filled them in on Carlos and Marisol. They talked about coming to *los Estados Unidos,* how they loved being here, but hated missing their families.

They asked to me stay for dinner. How could I refuse? It was good, arroz con pollo and homemade tamales bought from a street vendor. They used their own hot sauce, cooked up in the kitchen. Best damn hot sauce I'd ever had and I considered myself a connoisseur of hot sauce. They filled an old pickle jar with some for me to take home.

With a little bit of digging and a lot of schmoozing, I found the info on *Kidder's* competition. It was pretty much the same story Hartman was developing. He wanted to hire me to hit the producer of the competition, but even he didn't have enough money for me to do that. He flew into standard Producer's Rage #17, but was very grateful that I'd saved him from going ahead on his project. Instead of taking my full fee, I took half and asked him to read Derek Futterman's script. I dropped it off and Futterman still hasn't heard anything. I didn't have the heart to tarnish his dream and tell him that he probably never would.

I drove west, into the glaring sun because, as in most

westerns, the hero always rides off into the sunset. I was doing that, but I was also heading home. Molly jumped me as I
entered the house.

"Hey, Molly, you ready for your walk? The vet says we
don't have to *coupage* anymore."

She seemed to understand what I said, jumping at the back
door, or maybe the leash in my hand. And maybe it was only
my imagination or wishful thinking, but she seemed to favor
me over Jack now. She was finally becoming my dog.

The constant white noise of the TV news droned in the
background as I grabbed my jacket and headed for the door.
Something caught my attention:

"City Councilman Marc Beltran, who sources say was
about to be indicted for voter fraud and accepting bribes,
was found dead in his Hancock Park house early this morning. Beltran also had a relationship with Susan Karubian,
who recently jumped to her death from the Hollywood Sign.
Police say the councilman's death was also a suicide, though
no note has been found. They are checking into the matter.
In other news..."

Suicide? I wasn't so sure about that.

Molly and I went out the door into the sun streaked day.
I didn't really feel like walking the neighborhood. We might
run into the Goldsteins and Guillermo and Hillary. Instead,
we drove to the Santa Monica Pier. I bought hot dogs on
sticks for Molly and me and we walked to the end of the
pier. A young girl's hair blew in the breeze and she had to
keep pushing it off her face, reminding me of Marisol the
day I saw her here. The sun glinted on the water the way it
only can at magic hour. Bright. Blinding. Golden.

I stared out to the infinite horizon, to the sunny sea.

Proposition 187 won big time, but was ultimately overturned
by the courts. But I was sure that wasn't the last we'd hear

of the issue.

I had contacted Wilkman—who actually took my call—asking him to see about getting Eric's law license back. He said he'd try. And he was successful. Eric was pleased but wasn't sure if he'd go back to the law or not. Right now he and his girlfriend Lindsay were on a trip to San Francisco, maybe beyond. They were cruising his Beamer up Pacific Coast Highway. Jack and I chipped in to help pay for their trip. Without him who knows where this case might have ended up.

The ending still wasn't totally satisfying. Beltran took the fall, a deeper fall than I had expected him to take, whether or not it was actually suicide. The three bigwigs were getting away with it. But isn't that the way it goes? Supposedly the Cardinal had sanctioned Father Carrigan. I know he didn't do jail time, at least not for Marisol or Carlos. But I heard later that he was busted for having sex with altar boys. And we had gotten the triggerman of Carlos and Marisol and others. We had to be satisfied with that. Sometimes things didn't quite tie into as pretty a bow as we'd like. But I'd fixed a broken window—maybe it would hold for a while. At least until the next stone was thrown.

I wanted to go to the graves of Marisol and Carlos with Jack. He'd bought plots for them at Lawngreen-Pacific Catholic Cemetery, overlooking the ocean in Malibu. This was not the cheapest cemetery around.

He didn't want me to go. But I could picture him, standing over their graves, her grave, staring down at them one moment, out to sea the next. The ocean, seemed to solve a lot of problems for both of us. Sometimes we felt more at home there than on the land. And I knew Jack thought Marisol would enjoy her spot overlooking the ocean too.

My life wasn't too bad. I had Jack and I had Molly. I thought about Chandler. Another potential relationship that I probably blew.

I sat in my cramped home office, Molly at my feet, listening to "Because the Night" by 10,000 Maniacs, which I liked, though I preferred the Patti Smith version, but that's not what the radio chose to play. The phone rang. I thought it might be Detective Courval, who I still hadn't heard from. But it was some Hollywood producer looking for the renowned Duke Rogers. How'd he get my home phone? Well, they had their ways like I had mine. He'd been living with his girlfriend for six years. Now he wanted to dump her for a newer model—his words—and she was going for a palimony suit. Could I get the goods on her? Like I said, my life was good. I hung up, feeling the need to wash my hands.

Started off to do that, but sat back down. "Well, Molly, this is it," I said, picking up the receiver again. Dialing. I knew the number by heart, even though I hadn't called it in some time. My heart beat like it hadn't beat in ages, not even when I've gone down those dark alleys or sat as a sitting duck waiting for Miguel or his man.

"Hello," the voice at the other end said.

"Hello, Rita," I said, as the scent of honeysuckle drifted through the window from outside.

ACKNOWLEDGMENTS

I want to thank Eric Campbell, Lance Wright and all the other good folks at Down & Out Books for their support and all the great work they're doing.

Photo by Linda Campanelli

Paul D. Marks has written three novels, co-edited two anthologies and written countless short stories. He's won a Shamus Award, was voted #1 in *Ellery Queen Mystery Magazine's* 2016 Reader's Choice Award and been nominated for Anthony, Macavity and Derringer Awards. His story "Windward" was chosen for *The Best American Mysteries of 2018*. His short fiction has been published in *Ellery Queen Mystery Magazine*, Akashic's Noir series (St. Louis), *Alfred Hitchcock Mystery Magazine*, *Crimestalker Casebook*, *Hardluck Stories*, *Hardboiled*, and many others. Paul has served on the boards of the Los Angeles chapters of Sisters in Crime and Mystery Writers of America.

PaulDMarks.com

BOOKS

On the following pages are a few
more great titles from the
Down & Out Books publishing family.

For a complete list of books and to
sign up for our newsletter,
go to DownAndOutBooks.com.

Once a Killer
Martin Bodenham

Down & Out Books
June 2018
978-1-946502-75-9

Two ten-year-old boys are locked away in juvenile detention for the brutal torture and murder of a blind man in his own home. On release, and with new identities, one becomes a successful New York lawyer while the other becomes a career criminal.

Then their paths cross again…

Saying Uncle
Greg F. Gifune

Down & Out Books
June 2018
978-1-946502-90-2

Andy DeMarco and his little sister Angela worship their Uncle Paulie, an enigmatic savior who took the place of their absent father. But one summer day something unspeakable happens to Angela and the world changes forever.

Twenty years later, Andy returns home to bury his murdered uncle, and only now can he begin to understand who the man truly was.

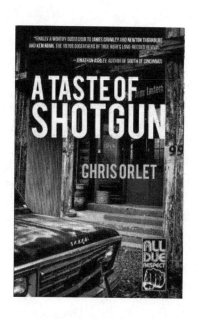

A Taste of Shotgun
Chris Orlet

All Due Respect, an imprint of
Down & Out Books
July 2018
978-1-946502-92-6

A local drug dealer has the goods on Denis Carroll. That shooting at his tavern five years ago? Turns out the cops got it all wrong. Now, after five years of blackmail, the Carrolls have had enough. When the drug dealer turns up dead, Denis is the prime suspect. As more bodies pile up, they too appear to have Denis' name all over them. Is Denis really a cold-blooded killer or could this be the work of someone with a grudge of her own?

In this darkly humorous small-town noir everyone has something to hide and nothing is at seems.

Dillo
Max Sheridan

Shotgun Honey, an imprint of
Down & Out Books
December 2017
978-1-946502-32-2

Artesia, New Mexico. Pop. 3012. There's nothing 14-year-old Doc Candy likes better on a hot summer afternoon than snapping pictures of dead armadillos off Route 82. Until a no-good grifter of a father he hasn't seen in eight years comes blowing up to his window at two in the morning in a hot El Camino talking about a family vacation in Miami.

But it isn't until they're hiding out in the Louisiana bayou that Doc learns the whole truth…

Made in the USA
Lexington, KY
13 September 2018